ETERNITY AND YOU: TIPS FOR THE YOUNG VAMPIRE

VAMPIRE INNOCENT
BOOK EIGHTEEN

MATTHEW S. COX

DIVISION ZERO PRESS

Eternity and You: Tips for the Young Vampire
Vampire Innocent Book 18

ISBN (ebook): 978-1-950738-64-9

ISBN (paperback): 978-1-950738-65-6

CONTENTS

NO ONE STEALS FROM ARTHUR WOLENT

TUESDAY

*C*omfortable is not a word I'd have used to describe my life for a long time.

Well, as much as anything can be a 'long time' for someone my age. It's weird how time feels different to people. When I was younger, the idea of having to wait five months for Christmas to arrive seemed like an absolute eternity while my parents lose track of years. A five-month wait for them is trivial. Someone out there probably got their doctorate degree based on a study of the exact ratio of a person's age to the time distortion tedium effect, and has it boiled down to a simple logical function. Plug someone's age into the equation and out comes exactly the ratio of perceived time to actual time.

I'm not that person.

Math is okay. I don't love it enough to torture myself by chasing advanced degrees in it. One semester of calculus ended up being a little past my limit. Made it through with a B, which I considered enough of a win. Speaking of semesters, the idea of going to school is starting to feel like more of a needless chore than something to help me fake feeling normal. Between running odd jobs for Mr. Wolent and wanting to spend time with my family while we are still a family, going to college seems a waste. Never mind the issue of a degree being functionally useless for me in terms of getting into a career I will need to survive. Undeath lets me sidestep that whole rat race.

It also means I'm stuck with my current perceptions of time. Meaning, I will never again feel like having to wait from April to December for Christmas presents is an impossibly long time. I'll also never be like my parents and have four years shoot by in a blink without noticing.

Not a big deal. I can unlive with that.

Anyway, comfortable can mean many different things. In some regard, my life has been totally comfortable. I've never had to worry about not having food on the table or being scared to go home to horrible parents. But those are the kinds of problems kids don't even think about unless they're stuck in a bad situation. I got really lucky. What I consider as being 'uncomfortable' for most of my life is totally normal bullcrap—stress over schoolwork, boyfriends, my body changing out from under me, that sort of thing. The last time I truly felt comfortable and carefree, I'd probably been nine or ten.

I'm having some moments now that take me back there. NO, not to feeling like a child. I mean comfortable. Vampirism seems to be a good fit on me, even if I'm like the absolute last person any self-respecting vampire would've chosen to be their progeny. At least, any vampire who cared about power or social status would never have chosen me.

Going to college is now more of a 'make the parents happy' thing than a 'make Sarah feel normal' thing. No, I'm not upset by this. Past Sarah™ thought she needed to do everything possible to feel normal and forget the whole vampire situation entirely as much as possible.

I'm getting used to it. Part of my brain must've been terrified at the idea of being a vampire and wanted to pretend it didn't really happen to me. I mean, I've never consciously felt like the Universe took a giant crap on me. All things considered, vampirism is pretty damn cool. I'm growing into it, so to speak. So, yeah, the whole school thing

—going to college right after high school like I'd planned to do for most of my life—no longer fills the role of a mortality security blanket. It feels like a chore now. Is this how the slackers felt?

Like, back when I was still a mortal going to high school, we had these kids who always talked about how much they hated going to school and wanted to be anywhere else. They never did homework and some of them even cut school sometimes. No, I am not saying they were right. They are still mortals and they needed school, so they didn't end up working at McDonald's for the rest of their lives—or going into politics. I guess since I don't *need* an education to excel at a career anymore, it's not the same. Maybe I don't understand why they felt that way about school. My problems are kinda unique.

Barring whatever craziness Sophia has done, I know my family—as it is now—won't last forever. The Littles will grow up and have lives of their own apart from being 'the children' in a family. My siblings are twelve, eleven, and ten. They've already spent more time as 'the kids' in the house than they've got left being 'the kids in the house'. I would rather be around to enjoy having my family while we are still a cohesive whole than chasing some useless college paper that won't do me a bit of good.

Question is, how do I break the news to the parents? I don't want to hurt them.

That aside, I've got more pressing worries than disappointing my parents—like making it through the next hour or so without ending up maimed. I'm on something of an attack mission for the boss—that's Mr. Wolent—so I fully expect to end up bleeding, naked, or some combination of those two things before the night is over. Not that I am eager to strip or anything. Just… vampire combat does *not* get along with clothing. I've considered trying to get my hands on some reenactor's plate armor, but that crap's a bit too heavy to fly in. It is also the opposite of subtle in the modern world. I'd feel as out of place walking around in that getup as if I'd gone to a funeral in my pajamas.

It's starting to make sense why Aurélie loves those multilayered, elaborate-as-hell dresses. They turn the wearer into a vampire equivalent of a Tootsie-Roll Pop: many layers to claw through before reaching the middle and causing a mortifying wardrobe malfunction.

Being a vampire back in the day had to have been a bit less stressful. They didn't have smartphones all over the place to capture photographic evidence of random unexpected nakedness. And yes, contrary to what some movies say, we *do* generally show up on cameras. I say generally because of Dalton. Some vampires—like him —can selectively alter the fabric of reality so they don't show up on cameras or video. It's a trick that I might be able to pull off someday, since he's my sire and all. Not that I'm planning to need the ability to hide from security cameras.

I'm a good girl.

Sigh.

There I go again. My intentions and the situations in which I find myself lately are often quite opposite. Yes, Follows Rules Girl *has* broken into a police station, broken into various places, stolen stuff, and even killed people… though I swear the killing people thing was a complete accident. I don't even remember doing it. Blast of sunlight to the face, total panic freakout, then blood everywhere. It's not like I made a conscious decision to murder people. It was an uncontrollable instinctual reaction from the most primal of primal natures… kind of like how one or two cupcakes disappear immediately off a serving tray if brought within the vicinity of my little brother.

Ashley's flying along beside me, being uncharacteristically quiet.

Yeah, she knows we're trying to sneak up on some bad guys. Such a scenario isn't guaranteed to make her stay quiet. I can't tell if she's taking tonight's job more seriously than usual or if something's really bothering her. I've known her for most of my life and she's not vibing like anything's wrong. Nothing is weird except for her unusual quietness. It's not like her to take anything seriously, even a job from Mr. Wolent to go track down some people who stole from him.

I'm not saying it's 'don't start a land war in Asia' stupid, but stealing from Mr. Wolent is not one of the top ten smartest things a mortal can do.

Dammit. Now I want to watch *Princess Bride* again.

Most of the difficult legwork for this job already happened thanks to a team of mortal employees—some of whom are in the police department. We already know the identity of at least one of the men responsible for the theft, thanks to his license plate getting caught on the security camera outside the antique shop. Yes, Mr. Wolent owns an antique shop. I mean, he owns a business entity that owns another business entity that owns the antique shop. The nice older couple who the general public thinks are the owners are on our payroll.

Feels strange to say that. 'Our payroll.' Makes me feel like I'm in the mafia or something.

So, this guy, Trevor Bishop, and his buddies broke into the antique shop and stole an urn of ashes. Seems kind of an odd thing to steal, right? Just... this urn happens to contain the ashes of a vampire who went sun-surfing back in the 1400s somewhere in Europe. I don't know all the details. Old-as-dirt vampire has become dirt in an urn. He became dirt in an urn a really, really, really long time ago. No, there's no bringing him back. The only thing I can guess here is that his remains are mystically powerful in the right hands.

Trevor Bishop's hands are not the right ones.

At least, I am assuming so. We still don't really know what we're dealing with here. Trevor might be a vampire. He might be a mortal. Whatever he is, he's pretty careless. Not only did he get caught on security camera using his personal car with his valid license plates, his internet presence is so over the top it's kinda cringe. He is apparently the lead singer for a no-name black metal band called *The Black Bishops*. Yeah. Sounds like something my little brother would come up with. Wait, no. Scratch that. Sam is abnormally intellectual for a ten-year-old boy. Then again, he's still a little boy, geeky or not. He might think that's a cool name.

Not entirely sure what 'black metal' is either. Probably something edgy. I couldn't even find them on YouTube, so really, it's just him and his friends playing in their garage. They haven't had the nerve to post their music online yet. Oh, and there's also the occultist stuff. His TikTok is full of that. I showed it to Sophia. She shrugged, got Coralie.

Coralie laughed at it. So, I'm guessing Trevor's not exactly a real mystic.

Still, he and his buddies knew enough to go after this particular urn—so anything could happen.

I stare down at the treetops silently gliding by beneath me. Ash and I are out in the sticks, somewhere in the western portion of Olympic National Park. The Quinault Reservation isn't too far from us to the south. Tracking this guy down online was the easy part. Discovering he and his friends were going to head out here to 'the cave' took me about twenty minutes. The actual 'finding the cave' part is a proverbial needle-in-a-haystack problem... or should I say 'moron in a forest' problem.

My mind wanders back and forth over what's going to happen in the near future—assuming we find this place Trevor referred to as 'the cave'. There's a decent chance we will, even if it's tedious. I mean, after all... we are vampires. We can smell mortals... or at least the fumes of their car exhaust, though I don't think anyone drove out to where we are now. It's pretty damn remote, what my dad would call the '3H club.' Hiking, helicopters, or horses are about the only way out here other than being a vampire who can defy the law of gravity. I suppose one of those jetpack suits might work, but they're still pretty expensive and don't carry enough fuel for a long trip.

This seems to be the sort of low-priority job Wolent would hand off to the intern. Hi. I'm the intern. My guess is he asked me to go get his bottle of ancient vampire ashes back because it's not a terribly important task. Also, sending me instead of one of his usual leg-breakers is probably a sign he's looking to keep the body count low. He knows I won't randomly shred a pack of mortals for kicks. Maybe he's thinking of me like a rogue in D&D who would be capable of sneaking in and out to steal back his stuff and not even get noticed doing it.

Yeah, Dalton's my sire. I suppose if vampires were characters in D&D, I'd be a rogue.

Definitely a swashbuckler, says Dalton's voice in the back of my mind. I feel him picturing himself dressed as a rapier-wielding pirate type character.

I chuckle mentally. Yeah. Can't argue with that. So, what does that make me? The cute little sneak thief?

You'd be one of those little moggies that stands there looking harmless and innocent, and nick the coinpurse as soon as the bloke turns his back.

I almost laugh out loud. He's teasing me. I'm way too old to be a grimy-dorable Dickensian pickpocket. Still, it would be nice if he showed up again at some point and maybe tried to teach me how to do the hiding-from-cameras thing.

Sure thing, luv. I'll schedule you in.

Heh. He says 'schedule' weird. Like… 'shedule' or something.

It is not 'weird.' It's British. This is the proper way to pronounce schedule. You Yanks are lazy.

"There," whispers Ashley, pointing. "I saw a flicker of light."

"Is it them?" I ask.

She shrugs. "Either a flashlight, a will-o-wisp, or a faerie."

I open my mouth to say something about neither will-o-wisps nor faeries are real, but decide against it and close my jaw. After running into freakin' leprechauns and brownies in Ireland… I'm not so sure what is or is not real anymore. Professor Heath said something to me near the end of my going to his class that really kinda rocked me to the core. All we know about history is based on old writings or, as he called it, educated guesswork. What happened on this planet as recent as 500 years ago could be completely different than anything we believe. That adage 'history is written by the victor' is pretty significant. If all the writings and historical records are propaganda or lies, anything might have happened and no one alive today would be the wiser.

There are certainly vampires around older than 500 years who know what really went on. For obvious reasons, they can't go public with such knowledge if, in fact, the history we know is not what really happened. Still, it's just as possible Ancient Egypt was a crazy buzzing metropolis where aliens from a dozen different other planets came to hang out and throw wild parties as it is possible it wasn't. Imagine the ancient pharaohs cruising around in flying hovercars and carrying laser pistols before a massive war blasted humans back to the Bronze Age.

Ashley grabs my hand and tows me into a gentle left turn.

She doesn't let go. No, she's not scared. We're just lame. It's not that unusual for girl best friends to hold hands while going places. It's just kinda unusual to keep doing it once we're older than tweens. Admittedly, we did stop that around age twelve. This is a newly returned clinginess. Ashley's been a bit weird lately. Not sure if it's a bad weird, a good weird, or just plain weird.

My alarm bells aren't going off, so I've decided to run with it and see what happens rather than interrogate her about her sudden shift in personality. It's not a massive shift. She's just stopped making 'adult jokes' or talking about really needing someone to ring her bell.

Sure enough, she's spotted the flicker of a flashlight ahead in the forest. No idea if it's Trevor. Still, there aren't exactly loads of people out here at night, so it's worth a closer look.

We lean into our flying, accelerating for a brief sprint to close the distance in a few seconds. We are as silent as ravens gliding in the wind, ninjas scaling the warlord's castle, or one of Sam's farts at the Thanksgiving dinner table—the ones that everyone always blames Uncle Hank for.

My iPhone beeps.

Ack!

Crap! I slam on the proverbial brakes and stuff my hand in my jeans pocket. Dammit! Ancient vampires never had to worry about an inopportune text message ruining their stealth right before they dropped out of the air on a hapless peasant.

With hand speed capable of snatching an arrow out of the air, I yank my phone out, flick the mute button on the side, and hold it up to see who's trying to get me caught.

It's Mom.

‹Are you going to be out all night, dear?›

"Unicorn sparkles!" whispers Ashley.

I smirk at her. She's started saying stuff like that because some old lady at the mall yelled at her for cursing. Ash stubbed her toe on the corner of a bench, muttered something along the lines of 'ow, shit' and this lady gets in our faces and starts giving us the business like 'teenagers using naughty words' is the sole cause of all that's wrong with the world. Of course, Ashley was involved, so things had to get extra. She freaked out as if she really had caused all the evil in the world, started crying (fake) and apologizing, acting like a five-year-old. Made a huge scene.

It's been two weeks and she's still 'cursing' like a little kid.

Roughly 300 feet ahead of us on the ground, a group of hikers all stop in their tracks and check their phones. Dammit. They heard the text beep.

I hastily send back a ‹Not all night. Home asaic›, and stuff the phone back in my pocket so the screen's not making light anymore, hoping Mom knows that means 'as soon as I can.'

The hikers don't seem to notice or question that none of them received a text. I'm honestly astounded there is signal out here... as much as getting one bar is signal. My guess is, it's only working because we're several hundred feet up in the air. As weak as any cellular reception is out here, any tree cover whatsoever would block it.

"How the heck did someone get a text out here?" whispers a man down below. "I don't have signal."

"Wasn't me." A woman grumbles. "Mine's not getting signal either."

Three other voices, all men, chime in agreeing about the lack of signal.

"Did we imagine that?" asks the woman.

"Someone's following us." The lead hiker turns in place, shining his flashlight around at the woods.

Good thing for us, he's not even considering the idea his stalkers are up in the air.

We hang in place, watching them search around for the source of the phone tweep. After a moment, I'm pretty confident they are not going to look up... so I drift downward for a closer look. As tempting as it is to be 'cool' or cute and land to perch like a gargoyle on a tree, that will make noise. Instead, we remain hovering near a tree without touching it.

I kinda feel like we're in a video game and using a cheat code to hack through the playable area. Don't remember who said it—possibly Dalton—but people generally don't look up when searching for threats. Oh, wait. I remember now... it was Sierra.

Yeah, my kid sister talked about military combat tactical blunders.

Not for her being in any sort of real life-or-death situation or even pretend military training. No, it's all from the PlayStation. Apparently, they have this whole issue with cross-platform gaming where PC gamers and console gamers end up in the same matches. The mouse & keyboard warriors figured out pretty quick that console gamers have a harder time looking around, especially upward, with a game controller... so the PC players go for the high ground and ambush the console people who can't find them.

It makes sense in reality, too. Having ambushed people in real life from the air, it's been my experience that they almost never look up. Does this point to human ancestors not having an evolutionary need to watch the sky for predators? Maybe. Guess that confirms vampires are an unnatural phenomenon.

"It's him," whispers Ashley without actually whispering.

I mean, she's moving her mouth like she's speaking, but not letting any air out. To any mortal, she didn't make a sound. The air moving through her mouth is enough for vampires to hear speech, though. Hey, not every vampire power is over the top. Sometimes, it's the really small things that come in the handiest—like super sensitive hearing.

Yep. Lead hiker guy is Trevor. Oh wow. Luck is with us tonight. Maybe we *will* manage to get home before sunrise. Can't say with absolute certainty, though I suspect the other three guys and the woman with him are the same group who broke into the antique store. At the moment, they all look painfully normal—just a bunch of twentysomethings on a hike in a national park. It's only odd due to the time. Not too many people go hiking this close to midnight.

Of course, whatever they intend to do at 'the cave' is going to happen at midnight. Because of course it is. Poseur occultists always do their rituals at midnight. It's like a thing with them. Here's hoping they're not pretending to be satanists and intending to sacrifice a black cat. Mr. Wolent wanted this to go down without any bloodshed. If one of them intends to murder a cat, Ashley is going to freak out and rip them apart.

I do kinda smell a cat. The scent is oldish, seeped into fabric. One of them has a pet at home. They didn't bring a cat with them here for evil purposes. Good. Hmm. Ashley and I could drop on them right now and be done with things pretty fast. No, not violence. They all seem to be mortals, which means they are one mental derp hammer away from staring into the Eighth Dimension while we rifle their belongings in search of the urn.

Curiosity makes me hesitate. For some stupid reason, I kinda want to see where they're going with this.

"What's the plan?" Ashley grins. "Pick them off one at a time from behind and see how many we can get before Trevor notices?"

I fight the urge to laugh. This is a direct result of Dad putting the movie *Predator* on for us last week. Sam's been teasing Sophia by making that weird clicking noise the alien did. Sure, Sophia is eleven, but she's still childish enough to be afraid a real predator alien is going to hunt her in our house. Of course, she's also old enough to catch herself before panicking completely.

It's a little funny to think about Ashley and I ambushing these hikers one by one and leaving them dazed in a mind fog. We could make a game out of trying to get all the way up their single-file line to Trevor before anyone notices the person following them disappeared. Still, lots of effort for no real payoff other than to say we could do it. Also, if one of the hikers did turn around and notice everyone else missing, they'd probably freak out. There are loads of bigfoot stories around here. The last thing Mr. Wolent would appreciate is us doing something to draw attention.

"Nah," I shake my head. "Curious what they're doing. Rather sneak in and yoink the urn without making direct contact."

Ashley nods.

We glide down to hover only a few feet above the ground, then follow Trevor and his friends. Vampire agility *might* allow us to walk and be quiet enough to avoid detection. Still, not worth risking it when flying is so much quieter. I'm not going to take the chance one badly placed twig snaps and gives us away. The forest here already has enough ambient strange noises to put mortals on edge. Heck, I'm undead and feeling a bit scared. Yeah, it's the bigfoot stories. Every so often, it really does sound like something big is walking around nearby. At least I can see in the dark, so it's not *too* scary. Whenever a random snap or thump happens, I look in that direction. Nothing there. So, it's either natural forest stuff happening, a ghost, or the source of the noise is much farther away than it sounds.

Trevor's people do not have the advantage of perfect night-vision eyes. They're all nervous.

Come to think of it, the area's got a particularly strong sense of foreboding hanging over everything. Feels like Ashley and I are a couple of neighborhood kids who got up the courage to follow through on a dare to go sneak into the abandoned 'haunted house' at the edge of town after hearing all sorts of stories about how children who go inside never come back.

Given that we are neither children nor mortals, it shouldn't be scary to us.

Or so one would think. However, I feel something with senses mortals don't usually have. Call it ESP, call it intuition, whatever. We're getting close to something seriously paranormal, and it seems angry.

Maybe tonight won't be simple after all.

2

EVERY OCCULT STEREOTYPE ALL AT ONCE

TUESDAY (ROUGHLY TWENTY MINUTES LATER)

*T*revor and his friends navigate the woods with the clumsy ease of people who aren't good at hiking in general but have taken this specific walk several times. I'd like to be all cool and vampire-like and claim to know this because of how they move or whatever mood pheromones they're giving off. Alas, the truth is more mundane. The woman, Casey apparently, keeps complaining about the remoteness of their ritual site, why do they keep coming to this stupid place, and why they couldn't do it somewhere closer to home.

Add that to their general awkwardness at hiking and it doesn't take a genius to figure out these people don't go for walks in the woods as a fun hobby all the time.

That strange mood surrounding us doesn't get any worse. It also doesn't get any weaker.

The group finally comes to a stop in the shadow of a three-story rock face. Yeah, there's a shadow. It might be dark, but moonlight is a thing. So, yeah. There's a shadow to vampire eyes here. Anyway, an old mineshaft tunnel leads into the rockface. It looks like the kind of thing you'd see in a documentary film about the gold rush days. Not the most stable looking of places. I certainly wouldn't be going in there if I remained a mortal. Even in my present existence as an immortal vampire, I'm not terribly keen on the idea. At least a mortal would die a quick death in a cave-in. If the ceiling fell on me now, I'd be trapped for… however long it took me to dig out.

I suppose it's reasonably safe. After all, Trevor and his friends seem to have been visiting this place frequently, and it hasn't collapsed on them yet. Or, maybe they just use the open area outside for their rituals?

Ashley and I creep up and hide behind a tree at the edge of the clearing in front of the old mine.

Trevor and his friends remove their backpacks and start taking their clothes off.

Say what?

Ashley covers her mouth to hold in embarrassed laughter.

It's a bit cold for nudism in Washington, but trivial things like temperature don't seem to be holding them back. The group strips down to their underwear as if it's a nice sunny day. Casey's a fellow member of the 'I hate bras' club. None of the guys react much to her being topless. Guess it's too cold for sexy thoughts.

Once everyone's standing around in their underpants, they rummage their backpacks and pull out these ridiculous black robes. I'm too stunned to even laugh as they wriggle into the giant-hooded garments. They look like cultists from a B movie.

Ashley leans on me, her body shaking from silent giggling.

Next, the group squirms around and removes their underwear out from under their robes, which they deposit atop their respective backpacks. Wow, I thought that whole 'naked under black robes' thing was just something cheesy Hollywood movies did. I've heard there's a sect of Wiccans who tend to do their rituals naked in the woods. So, there is some connection between rituals and nakedness. However, those witches don't do the black robes thing. They're also not evil, just nature-worshippers.

These guys? I'm not so sure they're evil as much as clueless. What's the deal here? If you're going to get naked for a crazy ritual, commit to it. Do robes count as clothes? Is it some sort of thing where they can't wear anything modern or it'll mess with the ritual? Are those robes magical?

Nah. Gonna guess this is just nonsense. Trevor's making up the rules as he goes along. Wearing black robes is cool and edgy, like naming your band 'The Black Bishops'.

Casey doesn't seem overly frightened. She's the only woman among them, but she's not here as some sort of sacrifice victim. It also doesn't feel like any of them plan on doing anything inappropriate to or with her here. She's just another cultist. Hey, stupid isn't limited to guys. Us girls can do dumb things, too. After all, I continued to date Scott after our first disastrous attempt to have sex when he demonstrated what an absolute uncaring jerk he was.

Dammit... I look around at their stuff. "Where's the urn?"

Ashley shrugs one shoulder. "No idea. Shall we knock them out and search?"

"That knockout thing only works in the movies," I reply, using our super silent whisper technique. "Punching someone hard enough to instantly knock them out causes serious permanent damage."

"No, dork." She nudges me. "I meant a derp slap."

"Oh." I lightly biff myself in the forehead to avoid making noise. "Duh."

Trevor heads into the mine opening, carrying the smaller of his two packs. Drat. The urn has to be in there. His friends form a single-file line behind him, holding their flashlights in both hands at their chests as if they were candles.

Good grief this is hilarious. The only thing missing is...

They start chanting.

Universe? Why did you make me fall into a *Monty Python* movie? Okay, to be fair, they are not saying 'Pie Jesu domine, dona eis requiem' before walloping themselves in the face with wooden boards. Still, I can't get the mental image of those monks from *Holy Grail* out of my head watching these guys.

Ashley grabs my shoulder. "Let's grab the last two, derp hammer them and take their robes."

Ugh. I give her side eye. "Can I please get through one vampire job without ending up naked?"

She grins. "We don't have to get naked. Just take our shoes off. Not like they're going to check under the robes."

"Why?" I exhale.

"To get into the cave without raising suspicion." She blinks at me like it's the most obvious thing.

"Umm… Or… you could just make them not see us."

She crosses her eyes. "Oh. Duh. Yeah. This just feels so much like I'm in an episode of *Scooby Doo,* it seemed like we should knock two of them out and steal their outfits. Wasn't really thinking vampy."

The last of the group disappears into the mine shaft, still chanting.

"Why do you look like you're about to bust out laughing?" Ashley raises an eyebrow.

"Monty Python monks."

She blinks, tilting her head slightly at me like a confused puppy. Four seconds later, her eyes open wide and she has to clamp both hands over her mouth to stop herself from laughing out loud.

Yeah, this is silly. I'll totally take silly over deadly or traumatic any day of the week.

I really don't care that much if we fail at stealth and they catch us. Not like five mortals are a threat. It's mostly the dread saturating the forest here that's making me try to stay quiet. It's not Trevor's people I'm hiding from… it's whatever is creating this dark mood. The energy is strong enough to the point where it's tempting me to race home and grab Sophia to come check it out. Of course, there's no way I'd do that. For one thing, she'd freak out. If this place is potent enough to make *me* feel like a scared little kid who just woke up from a nightmare, she'd lose her mind. For another, Mom would kill me. She was Not Happy™ with me for bringing Sierra on a Wolent job before. I really shouldn't do that again, especially not with Sophia.

Knowing exactly *why* this area feels so creepy isn't important… at least I really hope it isn't.

Ashley recovers her composure enough to concentrate on doing her charm aura deal. She stands out from behind the tree we've been hiding behind and approaches the cave. I follow close behind her. It's game time. Serious faces people. I can tell she's gotten serious because we're no longer holding hands like a pair of tween besties at the mall.

As we step around and over the backpacks, she gets this devilish grin.

"What?" I whisper.

"Oh, just thinking of pranking them." She does weasel hands. "Clothes up in the trees."

"Funny, but also kinda mean. It's cold. They'll get hypothermia."

She snaps her fingers in fake disappointment. "Yeah, true. I still kinda want to mess with them."

"Why?"

"I dunno. They're just so... mess-withable."

"That's not a word."

"Says who?" Ashley holds her chin up. "If people do something wrong and stupid, they deserve a little prankage."

"Wrong and stupid?"

She folds her arms. "They stole Mr. W's urn."

"Oh, well, yeah. Stealing is wrong." I give side eye to nothing in particular, thinking about Sophia yoinking a stupidly expensive ruby to power the enchantment she used on Sierra.

Honestly, it's just a rock. If nuclear war happened and civilization came to a primitive halt, no one would think a of giant ruby as valuable. Money is entirely an artificial creation of humans. Also, there's no way anyone could prove a then-ten-year-old girl stole something like that, especially not by using a teleporting kitten. We're completely safe from any legal ramifications. No one would even take such an accusation seriously. It's harder for me to wrap my brain around the idea of *Sophia* stealing. But to her, it wasn't stealing as much as she simply did what needed to be done to protect her sister.

Anyway...

We head into the mine shaft.

Two unusual symbols mark the wall on either side a few feet from the opening. They look like the sorts of occult symbols Puritans would carve into the tombstones of suspected witches with some extra squiggly bits. Looks like a sideways numeral eight with a line going straight down from the middle, and two horizontal lines at the bottom. I almost get the feeling the markings were intended as a barrier to keep something trapped inside this mine.

Can't tell if these carvings in the stone have any real power or not. If they're giving off energy of any form, it's too weak to pick up over the background ominousness.

"Umm." I point at the marking on the left. "Any idea what that is? And why do I feel like we're in a video game entering the place where some ancient society trapped a powerful evil being ages ago?"

She flaps her arms. "No clue. You're kinda right though. Feels that way."

"So, mood queen, progeny of Aurélie, are you reading anything?"

"Heh." She sorta eyerolls at me, then turns her stare into the mineshaft for a few seconds before doing a three-sixty spin. "Anger, mostly. Futility. Frustration. Torment."

"I sincerely doubt Dad is in this mine trying to beat *Ghosts & Goblins* on the 8-bit NES."

She almost stifles a snicker.

Seriously. That is the only time I've seen my father truly angry.

The chanting from deeper in the mine stops.

Ashley and I both kinda shrink downward like video game characters entering stealth mode. Trevor and his people have stopped making noise. Time to be super quiet. It's dumb. They won't notice us as long as Ashley is radiating charm. We could literally walk right into that room and none of them would react to us unless we did something to make a ton of noise or draw attention to ourselves.

Things like that take a bit of getting used to. It's hard to suppress the usual 'oh crap, be quiet' urge of a normal teenager sneaking around, afraid to get caught doing something they shouldn't be doing. Even though I am technically on the legal side here, Follows Rules Girl isn't used to running around doing 'jobs' for Mr. Wolent. She thinks any time I have to sneak, I'm doing something wrong. Why don't we just walk in there and ask for the urn back?

Yeah right.

Follows Rules Girl is also a bit of an unrealistic idealist.

I lead the way into the mine with Ashley right behind me. We pass multiple wooden support beams that look like they've been here for centuries. That's another thing making me want to keep quiet. Those braces look ready to disintegrate to splinters if one of us so much as shouted nearby. Careful not to touch anything but the floor, I make my way forward for about eighty feet to where the tunnel connects to a chamber about double the size of my living room at home.

Three other passageways lead off from the big cave, one going west, one east, and one kinda northwest. A single wooden post in the middle of the chamber supports an X-shaped wooden brace against the ceiling.

Trevor and his group have arranged themselves in a circle on the far side of the central support column. A small stone altar made from random big rocks he must've found outside holds the target of my mission: a burial urn. Not sure what kind of metal it's made from. Looks like brass or bronze, maybe even copper. It's an off-brown color with striations of various shades. The shape is obviously that of a crematory urn containing human remains.

"Amazing," whispers Casey. "I can feel the power coming from it."

The men murmur in agreement.

Hate to say it, but she's got a point. I can *definitely* feel something from the urn. I really hope the anger Ashley picked up on isn't coming from it. Really don't want to deal with another Oblivare soul jar if I can help it.

Trevor holds his arms out to either side and babbles in Latin. Maybe it's pseudo-Latin. I dunno. I don't understand Latin. The only Latin I know is the Monty Python monk line. That's definitely not what he's saying now.

Oh, shit. He's got a smear of pale grey dust on his forehead. Did he already open the urn? What the heck is he trying to do here?

The other three guys, plus Casey, stare at him expectantly.

Five seconds becomes ten. Then twenty.

Nothing's happening.

I mean, I'm not shocked. These guys are utterly clueless.

Trevor shifts his gaze left and right. If I could hear his thoughts right now, they'd probably be something like—it's not doing anything. Why isn't it doing anything? Something is going to happen, right?

Oh, wait. I *can* hear his thoughts. I peer into his head. Oh, boy. He thinks he's found a way to turn himself and his friends all into vampires. Smear the ashes of a supposed vampire on his forehead and chant some funny words he found on an occultist forum on the dark web. Yeah, I'm no mystic, but… something tells me that looking up magic on the internet is probably not going to give reliable results. Also, this guy doesn't know thing one about vampires. He has no clue Seattle already has an immortal society.

"Did you say it right?" asks a shortish black dude on Trevor's right.

"Yes, I said it right." Trevor sets his hands on his hips.

"Do you feel any different?" asks Casey, her voice ever so slightly shaking with apprehension.

I give her brain a poke. Hmm. She's not afraid of Trevor or the people with her… she's being affected by this mine. The same energy that's been giving me the heebie-jeebies is hitting her, too. She's on edge. If I clapped my hands, the sudden noise would probably make her faint. The other three guys are in similar states of fear. Casey's keeping herself from panicking out of hope that turning into a vampire will make her not need to be afraid of whatever is scaring her. The three guys are holding it together only because they don't want to look like chickens in front of their friends. Trevor's so busy being annoyed his internet magic failed, he's not even consciously aware of the supernatural dread all over this place.

"Urn's right there," whispers Ashley.

"Yeah. Keep me invisible. I'll go grab it."

She holds up a 'wait' finger and scurries left to the next nearest tunnel. "It's time for the messing."

"Huh?" I shift my stare to her while following.

"They're doing black magic… or think they're doing black magic…" She gestures at them.

Before I can tell her that they're not trying to summon demons but rather turn themselves into vampires, she does it.

And by 'it,' I mean…

Ashley makes her eyes glow with dark red light and gives off this growl in an inhumanly deep voice. It's well below the range even a mortal man could produce, straight out of a serious horror movie. Hell, I'm looking right at her. I know it's Ashley. I can see the stupid grin on her face at the time, and still, that growl makes me shiver.

I'm pretty sure people back in Seattle hear the scream that comes out of Casey. The short guy's scream isn't much quieter. One dude faints straight away where he stands. Trevor, the black guy, and Casey bolt for the tunnel leading out. The last dude runs directly away from us and goes down the eastward tunnel, too terrified to realize he's chosen the wrong passage.

Ugh. At least one of them peed themselves. I can smell it. Well, I suppose their silly ritual ended up being good for them. At least they still have clean underwear waiting for them outside.

Two seconds later, Ashley loses it and starts laughing.

I'm conflicted. On one hand, that was kinda funny. Also, maybe a bit cruel. Then again, having the hell scared out of them for stealing from Mr. Wolent is probably the tamest punishment possible, so I can deal.

The urge to laugh at this display of absolute panic almost makes it to my mouth. I say almost because of the scream coming from the side passage, followed by a heavy thud.

"Oh, shit." I stare across the room. "That guy fell down a hole."

Ashley stops laughing in an instant. "Oh, no…"

"Guys!" shouts the distant man. "Guys! Help! I'm stuck! Trev? Casey? Daz? Kev!?"

We stand still, listening for a minute. Sounds like the others are still running in a blind panic off into the woods. Maybe they're not going to come back.

I glance at Ashley.

She nods once. "We should get him out of there. At least bring him back up to this level."

"Yeah, that's what I'm thinking. His friends can get him back home. They're going to have a much harder time hauling him up out of a shaft than we will."

Ashley scurries over to the urn and stuffs it into the small pack Trevor carried it in. Like some sort of Girl Scout Master hiker, she zips it up and swings the tiny backpack on in one smooth motion. I was basically Sierra. Did the Girl Scout thing because Mom insisted but dropped it as soon as I was old enough to get away with not wanting to do it anymore.

We dart across the chamber to the eastward tunnel and make our way into the darkness. Just kidding. It's not dark to me. Several sets of wooden braces look like they got shot with a cannon, large bits gouged out of them. The damage is recent... so it must've come from this guy crashing into them while running in total darkness.

Uh oh. If a dude bumping into this wood broke it, we need to get the hell out of here. This place is the opposite of safe.

The mine shaft ends not quite fifty feet from the chamber at a dead end. Scraps of wood dangling from spikes in the wall and littered all over the ground suggest a crude elevator and pulley system might once have been installed here. Now, it's just a hole in the floor. Dude got seriously lucky, since the lower level is only about two stories down. This is not one of those super deep, treacherous shafts you see in some mines that seem to go so deep a balrog is going to be waiting at the bottom with a giant catcher's mitt.

I pick up on the scent of blood, and it smells like something faintly sweet. Kinda weird to get sweet from an adult.

"Let's go," I whisper, then step over the edge and fly/float down what is clearly a hand-carved vertical shaft.

Ash follows.

We land on either side of an average looking guy with black hair. At least, I think it's black. He's got a crapload of dust all over him.

"Gah!" The guy flails, clearly unable to see us... but he's obviously sensed something moving near him. "Go away! Leave me alone!"

"Relax. We're friendly ghosts here to help you," I say.

The guy freezes. He might be about to scream, but he doesn't get the chance before I wallop him in the brain with the Derp Hammer™. No need to make him forget anything. It's way too dark here for him to have seen us. His friends won't believe his stories about 'ghost girls' saving him. Even if they did, they all ran out here to the middle of nowhere to do a strange occult ritual with a stolen urn. It's not like they're going to tell anyone what happened.

"Help me get him up," I say. "Before this whole place comes down on top of us."

"Okay." Ashley moves to his left side, stooping to grab him... but she side eyes a wooden brace against the wall. "Are you sure? Looks sturdy enough." She pats it twice. "Solid wood. Holding up pretty well for being so old."

"Ash—"

The brace promptly slides away from the wall, toppling over sideways away from us and crashing down to the floor. It strikes the bottom of another brace, causing it to fall over as well, which in turn hits the next one, setting off a domino effect that claims six braces. By some miracle, the horizontal beams across the ceiling don't fall. Two of them sag, though.

She screams in shock.

Okay, I might've screamed too. Not a horror movie victim scream. Just... sudden loud noise startle scream. Here is me clawing the fragments of my dignity up off the floor and putting them back where they belong.

"Oops," deadpans Ashley.

I stare at her, shaking my head. Somehow, the whole mine shaft didn't come down—yet. I crouch and grab onto the guy. "C'mon. Let's get out of here while we still can."

"Oh, hey... it broke something," says Ashley, staring into the dust cloud.

"Yeah, I noticed."

"No, I mean there's like a box." She points. "That's so weird."

"What's so weird about a box?" I sigh, crouching there with a grip on this guy's arm and leg, and look over him into the churning dust cloud.

The last brace knocked over by the chain reaction seems to have smashed open one corner of a stone crypt, like one of those giant boxes they put caskets into in a mausoleum. As soon as I look at it, I get the weirdest feeling that we totally messed up, big time. This is 'borrow Mom's car without asking and smash it into a telephone pole' levels of dread. Fortunately, the weird emotion only lasts a few seconds before my brain dismisses it as irrational.

"Oh, that's really weird." I shift my jaw side to side, trying to figure out how anyone got that massive stone box down such a rickety elevator. Doesn't seem possible.

Ashley turns her head to smile at me. "I told you it's weird."

"What's a crypt doing in a mine?"

"That's the part that's weird." She sets her hands on her hips and nods. "Maybe the crypt was put here long before the mine and the miners just tunneled into some older tomb. Oh, look, there's something inside it."

I hang my head. "Are we going to get this guy out of here or not?"

"Just a sec. I wanna see." She cautiously scurries down the passage to the crypt.

Grr. I let go of the guy and go after her. For the record, I am not curious about what is in that crypt. I am going to grab my friend and drag her out of here before the mine falls on our heads. Ashley skids to a stop beside the crypt. I wrap my arms around her from behind and lift her off her feet.

She raises her right arm enough to point into the smashed crypt. "It's just a head."

I pause before hauling her away. Okay, maybe I am a bit curious, after all. The big stone crypt box is mostly empty—except for a single severed head. It's not a skull. Can't say the head is intact, either. It's brown and withered. Looks like an overcooked barbecue chicken wing. No trace of any hair on it. Pretty sure it belonged to a guy. It's impossible to tell how old he was at the time of death—or why anyone would put *just* his head in a box like this in an old mine shaft.

"That's pretty nasty," says Ashley. "Should we freak out, scream, and run?"

Mortal us would totally have screamed at such a grisly discovery.

"Umm. Ash. We *are* the monsters that go bump in the night. I think we're past shrieking at a severed head."

"Oh, true." She nods once.

The severed head abruptly rolls over to face us and its eyes snap open.

I'm *so* not ready for this that I let out a shriek worthy of Sophia's worst nightmare. Ashley screams her lungs out, too.

And yeah, we haul ass like terrified little kids.

3

RELEASING ANCIENT EVIL

*P*anic lets go of me about the same time I get within sight of the mine exit.

The instant I stop, Ashley crashes into me from behind. She gives me this urgent 'what are you doing' stare for half a second before her brain re-engages. Then, we both look at each other, feeling pretty-damn stupid.

"We shall never speak of this again," I whisper.

"Speak of what?" Ashley scowls—or tries to scowl. She doesn't do angry well.

I swear, even if she hadn't made the decision to join me in vampirism and aged up into her fifties… she'd still come off like an angry little kid when upset. Her angry doesn't worry people. It makes them want to say 'aww' and ask what's wrong.

Though, I might need to change my opinion of 'Ashley angry' now. Her red-eye growling thing *was* super scary. Guess that means there are multiple levels of anger for her now. If she's playfully upset, we get the cute scowl. If she's really pissed, the eyes will glow. Yanno, it's a really good thing that vampirism has freed us from the monthly visitor. I don't even want to imagine someone like Vanessa Prentice— a Fury—having to deal with that. I mean… Furies fly into blind rages at seemingly random things. The red faerie visiting a Fury vampiress would probably result in entire small towns being flattened.

"Exactly," I say.

"Huh?" Ashley blinks at me.

"I said we shall never speak of this again. You replied with 'speak of what'. I thought you were saying that on purpose."

She wipes a hand down her face. "Oh. Yeah. Totally."

We stare at each other for a few seconds as the last few drops of adrenaline wear off. It seems that the man who fainted when Ashley growled regained consciousness and ran away while we were downstairs.

"Oh, crap, the guy!" we blurt at roughly the same instant.

Ashley spins around to face into the mine again. "We should go back for him."

I bite my lip, the image of that desiccated severed head staring at me at the tip of my brain. "We should… but…"

Ash grabs my hand and pulls me after her as she walks across the chamber. "It's only a head. What's it going to do, come rolling after us?"

I can't help myself and let out a nervous chuckle. Yeah, true. Thinking about this angry evil severed head feebly attempting to chase people by rolling itself across the floor is hilarious. My imagination edits in various 'oofs' and 'grunts' as it bumps into rocks and such. By the time we get to the vertical shaft, I'm totally over the jump scare and having to fight the urge to laugh.

Speaking of the guy, he's still visiting the town of Derpville—and his friends have not yet returned.

The two of us float down the relatively narrow passage, avoiding the protruding remnants of the former mine elevator. Calling it an elevator is being generous. It seems to have been little more than a wooden platform, some ropes, and pullies. We land on either side of the guy. Before checking him over, I cast a glance down the tunnel toward the spot where we found the head. It's nowhere to be seen, likely still inside the stone crypt box. That makes sense. It's rather difficult for a limbless severed head to climb things.

Maybe it's the weird energy in this place, but now that I'm back on the lower level, the head—or the thought of it—is giving me the creeps again. I want to get out of here ASAP.

The guy appears to have suffered a broken leg. At least, I don't think knees are supposed to bend at such an angle. Also looks like he's sustained some impaling wounds from the wooden ruin of the elevator stuff. None of them are pierced near his vital organs. The worst injury is a stick about as big around as a broom handle sticking out of his right outer thigh. Not that I'm any sort of authority on medical stuff, though I think it's nothing a bandage won't deal with until his friends get him to civilization. One thing I *do* remember from Girl Scouts is that it's bad to yank out impaling objects.

Ashley grabs the guy on the other side. We exchange a nod, then lift off at the same time, flying straight up to the ground level. And yeah, we're probably moving a little too fast to be totally gentle with the guy—but he can't feel anything at the moment. Dude smells like S'mores. Well, his blood does. That's kinda weird, honestly. Adults don't usually taste like sweet stuff. Gotta be the hiking/camping vibe on the guy making me think of them. Wow. I can't remember the last time I had S'mores.

It is super tempting to sneak a few sips. Alas, we're in a hurry so I control myself.

We haul the guy across the first chamber to the exit tunnel and deposit him on the floor in sight of the way out. I don't really care if his friends are confused about how he got injured or if he remembers that he fell down a hole and can't explain how he made it out. He'll think the two 'ghost girls' saved him. Good chance his buddies will blame weed for that.

Did I mention most of Trevor's group reeks of pot?

Not judging, just saying.

Our conscience clear of leaving this guy to die down there, we rush out of the mine into the woods. Approaching voices tease

Ashley's curiosity enough that she stops and hides behind a tree. Argh! Really? With a sigh, I plod to a halt, swing around on one foot like a marionette, and creep back over to her.

Trevor, Casey, Daz, and Kevin (I am assuming their names based on what the dude who fell kept shouting) emerge from the woods into the clearing. They look weary and are kinda limping. Yeah, unless you happen to be a wood elf or a nymph, sprinting barefoot through the woods at night is not a great idea. It's not an awesome idea for vampires either, but at least we heal superficial injuries in a few minutes.

The group makes their way over to their backpacks without saying a word as they proceed to get dressed in a hurry.

Ash turns her head to look at me and whispers in super silent mode, "Tempted to growl at them again. Would that be mean or funny?"

I ponder. "Like I said, they stole from Mr. Wolent. Having the crap scared out of them is getting off easy."

"Yeah." She frowns. "But they might get lost out here... and their friend is hurt."

"True. Let's just go home then."

She opens her mouth, closes it, tilts her head, then shifts her gaze to the mine for a moment.

"Gaaaaaah!" screams a man's voice from inside the mine. "Guys!"

"Oh, shit! Nate!" yells Trevor.

He and the black dude—I think that's Daz—rush into the mine while still half dressed.

Ash nudges me with her elbow. "Should we really leave an undead severed head rolling around by itself?"

"What do you mean?" I raise both eyebrows. "It's been down there for who knows how long already."

She fidgets. "Yeah, but we kinda broke its box open. What if it's going to hurt someone? Or... maybe he needs help?"

Heh. "Uhh, Ash, that guy needs a bit more help than we can give."

She fusses at her hair while making Thinking Face™.

Trevor and Daz drag Nate out of the mine.

"Oh, shit," blurts Casey while zipping her coat up. "What happened?"

"Ran the wrong way," rasps Nate. "Think I fell in a hole, but… maybe I just dreamed it."

Ash and I stay hidden behind our tree, watching the poseur occultists finish getting dressed. They take a few minutes to bandage Nate up and help him put his clothes back on. The black robes get unceremoniously stuffed into backpacks. Daz pulls Nate's arm across his shoulders to support him. He takes a few testing hops. The poor guy doesn't act like he's *too* badly hurt. Huh. Looks like his right leg is not legit broken. I guess it just landed at a weird angle when he hit the ground so it appeared that way. Can't be broken or he'd be screaming his head off in pain. Seems like he doesn't want to put weight on it, though.

The group hikes off into the trees amid grunts of pain, questions about what the hell did they summon, and Casey repeatedly suggesting that Trevor find a better place for rituals that isn't so far away from home. It seems they've entirely forgotten about the urn. They'll probably remember it in the morning. Maybe they'll think the 'demon' they summoned took it.

As soon as they've gone far enough away that we can't see them through trees, Ashley again nudges me.

"What?" I whisper in the normal manner.

"The head? Shouldn't we do something?" She shifts her weight from leg to leg.

I picture the grisly thing in an effort to make some sense of this situation. Can't say I really got a good enough look at it. The more I try to remember it, the more my brain turns it into something from a campy 1980s horror movie. Thanks, Dad.

"What if it's a wounded vampire?" asks Ashley. "If it was our head in there, we'd want someone to help us."

I idly scratch at my collarbone. "Someone put a severed head in a box and stuffed it in an old mine. Maybe we should've left him there."

"Too late," singsongs Ashley while using her arm to pantomime a giant beam falling and smashing something. "Whatever mystical seals were on that old crypt are kinda busted now."

Irrational fear gets into a hair-pulling fight with my conscience. You know one of those 'girl fights' like in high school where no one's really trying to inflict serious injury, rather make the other person look foolish and publicly shame them.

"We either just released an ancient evil that some long-ago people tried to seal away... or maybe that's a vampire... or it could be something entirely new and messed up that we've never seen before. What do you think?"

Ashley starts walking toward the mine opening. "No idea. One way to find out, though. And even if we did unbox an ancient evil, running away is only going to make it worse. You've seen those movies."

Sighing, I chase after her. "What movies?"

"The cheesy ones Dad likes."

Yes, she refers to my father as Dad, too. He may as well be her father at this point. Her real dad is a jerk. I'm almost positive her clinginess with me is a direct result of him abandoning her when she was little.

"Dad likes a lot of cheesy movies."

Ashley ducks into the mine. "The ones where some random person finds something in a remote location, messes with it like an idiot, and releases the monster the whole movie is based on. Then they run away—or get eaten immediately—and evil grows unchecked until it is strong enough to attack more innocent people."

Sigh. Shaking my head, I follow her back into the tunnels. Yeah, this does really kind of feel like we're in one of those movies. We open the ancient box, let the thing out, run like hell... only for it to slowly make its way to the nearest town and start eating people. Again, the idea of a severed head chasing people down and killing them is hilariously campy, right up there with that *Sharknado* movie.

"You're sure about this?" I ask.

"Yep." Ashley stops at the edge of the hole, then spins to smile at me. "It's like dropping a match in the woods and running away. We should stomp the fire out before it grows out of control."

I step over the opening and float. "You're planning to stomp on the head?"

"No, dork. It's a metaphor." She sigh-giggles at me while levitating upward and drifting over the hole.

"Okay. Fine." I exhale. "Let's go make sure we didn't just unleash Gozer."

She laughs.

Her grin is contagious. I can't help but smile despite the eerie mood dripping from the walls in here. I really do have the coolest best friend. How many people my age have a bestie who would understand a *Ghostbusters* joke?

Thanks, Dad.

4

GREAT PAINS

ALSO TUESDAY

Gotta say, old mines are considerably less scary now that I can see in complete darkness. It's no more frightening than exploring an abandoned building in the middle of the day. The dust cloud from the earlier collapse of the support braces is still kinda hanging in the air in the lower-level passage.

This reminds me that the braces collapsed. It's probably a matter of hours before this tunnel caves in. Hopefully, my overamped sense of hearing will pick up on warning sounds coming from the walls in time for us to zoom the hell out of here before we end up being buried unalive.

Motion in the haze up ahead draws my attention to the floor. Oh, wow. The head got out of the crypt somehow. It's lying in the middle of the corridor. And yeah, it's facing us. Seems to be trying to talk. The mouth is opening and closing. His skin's crackling with the same noise overcooked fried chicken makes if someone bites into it. Hey, if I can hear that from forty feet away, I'm confident any dangerous noises coming from an imminent cave-in will give us enough time to get out of here.

Poor guy. Looks like someone cut his head off and threw it in a deep fryer. His skin's gone so rictus his teeth are permanently revealed. There's also a weird tumor-like growth above his left eye about the size of half a golf ball. Ick.

"Mood?" I ask.

"Hard to say." Ashley gazes around. "There's anger everywhere. I can't tell if it's coming from the head or just the environment."

If I try to pretend this mine is not saturated in dread and separate the head from that, it doesn't look threatening. Wow. Here I am staring at not only a severed, burned, head... but one that's moving— and I'm staying calm. There's more of Sophia in my personality than I like to admit. Dad sometimes makes the joke that my two sisters are like an alchemical distillation of my personality. Each sister represents one extreme end of my personality where I'm basically both of them in one person. Depending on the day, I gravitate more one way or the other.

I lose a minute or so astonished at myself for not freaking out... again. This shouldn't bother me. Not only am I a vampire who doesn't need to be afraid of the dark, I've beheaded vampires before. Just... the severed heads I created didn't move after being cut off. Decapitation is super inconvenient for vampires, but not the end of the world. Sounds strange to say but getting shot in the brain is much more dangerous since we lose consciousness. Having our head separated from the rest of us just makes controlling our bodies a teeny bit awkward.

Huh. Wonder where the rest of this guy is...

We creep closer. Ashley's bravado fades a little as we near the head. She grabs my arm in both hands, clinging to my side. Hmm. She has not yet made a crass semi-sexual joke about 'getting head' or something of that nature yet. Hope she's okay.

The head stops fidgeting and stares up at us. Not easy to read much of a facial expression from such a burned visage. Still, though. I can't help but imagine he's baffled at seeing a pair of teenage girls who aren't screaming and freaking out. Well, again. Being a vampire doesn't mean we're immune to jump scares. I guess there's also enough of *us* still in here that a gory severed head moving made us panic before until our rational brains recovered from the initial shock.

"Okay. Now what?" I ask.

Ashley crouches, leaning closer to it. "He's got fangs. Definitely a vampire. Doesn't feel very evil. I think the dark energy is in the mine."

The head attempts to speak, but makes no sound. Even the silent whisper trick isn't working for him. I don't think he knows how to do it… or maybe there are too many holes for him to control the air in his mouth.

"Sorry we screamed before," says Ashley. "You kinda startled us."

I glance around at the mine, not at all enjoying being at the site of a future cave-in. We should get out of here ASAP. "Oh yeah. Here we are having a casual conversation with a severed head like it's normal."

The head wags his jaw harder.

"What?" asks Ashley. "Can you say that louder? I can't hear you."

"Uhh, Ash?" I poke her on the shoulder. "He doesn't have lungs at the moment. How is he supposed to talk now?"

She blinks. "Oh. Duh. Umm, what about the silent whisper?"

The head furrows his brow.

"He looks confused." I take a knee beside Ashley. After a second or two to steel myself, I grab the poor guy and set him upright on his neck stump. Feels dry. Leathery even. Now that I'm holding him in both hands, I realize the 'tumor' above his eye is actually the head end of a railroad spike. Wow. This dude really pissed someone off. They drove a giant nail into his skull. Not sure what the heck they expected it to do, but here we are. Maybe it was some folkloric nonsense like that deal about iron harming faeries.

"Like this," whispers Ashley in silent mode. "Close off the back of your throat and move air around your mouth."

"He doesn't have a 'back of the throat' to close off at the moment." I wince.

The head shifts his eyeballs to the left several times, as if trying to indicate a direction.

"You want to go that way?" I point down the tunnel, deeper in from the elevator opening. At least the wooden braces forward of this spot remain intact.

He moves his eyeballs up and down, perhaps trying to nod.

"I think he's asking us to go that way." I glance at Ashley.

"What's that sticking out of his forehead?" She points at the spike.

"Looks like a railroad spike." I grimace. "Ouch."

Ashley shivers. "Oof. That's gotta be a headache."

With a fried chicken skin crackle, he makes a 'you have no idea how much that hurt' grimace. Okay, gore aside, I'm starting to feel sorry for this guy.

"Should I pull it out?" I ask.

The head moves his eyes up and down again, gazing up at the ceiling, then down at the floor.

Hmm. Better make sure he wants me to remove the spike before I do more damage. "Are you trying to nod?"

He does the same eye motion.

Ugh. "That's not helping. I don't know if that eye thing is a yes or not." An idea hits me. "Okay. If you want me to pull it out, close only your left eye."

The head closes his left eye.

"Did you mean the eye on our left or his actual left eye?" asks Ashley.

"Argh! Stop confusing me." I grab her around the neck and fake strangle her for a second, making her laugh. "I meant *his* left eye, which he closed. Okay. Spike comes out."

Ashley leans back.

"What are you doing?" I blink at her.

"I don't wanna get blood spraying all over me."

"Ash…" I indicate the head. "Any blood in there would have long ago drained out of his neck."

She keeps leaning away. "Since when has logic and vampirism ever worked together?"

"There's logic to vampirism. It's not *that* bad."

Ashley gives me side eye. "Okay. Rephrase. Since when has logic and *us* ever worked together? There is a teleporting kitten in the house."

"Fair point." I rest my left hand on top of the head, twist him slightly to the side, and grab the rail spike in my right hand. "One... two..."

I pluck the spike out. It crunches and crackles a bit, but pops free without too much fuss, taking only a little more effort than pulling a birthday candle out of a cake. He gives me this weird look, as if he hadn't expected me to be able to remove it so easily.

His eyes almost cross as the spike comes out. His expression is a mixture of relief and happiness. I usually only see that expression on a guy's face at certain intimate moments when the proverbial firecracker explodes. No, this guy didn't have a sense of arousal at the spike coming out. I guess it would be a better metaphor to describe his expression like someone who's been constipated for a week finally heaving ho.

A small ring of super hard scabby skin that tore away from the forehead surrounds the iron spike near the head. The lower portion of the giant nail is dark red, as if coated with a thin layer of dried blood so dense it's become paint.

And oof. This blood smells like ass.

Not literal ass. It's only a saying. Damn my overly heightened senses. A mortal probably wouldn't even smell this at all. For me, it's like... imagine the smell of a dead body. Take that smell and condense it into a liquid form... and then shoot it up your nose using one of those sinus spray things. The stench is so strong I can taste it.

Both Ashley and I gag and cough. I bury my face in the crook of my left elbow and fling the spike away. It lands in the distance, sending the echo of a ringing clank down the mine shaft.

"This,"—Ashley coughs—"dude isn't vibing like a bad guy. We should help him."

"I'm still kinda confused how he's even awake." I wince while examining the square hole above his left eye where the spike came from.

The edge of the wound is… undulating. Skin that looks as hard as fingernails twitches and fidgets about like it's trying to heal but can't move. At least I'm not able to see deep into his brain. The hole's full of dark red blood that's behaving like solidified Jell-O. Well, Ash was sorta right. There is still blood in there despite the open neck. That shouldn't surprise me. Vampires don't exactly bleed like mortals. Our blood is more like liquid soaked into a sponge. There's no blood pressure from a beating heart, so no reason for it to go spurting all over the place.

"There are some questions not worth asking." Ashley offers an innocent shrug and smile. "Especially when we're in such a dangerous place."

"Okay. How can we help? Do we just take the head home?"

The guy flicks his gaze side to side. Okay. If looking up and down rapidly means nodding, this has to be the head shake for no. He then indicates left with his gaze several times.

"Go that way?"

Eyeball nod.

"Okay." I pick the head up, stand, and start walking.

The passage goes on for another thirty feet or so before forking in a Y. Head sticks his tongue out and uses it to point left. It's simultaneously funny and disgusting. Can't blame him *too* much, really. He doesn't have any other way to point right now.

I go left.

Ashley trails after me, gazing around at the mine. "There are more of those strange markings cut into the walls here."

"What are they?"

"Like I have any idea about this stuff." She pulls out her phone and holds it up at the wall.

"Gah!" I yell, momentarily blinded by the flash.

Ashley yelps too, as if the consequences of a flash in complete darkness hit her as a complete surprise.

It takes about a minute for my sight to return.

Ashley blinks rapidly. "Oops. Sorry. Didn't even think about that..."

"Yeah. It's like dark in here or something." I make a goofy face at her.

Easy mistake for us to make. Things never *appear* dark for me anymore—except for the night sky. But that's not really dark as much as it is outer space.

"Umm." Ashley looks around. "All the markings are just the same symbol over and over again. Don't have to take any more pictures."

"Well, if you find something photo worthy, warn me... and close your eyes before you hit the button."

I resume walking, searching around for anything significant.

"Hey, another symbol. Get ready. Gonna snap a pic," says Ashley.

"Okay." I stop walking and close my eyes.

Everything goes bright red.

An iPhone camera flash in absolute darkness is still painful to vampire eyes when closed. Still, it's nowhere near as bad as it going off unexpectedly while my eyes are open. The blaring redness only lingers in my vision for a few seconds.

We continue walking. In only a minute or two, the head's goal becomes obvious: another crypt sits on the floor of the tunnel, tucked up against the wall on the left. Oh wow. I think someone dismembered him and put the different pieces in different sealed stone boxes. Maybe that's why he's awake despite being beheaded. This one does not look like an accidental discovery of an old tomb. Someone definitely put this here after the mine existed. There's got to be another, much bigger, elevator somewhere... or maybe an entirely separate mineshaft leading to the outside on this level. How the heck did they get a 2,000-pound stone box down here? Obviously, someone did. Well, whenever someone long ago in the past accomplished something modern people can't make sense of, there's only one 'logical' explanation—aliens did it.

I hurry over to the second crypt. This one is completely intact.

Ashley tries to get her fingernails into the seam between the lid and the rest of the crypt. Doesn't work. The seal is too precise. Those same crazy witch cross type symbols are all over the side of the crypt.

"Grr. I can't get a grip on the lid." Ashley glances at the beam nearby holding up the ceiling. "Probably a dumb idea to knock that out."

"Ya think?" I shake my head, then look down at the severed one I'm holding. "Is it a bad idea to break the beam?" Without waiting for him to react, I make him nod at Ashley.

She laughs. "Okay. Let's see if we can, uhh, re-boot this vampire."

"He's not a computer."

Ashley leans back and stomp-kicks the crypt, smashing a hole in it. "I was being literal."

"Ugh." I exhale hard. "Technically, wouldn't you have to kick it twice for it to be a *re* boot? Also, you're not wearing boots. Those are sneakers."

She holds up a finger. "True. However, the act of kicking something can be referred to as booting, regardless of the type of footwear involved." She lightly punts the crypt again. "There. Re boot."

Sigh.

We lean close to the hole and peer inside, our heads touching at the temples.

Eww. This crypt contains a de-limbed torso. No arms or legs.

"Think this guy's name is Jigsaw?" whispers Ashley.

I groan.

The head clacks his teeth. Not sure if he's annoyed at that or giving me a 'hurry up' sign.

"Now what?" Ashley swipes her hair off her face. "Do we have to do anything special or just, like, put the head back on the body?"

"Well, the user manual I got with my vampire starter kit didn't say much about recovery from dismemberment." I shrug one shoulder. "Guessing that means it's pretty obvious and simple."

"Try it." She sticks her hand in the hole she made, grabs the lid, and pushes it upward before dragging it off to the side, opening the entire box.

The head gawks at us.

"Relax, man." I hold him up to look me in the eye, and extend my fangs. "We're on the same team."

His expression gives off a sense of 'oh, that makes sense now'.

Poor guy appears to be naked, though he's burned up so badly this movie would still get a PG rating. Partially melted skin has stretched and split apart into strips so bad it resembles mummy wrappings made of old pizza cheese. Ick.

I lean over the crypt with the head in both hands. The torso twitches like a paralyzed dog waiting for its master to put the food bowl somewhere it can reach. Oh, that's super creepy. Trying my best to not be freaked out, I place the head where it belongs. Wormlike tendrils of flesh leap upward from the neck opening as well as extend down from the severed head. They weave together in mere seconds, creating a superficial connection. I'm guessing a good haymaker to the face would knock his head right back off. It takes a lot longer to fully heal. This is only enough to hold things in place while he heals.

He sucks in a deep breath, then chokes out a cloud of dust.

Ashley and I leap back, waving at the blast of grime.

"Seeeg," he rasps.

We tilt our heads in unison like a pair of confused Pomeranians.

"Saaaa." He coughs. "Baaaah."

Ash and I exchange a glance.

"What language is that?" whispers Ashley.

The limbless vampire coughs again before rasping, "Significant..."

"English, apparently." I fold my arms.

"Improvement," rasps the guy.

"Significant improvement?" Ashley scratches her head.

"Aye," wheezes the body.

I glance back and forth at the mine shaft. "I'm guessing your arms and legs are in another box somewhere?"

He attempts to nod, causing a seam to split open on his neck, then gives a grunt of irritation before rasping, "Yes," in a voiceless hiss.

"Any idea where?" asks Ashley.

"Right, fork," he wheezes.

"Okay. On it." I pivot away from the crypt and fast-walk back to the Y-fork in the tunnel.

Somewhere, an invisible clock is ticking down the time until this entire place collapses. I'd rather not be here when it happens. We jog down the corridor and swing around the Y fork into the other branching tunnel. A whole mess of mining tools lay around on the floor not far from the intersection. Old pick axes, rusted lanterns, some leather knapsacks, and so on. Fortunately, I don't see any bones or corpses. This looks like junk the former miners left behind, arranged in a somewhat organized fashion, like storage. Doesn't seem as if people dropped everything and ran. Hoping that's a good sign.

We find another crypt almost sixty feet away from the Y.

"Wow."

Ashley glances at me. "What?"

"Someone dragged not one, but three stone crypts into a mine." I whistle. "This dude really got on someone's bad side."

"Hmm." She rubs her chin. "He seems nice enough to me."

It could be said that a vampire in his position would be nice to anyone to get them to help put him back together. No idea if he will remain nice when fully assembled. However, Ash is pretty good at picking up on moods. If she thinks he's not a bad guy, he's probably okay.

We stomp kick the crypt open. Thankfully, this one contains both arms and both legs. However, each limb has been wrapped in burlap and bound in rope. Something like tar seals all the knots.

"Whatever this guy did to annoy someone must have been epic." I pull a bundle out, pop my claws, and shred the fabric off.

"No kidding." Ashley tears one of the legs free of its burlap. "Been down here a while. This cloth is falling apart."

It doesn't take us too long to 'free' the limbs from their elaborate packaging.

"Well, you know what they say..." Ashley picks up his left limbs. "Vampire healthcare costs an arm and a leg."

"Boo," I mutter.

She tosses me his left arm. "Here, I'll get the legs. Mom would kill me if she thought I was trafficking in arms."

"Wow." I shake my head. "Just wow."

I pick up the right arm. They don't weigh very much, all dried out.

"Hmm." Ashley peers into the crypt. "Where's his dingus? I didn't see it on the body."

Oof. I cringe. "Pretty sure it burned off. I don't think that counts as a separate limb."

She gives a disgusted laugh. "Some guys seem to think so, but yeah, you're probably right."

We hurry back to the crypt containing the head/torso. The arms start twitching in my grasp, more and more feverishly the closer we get. As much as they can, they flail about, grabbing anything within reach.

"Relax, relax. Gonna put you back together. Stop squeezing my ass."

As soon as I say that, the arms go still, almost giving off a vibe of 'oops, sorry.' No foul. He can't exactly see what he's reaching for right now.

We rush back to the crypt containing the head and torso. Ash and I kneel beside it and set the limbs down, watching them do the fleshy-wormy thing as they superficially reattach themselves.

"Weird," whispers Ashley.

"Just a bit." As icky as this spectacle is, I can't look away. It's fascinating.

She nudges me. "No, I mean... if someone was mad at him enough to do this... why do this and not like leave him out in the sun?"

"Good question."

"Thank..." rasps the guy, before losing consciousness again.

Any sense of him being an animated undead being is gone. Now, he looks and feels like an ordinary corpse. No idea if he just died for good or if his body has gone into deep sleep recovery mode now that it's in one piece. Could be either.

"Humpty Dumpty's back together again." Ashley pats the crypt wall.

"He probably wouldn't appreciate you calling him that." I gently touch his chest. Cold, hard, like week-old fried chicken left on the kitchen counter. "Now what? This guy is *out*."

"Did he die?"

"Maybe. Or he's recovering."

"Should we take him home?" Ashley tilts her head.

I wince. "Not a good idea to try moving him. He'll fall apart. If he *is* recovering and not permanently dead, he needs to be left at peace."

She stands. "So, we just what… leave him here? What if the mine collapses?"

"It's been here this long without caving in." I exhale, not really liking any option here.

"Yeah, but we knocked out a bunch of beams." She flashes a sheepish smile.

I give her a playfully accusatory look. Technically, *she* knocked out the beams, but I accept the collective 'we' there.

"We could lug the whole crypt up to the top level, so if it caves in down here, he should be safe."

Ashley nods. "Yeah. Good idea. Or maybe we could just call Wolent? See what he thinks?"

"No signal out here." I grumble. "We'd have to fly up pretty high, and even then, the signal's probably too weak for voice."

"True." She twists her hair around her finger a few times. "So, let's bring him upstairs, at least."

Moving a stone crypt normally requires forklifts. Fortunately, vampires and forklifts have some similarities. We're also a lot more agile.

"Problem." I tap my foot. "We might be able to lift this crypt, but we sure as hell aren't going to be able to fly with it."

"Oh, yeah." She frowns. "So, we just grab him then and be gentle. Hopefully, he doesn't fall apart."

I think about this for a minute. "He probably wouldn't withstand a long flight in this condition. Moving him upstairs shouldn't be too bad if we are gentle."

She nods.

We carefully collect the corpse from the crypt and carry him back to the elevator shaft. He's probably not more than sixty pounds right now, so it wouldn't really be a burden to fly him all the way back to Seattle. Biggest problem is that wind exposure would rip him apart. I am not flying at walking speed. It would take us days to get home.

After depositing him in a secluded spot a little north of the chamber where Trevor and his friends tried to do a ritual, Ashley and I head out of the mine. He should be safe there in the event the lower level gives out and caves in. I stop to gaze up at the sky in worshipful delight. I'm not exactly claustrophobic; however, I do not like being in old mines on the verge of collapse.

Ashley makes a face at the mine.

"Aww, it's fine. Don't feel guilty about leaving him there. He'll be okay now. It's beyond dark and no one will find this place. It's way out in the middle of nowhere."

She turns in a circle, staring out at the trees. "Should we maybe put up a sign warning people there's a wounded vampire in this cave about to wake up and they should avoid the area?"

I grimace. "Not a bad idea in theory, other than saying the V word out loud. You know, we're not real creatures."

Ashley peers at me.

I brace for her to scream 'vagina' like a goofball making a 'v-word' joke, but she doesn't.

"Umm. All right. If you think it'll be okay." She bites her lip. "I'd feel guilty if someone got hurt."

Yeah. Me too. But... this is a vampire who was burned and dismembered. He's crashed *hard* now that he's in one piece again. When he wakes up, he will more than likely be out of his mind with hunger. It's an almost certainty that *someone* is going to die. Just like when I ripped up those drug dealers, he won't have any active control over it. Maybe fate will be kind and the unsuspecting blood meal will be a bear or some other animal. Even if we knew that vampire was going to kill a human hiker, what do we do? Destroy him permanently? That's just as morally bad as walking away and letting him kill someone in a mindless rage.

Oh, wait…

"What's that look for?" Ashley raises her eyebrow at me.

"I think we can stop him from murdering a bunch of people."

"How?" She perks up.

"Where's the closest Walmart? We need a couple thermoses." I wag my eyebrows. "Gonna leave him a snack for when he wakes up."

5

THE STRANGE UNDEAD
ROLLERCOASTER

WEDNESDAY

*P*eaches and Cream bath bombs are the bomb.

Being a vampire is amazing—most of the time. Running around Forks (that's a small town) bleeding a half dozen people into Thermoses wasn't the most fun thing I've ever done. Relax. None of them are dead or seriously hurt. They all walked away with a strange compulsion for chocolate chip cookies and orange juice. Aurélie coached Ashley over their sire-progeny mind link how to add a drop or two of her blood to each Thermos to 'preserve' the fresh blood inside it. Aurélie uses the same trick with all her wine bottles. She's like the vampire version of a Sam's Club shopper: she does all her feeding once a year, then lives off the bottles.

So, hopefully, whoever that guy is won't go completely and totally crazy when he opens his eyes again. We helped a vampire in need and my conscience is clear that he's not going to hurt anyone accidentally.

Yay for peaches and cream bath bombs.

I love lying here in the tub completely underwater. Breathing is for losers. I've never been *overly* short. I'm not exactly tall, either. Guess most average people would think of me as 'a little short' but I'm not 'has to climb up on the counter to reach the cabinets' small. I'm the perfect size. Perfect, that is, to get all my body underwater without anything sticking out into the air in a standard size bathtub.

This is relaxing.

Good for the skin, too. Gotta take care of my body. I'm going to have it for a really long time.

I'm ever so slightly on guard for the bathtub to betray me like it did Sierra. One moment she sat here taking a nice warm bath, the next, she found herself on top of the Space Needle. Sophia isn't sure exactly what happened. It obviously has something to do with residual magical energy soaked into the bathtub. After all, she used it in the ritual that enchanted Sierra into whatever she is now.

Hmm. That's a bad way to phrase it.

Sierra is still a mortal human. She's merely… boosted. My tween sister is almost as strong and fast as a vampire. She's tough, too. Took a fall from a second story and didn't even bruise. Hell, a car hit her head-on and she laughed it off. Thankfully, her lack of injury was so unbelievable to normal people everyone at the school believes they saw it wrong and the car only grazed her. I mean, nothing else makes any sense, right?

So, yeah. This bathtub might be magical still. Maybe it's an interaction with Sierra. The magic in her resonates with the magic residue in the porcelain. Or, perhaps this tub is likely to teleport anyone in it somewhere randomly whenever it feels like. If it happens again, I hope it gets me instead of anyone else in the family. Wouldn't be the first time for me to end up stranded outside naked. At least I can fly up where no one can see me and the cold doesn't bother me.

Not that I want this to happen.

Just saying, if it does, better me than Mom, Dad, or the Littles.

If it did it to Chloe, she'd be furious. Or, maybe think it hilarious. She's little enough that she might not be embarrassed at all. She can also fly herself home at an altitude where no one will see her. Of course, she's still a little too little to take a bath by herself… so I'd be in here with her and could grab her if she started to fall through. Or maybe she could be left on her own if she wants. Not like she's at any risk to drown. I chuckle at the idea.

Sophia's been trying to 'fix' the tub so it doesn't do that. Sierra is a little gunshy about this tub. Lately, she's been taking showers instead of baths, using the basement bathroom. Speaking of Sierra, she's still coping with her demonic nightmare. On an intellectual level, she knows no actual shooting happened at her school. The entire thing only existed as a waking nightmare forced into her mind by a piece of crap demon. Most of the people at school don't even really know why she had a panic attack in class. I mean, to them, it looked like she had a panic attack—not a demon-induced nightmare.

Since she had a freakout in the middle of class upon waking up, the school kinda insisted she see a therapist. Not sure if it's helping. Can't be hurting. Sierra hasn't complained about the therapy sessions yet. For the most part, she's latched onto art. Lately, she's been spending as much time drawing and such as she does playing video games. I'd be worried that a nightmare affected her more than a literal trip into the demonic underworld... but she's had a thing about school shootings for years. That stupid demon sensed a weakness and went after it.

Why do kids fixate on certain fears like that? For me, it used to be closets. When I was super little, like four, I could've sworn the doorknob on my closet rattled one night. Ever since, I was terrified some monster was in there and wanted to get me. I couldn't bear the sight of the closet being open in the dark. I had to close the door and drag my toy chest in front of it in order to sleep. For all I know, I totally imagined the rattle.

Practice drills for school shootings traumatized Sierra.

I'm kind of amazed Sophia brushed it off. Go figure my 'tough' sister was the one who had an irrationally strong fear reaction. It's probably got to do with how much she hates feeling powerless or helpless. Sophia's used to it. I think part of her kinda likes being seen as the weak damsel from a faerie tale who needs to be saved. Sierra is very much a self-saving princess, and if she isn't able to save herself from whatever situation, she can't handle it.

So, yeah. Soph's been investigating our bathtub to try and stop it from randomly warping anyone else out of the house in the middle of a bath. Maybe it's karma biting us in the butt for stealing a super expensive ruby, or maybe she's still struggling with stray magic. Soph said something the other week about having a 'minor control issue' that lets scraps of magic leak out into the world whenever she does something big.

Ugh. I don't understand magic. I'm not going to even try to make sense of it.

Ashley, though. She's kinda confusing me lately. At the moment, she's still down in the basement with Chloe. I think they're playing dolls. To say she's been acting odd lately would be an understatement. My best guess is that she's going through a similar phase to what happened to me a few months after going vampire. I had this crazy mood thing where I'd think about my mortal life like it happened a really long time ago, full of nostalgia and longing. Maybe it came from the mortal part of my brain slowly dying and screaming at me that I should be sad for dying and losing my family and never being able to go back to those days. Who knows? I had all the mood swings. Needed my stuffed animals again. That mess is mostly gone. About the only remnant still rattling around my head is extreme possessiveness toward this house and my family.

Like, I don't wanna move out. Ever. This is my home. My security blanket. My fortress.

All problems I'll ever run into can be solved (or avoided) by hiding in my sanctuary of sanctuaries: my bedroom. No, I know that's not really true. But it feels that way to me. I wonder how that feeling will change when my parents eventually get old and die and all the Littles are grown up and moved out on their own. Will I still feel the same way about this house when it's empty, or will the emptiness serve only to make the absence of my family even worse? Will I have to run away from this house to escape sadness? Or will Ash and I live here with Chloe and just act like the 'rents are off on vacation with the Littles for a really long time?

I'm a permanent teenager. Can I even function without there being parents in the house? That's like the entire *point* of being a teenager. I'm an adult when it's convenient and I'm a child when I'm scared/lazy/overwhelmed.

Maybe Mom and Dad will stick around as ghosts. I could work with that.

They say nothing in this life is forever and I should get used to that. I say they can go to hell. Vampires are a thing. We are forever. Okay, splitting hairs here. I guess vampires aren't really in 'this life.' Nothing in *life* is permanent, but I'm having an unlife. Not exactly the same, no matter how much I try to pretend I'm normal.

I'm also a teenager. I should not be obsessing over decades in the future. I live in the here and now, dammit. Come on, brain. Stop tormenting me.

Anyway, Ashley. She's not getting all nostalgic and talking about the past like I did. Nope. Her personality is changing. From like age sixteen on, she sorta fixated on sexy stuff but had been too embarrassed to really talk about it. In the months leading up to her decision to go vamp, she'd gotten more uninhibited and open about it. I'm sure having a romantic encounter with Aurélie broke her inner freak loose for a while. All the stuff she'd always sorta daydreamed and fantasized about, she decided to leap into. Then again, it might not have been sleeping with an elder vampire as much as it was her believing I died for a few days. A mortality check could also help someone get over inhibitions and want to 'live a little' before their ticket got punched, too.

So yeah. Two months ago, Ash was a little redheaded sex kitten. Now? She's sliding way hard in the other direction. Honestly, it always did get awkward hearing her talk about that stuff. Even though we're the same age, she's always kinda felt like a kid sister who needed protection from the world around us. Her being so into rainbow unicorns and glittery stuff didn't help her come off as any more mature, either.

Lately, she's been embracing her inner fourteen-year-old. She hasn't said two words about wanting a boyfriend or girlfriend, getting laid, or even touching herself in… at least three weeks. Not that I went prying, but it was pretty obvious whenever she wanted some alone time with one of her plastic boyfriends. That hasn't happened in a while, either.

Ashley's kinda acting like she did when we were fourteen or fifteen. Which, for her, means basically not much has changed other than the absence of sexy type jokes or conversation. Case in point: she didn't make a single NSFW joke about 'head' the entire time we were in that mine.

My guess is she's going through mental stuff associated with the conversion to vampirism. Her brain is sorting things out, trying to make sense of everything. Sooner or later—could be months—her personality will settle down to its permanent state post-vampirism. I assume this will end up being a lot closer to normal Ashley. Three steps back from 'sex kitten' Ash and a few steps forward from plush-unicorn-hugging tween. She'll be able to talk about sex again, even if not without blushing and giggling.

More or less, she should settle back into a personality quite close to how she was during our last year of high school. I wonder if she'd been so desperate to find a lover because she expected us to follow the usual route of growing up like the 'rents did. Go to college in a different city than their friends, meet someone, get married, and rarely see their friends again into adulthood. As I said, Ash has some serious abandonment issues thanks to her father just up and leaving them one day out of the blue with no warning. She figured we'd grow into adults on our own paths and she needed someone else to cling to if I wasn't going to be there.

Or so I guess.

Well, that's not a problem now. We're besties forever. Literally.

I don't mind, even if it is a bit *Groundhog Day*. Can't miss what I don't know, right? Besides, the 'rents are always complaining about this that and the other thing. Job sucks. Bills suck. Getting old sucks, and so on. They don't exactly make a strong case that I am 'missing out' on anything by not growing older. I'm sure some people think it's somehow 'sad' or tragic that I'm never going to get older. Those same people also think it's sad and tragic that Chloe is stuck as a seven-year-old forever. The two of us are in the same boat: fate left us a choice between vampirism or permanent death. I think we both got lucky. Besides, Chloe doesn't know enough to be upset about anything. I barely remember being seven, but I do remember enough to know it wasn't an age where I 'couldn't wait' to grow up and do stuff. That crap didn't start until like twelve or so. No, Chloe's unlife isn't tragic. She gets to enjoy permanent innocence, an existence completely free of worries, cares, or responsibilities. You wanna talk tragic, there's that vampiress in London—Charlotte. That poor woman has the body of a twenty-one-year-old but is mentally like Chloe's age.

Talk about messed up. I have no idea what happened to her to cause that, but I hope whoever did that to her suffered for it.

As far as Ashley goes, who knows what will happen as she works her way through the mental adjustment period? This whole vampire thing is sorta random and weird. I suppose it's possible she could end up like this forever, too. It's not likely, but I need to prepare for the possibility. We spent all last night talking about regrets.

I don't have that.

My death wasn't exactly by choice. Sure, an argument could be made that taking Scott off somewhere alone in the woods to tell him we were done might have been stupid and risky. I never expected him to stab me to death. He'd always been a jerk. Never saw him as violent before that, at least not to a murderous level.

But, yeah. I didn't ask to be made a vampire. Ashley did. She chose to give up her mortal future, all those dreams she had about becoming a veterinarian and a mother. She's got stuff to deal with. I don't think she truly regrets choosing to join me in undeath. We've been inseparable since the day we met. Somewhere in her daydreams of having a family and a career helping animals, we also still lived in the same houses we do now and still hung out all the time like we did growing up. I don't think it really occurred to her that adult life seldom works out like that. Maybe once she realized adult life would more than likely pull us apart, she finally chose to stay with me in a permanent summer-after-high-school life.

Talking about potential regrets is totally from that whole mental process that made me super nostalgic for crap that only happened a few years ago. I know exactly where those thoughts are coming from, so I did my best to talk her through it. Some girls might have spent the night drowning their negative emotions and fears in weed and booze. Us? We watched movies and ate excessive amounts of rocky road. What finally broke the glum mood was me commenting about how we didn't have to feel bad for eating an entire box of ice cream. All I said was something about how we wouldn't gain any weight, merely have an incredibly weird and uncomfortable few minutes in the bathroom later… and she burst out laughing.

For the record, any Innocent vampire who eats rocky road ice cream (or any food) should make damn sure to thoroughly chew any hard bits like nuts. Sharp edges are *not* cool.

Ashley couldn't stop laughing for the rest of last night until the sun knocked us out. Yeah, my best-friend-slash-sister is going through a phase. For the time being, I'm rolling with it and treating her like she's fourteen again. And yeah, that kinda means we are both acting a bit childish. It's a force feedback loop. Her attitude affects my attitude, which reinforces her attitude.

Yeah, it really did feel weird to have 'sexy Ashley' around. Is it strange that she's gone hard in the other direction now, being all innocent? Meh. The first year or two of vampirism can be a wild ride emotionally. Fingers crossed she stabilizes somewhere between the two extremes.

Me? I feel pretty normal now, more or less how I was before Scott killed me… if a bit more confident. I'm not exactly the most objective critic of my personality; however, I feel more or less like the old me with some minor changes. For one thing, I don't give a flying duck (yes, my brain has autocorrect) what other people think of me anymore. If I do something stupid and embarrassing in public, I can make them forget it.

Heh.

Unlife is sweet.

It's also crazy. Still, beats having to grow up the rest of the way and waste my life in an office cubicle somewhere. Right now, I have no cares or worries beyond enjoying this peaches and cream bath bomb.

Oh, wait. That's not true. I've got some homework to finish off.

Grr. Screw it. I sink deeper into the tub. The homework can wait for tomorrow.

6

CAKE

*N*othing starts off feeling surreal.

I mean… something that's going to eventually strike me as surreal doesn't do so immediately. It takes a while before my brain skips a gear and gets all tangled like the chain on Dad's mountain bike. I can usually fix it—my brain, that is—much faster and with a lot less swearing. Only thing is, once Dad gets the chain back in place, he can keep riding like nothing happened. Once I've experienced that flash of surrealness, it's not as easy to re-immerse myself in the moment.

This particular moment is happening at Mrs. Carter's house.

Oh, that's weird. Why did I call it 'Mrs. Carter's house' and not 'Ashley's place.' Guess I've adjusted to Ash living with us now. Her bedroom here is still intact. Sophia essentially copied it with magic, like duplicating an image file on a computer. From the outside, our house looks normal. No extra rooms appeared. That would've attracted attention. Besides, windows aren't a great idea for vampire bedrooms.

Ash's new bedroom is basically under our backyard, branched off the basement. I don't know what happened to all the dirt and such it displaced. Some of it got compressed into like a seriously dense wall around the space but it seems odd for that to be all of it. What happened to the rest? Sophia had to send it somewhere. She probably doesn't even know where it went.

Anyway, yeah. Strange for me to think of this as Mrs. Carter's house, but that's not where the surreal feeling came from. No, that's the whole birthday party going on now. Ashley and I have been acting like children since we woke up. Not *little* kids. Just like... I dunno, like girls too young to care about having boyfriends.

We weren't exactly the most social creatures in school, though we did have a few ancillary friends in grade school. Nothing that extended past school hours, though. We'd hang out with them at the school but never bothered trying to get together otherwise. Our actual childhood birthday parties involved between two and four kids from school. Once we got a little older into our teens, birthday celebrations dialed back a bit—often being just something with family. A few minutes and cake, so to speak.

Today's a mix of both worlds. We're having a party like we're still in eighth grade, but we didn't invite a ton of people. This is mostly due to everyone we knew from high school being out of state in college and/or simply being too old and mature to have any interest in silly party games or watching cartoons. The goofiness is the point. Also, we're kind of catering to Ashley's need to embrace childishness. It's a small party type affair with just the two of us plus Ashley's mother, Chloe, and Michelle. Haven't seen 'Chelle in a bit. She's been super busy with school and work. Becoming a lawyer is not easy. She's definitely smart enough for it. She's also the opposite of lazy... unlike me. I'm probably smart enough to be a lawyer. I merely lack the motivation to punish myself that much. Also, getting up in people's faces confrontationally isn't my deal.

I had such a hard time convincing myself to dump Scott, after all, didn't want the argument. Also, public speaking freaks me out.

Combining arguing with public speaking—arguing in public—would make me want to shrink into a black hole and disappear.

Not saying I am *totally* lazy. My brain walks a fine line between motivation and feeling like something is far too much work for too little return. Case in point: becoming a lawyer, or a doctor. Even if I have the smarts for those careers, way, way, way too much work for me. Also, in the case of doctor, far too much responsibility. Thoughts like this are the reason mortal me graduated high school and still had no idea what to choose for a major in college. Felt like everyone else in my class who wasn't planning to spend their life at dead end jobs or join the military knew what they'd be majoring in before senior year even started. Not me. I knew I'd end up in college because that's just what my whole family expected. Not a damn idea what I wanted to do with the rest of my life.

Oh, there's a bit of Sierra's artist coming out. I'm about to grumble about how our society only places value on what a person is going to do for a career. Sigh. We're so work focused. Kids don't even have the chance to finish high school before they're under pressure to make a decision about how they're going to spend the entirety of their adult life. I mean, if you're younger than twenty-five, you're not allowed to rent a car. If people aren't 'responsible' enough to rent a car, how can they be trusted to settle on a career path?

Meh.

So here we are. There's a pink cake on the table. Ash is all about pink. And unicorns. Did I mention the cake has little cartoon unicorns made of white chocolate all over it? It's the kind of thing someone gets for their daughter's ninth birthday. Ash let out a squeal of delight when she saw it.

For the first hour and a half or so of this party, nothing seemed weird about it. At all. This could have been any ordinary day in our life during the first two years of high school. It's even around the same time of day as our birthday parties used to be. Of course, now it's because we are physically incapable of being awake before two or three in the afternoon, not simply because 'we'd been at school' all morning. Everything feels so normal. Dunno if Ashley charmed me accidentally or if I willingly surrendered to the delusion of being thirteen again.

Chloe's in heaven. She hasn't been to many birthday parties. I'm going to stop there because if I think too much about her past life, I'm going to be in a bad mood for a week.

So yeah, here I am sitting on the sofa watching *The Last Unicorn* and that sense of surrealism hit me out of the blue. My brain rejected the Matrix simulation. I am not a tween. We didn't go to high school this morning. We're not even alive anymore. This is kinda weird. The cake looks like it's meant for a kid except for the 1 and 9 candles. Yeah, this is Ash officially turning nineteen. Like me, she's still biologically eighteen... will be forever. Also like me, everyone thinks she's even younger than that. It's a crazy interplay between the Innocent bloodline and us being young, I think.

I have no idea what would happen if someone well into their forties turned vampire and happened to end up as an Innocent. I'm sure they wouldn't physically de-age back to their teen years. Every other vampire bloodline—except Shadows—gets the hotness. Even if they'd been fairly plain in life, going undead makes them either gorgeous or smolderingly handsome. Some of it is actual changes to appearance. Some is mental charmy type stuff. Vampires are all about manipulating mortals to make feeding easier. It's what we're designed for.

Ashley really puts the 'aww' in shock and aww.

Chloe, too. The kid is adorbs.

Surreal doesn't even begin to describe how I'm feeling all of a sudden. For a moment, my brain gets its bike chain tangled up and it feels like I've gone back in time before any of this vamp stuff happened. This is Ashley's thirteenth birthday—but who is this little girl with black hair? Then I recognize Chloe and have this 'oh yeah, vampire stuff happened' moment.

I peer over at Mrs. Carter. Ashley's mom is more or less how I'd imagine an adult Ashley would've looked. They've both got the same shade of red hair, blue eyes, and pale skin. I think Mrs. C is forty-one or two. She hasn't had much luck dating since the jerk left. Not sure if it's because she didn't really try too hard or she simply couldn't find a guy she trusted. It doesn't seem to bother her being on her own.

Watching her sit there smiling at us makes me feel a little better. I've been wondering how she felt about Ashley's decision to become a vampire. There went any dreams of having grandkids. Gotta say, though, Chloe is doing a lot to scratch that itch. I've even caught her calling Mrs. C 'Grandma' on occasion. It kinda works. Ashley and I are technically somewhere between mothers and big sisters to the kid, so Ash's mom is basically a grandmother.

Mrs. C doesn't seem to mind the title and she adores spending time with the kiddo. Wonder if Chloe does it on purpose because she read the woman's mind and knows she likes it. On that note, we are *so* lucky the kid is not a brat. Imagine a mortal—my parents or Mrs. C— watching her while Ash and I are out doing Wolent stuff and them trying to discipline a misbehaving vampire kid who could just charm them to shut up and go away?

Yeah, messy. But that's less of a problem with a vampire kid being bratty and more of an idiot problem: leaving said brat with a mortal caretaker they could manipulate. If ever a selfish brat of a kid gets turned vampire, they should not be left in the care of ordinary mortals. Hopefully, one can count the number of child vampires in the entire world on one hand.

It's good to hang out with Michelle again, too. Since I've kinda snapped out of the 'acting like a tween' mentality, I start up a conversation with her, leaving Ashley and Chloe to be enamored with the movie. I've seen *The Last Unicorn* more times than I can count, so it's not as if I'm missing anything.

'Chelle seems to appreciate the somewhat more adult conversation/attitude from me. She mostly vents about how much work she has to do. Apparently, the amount of schoolwork and actual job work on her head at the moment is cutting into her time so much she's no longer going with her parents to church on Sundays. I'm sure her mom *loves* that. Michelle's not what you'd call anti-religion, though she doesn't really buy into it the way her parents do. Doubt she'll continue with it once she's living on her own.

For the most part, I try to sound sympathetic. I can sorta understand what it's like to have chaos raging around me and more demands on my time than I have time. There are some commonalities between being the most junior underling of the area's vampire boss and a law student. Though, technically, she's not a law student yet. She needs to graduate basic college first, then comes law school. Still. She's really loading up on everything she thinks will give her an advantage.

Me? I'm not that competitive. Another reason I wouldn't have made a good lawyer.

There's also an odd distance to her. She's not exactly acting like she really can't wait to leave or didn't want to be here. It's more like she feels out of place and doesn't understand why. That could be due to her remaining mortal and having no plans whatsoever for this to change. It could also be the odd childishness surrounding Ashley. I mean, Ash isn't overacting being a little kid. She's just… innocent. Or acting like it, anyway. The girl isn't baby-talking or pretending to be a child. Ash is simply being Ash without making any sexually charged jokes or talking about that sort of thing.

Michelle's vibing like she's the older aunt who showed up to a tween's birthday party who's too old to really hang out with the kids and too young to hang out with the parents. I gear shift into a more mature teenage headspace for the time being, acting like a bridge between them. It works, mostly. 'Chelle pauses a few times like she's got something in her mind she's trying to decide if she should say, and each time, she decides against it.

Ugh.

I know that face. It's the same face I wore when trying to summon the courage to break up with Scott and chickening out. This is possible pessimism on my part, but it really feels like she's trying to hit me with the 'we probably shouldn't hang out much anymore' thing. Could be that she's hoping to avoid being dragged into any supernatural craziness. It also might be her trying to finish growing up and get her adult on. One of those 'as fun as it would be to remain a teenager forever, that's not in the cards for me' deals.

It could be. All she has to do is ask and we can make it happen... I think.

Meaning, it's not—as far as I know—required for us to get permission first.

However, as long as she maintains her desire to stay mortal, I will respect it. Wouldn't be much of a friend if I forced that on her against her will, after all.

Mrs. C surprises me with how at ease she's being over Ashley's vampification. It helps a boatload the Universe was kind to us and let her go Innocent. She doesn't look any different while awake. Her mom probably wouldn't be too keen on seeing us sleep. Not that we go super gross or anything. Just... any normal person seeing us while we're sleeping in the daytime would think they've found corpses.

Yeah, I don't have to feel guilty about what Ashley's choice may have done to her mother. Sure, she won't have grandkids... but she also gets to have teen Ashley around forever. Also, she never has to worry that something crazy or tragic will happen to her daughter. We won't get mugged, kidnapped, murdered by a crazy husband, or nailed in the head by a de-orbiting toilet seat falling from the disintegrating remains of a Russian space station.

"Be right back," chirps Ashley. She bounces up off the sofa. "Bathroom."

Chloe pauses the movie, then twists around to peer up at me. She's sprawled on the floor in front of the sofa. "Can I have another piece of cake?"

"Sure." I stand to get it for her. This is 'parenting' made easy. No reason to really enforce restraint on cake. Kiddo won't get sick, fat, or too hopped up on sugar to sleep later. She is, however, too young to wield a knife by herself. Yeah, I know, she'd heal any damage she did to herself. Still, it feels wrong to hand a child her age a giant knife. "Mrs. C? 'Chelle? You guys want more cake?"

Michelle makes a pinchy gesture as in 'small piece.'

"No thanks, dear." Mrs. C smiles. "It will go straight to my backside. One piece is enough."

I smirk. "It's going straight to my backside, too, but not quite in the same way."

"Oh…" She covers her mouth to chuckle while blushing slightly.

Michelle manages a weak smile.

"Sorry. Didn't mean to make you uncomfortable," I whisper.

"I'm not uncomfortable." Michelle stretches, then winks. "Just jealous. I'm gonna end up paying for that cake with another hour on the treadmill tomorrow."

"Oh, you…" Mrs. C waves dismissively at her. "You're still young. Wait until you get to be my age. If I even *look* at cake, I gain a pound."

Since I'm up and cutting cake anyway, I decide to have another piece as well. It's cake, so we're not stealing real food from people who need it. Also, calories don't matter. I will enjoy the chocolatey-raspberry awesomeness with zero guilt.

I hand Chloe a paper plate with a kid-sized piece of cake on it. She grins, thanks me, and heads back to her spot on the carpet. I give Michelle a piece the same size as the one I cut for Chloe, then section off a 'normal' sized one for myself before sitting back on the sofa beside Michelle.

Two bites into the cake, she stops. "Um, Sare?"

"Hmm?" I mumble over a full mouth.

"Ashley went to the bathroom," replies Michelle, scarcely over a whisper.

"Yeah? So?" I give her side eye.

Michelle peers over her left shoulder at the hall where the bathroom is, then looks at me. "Don't you guys like not need to do that anymore?"

"We had cake. And she had some chocolates." I cut another bite off with my fork. "Cake wants out."

Michelle cringes. "Ugh. I don't think any food tastes so good that I'd eat it knowing I'd have to yak it up later."

I examine my fingernails. "Umm, 'Chelle, we don't yak it up. We're special. You know this already."

She raises a hand at me. "You can spare me the details."

After another bite of cake, it hits me that Ash has been gone for a while, a bit too long to simply get rid of cake. I set my plate on the sofa beside me and stand. "Gonna go make sure she didn't fall in."

Michelle chuckles.

"Oh, to still have a backside so narrow falling in was a risk." Mrs. Carter sighs.

"Stop. You're not even close to fat." I roll my eyes at her.

Mrs. C pats her leg. "I can't wear any of the things I used to wear at your age anymore."

"That's pretty common. Most adults can't fit into their high school wardrobe." I head for the hallway. "Don't take my dad as an example. He's a genetic anomaly of skinny."

"Your mother, too," says Mrs. Carter with a note of friendly jealousy.

I pause to smile back at her. "In Mom's case, it's only about half genetics. The rest is stress from her job."

Michelle gives me side eye. "If stress keeps lawyers thin, maybe I could've gotten away with a whole second piece of cake."

"Careful what you wish for." I wink at her. "Mom says law school was like a vacation compared to some of the cases she's been on."

"Oof." Michelle shivers, though she's clearly acting. She's laser focused on her goal of becoming an attorney.

I head down the hall to the bathroom. It's empty. Uh oh. Something's wrong. It's too daylightey in here for me to fly, so I do the next best thing and run to the stairs. There's only one place Ash goes when she's upset: her room. Well, suppose there are technically two places she might go now. She has two almost identical bedrooms. The only differences between them are that her original bedroom has actual windows, and whatever small objects might have been added or moved after Sophia's magical 'copy and paste'.

Sure enough, I find her curled up on her excessively pink puffy bed, crying into her pillow.

This is not entirely without precedent for her birthdays. She's not quite as sensitive as she used to be. For her ninth birthday, she thought Kelly Martin, one of those tangential school friends, might not really like her... so she ended up in tears over that. Did I mention she has daddy issues? She really needs to be liked. She can't handle it if she thinks someone does not want her around or dislikes her—unless she knows she did something to deserve it first. Pretty sure that's not the case today.

"Ash?" I ask in a low, comforting voice. "You okay?"

She sniffles, pauses a moment, then says, "I'm sobbing into my pillow. That means I'm not okay."

I walk over and sit on the edge of the bed. "Wanna talk about it?"

"Okay." Ashley pushes herself up to sit amid her stuffed animal army, then wipes her face. "I'm just being a drama queen."

"About what?"

"Was just sitting there watching the movie and thinking about how the party felt so normal… like any other birthday I've had."

I lick some cake off my teeth, trying to be subtle about it. "Yeah. It's been pretty normal."

"Except…" She stabs her elbows into her knees and catches her chin in both hands. "Tonight, I realized that Mom is going to get old and eventually be gone. Michelle's gonna get old and eventually be gone."

My willpower is stronger than I thought. My mouth does not release a 'well, no kidding'. I also refrain from calling her Captain Obvious. Can't tease her. Thoughts like that have been swirling around my brain ever since I woke up in a morgue. Okay, maybe not right away. But ever since a couple days after I went home.

"Yeah." I smooth my hands down my jeans in a repetitive, soothing manner. "It's true. There's no real easy way to deal with that."

She shifts her eyes toward me. "Did I do the right thing? Was it dumb of me to go vamp?"

I lean back on the bed, staring up at the pink ceiling. "Well, if you didn't do it, you'd have grown up and not had birthday parties at all anymore. It's not the sort of thing that adults really do. So, now you get to have a birthday party every year for eternity."

"Hah." Ashley pokes me in the stomach. "I'm being serious. It's not about the birthday parties." She makes a contemplative face. "Though, you do have a point. We're never going to think birthday parties are lame."

"Also…" I roll on my side to face her. "Even if you didn't go vamp, your mom would have eventually grown old and gone away. That's normal. Michelle not so much. Would've been a coin flip which one of you checked out first. It's possible she'd have died before you and you'd have had to deal with that, too. So really, none of that changed."

"Yeah." She sighs. "Is this that stupid emotional rollercoaster you talked about?"

"Probably."

She stares glumly at the wall for a little while, then perks up. "We can still have birthday parties?"

"Yeah. Of course. I mean, it's just going to be us and Chloe eventually… but that doesn't mean we can't have cake."

I sigh to myself, not really knowing what the full story is with the Littles just yet. Seems like they might end up sticking around a bit longer than normal mortality would allow, but I don't want to get my hopes up just yet. I'd rather be glum about theoretical normality and happy when they break the rules.

She picks up a giant plush unicorn and hugs it. "If I stayed mortal, there wouldn't be any birthday parties, so I guess I'm ahead."

"That's a good way to think about it."

Ash mushes her face into the top of the unicorn's head. "When does it stop being sad to think of everyone else getting old?"

"Oh, boy. Going for the easy questions."

She chuckles, then sniffles.

"I dunno." I idly scratch my stomach, gazing into the mountain of plush cuteness surrounding Ash. "This might sound morbid, but I think it's kinda like learning someone you love has a terminal disease. Some people spend years trying to come to terms with imminent death."

"Mom's not sick."

"Yeah, I know. I mean, compared to us being immortal. We know time is going to catch up to her, eventually. A day will come when no one we knew in our mortal lives will be around anymore."

Ashley bonks me over the head with the big unicorn. "You're going to make me start crying again."

"When will we stop thinking about that? No clue. I'll let you know if it ever happens."

She's quiet for a moment, peering down at her hand on the pink bedspread. "Is this why most vampires play dead to their families?"

"Nah. I don't think so." I sit up. "I'm pretty sure that tradition got started because back in the old days, people would freak the hell out and try to burn vampires to death. Like, 'hi Mom and Dad, I'm back home and not really dead'. Followed by 'no you're not, you're a monster' and a lot of stabby stabby."

She blurts out a laugh.

I check the door to make sure no one is listening, then whisper, "Imagine Michelle going vamp and trying to tell her parents."

"Ooh. They'd totally freak out." Ashley seems horrified but also like she wants to laugh. "Do you think they'd kill her or try to ram a stake into her heart?"

"Probably not. I mean, it's not as if she'd be telling them she's gay." I examine my fingernails. "Just an undead creature of the night."

She gawks at me, then cracks up laughing.

"Now, go back 300 years when the average person was way more religious than 'Chelle's parents... vampires would not have been tolerated. So... secrecy."

"Nothing 'abnormal' was tolerated," says Ashley with a bit of a scowl. "They tortured people for being left-handed."

Sigh. Sad, and true. "But, yeah. I think playing dead is worse for the families. At least the way we're doing it, we get to have time with us. It would suck way more to make them think we're dead and watch them deal with the grief from a distance."

She takes a deep breath, then sets the big unicorn plush aside. "Yeah. You're right. Let's go back downstairs. We're missing the movie... and I wanna spend time with Mom."

"Cool." I hop to my feet. "What movie do you want to watch after this one? Or is it board game time?"

"Hmm." She taps her finger to her chin. "Let's see how I feel when the movie is over."

7

THE RESTLESS DEAD

WEDNESDAY

*I*t's been a while since I had to rush from school to a job.

Still sucks. And there's another reason life as a lawyer isn't for me: I hate being under pressure or on tight schedules. Maybe it's a bit of a stretch to compare waiting tables to running errands for Wolent. In the grand scheme of things, this likely doesn't count as a job. Not like I'm getting paid now. Of course, vampires don't need money the same way normal people do, so that's not a big deal. There's also the upside of not having to dodge middle-aged men hitting on me anymore. Few times in my life were as uncomfortable as that waitress job I had when I was sixteen. I'd get a table with four dudes almost my dad's age out for some guys' only celebration or whatever… and they'd spend the entire time trying to flirt with me.

Usually, dropping a random comment about my age would get them to stop. Not always. Ugh. Creeps.

Don't have that problem now. For one thing, I'm not working with the general public. For another, even if I *did* run into a creep, I'm more than capable of dealing with the situation myself. Sure, the tips aren't as good running messages for Wolent, but I'll take it.

I'd been wanting to spend some time with Hunter tonight since he had the night off from his job waiting tables at Mi Tierra. Of course, somehow, Wolent's people sensed this and called me in. Grr.

Ashley's more than willing to run around with me despite not being officially part of Wolent's organization. I mean, Aurélie sired her, so there's no disputing she's a 'society' vampire. The lines get blurry there as to whether or not she counts as 'one of Wolent's people'. To split political hairs, Aurélie doesn't consider herself part of his group either. She's like the queen of a neutral nearby kingdom that's on friendly terms with Wolent. I mean, that's really overcomplicating it. The vamps around here don't act like royalty… at least not compared to the way things are in London. Over there, a legit political structure exists. Here in Seattle, Wolent has no official title. He's just kind of in charge because he's in charge.

I'm working for him because he's in charge and, well, he's honestly kind of a nice guy under the tough exterior.

Follows Rules Girl just kinda reflexively fell in line with the power structure. I'm not a power-seeking vampire. The thing I want most is just to exist in as (relatively) normal a manner as possible. If attaching myself to Wolent's empire helps me do that, so be it. Having been turned into a vampire unwittingly (as opposed to seeking it out on purpose) came with a degree of pity from other vampires. Being an Innocent keeps them from worrying too much about me trying to scheme or stab anyone in the back. Even if I got the idea to do so, the general perception of my bloodline is that we're pretty weak and harmless.

I don't feel weak. Yeah, I'm good at pretending to be harmless, though I'm not that either.

Now, if you compare me to someone like Aziz… I am as weak as pond algae. That man could throw a car overhand. Beasts aside, my bloodline isn't too much weaker than any other. We just miss out on the really cool, umm… 'high level spells' as my brother put it. Once a vampire reaches a certain age, they get all these neato tricks depending on their bloodline and other factors no one seems to fully understand. Kinda like how that Oblivare, Ladonna, shapeshifted into a raven and flew away.

I'll never be able to do anything like that.

Again, oh well. I can fly anyway, so who needs to turn into a bird? It's cool and flashy, but I'm happy without it.

So, yeah. I'm probably the permanent 'kid' on Team Wolent. Also, no big deal. It's not like I'm vying for power and respect here. Just want to be left alone to goof off and have fun. How many plush unicorns can a girl hug in an eternal unlife? I don't know the answer to that question, but I suspect Ashley intends to conduct thorough research on the topic.

Tonight is a fairly standard messenger deal. For some bizarre reason, vampire elders don't seem to understand email is a thing. They've got this habit of sending literal scrolls, wax seals and everything, like we're still in 1493. I mean the fantasy geek inside me adores that, as impractical as it is. Handwritten calligraphy on scrolls feels like I'm stepping into *Lord of the Rings* or perhaps Bram Stoker. I can just picture Mr. Wolent huddled over an enormous desk, his face aglow in the flickering light from an oil lantern, as his quill pen scribbles furiously.

Email would be so much faster... and it wouldn't be keeping me away from Hunter.

Maybe they're afraid of the Persons in Black snooping on them. Maybe they don't trust computers the way Uncle Hank hates all technology more advanced than a television set. Could be they simply enjoy the reminder of days gone by the same way Dad still loves to play video games he grew up on and watch movies from the Eighties. It might even just be the coolness factor.

Whatever the reason, I'm the one who has to run around with the tote bag like some sort of undead postal worker. At least we can fly. Having to do this in a car would take all damn night.

For our fifth stop, we glide down out of the sky and land at the back corner of a parking lot where one conveniently nonworking lamp leaves it nice and dark. Took me a bit to get used to, but we *can* tell degrees of lightness even though nowhere is dark to us. The trick is colors: the more vibrant the colors, the more actual light is there. Darker areas have muted, faded colors like old photographs.

"Damn," whispers Ashley as soon as her sneakers touch the ground. "Now I'm hungry."

Takes my brain half a second to match her words to the aroma of Italian food in the air. Ooh, yeah. This place smells really good. It's gotta say something that the smell of ordinary food is making a vampire hungry. At least, I assume she's hungry for ordinary food. Safe bet this is a 'problem' unique to Innocents.

"Actually hungry or food hungry?" I whisper.

"Food hungry." She starts walking toward the restaurant. "Kinda craving something with shrimp and pasta."

I hurry after her, falling in stride once I catch up. "It's a bit late. They're probably getting ready to close the dining room. It's almost eleven."

"Think so? This place serves alcohol." She gestures at the fancy entryway. "Might still be cooking."

They've got this little loop driveway deal under a massive roof extension, all fancy fake stonework columns and whatnot with tiny potato-sized putti all over them. That means naked babies with wings. Yay for art history class, right? Place is called Garibaldi's, though I'm sure no one named that works here or even knows about it. One of Wolent's underlings probably grabbed the first hoity-toity Italian sounding name they could find and slapped it on all the marketing materials. This is the kind of place Mom's boss might take someone to on a date, the kind of place one almost never sees children inside of.

It's also the kind of super fancy, super expensive restaurant that wouldn't let two teenage girls in the front door unless we happened to be wearing dresses that cost more than some cars. My T-shirt and jeans ensemble isn't up to standard. Guys have it easy. It's easier to get a passable looking cheap suit than it is to fake an expensive gown.

Fortunately, I don't care about fashion. I'm also not here to eat.

We're not quite halfway across the parking lot when Ashley looks over at me, seeming confused. "Does Mr. Wolent intentionally try to act like the godfather, or is that just us thinking of him that way because he kinda acts like the godfather?"

Can't help but chuckle. "There's a question we could debate for years and never answer."

A scuff comes from the ground close by on my left side. I reflexively turn toward the sound and brace for attack. Good thing, too. There's a body flying at me. The pounce is too fast for me to see much detail about the man leaping on me before he slams into me in an attempted tackle. I twist counterclockwise, letting his weight and momentum pull me around while redirecting most of the force into spinning. Without even thinking about it, I widen my stance for extra balance and jam my fist into his ribs as if I had a dagger. Alas, I do not have a knife on me. Despite the lack of weapon in my hand, his rib cracks.

Thanks, Dalton.

My sire's experience and memories of dozens of times getting jumped at the wharfs of old London come in quite handy sometimes. Even though the memories aren't mine, feels like I'm a veteran at defending myself from sudden ambushes.

Ashley's not so lucky. Another man has leapt on her, flattening her to the ground like a helpless, undefended target. She basically just learned what it's like to be the San Francisco 49'ers quarterback. No, I'm not a huge football fan, but I *am* from Seattle. Go Seahawks.

The guy who jumped on me loses his grip and tumbles to the pavement nearby, flailing his arms in an ungainly, lopsided stagger. Everything about him feels brownish grey. I'm still processing what I see when the smell hits me.

Death.

"Eww!" screams Ashley, sounding way too much like Sophia touching something disgusting. "Get away!"

The man on top of her rockets nearly straight up from the force of her shove. At that moment, the guy I threw to the pavement emits a raspy moaning wheeze and wobbles to his feet. He spins to face me, and I find myself staring into dead, yellow eyes set in a withered excuse for a face. His skin is browned from age and what appears to be long-term exposure to wet dirt. A rat's nest of light brown hair sticks out in clumps from beneath a weird old-timey hat. His outfit looks a century or two out of place, rags mostly. I can barely tell what it used to be since it's decayed into a mess of generic tattered cloth.

One of his three remaining teeth flutters in the wind coming out of his lungs. Oof. I thought his presence stank. His breath is an order of magnitude worse.

"Dude. Breath mints." I cough. "Get some."

Whud.

The guy Ashley launched lands some distance away from us.

She scrambles to her feet, spinning to face the dead guy looking at me. "What the actual hell is this?"

"A couple of waterlogged mummified corpses who didn't quite get the memo about being dead, I think." I consider sprouting claws, then reconsider. Cutting these things open is going to smell horrible.

"Eww!" Ashley shivers. "Now I really want to go home and shower. It touched me."

"He's going to try to touch you again." I shift my weight, getting ready for this thing to come charging at me.

The second walking corpse picks itself up and speed-staggers toward Ashley.

She spins to face the one that tackled her. "Emphasis on *try*."

As soon as it's in range, she emits a faint little snarl and punches it in the face. The dead guy's entire head explodes in a blast of muck, dust, and bone fragments. The rest of the body topples over and goes into a flailing, convulsing fit.

Hissing, the other corpse reaches under the lapel of its long coat for something, seeming caught off guard upon discovering whatever weapon it wanted to grab isn't there. He's got just enough time to look back up at me with an 'oh crap' face before I do the same thing Ashley did.

One vampire-strength punch to the nose detonates his head. His skull is brittle, smashing to bits like I'm pounding my fist into some breakaway stage prop made of sugar glass. He, too, collapses to the pavement and flops around in the manner of a freshly caught salmon on dry land. The one Ash clobbered bursts into a haze of dust and a spattering of dark greenish-blue slime. Not quite thirty seconds later, the other one does the same thing. Soon after, the slime spatters dry out and flake apart to darker dust. Little trace of the creatures ever having existed remains.

"Oh, that's convenient." I dust my hands off. "No mess to clean up."

Hissing rapidly closes in on me from behind. Sigh. Another one?

I spin, my vampire reflexes making everything around me feel like slow motion. Another dead guy comes charging at me with his right arm up over his head, holding what appears to be a wooden stake. I have enough time to think 'what the actual f is going on here' before he gets close enough to where I need to do something more than stare at him in dumbfounded shock.

He's a little faster than a mortal, but not that fast.

I sidestep his downward stabbing stake, grab him by two fistfuls of coat, and swing him around off his feet before hurling him as hard as I can throw at the nearest giant steel lamp post. The corpse thing flies at least twenty feet across the parking lot before he hits the post horizontally, basically ass first. His body gives out with a painful sounding *crack*. Legs and upper torso whip around the pole, the back of his skull crashing into his boots before the body splits in half at the waist.

Both halves disintegrate into a shower of fine gray dust before reaching the pavement.

I glance toward the restaurant. "Gee, I hope one of our guys is in the security room tonight and deletes the surveillance video."

"Seriously," mutters Ashley.

"You okay?"

"Yeah. Fine." She dusts herself off.

"Hmm." I look around for any signs of more threat. Nothing seems to stand out. "Something's wrong."

Ash blinks at me. "Ya think?"

"Heh. I mean… usually when I'm randomly attacked, it doesn't end so fast. Am I getting more powerful or were those things weak as hell?"

She squeezes my bicep, pretending to measure it. "I think it takes more than two years to level up as a vampire."

I laugh. "This isn't a game."

"You know what I mean." She flashes a cross-eyed grin.

Too many questions, too few answers. I gaze down at my hands. "I don't really feel uber. Guess those things were weak."

She kicks at the dust on the ground. "What the eff was that?"

"Umm, I kinda wanna call them ghouls." I fidget. "Maybe zombies... but they didn't really act like zombies. Whatever they were, I'm thankful they were so flimsy. Really don't feel like having my ass kicked again."

"Right?" Ashley whistles.

"Oh hey!" I strike a model's pose, showing off my outfit. "Vampire combat happened, and I didn't suffer a wardrobe malfunction."

She smirks. "Did that really count as combat? It was over in seconds."

"Umm. I dunno."

Ashley makes a silly face. "Scott would've said it still counts as combat, even if it's over in ten seconds."

I laugh. Yes, I'm over him. Her joke doesn't bother me. And hey, a sorta sexy joke. Ashley is still in there somewhere.

"What's the difference between ghouls and zombies?" She scrunches up her nose. "And I still really want a shower now."

I resume walking toward the restaurant. "If a ghoul rolls a natural twenty on its attack, you have to make a saving throw or they can paralyze you."

She groans at me. "No D&D jokes. I'm being serious."

"Totally guessing here, but ghouls are more agile and faster." I peer back at the spot where the attack happened. "One of them seemed to be reaching for a weapon under his coat. Might not be quite as stupid as zombies."

"Two of them watched me destroy the first one in a single punch." Ashley holds her chin up. "And they still came after us. That's pretty dumb to me. So, ghouls, huh?"

I grab the doorknob, pausing before opening it in case there are any mortals inside who might hear me. "Just calling them that. Dunno for sure. I'm still pretty new at this whole 'supernatural stuff is actually real' thing."

She nods once.

We go inside.

Even though it's almost eleven at night, the place has a decent crowd. And by 'decent crowd' I mean six tables are in use. Hey, it's late after all. Not too many people eat dinner at this hour. From the looks of things, these are the parties who stayed well after they finished eating to hang out and maybe keep drinking.

Some of the patrons and most of the employees in sight stare at us in varying levels of contempt. Yeah, yeah. We're daring to walk in here in ordinary non-expensive clothing. Whatever. I'm only a courier.

Several vampires lurk around the room, pretending to be security or managers. The majority of the wait staff and cooks are mortals. I don't think they *all* know about vampires beyond a few key people in charge. There's sort of a *Men In Black* thing going on with vampires and mortals. As long as they work for us, they get to know stuff. As soon as they want out (or get fired), they lose all memory of vampires being real.

Oh wait. Got a feeling the mortals who are still here at this hour are tonight's designated nom-noms.

I cross the dining area to the bar at the back. Once there, I lean against the shiny black wood and nod at Michael, the bartender. He's one of us. Handsome guy really, but too old for me to do anything with other than admire. Almost thirty. Black hair, slicked. I dunno if Wolent is trying to go for a mafia theme on purpose, but this guy totally looks the part.

He offers me a polite smile and nod while setting a scroll on the bar. I check my bag. Got two scrolls for this place, so I pull them out and place them on the bar beside the outgoing one, which I then grab and stuff in the bag.

Ashley waves at him.

"Thanks. Night." I wave at Michael and head for the exit.

"Good night, Sarah." He smiles.

Most mortals at the tables who noticed us and our lack of sufficiently expensive clothing probably assume we went to the bar and got chased out for being underage. Or maybe they realized I'm a glorified FedEx delivery person. Really, I couldn't care less what they think.

We head outside to the parking lot, going straight toward the dark corner.

"So, who sent ghouls after us?" whispers Ashley.

"Are you sure they came after us? They might have just been there." I gesture around at the room. "You know who runs this place. Those things could've been out there for any number of reasons, from attack to accident."

Ashley wags her eyebrows. "Ghouls' night out?"

I groan. "C'mon. let's get moving. Faster we go, faster we get home."

"Eww." She brushes a hand down her shirt. "I can still smell that thing. Definitely taking a shower when we get home."

8

A TEENSY BIT OF STRAY MAGIC

SO HAPPY IT'S THURSDAY

So, it's been a few days. Made it to another Thursday without being lit on fire or our house getting sucked into a parallel universe. I consider that a win. Something's in the air today and it's worse than static electricity. The feeling I'm about due for a giant dose of weird woke me up early—it's a few minutes before two in the afternoon.

Hey, that's early for me.

No, I'm not an unemployed bum. I'm a vampire.

Waking up at 1:57 p.m. for me is like a mortal jumping out of bed at 4:30 in the morning. I have no idea why anyone in their right mind would wake up so damned early unless they were like a doctor, a cop, or in the military and had no choice. Setting an alarm clock to such a horrible time should be considered a violation of the Geneva Convention.

Speaking of war crimes, I wonder what became of Tobias Krüger. Haven't seen or heard any sign of my former cell phone haunt since Sophia set him loose. He's probably out there enjoying being a free ghost. Or maybe he got yoinked into the cosmic spirit recycling apparatus to be reincarnated. Hmm. I wonder if the Universe cares about how good or crappy a person was in life when deciding how to reincarnate them. I mean, do former Nazis come back as toilet seats in sketchy Mexican restaurants? Poetic, but something tells me the cosmic machinery couldn't care less about any sense of human morality. Killing and eating a person is horrible, but if we were fish, cannibalism wouldn't be a big deal.

Maybe that's why fish don't have civilization.

They're kinda working on it. I mean, they go to school, right?

Ugh. Dad.

I lightly slam my face into my pillow a few times. Bad puns are definitely in my genes. At least no one heard that one. So yeah. Fish don't have reality television shows. Does that mean they're more advanced than us?

On another unrelated note only tangentially related to the concept of weird, I've drawn a total blank on trying to understand what happened with those three ghouls. Whether or not they truly *are* ghouls, I have no idea. The term works for me, so that's what I'm going to call them unless someone out there happens to have a copy of *Tobin's Spirit Guide* and can tell me what the hell they were.

Damn. Now I kinda want to watch *Ghostbusters* again. I'm sure Dad won't mind. Sophia might, though. I mean, that's a kid-safe movie by any reasonable standard... but six-year-old Soph developed a dread fear of Slimer. She used to be afraid he'd come out of nowhere in our house and chase her around. I have no idea how anyone could be afraid of such a cartoonishly cute ghost. Then again, this *is* Sophia. Her worst nightmare is a giant black pom-pom with itty bitty wings.

Which, okay, that sounds extremely silly... right up until I saw Fuzzydoom in action.

Don't look at me like that. I didn't name it. Sophia did... when she was three years old.

Hmm. There's a chicken versus egg problem. Did Fuzzydoom always exist, or did Sophia create him? Ehh... she probably created him for real without meaning to once her magical ability got unlocked. Another question: how many people have magical potential waiting inside them? It's not like Sophia could have unlocked it on her own. At least, if the means to do so remained, there aren't many mortals out there who know how to do it anymore. The mystics that yoinked her soul out of her body so they could hijack it and spy on me weren't intending to 'activate' her. They had no idea she had such potential.

It's pretty damn difficult—and rare—for a person to have their soul yanked out of their body forcibly while they're still alive. There are only two ways to do that: piss off a bunch of mystics or participate in a live studio audience at a taping of Dr. Phil.

Dalton had no idea what the hell those ghouls might've been. He'd never seen anything like them. Aurélie didn't know for certain either, though she did suggest a bizarre idea. According to her, those three ghouls had probably been vampire hunters in life and somehow ended up cursed with the bad kind of undeath by whatever vampire they attempted to destroy. By 'bad undeath' I mean crap like zombies, ghouls, and health insurance CEOs. Literal monsters.

Went to sleep last morning with Ashley clinging to me as though she feared being swept out to sea if her grip faltered. It was less desperate child and more possessive cat doing a 'this is mine.' I woke to find her draped across me horizontally, her body halfway off the bed, mouth gaping open. Her hair had mutated into an enormous wild tangle of red, arms and legs splayed in the pose of a crime victim. Chloe's still curled up in a ball tucked under my right arm.

Kinda rare for a vampire to move in their sleep, though to be fair, Innocents are the most prone to it. She must have had a doozy of a dream. Then again, Ash always did sleep hard. I used to slightly envy that about her, how she could fall asleep so fast and remain asleep through almost anything. Prior to becoming a vampire, I'd almost always spend anywhere from thirty minutes to two hours staring at my ceiling before passing out. Dad told me that difficulty falling asleep fast is a sign of intelligence. I dunno what it means, but it was really damn annoying.

Waking up earlier than usual is not a good sign. That's only supposed to happen in the presence of an imminent threat. Last I checked, psychic premonitions aren't one of my abilities. It's quiet. I lay there listening for a while. Dad's upstairs in his office typing away. The kitchen fridge whirrs. Our central heating unit is humming. No sound comes from anywhere else in the house. A lack of video game noises tells me Blix went to school with Sam again. The Littles aren't home yet. I'm half tempted to rush upstairs and do some cleaning before they get here. Mom doesn't really like it when I clean my siblings' rooms for them. She wants them to do it themselves. I'm not spoiling them. Just trying to be nice.

Sophia doesn't mind cleaning her space. Her stuff is usually neat. Heck, that girl didn't even complain when Mom added 'upstairs bathroom' to her chore list. No, it's not child labor. Each sib only has to clean the bathroom once a month. It's more so they learn how to do it, so when they're living on their own, their home doesn't end up on a television series like *Hoarders*.

Sierra doesn't necessarily dislike cleaning. She's just… well… okay maybe not lazy. She's just distracted with other things like video games, and these days, art. She's totally going to end up living in a mess. That girl doesn't budget time for annoying but important things like cleaning up. She gets fixated on what she wants to do and cuts every corner possible to get back to it as fast as possible.

Surprisingly, Sam is also fairly okay with the chore thing… though he does make child labor jokes while doing it.

Meh. I'm on edge again and I don't know why.

I reach out and grab a fistful of Ashley's nightgown, then pull her upper half off the floor and back into bed. She flops around like a full-sized doll, no sign whatsoever of any life in her. Yeah, it might look alarming to someone who wasn't a vampire, but this is normal for us when we feel safe. I rearrange her into a normal sleeping pose, slip out of bed, then tuck Chloe in before squishing her rabbit plushie into her grip where my arm had been.

For a moment I stand there beside the bed, watching them sleep. I am *so* grateful that Aurélie was able to reprogram Chloe's brain, so her body no longer reverts to how she looked at the time of her mortal death whenever she falls asleep. Hopefully, someday, I will stop thinking about how her bio dad beat her to death. It's out of character for me, but I'm kinda angry the guy who turned Chloe into a vampire already killed her parents. I really want to kick that guy's ass again. The dad, not the sire.

Grr. The only revenge I can get against that piece of shit is to make her happy.

Great. Now I'm pissed off. I'm also groggy and restless. Want to sleep. Can't sleep.

Grumbling under my breath, I stagger out of my room into the basement, turn right, and walk the length of the big room to the stairs leading to the kitchen. A blast of daylight slaps me in the face when I open the door. I snarl at it, feeling irritated. The sun is like that annoying guy my Mom talks about at the office who swoops over to her desk at 8:02 a.m. all chipper and happy and starts yammering ninety miles an hour about random nonsense.

No one should be *that* happy or energetic so early in the morning.

Going offline only makes me feel *more* groggy. Hey, at least the daylight isn't hurting anymore. I'm getting pretty good at the whole faking mortality thing. Ashley likes to make D&D jokes about vampirism, so I guess I'm spending all my skill points on sun tolerance. Had a stray point last level since the next rank of 'ignore sun' cost five points and I only had two left, so I threw some at lockpicking.

Heh.

Crazy how reality can sound so much like a game sometimes.

Out of old habit, I shamble over to the fridge. Is this what it feels like to be a ghoul? My arms and legs barely want to listen to what my brain is telling them to do. Dad would say this is normal for a 'pre-coffee' state. Sadly, caffeine doesn't work on me anymore. Though, maybe it would have a placebo effect. Screw it. Even if it doesn't wake me up, I love the taste.

I set up the machine to brew a pot, then pull open the fridge door and stare into the cold box.

Nothing there catches my interest. Leftovers. Soda. Milk. Apples.

A stack of square Tupperware boxes with Mom's lunches for the rest of the week. Two cucumbers. An onion. Huh? Who put an onion in the fridge? The pink plate formerly holding ¼ of Ashley's birthday cake is still in the fridge, covered in crumbs.

Ugh. Really? If you're going to finish off the cake, at least pull the plate out of the fridge and toss it in the machine. Shaking my head, I grab it, dust it off at the trash can, and pop it in the dishwasher. I go back to the fridge and open it again, staring into it. Nothing's different.

Sigh.

"Hey, kiddo." Dad enters the kitchen and smiles at me over the top of the fridge door. "Closing and opening the door won't make the contents change."

Aha. The smell of brewing coffee has summoned Dadzilla from his cave.

I close the door. "With Sophia around, you never know."

He starts to say something, pauses, then chuckles. "Good point. Everything okay? You look like you had a rough night."

"Woke up a bit early. Not sure why."

Dad looks around, overacting searching for hostile forces. "Looks clear."

Heh. I chuckle and hug him. "Yeah. We're pretty safe here with Max and Blix and Coralie looking after us."

"Most catastrophes are going to come from Sophia, I fear." He winks.

The man is not wrong. However, anything crazy she does won't be coming from a place of malice.

"Question." I peer up at him.

"That was a statement."

Ugh. I shake my head and end up chuckling at the fake serious look he's giving me. "How important is it to you and Mom that I do the college thing?"

"It's only important to us for how much you need it." He pats me on the shoulder. "I know your mother doesn't like to really think about it, but we're aware your situation is... special now."

"That's one way to put it." I laugh into another sigh.

Dad escorts me over to the table and encourages me to sit. Then, he grabs the coffee pot, two mugs, and the milk before joining me. "Let's analyze it. Why did you want to go to SCC?"

I pour coffee into each mug. "Honestly? I was trying not to think about what happened to me and keep things as ordinary as possible. Also, I thought you guys really needed me to go and would be disappointed if I didn't."

He adds milk to his coffee. This is a treat for Dad. He usually has it black. "Advantages to continuing?"

Hmm. I take a few sips of coffee while thinking. "Exposure to new ideas. Learning stuff for the sake of learning stuff."

"Okay. What are the cons of continuing?" Dad leans back, takes another sip of coffee.

"Time, mostly. I'd rather be home with everyone before the Littles grow up and you and Mom are... you know." I look down.

"Three or so hours a night isn't like you're going away to California." He smiles. "Is that sincere, or are your emotions going haywire again?"

I smile into the cup. "Oh, it's totally irrational clinginess. What eighteen-year-old obsessively wants to be around her younger siblings all the time before they grow up and move away? I know it's weird."

Dad slides a hand across the table and squeezes my forearm. "Most eighteen-year-olds are also not immortal. Honestly, you've got all the time in the world and a college degree probably isn't going to make any difference whatsoever in your future other than collecting knowledge as a hobby. If you'd really rather spend your time here, it's fine with me. Your mother and I didn't want you to go to college so we could brag to our friends. We wanted you to have a good life."

"Really? You're not upset?" I look up from the coffee, making eye contact. Weird. He seems happy.

"Of course not." He raises both eyebrows, giving a small sigh. "You're not the only one dealing with some elevated levels of clinginess. I thought we lost you there for a few days. Having you back at all is a thousand times a win. Whether or not you finish college isn't even on the scale of importance compared to that."

"Aww, Dad…" I slip out of my chair and hug him.

He almost starts to cry. His grip is unusually strong—a momentary flash of the grief he experienced when everyone believed I'd been killed. It passes in the span of a few breaths and he goes back to his normal not-quite-serious self.

"Besides." He winks. "We've still got three rounds in the chamber."

"Huh?" I blink. Kinda odd for my father to make a gun reference. The only firearms he's ever touched have been in video games.

The front door swings open as the Littles arrive home from school.

"Dad, we're back," calls Sam.

"Another day flushed down the toilet of industrialized conformity," yells Sierra.

"I like school," chirps Sophia.

All three of them go upstairs after removing their shoes.

"Oh, duh. You mean the Littles." I chuckle. "Three rounds in the metaphorical chamber."

Dad grins. "Your mother and I took a shotgun approach. One of you four is bound to get a degree."

I laugh. "Bet all three of them will."

"Sierra?" Dad tilts his hand in a so-so manner.

"She's really smart. Just doesn't like to show it."

Dad does a parody of the 'Kermit sipping tea' meme with his coffee. "It's not her brains I'm worried about. It's her inertia. Anything that feels like work…"

"Right." I chuckle. "Though, I have a feeling she'll go after an art degree."

"Oh, well. At least she won't be getting something useless." Dad makes a silly face.

"Art degrees aren't useless." I give him side eye. "Could be worse. She could major in a 3,000-year-old-dead language… or anthropology."

Dad winces.

We stare at each other for a moment in silence, then burst out laughing.

"In all seriousness, hon," says Dad, "it would be different if you needed a career and a degree would've been a stepping stone to a better life. You've kinda got that whole thing handled now. Don't feel compelled to go to college just to make your mother and I happy."

I nod. "Yeah. I kinda got over that whole needing it as a security blanket to feel normal thing. Been going just for you and Mom. I think I'll finish this semester out, then take a break."

"Sounds good, hon." Dad smiles. "As long as—"

Reality abruptly shifts into black and white.

Dad stares at me for a few seconds, then looks around the kitchen.

I twist to my left to look out the patio door. Our backyard is also in black and white… though the trees a distance past our fence appear green. It's as if a circular zone of anti-color has fallen onto our house and immediate surroundings.

Dad and I exchange a long stare when I turn back to face him, then we say, "Sophia" at the same time.

We stand in unison. I take a step toward the hall, though Dad pauses to chug the rest of his coffee.

"Letting it get cold would be coffee abuse," whispers Dad.

"Ice coffee is a thing." I march into the hallway.

Dad snaps his fingers. "Yes. That is true. However, there is a forbidden zone between steaming hot and ice cold where coffee shall not be allowed to dwell."

Did I ever mention that my father used to run *Dungeons and Dragons* games for his friends when he was younger, and within his game world, he added a religious sect that worshipped coffee? Monks of the Sacred Bean, he called it. Took his friends a while to catch onto the joke. I think what finally gave it away was when their high priest summoned the Great Celestial Deer as an avatar. Dad described it as basically a silhouette of a male deer full of outer space… a star buck.

Sigh.

We hurry upstairs.

"How bad do you think this is?" I ask.

"Can't be too bad. Everything's gone black and white, but our clothes didn't change to look 1950s."

I zip over to Sophia's bedroom door and open it. "True, but this is visible outside. Neighbors are going to freak."

Sophia is in the middle of her bedroom, barefoot in the same pink dress she wore to school today—and she's floating off the ground. Her head's inches from the ceiling. Did I mention her eyes are glowing bright blue? She's got her arms out to either side, palms upward. Small arcs of pink-purple lightning snap around her body before jumping to the crayon-candles standing up on end around the pentagram she's created on the carpet out of Barbies, rulers, plushies, and scraps of construction paper. Her butt-length blonde hair blows backward, fluttering in a wind that doesn't exist.

A soft stream of whispered pseudo-Latin comes from her mouth. She sounds like what Dad's parents thought they'd hear if someone played a heavy metal album backward. I'm still not sure how the heck anyone could play a CD backward.

"Oh, my," says Dad, doing a George Takei voice. "I didn't think she was old enough for this to start."

Takes me a second to catch his meaning, then I laugh. "She's not having her period, Dad."

"Are you sure? Your mother's done this a few times when it's been really bad for her."

I wipe a hand down my face. If Mom's eyes glowed and she levitated off the floor, it would have been entirely metaphorical. Yeah, I've had one or two like that, myself. You know the red faerie is being particularly nasty that month when you start speaking in tongues.

Sophia stops chanting. A few seconds later, she glides silently downward until her feet touch the carpet. She lets her arms fall slack at her sides and her eyes stop glowing like tiny Maglites. The instant her eyes go back to normal, the burning crayons also go out. Wisps of wax-scented smoke trail upward. She flashes a super innocent smile.

"Sweetie?" asks Dad. "Didn't we ask you to warn us before you invoke any major enchantments?"

"Uh huh." Sophia nods eagerly. "You did. But this one wasn't major."

I point a thumb back over my shoulder. "A circle roughly a hundred yards out from the house in all directions turned black and white. You call that small?"

"Yeah." Sophia idly swishes side to side, making her arms flop and dress flare out. "The spell is minor compared to like boosting Sierra."

Dad rubs his chin. "That's a technicality, but I'll bite. What did you do?"

My kid sister grins and points with her toe at a small lock of black hair in the middle of her ritual circle. "Enchanted the house and space around it so anyone who doesn't live here—or doesn't spend a lot of time here—will forget seeing Chloe."

I note more 'hair samples' in the circle. If I had to guess, it's one from everyone in the family, plus Ashley as well as Ronan and Hunter. Mrs. Carter's probably in there, too.

"Oh, neat." Dad makes weasel hands. "I don't suppose you could enchant the house so the IRS forgets we exist."

Sophia taps her chin in thought.

"That was a joke." Dad scratches the side of his head. "Do not mess with the federal government."

I snicker. "Yeah, the PIBs would come knocking."

Dad glances at me. "Do you think there are any mystics out there who did it?"

"They probably ended up in prison like Al Capone." I fold my arms. "You know, operating a crime syndicate is not a big deal, just don't cheat your taxes."

A small lump rises in the carpet by Sophia's left foot. It's about the size of a hamster under the rug. Half a second after it appears, the lump—in an extremely *Bugs Bunny* cartoon manner—races forward, zooming out the door and off down the hallway to the stairs.

"Shit," whispers Sophia.

"Eek! What was that?" I blurt.

"Space herpie," says Dad into the back of his hand.

I stare at him. "What?"

"Movie reference. You have seen *Ice Pirates?*" right?

"Of course. You screen it every three months." I chuckle.

Dad beams at me. "It's a good movie." He turns his gaze back to Sophia. "What just happened?"

"Umm. Oops." Sophia bites her lip and grinds her right big toe into the carpet. "Probably just some stray magic."

I tilt my head at her. "No, I meant *you* said a bad word."

Her entire face goes tomato red.

Dad gawks. "Uh oh. It's got to be a catastrophe if *Sophia* dropped a bad word."

She almost starts to hyperventilate, but manages to fight for control. This is standard Soph. She's terrified of getting in trouble. Most likely, she's more afraid of being punished for saying the S word than whatever that magical lump might do.

"I'm sorry!" She looks down. "It's probably not that bad, I'm just frustrated. I can't figure out why the leaks keep happening and they won't stop."

Dad purses his lips. "That's really not supposed to start until you're over fifty."

"Huh?" Sophia looks up at him, clueless.

I bonk my head into Dad's arm, making him laugh.

"Is my magic going to get hard to control when I'm really old?" Sophia blinks.

"No. He's just making a bad joke." I chuckle, then smile to myself. Yay for urine retention humor. Oh, there's one more thing I'll never have to worry about dealing with. Points for vampire me.

"Oh." Sophia exhales in relief, then cringes. "Am I gonna get in trouble?"

"For swearing?" asks Dad. "I'll let this one go. It slipped out without thought. Do try and catch whatever that was before it does something crazy."

Sophia balls her hands into fists, sorta-smiles, then nods. "Okay. I'll try to collect it before mayhem ensues."

She races between us and hurries off down the hall in the direction the lump went.

Dad and I exchange another long glance.

"How bad do you think this one will be?" he asks.

"Why does everyone keep asking me about magical stuff?" I flail my arms. "I have no idea."

He leans against the doorjamb, arms folded. "Should I call Darren Anderson?"

"I don't think he'll know either. Soph's magic is kind of uncharted territory." I offer a helpless shrug. "Oh, Dad. I made two *Ghostbusters* jokes in the past week. I think it's time we screened it."

"Excellent idea. Hmm. I'll add that one to the rotation soon..."

"How about tonight?" I fidget. "Don't *think* I'm obligated anywhere but school. Oh shit!"

"What?" asks Dad.

"It's freaking Thursday!" I look around in a panic. "No wonder I woke up stupid early. I have class at three!"

Dad puts an arm around my shoulders. "If you're going to take a break from college—and by that, I mean probably quit and never go back—why stress out over missing one day?"

I grab two fistfuls of my hair. "Not that. I mean, that explains why I woke up. I've been worrying like crazy something weird was going to happen."

He points at the ritual circle. "Something weird *did* happen."

"True. Not what I meant..." I look at the alarm clock on Sophia's desk. It's 2:49 p.m. "Crap. I'm never going to make it to school on time."

Blix appears in a puff of smoke, levitating between Dad and me. "Ooba?"

He's offering to help me take a mirror there.

"You're awesome. Yes! Okay. Let me get dressed." I glance down at the oversized knee-length T-shirt I use as a nightgown. "This is a bit informal for class."

"Still going?" Dad's smile looks impressed.

"Well, I started this semester. I might as well finish it." I start off down the hall. "Quitting in the middle of class feels worse than just not renewing for another semester."

9

UNLIFE ALERT

STILL THURSDAY, LATER AT NIGHT

*A*ttending class from three to six in the afternoon wasn't the greatest idea of mine.

At least it's chemistry with Dr. Tatiana Markov. The subject matter is interesting enough to keep me awake. I consider it vampire training, working on my 'resist sun' skill. For the most part, I'm good. The only complication to worry about are things like a sudden massive shift in clouds that cause a rapid brightening sunbeam to hit me. My power to resist the fireball in the sky can handle brighter sun than this, but it hates abrupt changes from dim to scalding. It takes my body a couple seconds to realize the dial just got turned up to eleven and compensate.

I've had two smoking incidents since this semester started.

Somehow, I managed not to scream. As far as I am aware, no one noticed where the smoke—or smell of overcooked beef—came from. I am, however, responsible for at least one guy deciding to hit a steakhouse for dinner.

Yes, I wanted to bite him later but didn't get the chance. Class ends at six, so the sun's still up. I can't fly while offline—without the use of mechanical assistance. Thankfully, the clouds didn't mess with me today.

Class was normal, even interesting.

There's a sense of freedom that comes with knowing I'm going to set college aside after this semester. It makes going to class no longer feel totally like a burden of time stealing. Maybe it is kinda silly of me to insist on finishing the semester. I get that from Mom. She hates leaving things unfinished. Also, if she says she's going to do something, she moves mountains to make sure she does the thing. I really would feel like a failure if I walked away in mid-semester, despite college being functionally useless for me as a vampire.

Anyway, Dad picked me up after class since I mirrored to campus with Blix. Even with the mirrorverse travel, I ended up being two minutes late. Not a big deal, really. I blamed traffic.

It's a little after eleven at night now. Tonight was awesome—for a nerdy homegirl like me. Got back from school in time for dinner, then we watched *Ghostbusters*. Yeah, the first one. Sophia still screamed at Slimer. She's a bit older now, so he didn't scare her as much. It probably won't give her nightmares. It's kinda hard to have nightmares about something everyone around you is laughing at. Of course, this *is* Sophia, after all.

Wow, she's lucky Sam is an angel. Lots of girls I went to school with told stories about how their older or younger brothers would mess with them all the time. If Sam happened to be one of those kinds of boys, he'd totally put Blix up to cramming himself into a Slimer plushie and making it fly around the house chasing Sophia. It really is kinda funny to imagine. Wouldn't do it to her, though. Sophia is too brittle and sweet. She'd cry and I'd feel awful.

I'm presently flopped on the living room couch with Chloe and Ashley. One of the *Hotel Transylvania* movies is playing... again. Volume is super low not to disturb the 'rents or Littles trying to sleep. Super low volume is not a problem for Chloe. The movie isn't really holding my attention because we've watched it fifty times. I'm grumbling to myself about unfinished homework I have to do for my writing class.

Slacker Girl and Follows Rules Girl are having a wrestling match in my brain right now. Do I do it because I need to finish the classes or do I blow it off because I'm going to stop going to college? I think Follows Rules Girl is going to win because Slacker Girl is too lazy to put any effort into the fight.

A man's voice screams right before a heavy thudding crash.

Both sounds are so faint they blend into the movie… but don't fit anything happening on the screen. I'm not entirely sure if something happened in reality or if Netflix had a sound glitch.

Ashley looks over at me. "Did you just hear a scream?"

"Was that a Wilhelm?" I scratch my head.

"Kinda sounded like it."

Chloe looks at her, then me, then her, then me. "What's a Wilhelm?"

"The Wilhelm Scream is a sound effect they put into movies all the time," says Ashley. "Rather than having actors scream for themselves, they just keep re-using this one guy's yell. It's kinda become a running joke."

"Oh." Chloe shrugs, clearly unimpressed.

A loud moan comes from the distance.

Ashley pauses the movie.

"Hey," whines Chloe.

Seconds later, another moan happens. It's definitely coming from out front.

"Okay, that was definitely not the movie." I gesture at the screen.

Ashley scrunches her nose. "That sounded like Niedermeyer."

Hmm. Neighborhood kids have been known to prank him by throwing stuff at his windows. "I didn't hear breaking glass." I look up at the ceiling. "Blix? Are you messing with Niedermeyer?"

"Wanna check on him?" Ashley scoots forward on the sofa.

I look down at myself. Baggy T-shirt and sweat pants. Good enough to go outside in. Ash is wearing this neon green top that can't decide if it wants to be a too-short dress or a huge shirt over black yoga pants.

"Suppose we could."

Blix flies down the stairs, bounces off the front door because he can't stop in time, then comes tumbling through the air to hover in front of us. Chloe laughs at him. Oh, maybe he did that on purpose because it makes her laugh.

The imp looks at me and shakes his head.

"You're not messing with him?"

He shakes his head again—long ears flapping—then points at me, points at his eyes, then points at himself.

"Watch you?"

He nods.

Blix zips back up the stairwell and flings himself down the steps like a grey demonic tumbleweed. He faceplants the wall at the bottom of the stairs, sticks for a second, arms and legs splayed out, then peels away and lands on his back. Next, he grabs his hip and makes pain faces.

"Oh, shit." I jump to my feet. "You're saying he fell down the stairs and broke his hip?"

Blix nods.

Ashley grabs her phone from the coffee table. "How do we explain this?"

"Explain what?" I rush for the front door and run outside, not bothering to waste time putting shoes on.

"How we knew he needed help." Ashley flies to catch up with me, then lands to run alongside.

I dart across the cul-de-sac and jump-fly to Niedermeyer's porch. Yeah, he's definitely wailing in agony inside. As much as a jerk as this guy was to me as a child, it's tempting to make some sort of karma joke here or even ignore this situation entirely. I don't have it in me to be like that, though. Even if he's an angry, toxic jackass, he's still a person in pain.

Yes, I'm a softie.

His front door opens as though he left it unlocked. He doesn't leave his door unlocked. The guy does not like people. There are two deadbolts on this door. But I have a way with locks. Barely had to think about it. I barge right in like it's my house.

Mr. Niedermeyer lays sprawled on the floor at the bottom of the stairs leading to the second floor. He's got one leg up in the air against the wall, his head on the landing. His face is bright red in pain—and possibly rage. One beat-up leather slipper dangles from his foot. The other one's sitting on top of the coffee table. Probably went flying as he fell.

Ashley calls 911.

Niedermayer stops howling long enough to glare at me. For a second, he seems furious that I'm barging into his house. Then, he seems to process the reality of his situation—and remembers he'd been shouting for help. Bet he's upset that a 'kid' is here and not an adult. Really don't know what the guy's problem with kids is. Dude probably just hates being old and kids remind him that he's old. I didn't see anything really bad in his mind the last time I looked.

I head over to the landing. "Hi, Mr. Niedermeyer. It's going to be okay. We got you. Ash is calling for an ambulance now."

He seems bewildered, almost as if he's not really sure how he ended up on the floor or why he can't stand back up. I sit on the first landing step and take his hand before giving him a light tap from the Derp Hammer. It's not enough to put him into a feeding trance, only enough to dull the pain.

Breaking a hip has to hurt like hell. There's another item on the list of stuff I'm glad I never to deal with as a vampire. Well, I suppose having my spine smashed into pieces by a troll is probably *more* painful than an old person breaking a hip. I also had a katana blade entirely inside my body once. That truly sucked. Okay, so maybe being a vampire isn't a free pass away from painful experiences. At least I'll never get old, fall over, and die alone in an empty house because no one noticed me.

Sigh.

Mr. Niedermeyer squeezes my hand. He's not going to say it, but that's a thank you.

"They'll be here soon. Try not to move," I say in a quiet voice.

"Why am I on the floor?" he rasps.

"You fell down the stairs."

"No, I didn't." He grumbles. "If I fell down the stairs, I'd remember it."

Something in his voice tells me he's not lying to save dignity. He really doesn't remember the fall. I hope it's just like a traumatic blackout of memory from the fall itself and he's not developing something like dementia or Alzheimer's. The guy's been an absolute jerk to me for most of my life—and every kid in this area—but I still feel bad for him. Here, tonight, he looks so weak and vulnerable, a far cry from the guy I used to be terrified of when I was small.

"Where's Margaret?" he asks, seemingly at no one in particular.

I pat his hand. "I'm not sure who that is."

"My wife. She's been out for a long time."

Aww hell. I peek into his mind, cringing at the overwhelming presence of a headache. I think he whacked his head into the wall. He's not quite sure if his wife died sixteen years ago or if he imagined the whole cancer thing. Time is kinda flipping over itself in his thoughts. I'm unsure if it's because he hit his head or if something deeper is going on in there.

I keep reassuring him that he'll be okay and telling him not to move if he can help it. Ash stands close by on the phone with 911 telling them about Niedermeyer's condition.

Finally, sirens approach in the distance outside. Ashley darts out onto the porch to flag down the EMTs. They soon hurry inside with a stretcher. I move out of their way and let them take over. A pair of cops walk in while the medics are examining Mr. Neidermeyer.

"That your grandpa?" asks the slightly older cop.

"No, officer." I say. "We live across the cul-de-sac. Heard the scream when he fell."

That is not a lie. It's just kinda difficult to believe if one ignores the existence of vampires with overamped senses.

"We were out on the patio stargazing," adds Ashley, hoping to add some believability.

Cop two looks at the front door, likely checking for signs of damage. "Good thing he left his door open."

The medics shift Mr. Neidermeyer onto the stretcher and strap him down. I think they gave him pain meds already.

"He didn't." I fidget my hands. "Ran up on the porch and peeked in the window. Saw him lying there on the floor screaming. Ash called you guys while I slipped through a window. Hope that's okay."

Both cops nod at me in a 'yeah, no worries' manner. Sometimes, breaking into a house is legal. Nice. I didn't even have to charm them.

We give our names and address, then answer a few routine questions. Mostly about Niedermeyer... specifically us not knowing if he has any family or relatives at all. Eventually, the cops send us home. And yes, they do watch us walk across the cul-de-sac toward home and go inside.

Once back in our living room, Ashley leans against me. "Helping an old man who fell. Truly, we are evil creatures of the night."

I chuckle. "Yeah…"

"As much of a prick as he is to everyone…"

"He's still a person." I head over to the couch and flop. "Poor guy lost his wife years ago to cancer. Maybe that's why he's been so angry."

Ashley 'awws.' She jumps over the sofa back, goes cross-legged in midair, then levitates down to sit. "Yeah, that would do it."

Chloe cuddles against me and sticks her feet into Ashley's lap.

This, of course, results in immediate tickling and squeal-laughter.

Once that settles down a few minutes later—and Chloe has cocooned herself into a blanket for defense—Ashley peers over at me. "Would you do the same for Uncle Hank?"

"Yeah," I say without too much thought. "I mean, I don't wish harm on the jackass. Just wish he wasn't such a bigoted, self-important jerk."

She groans. "Totally. Oh, hey, speaking of creatures of the night. Hungry?"

My stomach clenches up. "Yeah. I went to day classes. Definitely could use someone to eat."

Chloe bounces. "Let's go bite an Irish person!"

"What? Why?" Ashley snickers.

"Because." Chloe sheds the blanket and hops to her feet. "I want McDonalds!"

10

A FATE WORSE THAN DEATH

FRIDAY

*S*ierra watched the volleyball bouncing among the other kids around her in the enormous pool.

Small waves created by her classmates jumping after the flying rubber sphere lapped at her neck. Thankfully, the game stayed in the 'shallow' section, where the water only came up to her shoulders. The 'action' stayed away from her for several minutes, a fact she didn't really mind.

How she'd been talked into going to Amanda Clarke's twelfth birthday party, she couldn't explain. Why her classmate even invited her also remained a mystery. Sierra and Amanda didn't really hang out as friends. They also didn't have any problems, either. In fact, they rarely spoke to each other on any given day at school. Amanda was a nice enough girl, one of those kids like Sophia, who always tried to make everyone happy. Unlike Sophia, Amanda was neither shy nor easily frightened.

The girl invited more-or-less their entire sixth grade class to Orbital Fitness so they could have a pool party in October. Rumor had it Amanda's mom knew the manager here, or perhaps her parents simply paid for guest access for twenty-or-so kids and four parents. They certainly hadn't bought everyone a gym membership. A fitness center did seem like a weird place for a birthday party. Amanda insisted on a pool party, not an easy task for a kid born in October.

Sierra spent the past two weeks leading up to the party trying to come up with an excuse not to go that wouldn't hurt Amanda's feelings or seem stupid. She chickened out every time. Going to a pool party wasn't the worst thing in the world, even if it ate into after-school time on a Friday. Her biggest problem was not having any close friends among her class group. Of course, she couldn't blame anyone for that but herself. Several years of being paranoid about a school shooter kept her quiet and withdrawn. She'd figured if she didn't make close friends, losing them wouldn't hurt as much.

Now, she felt dumb for keeping her distance. The therapist suggested she consider making some friends. Maybe that's why she kept chickening out from telling Amanda she couldn't go. It certainly didn't help she'd felt strangely emotional earlier that afternoon when Amanda approached her to confirm she'd be at the party later. It had taken every ounce of her strength not to cry in front of the girl. That sense of 'wow, you actually want me there' came out of nowhere. Since when did Sierra care what anyone thought of her?

Yet, here she found some solace in having no one pay any attention to her, effectively alone in a pool with a bunch of her classmates—and a handful of adults at the other end. The grown-ups in the pool did boring things like swimming for exercise. The fitness center wasn't about to close down completely so only one kid's birthday party would be inside. Ordinary club members still went about their workout routines, oblivious to some random kid having a birthday pool party in the building.

Her classmates played a crazy game somewhere between netless volleyball and dodgeball. The rules seemed to get invented on the fly. Making the ball hit water without the other team keeping it in the air scored one point. Beaning someone in the face scored five points. The face-beaning rule got suspended pretty quick. Go figure, Amanda's mother didn't want to be responsible for bloody noses. Let's face it, giving sixth-grade boys an excuse to hammer each other in the face with a volleyball had bad idea all over it.

Essence of birthday cake bubbled up in the back of her throat. She re-swallowed it, still keeping her eyes on the zooming ball in case it suddenly came toward her. Thanks to Sophia's enchantment boosting her strength and reflexes, she pretty much aced any physical sport that didn't require specific training to master. Inhuman speed and agility made something like preventing a ball from hitting the water around her trivially easy.

That's probably why they're keeping the ball away from me. They'll know I'll hit it and score.

Her gut tightened up.

Ugh. Cake is angry. I shouldn't have had such a huge piece. She grimaced, rubbing her belly. *Maybe Mom was right after all... stupid to go in the water so soon after eating.*

Amanda's mother sat on a folding chair nearby, dutifully watching the kids in the pool. Two fitness center lifeguards also kept an eye on things. They only looked a little bit older than Sarah, one guy and one girl who were both probably still in college. Another two moms and one of the dads stood in a conversation cluster by the folding table holding all the soda, pizza, and cake.

Sierra idly swished her hands back and forth under the water.

The general sense of malaise building in her gut grew worse over the next few minutes. One moment, she felt about ready to throw up, the next, her lower back hurt as if she pulled a muscle the last time she leapt to hit the volleyball. Then it all stopped only to return a minute or two later.

Ugh. I'm either going to throw up or have diarrhea. I should get out of the water.

None of the other kids seemed to notice her making uncomfortable faces. They kept bouncing the volleyball around. A few boys also got tired of the ball not going anywhere near them and started yelling things like 'send it here' or 'I'm open'.

The more she stood there feeling uncomfortable, the more she decided she'd had enough party and wanted to go home. It had to be almost over by now, anyway. She could spend the last twenty minutes or however much time remained wrapped in a towel. Everyone else could scramble from soaking wet bathing suits into their normal clothes. She'd already be mostly dry by then. It *was* October, after all. Going outside wet would be awful.

Sierra paddled toward the nearest ladder. Whatever war raged in her stomach refused to settle down. She wanted to be in the bathroom —or at least on dry land so she could run—before anything went too far.

A dread thought stopped her in the middle of the pool, still fifteen feet away from the ladder to safety. Could this be Sophia's magic unraveling? Her sister seemed really confident the enchantment was permanent. The magic making her strong, fast, and tough shouldn't wear off at all, much less mere months after it started.

No. It's not that. It can't be that... please. She closed her eyes and made a wish. *Anything but that.*

Her stomach seemed to settle.

Just too much cake and pizza. Shouldn't have gone back in the water so soon. "I'll be fine. Just need to sit down for a bit."

She trudged over to the ladder, grabbed onto the plain steel rails, and hauled herself up out of the water. As soon as she found herself standing on the wet concrete edge between the ladder's handrails, it occurred to her that the entire place had gone silent. This side of the pool happened to be near the wall, so she couldn't see anything out of the ordinary.

That's really weird.

Sierra turned around to look at the fitness center.

Every kid in the pool stared at her, their expressions somewhere between concern and shock. All three moms and the dad also had their attention fixed upon her. Most of the adults who'd been swimming for exercise also stopped what they were doing to look at her. Even some people on stationary bikes within sight of the pool area made faces of 'oh no' or 'that poor kid' at her.

Umm... what the heck?

Sierra scrunched her nose and glanced around at everyone. The adults all gave off varying degrees of concern. A few of the men appeared to be averting their gaze from her, as if embarrassed. Several girls among her classmates giggled. The rest seemed either confused or worried. Except for one boy, Parker Williams, the boys all wore expressions of utter bafflement. Parker gave off more a sense of 'uh oh'.

The heck is wrong with everyone. Why are the guys afraid to look at me? Eek! Did my suit bottoms fall off?

A wave of heat ran down her body at the expected mortification of missing the most critical part of her swimsuit. Why else would guys be trying not to look at her?

She peered down at herself.

Blood ran in multiple dark trails down both legs, cascading over her feet to the concrete where it bloomed out in a crimson aura. A long smear of red hung in the pool, a trail from the ladder extending about fifteen feet.

Her bikini bottoms remained right where they should be, albeit bloodstained.

Sierra gripped the tall ladder posts on either side of her to keep from fainting... either from blood loss or embarrassment. She couldn't bring herself to move, too crippled with mortification. Thanks to Mom, she knew *exactly* what just happened.

How much trouble would I get in for killing all the witnesses?

The amount of blood in the water and still running down her legs seemed abnormal. Way, way, way too much for how Mom described it would be. Is that because of her being in the water? Or had something else gone wrong with her? She didn't feel woozy or anything worse than sick to her stomach. Again, she looked down at herself. The bleeding appeared to have stopped, though she remained covered in it. Her guts tingled the same way her arms and legs did after the car hit her. Sophia's magic made her body heal itself. The enchantment had to be having a brawl with the red fairy. That might explain why so much blood came out of her. Whenever the magic healed her, she got hungry. Getting hungry while cramps knotted up her insides and she already felt ready to puke made the sense of nausea infinitely worse.

Most of the boys in her class started giving her 'are you okay?' looks.

"Ohmigod," whispered Ainsley Rush, "Sierra just had her period in the pool!"

A few boys close enough to hear the girl's whisper started laughing.

Sierra wanted to implode, to teleport out of there, but she couldn't even make her hands let go of the ladder. She also didn't have powers of teleportation. Her body refused to do anything other than stand there shivering in embarrassment.

Parker Williams came out of nowhere, right beside her. "Hey, Sierra. Here..."

Somehow, she managed to turn her head away from the staring crowd to look at him. The boy was kinda skinny, but athletic. A pattern of giant blue flowers decorated his enormous black swim trunks. Not a trace of wanting to laugh at her radiated in his expression. He appeared entirely concerned—and held out a towel.

She dry swallowed. "Umm... thanks."

The vulnerability infuriated her, though no anger showed on her face past the shock and embarrassment. She hated needing help. However, she wasn't going to bite his head off for trying to be nice. All the other boys found this situation hilarious once they realized she hadn't been hurt and simply had a 'girl issue'. Evidently, word got around about what happened. Weird that a boy wasn't laughing at her. This gangly kid with a warm smile and short dreadlocks appeared to be sincere, not trying to set her up for an even more embarrassing prank.

Parker gestured as if asking if she wanted him to wrap the towel around her or if she would rather take it from him.

Sierra made herself let go of the ladder so she could take the towel and wrap it around her waist.

Amanda, the birthday girl, covered her mouth. The expression on her face said 'omg you poor thing.'

Mrs. Clarke and another class mom, Mrs. Wilson, came running around the pool toward her.

Ugh. Sierra looked down at the blood all over the concrete around her feet and off into the water where it gradually diffused from a trail to a haze. The other kids hurried away from it, acting as if someone set piranha loose. Some even screamed.

So much blood... that can't be normal.

The moms appeared to be freaking out with worry, until they noticed she didn't look abnormally pale—in fact quite the opposite. She doubted her face could be any redder.

"Attention, everyone," called the male lifeguard over the PA system. "At this time, we need to ask everyone to exit the pool so the water can be decontaminated."

Sierra shrank in on herself. If it were possible to die from embarrassment, she'd be a ghost any second now.

"Sierra!" Amanda's mother reached her first and gave her a hasty look over before feeling her forehead. "Hang on, sweetie. You're going to be okay."

Even if she had any idea how to explain where *all that blood* came from, Sierra couldn't make herself speak.

Mrs. Wilson stared at the blood. She seemed close to having a panic attack.

"She's hot to the touch." Amanda's mother leaned around to look her in the eye. "Do you feel lightheaded? Like you're about to faint? Dizzy?"

Sierra managed to shake her head. Other than wanting a hole in reality to swallow her into an endless void, she felt reasonably healthy... if a bit queasy.

"C'mon honey, let's get you to the locker room." Amanda's mother grabbed her hand. "I think they have a nurse on staff here, just in case."

Despite wanting to *stop standing there where everyone could see her,* Sierra couldn't move. She merely stared at the woman trying not to notice the tickling sensation of water droplets running down her body.

"Sierra?" Mrs. Clarke patted her shoulder. "Are you okay?"

"She lost an awful lot of blood, Ann," said Mrs. Wilson. "She might be in shock."

Mrs. Clarke pressed a hand to her forehead. "Oh, she's in shock all right, but I don't think it's medical shock. She's not turning pale and she's not cold. Sierra, hon? You okay? Why aren't you talking?"

Sierra took a breath. "I'm not dying. Just trying to fight the urge to kill all witnesses."

The class moms smiled and made aww faces at her.

"Wanting to kill everyone around you is pretty normal." Mrs. Clarke set her hands on her hips. "Especially for the bad months. I've had a few times where I thought about murder sprees, too. Nothing to be ashamed of. Happens to all of us. Part of nature."

"Nature's an evil witch," muttered Mrs. Wilson.

"C'mon dear." Mrs. Clarke tugged at her hand. "Let's get you to the locker room so you can shower off and clean up. Or should we go to the nurse first, you think?"

"Shower, please," said Sierra in a small voice.

Mrs. Wilson nudged Mrs. Clarke. "Stay with her and call 911 if she faints. While you get her to the lockers, I'll call her mother to come pick her up."

"Okay." Ashley's mom gave her hand another squeeze. "C'mon, hon."

She numbly let the woman lead her off, head down. *Great... I can never go to school again.*

When they passed Parker standing at the corner of the pool, she looked up, ready to snap at him for staring at her.

His 'everything's gonna be fine' smile stole the vitriol off her tongue.

"It's okay. I got an older sister. Know how it is." He nodded once. "Keep the towel."

Sierra almost smiled back at him.

11

ALIEN CREATURES

*S*tupid writing project.

      I'd scream and rant about how unfair it is for a vampire to have freakin' homework, but it's entirely my fault. Go to college so I feel normal. Yeah, great idea. Ugh. Oh, well. I made this bed, time to lie in it. The truly weird thing is I never really hated homework. I don't enjoy it like Sophia does. Just… never really grumbled about it… much. Now, it feels pointless and annoying.

Both of my sisters tend to do their homework immediately upon getting home from school. Sophia does it because she finds it fun. Sierra does it right away to get it over with. I'm taking a page from her book. No sense procrastinating and having this stupid assignment hanging over me for half a week only to scramble to get it done the day before it's due.

Writing… writing… writing…

A loud slam from upstairs smashes the silence hard enough that I jump halfway off my chair.

"Everyone pack!" yells Sierra. "We have to move to the East Coast."

The stomping thuds of a scrawny tween hammer the stairs up to the second floor.

"What? Why?" calls Dad.

"Because I can never go back to that school again!" screams Sierra.

Uh oh. Did something happen? I bet someone picked a fight with her and she had a vulgar display of supernatural power with witnesses. It's not like Sierra to be a drama llama. This has to be serious. Hopefully, I can erase memories before the Persons In Black need to get involved.

I leap away from the computer and rush upstairs. Someone's already closed the front door, but there's no one in the living room. Dad's poking his head out from the office. He gives me this 'what the heck is going on?' face. I shrug at him and keep going, grabbing the banister post at the bottom of the stairs to swing myself around before running to the second floor.

Sierra and Mom are in her room. My kid sister is sitting in the middle of her bed hugging a massive teddy bear almost as big as she is. Her face is red, eyes watery, she looks equal parts furious and devastated. She hasn't even had a boyfriend at all yet, so she couldn't have been dumped.

Mom's got an arm around her, being a beacon of silent comfort.

I skid to a stop right inside the door, one eyebrow up. "What happened?"

"Your sister just had her first period," says Mom in a quiet, matter-of-fact tone.

"Period?!" Sierra buries her face in the teddy bear. "That wasn't *just* a period! It was a damn *exclamation point!*"

Mom's face is absolutely priceless. I've never seen anyone work so hard to stop themselves from laughing before in my life.

Sierra lifts her face away from the bear and stares daggers at me, then points like the Evil Monkey. "You. You will make everyone forget!"

Head tilted, I approach the bed. "Make everyone forget what?"

She huffs and smashes her face into the bear's plush head again.

Mom rubs her back. "The red faerie ambushed her at the pool party."

"Everyone saw me," whimpers Sierra into the bear. "They had to close down the pool to *decontaminate* it." She lifts her head away from the bear, then slams it into the plush several times. "Ugh!"

"Aww, honey." Mom pats her back. "Don't take it personally. They do the same thing at the pool if someone pees or cuts themselves. No one was calling you a contamination."

"Eww," deadpans Sierra. "Still. My stupid uterus shut down an entire Olympic sized swimming pool! Everyone hates me."

Mom lets out a soft sigh. "No, they don't hate you."

"Sare." Sierra peels her face out of the plush teddy to look at me. "You gotta make them all forget. Please! I can't go back to that school ever again otherwise."

Oof. Red faerie, indeed. The drama is strong with this one.

"I'm not sure how realistic that is, dear." Mom gives me side eye. "She'd never be able to track down everyone."

I wince. "Umm… maybe if I'd been right there when it happened. Unfortunately, vampire mind powers aren't faster than the speed of texts. I won't be able to get to everyone who knows it happened."

Sierra's face goes as white as Ashley's as if she hadn't even thought about the kids who witnessed it texting their friends. "My life is over!" She wails and power-slams her face into the teddy bear's head. A moment later, she whimpers, "Can I be homeschooled?"

"It happens to us all. They won't remember it in a few weeks," says Mom.

"Are you crazy?" Sierra lifts her head, sniffling. "They're going to call me *Carrie* until I'm out of high school."

"Carrie?" asks Mom.

Sierra glares at nothing in particular. "Yeah. Carrie. I'm standing there *covered* in freaking blood while everyone's staring at me."

"It couldn't have been *that* bad." Mom examines her fingernails. "My first time was just a little bit of blood. One tissue managed it."

"Mom…" Sierra's eyebrows form a flat line. "It looked like a damn shark attack. Mrs. Wilson almost called an ambulance because of how much blood came out of me. Mrs. Clarke insisted I have another whole piece of cake and some juice."

"That's smart. If you lost a lot of blood, you really should eat." Mom ruffled her hair.

I sit on Sierra's other side. "Are you feeling okay? Light headed? Cramps? Random unexplained emotions?"

She looks down. "Maybe some crazy emotions. Felt like I was gonna throw up. Maybe some cramping. No, I don't feel light headed. I think it was the magic."

"Red faerie attacks are not magic," says Mom. "Quite the opposite."

"Duh." Sierra rolls her eyes. "That's not what I mean. *All the blood.* It had to be the magic. Crazy amounts of blood. Sare. Bite me."

"No," I say.

Mom blinks. "What?"

"When a vampire bites someone, they can tell if they're low on blood, right, so you know not to drink too much? Bite me so you can tell if I'm low."

"The nurse at Orbital seemed to think you were fine, even though she couldn't explain it." Mom rubs Sierra's back.

"That's true, but I'm not going to bite you." I lean close and sniff at the side of her neck. She still smells like strawberries. "It's still daylight out. And you are my sister. I am not going to bite any of you. You're not low on blood. I can smell it."

"Umm." Mom fidgets, unsure how to react to the vampiness. "Well, I suppose that's good then if she's got enough blood."

I pat Sierra on the arm. "You should be thrilled this happened."

She glares death at me. "My life is over. I am not thrilled. Why the hell do you think I should be thrilled about this?"

"Weren't you worried that Sophia's enchantment was going to freeze you permanently at twelve?" I grin. "Doesn't this mean you're not going to be stuck as a child forever?"

Sierra's anger recedes. "She didn't freeze me as a kid. Said it would take me a really long time to grow up. I'm probably going to look just like this when I'm a senior in high school."

"Still. Your first visit from the red faerie is a sign of maturity." I hold my chin up. "Wear it with pride."

"Yeah right." She grumbles. "That bitch betrayed me in front of everyone."

"Do you want a period party?" asks Mom.

"Hey!" I set my hands on my hips and playfully glare at her. "You didn't give me the choice, just kinda sprang it on me when I wasn't ready for it."

"Firstborn problems." Mom examines her fingernails. "I was too proud of you. Also, you weren't so upset that you wanted to move across the country after it happened."

I bite my lip. "I also didn't shut down a pool."

"Augh!" Sierra powerslams her face into the teddy bear again.

"No, no, you didn't." Mom rubs Sierra's back.

After a moment or two of silence, my sister lifts her head away from the plush. "Sare, where did it happen to you?"

"Right here at home. I woke up in a puddle of blood. Had to get a new mattress and everything." I cringe.

"We just told you that," says Mom. "Your father only flipped it over after it dried out."

I wince. "Eww. That's… not right."

"It's only blood." Mom shrugs. "Not like we're alien creatures that secrete deadly acid once a month."

Sierra manages a laugh. "So, when are we moving?"

"If anyone picks on you, I'll deal with them." I flash a wicked smile. "Or we could sic Blix on them for payback."

"Ooh." Sierra does weasel hands. "Okay, fine. We don't have to move. But I demand not to be grounded if I get suspended for punching someone who teased me over having a period."

Mom holds up a finger. "I will let it slide on one condition: you don't hit anyone harder than an ordinary kid could hit them."

"Fair." Sierra offers a handshake.

Mom shakes on the deal.

"And…" Sierra shrugs one shoulder. "If you really want to do the red cupcake thing, we can. Just don't make a big event out of it with like a bunch of people."

"Really?" I raise both eyebrows. "You're not embarrassed?"

"Of course I am, but chocolate cupcakes are still chocolate cupcakes, even if they have red glitter frosting." Sierra examines her fingernails.

Mom nods toward the door. "Are you ready?"

Sierra blushes. "No, but I suppose we might as well get this over with."

"It's a skill you will need for most of your life, and it's kinda tricky." Mom tugs her to her feet.

They make their way out to the hall bathroom.

Ahh. It's time. Mom's going to help her learn how to use a tampon. I trail after them to play door guard in case Sam, Ronan, or one of his friends tries to run in there without knocking. Poor Dad and Sam. It won't be too much longer before they'll be dealing with three monthly demons. When living together, we girls tend to synch up and pop off at the same time.

At least Ashley and I are out of the loop now.

One more point for team vampire.

12

SQUISHY

I make my way upstairs into the kitchen.

Upon spotting the large plastic container on the table holding red-frosted cupcakes, I decide to make myself a mug of coffee and have one. Chocolate is still awesome. More so now that I can't get fat. Oh, there's another thing I can blame Dad for. Chocolate cake makes me want coffee. It feels strange not to have them together for some reason. Having coffee makes me think about something chocolate but I can have coffee without the chocolate just fine. If I have chocolate cake or a brownie, it genuinely feels like I'm doing something wrong if I don't have coffee as well.

Sierra's little 'period party' was pretty much only the family plus Nicole, Megan, and Priya who happened to be hanging out with Sophia when they got home. Sierra wasn't too thrilled about having extra girls know what happened… but she got over it pretty fast. Poor Priya had no idea that periods were even a thing. Evidently her parents can't or won't talk about that sort of thing with her. Not sure if we overstepped boundaries there, but Mom decided to give her a basic education.

I'd joke that Dad, Sam, and Ronan spent Friday night camping out in the backyard with helmets on, but they didn't. Dad's one of the four men on Planet Earth who can talk about girl stuff like that without wanting to run for the hills.

Sophia made the cupcakes. They're really good. I'm not supposed to tell anyone that she got the ingredients from Cat-ma-zon. That is to say, Klepto stole them from a store somewhere. The whole thing came together in a rush, after all. Oddly, Mom didn't ask where the mix and frosting came from. Not sure if she assumed we had it already or if she condoned the yoinking, believing it a small price to pay for Sierra's emotional health.

I finish off the cupcake, briefly consider having a second one, and decide not to. Wouldn't be fair to the Littles.

Huh. Weird. The house is oddly quiet for a Saturday afternoon. Chloe and Ashley are still sleeping downstairs, so they're not going to make any noise. Half-mug of coffee in hand, I snoop around. No sign of the 'rents. No one in the living room. Looking out the kitchen patio doors reveals the backyard is empty as well. Max is probably still there. He's invisible, so I can't tell.

I pause at the bottom of the stairs to take a sip of coffee, then go up, peering into bedrooms.

No sign of Sam or Sophia.

Sierra's at her desk, huddled over her latest drawing project. Every so often, she lets out a small sniffle. Doesn't seem like she's actively crying, though she's clearly not in the greatest of moods. While this could be aftershocks from the red faerie's first attack, I am compelled to check on her.

After that demonic nightmare, therapy sessions, and a worst-case scenario period-mageddon event, I break my rule and peek into her thoughts. It's daylight up here so tapping into mind powers requires I temporarily weaken my sun shield. Ow. Ow. Ow. This is stupid. Only a quick snapshot peek, merely a shallow skimming of what's right on her mind. Don't want to pry. This is a wellness check. I'm not fishing for gossip or blackmail. Also, ouch. Stupid sun.

Surprisingly, she's really into the idea of becoming an artist. Like, I don't think this is a phase she'll be done with in a few months. All the energy she put into wanting to become a video game programmer kinda died when she learned programming requires tons of math. She's salvaged that dream and poured it into art. Video games need artists to design all the visuals, right? She can still be part of a video game company without having to do heavy math. Win win.

Her emotions are swirling around in an unpredictable, strong way that has to be the work of the red faerie. There's also some guilt in there, too. The reason for the guilt lurks deeper into her head than I'm willing to go.

I let off the telepathy and exhale a sigh of relief as the burning stops. All done in two seconds. Not enough time for any smoke to happen.

"Hey," I say. "What's up? Where is everyone?"

"Umm, no idea," says Sierra without looking up. "I think Soph went to Priya's or Meg's. Sam's with the turd brothers."

I chuckle. Daryl and Jordan are not related to each other, though she calls them the turd brothers since most of the time she sees them, they're on their way to or from our bathroom.

"Okay, so a pretty normal Saturday, then. Everyone's off doing fun stuff." I lean over her shoulder to look at the table.

The drawing she's working on is an action shot of some sci-fi superhero like girl surrounded by six not-quite-human alien monster things. Hero girl has got one of the aliens up in the air over her head by a one-handed chokehold grip on its neck and she's firing a tiny missile off her left arm at one behind her without even looking at it.

Sierra's not a professional artist yet. I mean, this is amazing for a twelve-year-old who's never taken a serious art class in her life. She's put enough into it that I suspect 'hero girl' is based on me. I'm not *that* skinny, am I?

Anxiety blooms out from Sierra all of a sudden. She shrinks in on herself, biting her lip, staring at the big piece of paper in front of her.

"Oh wow… That looks seriously cool." I give her a shoulder squeeze.

She seems to relax a little, then frowns and points at a comic book leaning up against her computer. "It looks like a kid drew it."

"Well. A kid *did* draw it." I smile. "Honestly, though? No one starts off out of the box being a professional artist. For every comic you see like that, there are thousands of hours of practice drawings, most of them not even as good as what you're doing now."

"Really?" She peers up at me.

"Yep. And you're only just starting to take this seriously." I glance at the image, then twist around to show off my butt. "Is my rear end really that small?"

Sierra bursts out laughing—and blushing.

"That's supposed to kinda be me, right?"

She fidgets.

"It's fine." I put an arm around her and squeeze.

Sophia, as younger siblings occasionally do, idolizes me for some reason. She makes no secret of it. If I happened to be the bitchy sort of annoying older sister who constantly screamed at my siblings to get out of my room or go away, Sophia would spend half her day crying into her pillow all the time. I'd be lying if I tried to say mortal me never caused her to have a meltdown because I wanted time away from 'little kids' to hang with my friends. Though, I don't think it ever came off mean.

Anyway, Sierra's kinda got that thing going, too… but she doesn't say it out loud. Ever since that night we ended up fighting a group of vampires together, we've kinda got this special secret relationship. She confides in me all sorts of stuff she's too embarrassed to tell anyone else. Even Mom. I'm kinda surprised she didn't insist that I be the one to show her how to use a tampon. Then again, Mom was right there and all 'let's get this done with now.' Perhaps if Sierra had been left to ask for help, she would've come to me.

Thankfully, Mom is awesome. She's determined to make sure all four of us have everything we need to survive in this world.

"You okay?" I ask.

Sierra leans back in her chair and wipes both hands down her face. "Ugh. Am I that obvious?"

"Not really. Just making sure."

"Umm. It's stupid."

"Nothing's stupid if it's making you sniffle."

Sierra spins a colored pencil around between her fingers, staring at it for a minute or so before speaking. "I keep wanting to thank Mrs. Burke for trying to protect us… but there wasn't really a shooter. It was all a nightmare the demon gave me. I know it wasn't real. It felt too real. Every time I see her in school, I want to cry."

"You're right. It wasn't real. Whenever you think about that awful hallucination, just remember watching the stupid demon that caused it screaming and breaking apart instead. And if that doesn't help, think about Dad with his headband and giant Nerf cannon playing Rambo."

Sierra sets the pencil down, then pushes off the desk so her chair spins to face me. "Sare, can you make me forget seeing Mrs. Burke get shot? The stupid therapist just tells me to say 'it didn't really happen' over and over. That doesn't work. She's used to normal crazy people, not victims of a demon."

Oof. Umm. I sit on the carpet beside her chair, peering up at her. "If it's what you need, I can try."

"Try?" She blinks. "You don't think it's a good idea?"

"Well…" I shift my gaze to the drawing. "They say no good artist had a sane childhood."

She rolls her eyes. "I think our lives are wacky enough without a memory of watching one of my teachers getting blasted trying to protect us." She huffs. "Stupid demon nightmare."

"We destroyed that demon."

"And the worst part…" Sierra makes a fist but doesn't seem to know what to do with it, so she relaxes again. "I don't even really know if Mrs. Burke would really have tried to throw herself at a shooter or if she'd have been hiding under her desk. It's like, I really want to thank her for doing that, but she didn't really do it… and she might not even be that brave."

I scratch my fingernails idly over the rug by my knee. "You must believe she would do that or you wouldn't have dreamed it that way."

A long, slow sigh leaks out of my sister. "Yeah, I suppose. Or, maybe she's just the teacher and I expect that's what they'd do. Whatever. I've got enough emotional baggage already. I could really live without remembering that nightmare."

Ugh. She's going to demand that I erase her memory. This is not going to end well. The odds of making things worse are so high it's not a risk worth taking. How can I fix this without tinkering in her head? I have to talk her out of it somehow.

"Sare?"

"Hmm?" I look up at her again.

"Why did you say try? Do your mind powers not always work or something?"

"It's complicated."

Sierra grins. "I'm not asking you about your boyfriend."

"Hah." I chuckle. "So, okay. I said try because it's the kind of memory I might not be able to get rid of. If something is deep enough or traumatic enough, it's really hard to erase. Memories are squishy things. I'm afraid of poking it and causing it to mutate into something even worse."

She cringes. "What could possibly be worse?"

I'm not going to feed her fears with a serious answer, even though a few thoughts of true 'worse' come to my mind. "The nightmare could change from a school shooting to something like you being trapped in pink Barbie world, stuck in a frilly pink dress you can't take off and there are no video games."

Sierra stares at me. For half a second, her expression says 'you're not serious,' then she seems to realize what I'm doing and acts horrified. "Oh, yeah. True. That would be horrible."

"If you really can't get away from thinking about that nightmare and it's making life hard, I will try." I purse my lips. "Or maybe we could ask Aurélie to help. She's had a bit more practice at memory tinkering than me."

"Are you sure she wouldn't sneak in some bit of side programming to make me like fancy dresses?" Sierra grins. "Oh shit."

"What?" I blink. "And no, I'm sure she wouldn't do that."

"Sophia enchanted me to resist vampire mind control… after what happened at the airport." Sierra closes her eyes and sighs. "You might not even be able to change my memory."

"Oh. Uhh. Damn."

Sierra waves both hands in a 'never mind' gesture. "Forget it. I'd rather cope with this bullshit dream than potentially be mindwanked into hurting you, Soph, Sam, or the 'rents."

"Mindwanked?" I chuckle. "Where did you hear that?"

"Online… and Dalton likes the word 'wank.'" She grins. "It's kinda funny."

"Do you know what it means?"

She smirks. "I'm twelve, Sare. Not four. Yes. But it also means other stuff. Like when Dalton says 'a bit fat bag of wank,' he means nonsense."

"True."

"So, umm… yeah forget it. You can't make me un-remember." Sierra picks up her pencil again. "When I'm drawing, I don't really think about the nightmare, so I guess I'm gonna be drawing a lot. So, honestly, do you think this is any good?"

"It's great… for a kid."

She sighs. "That means it sucks."

I grab her hand. "No, it doesn't. You asked for honesty. This is not polished enough to be printed in a professional comic book or video game, but you are only twelve, and you've just started. You're already this good. Definitely better than I could draw. I'm totally confident that you will be able to do this for a living if you love it and keep at it."

"I kinda think I do." She narrows her eyes at me. "And if you tell anyone you caught me crying, I will… do something."

I play innocent.

"Oh, come on." She smirks. "I know you were watching me for a minute or two before you walked in."

And she didn't freak out at being caught sniffling. I am in the center of her circle of trust.

"Not a word," I say.

Again, she kinda blushes a little. "So, I'm doing this character that's kinda based on you, but I'm turning all the vampire stuff into science fiction, cybernetics, and technology. Can't let the secret out, right?"

"Right." I grin.

She leans forward in her chair. "One more serious question?"

"Sure."

"Do you think I'd really freeze up like a scared little girl if a shooter ever attacked my school?"

I cringe. "Umm. I really hope you never, ever learn the answer to that question."

She's quiet for a minute, lost in thought. "Umm... I don't think I will, 'cause of Soph's enchantment. Just curious what you think."

I make a sword slashing gesture. "Well, you did run *at* literal demons when we went to the abyss, right? Those are a lot scarier than some psychopathic human. I think you'd get super pissed off that someone had the audacity to attack your school and kick his balls into his throat before you had time to even think about being scared."

Sierra fidgets. "Really?"

"Yeah. Almost always, your first emotional reaction to a situation that's bad or out of your control is getting angry. The demon that gave you the nightmare specifically made you feel overwhelmed with fear."

Eyes closed, Sierra lets out a long breath. "Not real. Not real."

Tears form and roll down her face.

I lean up and take her hands in mine. "It's okay."

"I'm fine," says Sierra, without opening her eyes. "My stupid uterus is being annoying again, making me super emo."

"Ahh."

"Who needs demons messing with them when they have one of these?" She opens her eyes and pats her belly. "Ugh. When does it stop?"

"Sometime in your late forties or early fifties."

She glares. "No, dork. I mean right now. Like this particular phase of being super emotional about everything."

"Usually anywhere from one to three days. It's even different from one month to the next. Sometimes, you'll barely notice it. Other months, you'll want to rip the faces off anyone who dares speak to you."

"Ugh…" Sierra squirms in the chair like she can't find a way to sit that's comfortable. She fires off a long, frustrated sigh at the ceiling, then looks at me again. "Go ahead and just vamp me now, so I don't have to deal with this crap."

I chuckle, since I'm ninety percent sure she's not serious. "Mom would kill us both if I did that."

"True." She snaps her fingers in fake disappointment. "I'll have to find some other way to kill the red faerie."

"Umm." I hold up a finger. "I would strongly advise against asking Sophia to try to 'fix' that with magic."

Sierra gawks at me as though I suggested the dumbest thing ever. "No kidding. I don't want to be stuck as a little kid forever."

"Either that or her spell would go sideways and you'd end up having a litter of kittens."

She snort laughs, then bursts into a fit of giggling.

We laugh together for a little while, then go off on this wild wandering tangent about all the crazy ways Sophia's magic might go cartoonishly wrong trying to get rid of periods.

Yanno… I think she's going to be okay.

13

CHEAP SHIPPING

SUNDAY NIGHT

*T*hey say that teenagers are impulsive and often do things on a whim without really thinking.

Often, such impulsive things tend to be dangerous, reckless, or random. Not so much for me. I'm kinda lame. The most 'illegal' thing I've ever done on a whim—at least in life—was to scribble a bunch of goofy nonsense on one of the whiteboards at school while the room was empty. Ash and I thought it hilarious and so rebellious—even if we did use dry erase markers.

I was also terrified of being suspended for that.

No one cared.

Probably the worst thing I did on impulse post-vampirization was lighting my ex-boyfriend on fire and watching him burn away to ashes. That doesn't count as murder. Honestly. Scott was already dead. It wasn't even really Scott anymore. Scraps are primitive creatures with only a fragment of their former personalities left intact, helpless to resist acting on whatever bestial urges bubble up from their deeper subconscious. Kinda like the people who end up on the stage talking to Jerry Springer... plus fangs.

Oh there was also the time I caught the guy about to kidnap and kill Ashley. Most reasonable people would probably consider that a murder, but I don't. The things he was going to do to Ashley disqualified him from counting as a human being. I stepped on a nasty bug, nothing more. Ugh. That's gotta be the vampire side of me taking over a little. Not like me to be so blasé about something like that but. Grr. Ashley. I'd do anything to protect her.

Bleh. Enough somber thoughts.

Tonight, I'm being impulsive again, but it's a good thing.

So, Sierra is pretty serious about becoming an artist. She wants to someday work in the video game industry. Now, I'm no expert, but something tells me there isn't too much physical paper-and-media drawing going on out there. Figure she should get comfortable using computers sooner or later. Now, I was almost ready to order her a super top-end amazeballs system with a massive drawing pad.

Ashley—crazy as it sounds—became the voice of reason.

Yeah, even though I peeked into Sierra's thoughts and I'm pretty sure she's not going to lose interest in the art thing anytime soon, throwing like six grand at a top of the line 'creation station' for a twelve-year-old is pretty ridiculous. It would be like if my Dad bought me a Ferrari for my first car. Not like we could afford it, just saying. It would've intimidated me so much I might not have wanted to drive much.

Also, despite me having a bunch of money, spending big like that leaves a paper trail. Vampires have a certain way to buy stuff that doesn't leave much trace. I'm not experienced enough at being undead to pull that off. Maybe I'll never understand it since those sorts of advanced accounting tricks are a bit over the head of the average teenager. I'm not one of those Wall Street whiz kids who makes their first million before they're out of high school.

So, I found a nice compromise. This guy, Danny Ruiz, down in Eugene—that is a city in Oregon, by the way—is selling his old system, complete with a drawing tablet and software. He initially wanted $1200 for the setup, but the computer is like four years old. I don't care if it is an Apple, computers lose value fast. We talked online for a bit. Once I mentioned my interest in it was for my kid sister who's got dreams of becoming a digital artist, he dropped his asking price to $600.

Behold the power of cute.

Nah, I didn't send him a picture of Sierra, just hearing a tween-age girl would be using it was enough. I think the guy was more interested in 'bequeathing' the system to someone who would use it for digital artwork rather than just as a generic computer. I mean, it is a Macintosh, so it's not like anyone would be gaming on it. The guy also works in the field, so there's probably some bit of 'helping the next generation' in there, too.

The only catch in such a deal is he's not going to ship the system. I have to go get it.

Could be worse. Eugene, Oregon isn't *that* far away from home—as the vampire flies. Road tripping it would be annoyingly long, more so since the sun enforces mandatory rest breaks.

Sunset tonight happened at 6:23 p.m. It's now 8:32 p.m., and we've reached the outskirts of Eugene.

Ashley and I fly down from our cruising altitude over the city. A two-hour flight ended up being a better option than asking Blix for a trip through the mirror. The longer the trip, the crazier the mirrorverse gets. I didn't really feel like getting into a fight with nine-foot-tall anthropomorphic mice, multi-headed tarantula-dragons, or talking mushrooms. I mean, just about *anything* could happen there. That dimension reflects stuff back at us from our subconscious minds, as well as the nightmares or thoughts of everyone nearby in the real world.

Blix finally explained why the mirrorverse can change so abruptly from 'room' to 'room,' like going from a twisted *Alice in Wonderland* in one area, then you walk across a corridor into an MC Escher drawing. It's because the place feeds on the thoughts of every human all the time. Every physical location in the real world is linked to its 'shadow' in the mirror world. The people in the real world warp the nature of the mirrorverse based on their thoughts and mood.

Even worse, there are things native to the place—like that demon slug that paralyzed Ronan.

Yeah, just risky all around. I'm willing to go above and beyond for my siblings. Getting her an art computer is not a matter of life and death. Some risks are simply excessive, so I will take the time flying.

I pull out my phone and check the navigation app. Danny gave me his address. I might've lied a little bit to him. Nothing major, only said he lived 'close enough' for me to pick the computer up tonight. Does that count as a lie? I mean, considering I can fly to Eugene in two hours, it technically *is* close enough. He has no idea we're from Cottage Lake, likely assuming we're an hour or less by car away from him.

Doesn't make any difference.

And yeah, I'm going to the home of a total stranger I met on the internet. Sounds really bad when put that way, doesn't it? I'm not worried. Danny was nothing but professional in our conversation. And even if he tries anything crazy when we get there, it's not like I'd be in danger. Becoming an immortal vampire does wonders for a girl's sense of personal security.

Ashley, of course, came with me for several reasons. Girls never go anywhere alone. I am probably going to need help carrying stuff. Also, this is Ashley. We're inseparable. Mostly. Going to the bathroom, showering, and having sex with our respective romantic partners are the exceptions to her wanting to always be around me. To be fair, the taking showers or baths together thing had some exceptions—but only in emergencies when we were really in a hurry—or got blasted by a freakin' skunk.

We're both carrying giant hockey bags full of old blankets and towels to protect the technology on our return flight.

Upon locating Danny's house—in a nice suburban area southwest from the city center—we aim for a cluster of trees next to a small, empty playground at a street corner about two blocks away. The spot is nice and dark with no one nearby enough to see us drop out of the sky.

A short walk over a sidewalk ravaged by tree roots brings us to his house. It's not the biggest place, but if anything my Dad says is true about the economy, owning a house at all these days is pretty impressive.

Like a pair of Girl Scouts selling cookies, we head up onto the porch. I ring the doorbell.

Not long after I push the button, the door opens to reveal a thirtysomething guy with curly black hair and a mild suntan.

He blinks at us, seemingly lost for words.

"Hi." I offer a hand. "I'm Sarah. Are you Danny Ruiz? We chatted online about the Mac?"

"Oh." Danny chuckles, then shakes my hand. "Sorry, thought you were someone else. You don't really look eighteen."

Ashley and I sigh at the same time.

"No worries. I get that a lot." I fake an annoyed eyeroll. "Going to suck when I'm twenty-one. No one will ever believe me if I try to buy beer."

He chuckles, then glances at Ashley. Some of the life leaves his eyes. For a moment, he stares at her entranced. It doesn't feel like a creepy stare; however, I still check by peeking into his head. Nope, we're safe. The artist in him just finds her captivatingly beautiful but in an 'adorable' sort of way like how Ashley ends up staring at kittens or puppies whenever she sees them.

Good chance the next time Danny has to do a character design, it's going to be based partially on Ash. Yay. My best friend is about to become a famous cartoon character. Also, no, Ashley is not abnormally cute or sexy. She is Aurélie's progeny. Even if she doesn't mean to do it, she's always giving off a tiny bit of charm. It doesn't do a thing to other vampires or even mortals who are around her often. Total strangers seeing her for the first time usually end up entranced for a little while.

So, yeah. I guess you could say my best friend is part succubus now.

The major downside is, of course, some people with weaker than normal self-control might act out depending on their personality. Like, this dude wants to draw her face or use her as an inspiration for a character he makes up. A creep might not be able to resist trying to grab her. Someone who thought she looked like the human version of a lost kitten might not be able to resist going in for a hug or asking her what's wrong. That sort of thing. To the average mortal with strong nurturing instincts, Ashley is truly aww-inspiring.

I imagine that's going to get annoying after a while. Of course, neither she nor I are social butterflies. Our idea of a great night is staying at home watching TV, playing video games, reading, or just goofing off and talking. So, perhaps it won't be a big deal. Maybe she'll even learn to control it eventually.

He snaps out of it after about forty seconds, eyes fluttering. "Don't just stay out there. C'mon in. Do you girls want some tea or something? Soda?"

Not too keen on spending all night here, but the guy is only trying to be polite. I have not yet tried to consume fizzy drinks since becoming a vampire. That might have bizarre consequences.

"Tea would be nice, but it's not necessary," I say.

We go inside. Danny walks ahead of us across the living room to a dining room where a computer, a monitor, and a big slab of technology are on the table. I smell the presence of a woman here as well. Oh, and they had something with chicken and saffron for dinner.

"Sorry I don't have any of the original packaging anymore. Threw that out years ago." Danny pats the computer. "This is the rig that I've been using for the past few years. Lot of hours on it."

For a four-year-old computer, it looks to be in fairly good shape. Bet he cleaned it recently. Yeah, I can smell the Formula 409 on it. I glance at the big slab thing. Looks similar to an iPad but much larger.

"Guessing that's the drawing tablet?" I point at it.

"Yep. If your sister is used to working with physical media, it will take a bit of adjustment... but once she's past the difference in feel, it's just like drawing or painting on paper."

"Cool." Ashley smiles.

"Better than paper, I think." Danny gestures at the chairs in a 'have a seat' manner and heads for the kitchen. "Paper or canvas don't have undo buttons."

We chuckle and sit down.

A woman wanders in from a side hallway. She's blonde and, despite not being too deep into her thirties, is giving off mom-ish vibes. I don't smell kids, so my guess is they're still trying. Or, perhaps, they're happy not having any children. Who knows?

She gives us a big smile, then pauses, glancing back and forth between me and Ashley like she's trying to figure out which one of us is eighteen and which is the twelve-year-old artist sister. She apparently can't decide. "Oh, hi there. Are you the kid who's trying to get started in the art world?"

"Not me," I say. "It's for my little sister, who's still home. This is my friend Ashley."

"Hello. I'm Madison." The woman shakes our hands, then looks at the kitchen. "Hon, what are you doing in the kitchen?"

"Grabbing tea," calls Danny.

"Oh." Madison turns back to me. "Are your parents waiting outside?"

"No, they're at home. We came here on our own." I try not to sigh too loudly. "We might not look like it, but we're eighteen." I feel dumb as soon as the words leave me. As if there's some rule or law about turning eighteen magically makes it okay to go somewhere at night without a parent.

Danny reappears at the archway to the kitchen carrying a pitcher of iced tea and a stack of plastic cups. He and his—I assume—wife exchange a 'yeah right' stare.

Ashley gives me side eye with a grin. "That's never gonna get old."

I smile cheesily and silent-whisper, "Neither will we."

She covers her mouth to hold in a laugh.

Danny holds up a big red Rubbermaid pitcher. "Had to make a new batch. It's from a mix. Hope that's okay. Not quite cold yet."

Madison takes the cups from him and de-stacks them, giving us each one.

"No worries." Ashley grasps her cup in both hands.

Ice rattles around the big plastic pitcher as he pours everyone a drink.

We sit there for a while sipping iced tea and talking about the computer, art stuff in general, and Sierra. I don't go into too much detail about her other than to say she's really interested in doing artwork for video games or maybe even CGI type work for movies. Danny rambles about his present job, freelancing as a bulk animator for a handful of cartoons. Basically, the lead artist comes up with the character designs and draws the key frames. Danny fills in the dozen or so intermediate drawings in between each key frame.

It's kinda interesting to hear him talk about working in animation… kinda like we stumbled on a YouTube video about it. I think he's about to whip out a giant portfolio book and show us some of his work until Madison interrupts him.

"I don't think these girls want to be here all night. It's already dark out." Madison tosses a nervous look at the front room. "It's not safe outside here after dark. Some craziness is going on. There have been numerous attacks, especially on women."

Whoa. She is legit worried. Like, almost to the point she's about to insist we spend the night and not leave until daytime unless our parents show up. That would create a whole bunch of problems. I stare into her eyes and nudge her brain a little. We're going to be perfectly safe. You don't need to worry about us.

While I'm settling her nerves, Ashley does the same to Danny.

"Yeah, it is getting late. We should probably head out soon," I say.

"All right." Danny pats the computer box. "Want a hand carrying it to your car?"

I point at the bags we brought with us. "Thanks, but we got it covered. Want to make sure it gets home intact."

He does help us pack the computer, drawing tablet, and keyboard in our giant hockey bags. I'm using the same bag that I brought Chloe home in. She wasn't terribly thrilled about being bagged, mind you. Still, she preferred it to a sun bath. The monitor is, alas, too big to fit in the bag. One of us is going to need to carry it. I'm not worried about it being heavy… flying at over 100 MPH with a big slab of technology in my hands is going to be a challenge. It'll act like a wing or airfoil. Hopefully, we don't have a close encounter with a pigeon.

Then again, for $600, I'm not too worried. If need be, I can order a new monitor. That won't cost as much as a whole top-end system. This old Power Mac was probably close to four grand when he got it new.

Speaking of money, I pull my phone out. "Is PayPal okay, or should I run to an ATM?"

"That's fine." Danny gives me his email address. I send him $600.

"You're very welcome." He smiles at his phone when it beeps in response to the money arriving. "If your sister needs any advice or pointers, she's welcome to email me. Some of the software on that thing isn't terribly intuitive. Pretty much need to be taught how to use a lot of it."

"Cool. I'll let her know. Thank you. I'm sure she's going to have a ton of questions I won't be able to answer." I shake his hand again. "We better get going before our parents start to worry what's taking us so long."

That may or may not be an exaggeration.

Well, it is considering I didn't tell either of them where we were going. Sierra doesn't know about this either. It's going to be a surprise.

After a polite goodbye, Madison Ruiz escorts us to the door and sees us out. Ashley and I walk across their front yard to the sidewalk. I turn in place, looking around at the neighborhood. This seems like the sort of place nearly every Stephen Spielberg film happens in. Safe. Ordinary. Quiet. Not that I doubt there's something odd going on around here lately. This neighborhood simply doesn't look or feel threatening.

According to my phone, it's 9:41 p.m. We should be able to make it home before midnight. Perfect. Sierra will be asleep. That means I can sneak into her room and set the computer up, so she wakes up to a surprise.

"So, are you thinking what I think you're thinking?" asks Ashley.

"I can't read your mind." Here, hold this.

She takes the monitor from me. "There's some sort of psycho attacking people at night around here. Are you saying you don't want to pretend to be a superhero again?"

I adjust the way the big bag hangs on my back, then reach for the monitor again. "This is kinda out of my jurisdiction."

"Hah." She snugs her bag tighter to her back as well. "You don't really care about that if someone's getting hurt."

"No, not really, but... computer. Don't want Sierra's stuff to get smashed. We could come back here tomorrow night and play helpless victim bait."

Ashley nods. "Okay."

We head left and meander down the bumpy sidewalk toward the little playground.

"Ugh," mutters Ashley.

"What?"

"Just thinking about a two-hour flight while lugging this stuff."

I chuckle. "It's not exactly heavy. Besides, consider all the money we're saving on shipping."

We're about forty feet away from the cluster of trees where we landed when a muffled scream comes from the opposite side of the playground. Without missing a beat, Ashley reaches out to take the monitor from me.

Sigh.

One sec while Follows Rules Girl gets her spandex costume on. That's a metaphor, by the way. I'm not actually changing clothes. I hand off the monitor and hurry toward the sounds of screaming and struggling.

Ashley jogs along beside me.

We reach the next street over past the playground in time to catch sight of a man dragging a struggling woman into a dark space behind a Wendy's where the dumpsters are kept.

"Dammit." I sigh. "I *just* bought this computer for Sierra, and it's going to get trashed before we even get it home."

"I'll watch the stuff," says Ashley. "You deal with the creeper."

"Fine." I shrug off the hockey bag and set it on the ground—gently —before sprinting across the parking lot to the dumpster alcove.

A purse lays on the pavement at the opening in the concrete wall. Not far past that, a man in a dark jacket and jeans is on top of a woman, trying to pin her down. She's kinda slim and nowhere near strong enough to throw him off—though her size isn't stopping her from trying really damn hard.

"Hey!" I yell. "Get off her."

Most creeps like this startle quite easily. Another person catching them in the act is very likely to make them bail out and run for their lives. On the other hand, it also might escalate things directly to gunfire... or stabbing.

This guy shifts his weight enough to glare back at me. He doesn't appear spooked at all. The woman, who's probably in her middle twenties and dressed like a waitress from a chain restaurant—white polo shirt, black pants—continues struggling despite being completely unable to budge this guy.

"I said, get off her." I lean forward, trying (and probably failing) to be intimidating. I do 'girl next door' really well. Scary, not so much, especially not after becoming an Innocent vampire. Ironic, right? Turning into an undead creature actually resulted in me being *less* intimidating. "Don't make this get ugly."

Dude sprouts fangs. His eyes light up red, and he growl-hisses at me.

"Oof," says Ashley a short distance behind me. "He made it ugly."

I fold my arms. "Real subtle."

The guy stops growling and makes a face like my head just split open to reveal a little green alien working the controls inside. It seems he can't handle a 'kid' not being the least bit scared of him.

His victim picks that moment to find enough mobility to ram her knee into his groin.

He grunts and swings his head around to glare down at her... at which point she saturates his face with pepper spray. This doesn't seem to bother him... much.

Again, he snarls at her... and this time she goes derpy, falling slack in a semiconscious state, gazing up at the stars.

Dude shifts his glare back to me and hisses, louder.

"What the heck are you doing?" I ask.

He blinks. "This is the part where you scream and run away."

"Try being scary," chimes Ashley.

This Oregonian vampire couldn't look more clueless if he'd been on *Who Wants to be a Millionaire* and got asked to sing the Zimbabwean national anthem backward.

I walk closer to the guy, gesturing at this mess. "You're just having a snack here? Not going to hurt her?"

"What the hell is going on?" asks the guy.

"That's what I want to know." I tap my foot, then extend my fangs. "Relax."

"Oh..." He exhales in relief. "That explains why you're not freaking out. Damn, kid, you look tasty enough to bite."

I lean back. "Say what?"

"I mean... I thought you were a damn mortal."

"Oh." I examine my fingernails. "Yeah, I get that a lot."

"Chill, kid. Just feeding." The guy reaches up and wipes pepper spray off his face. "Damn, I hate this shit. Never liked spicy food."

"Maybe if you tried starting a conversation before swinging the derp hammer instead of grabbing them like a freakin' mugger..." I gesture at the woman. "You wouldn't get pepper sprayed so much."

He sighs, his expression flat. "The hell is a derp hammer?"

"What you just did to her so she went catatonic," says Ashley.

He still looks confused.

Oh, come on. Really? This guy never even thought of that? His first instinct was to just grab people and drag them off? Maybe it's not that weird. I mean for a guy his size. For me, Ashley and especially Chloe, manhandling our prospective meals isn't a feasible option. We have to rely on subtlety. Still, even though this guy *can* drag people off into the dark, he probably shouldn't.

"I think we found the cause behind the dangerous area." Ashley wanders up behind me.

"Did you guys steal a computer?" asks the vampire.

"No, we just bought it from some guy." I shrug. "Was about to go home when we heard the scream."

The woman screams again.

Vampire dude snarls and re-derps her.

"I think he's being honest." Ashley nods at me. "Not going to kill her."

"Nah. I don't kill anyone." The guy starts to lean down toward her neck, then stops before looking back at us. "Do you girls mind? Kinda hard to do this with an audience."

That sounds so wrong, but I know what he means. It's awkward having people watch me feed. Honestly, I think it would bother me more if one of the 'rents walked in on me feeding on someone than if they caught me and Hunter in the middle of things. I hear Maury Povich's voice in my head a second after that thought saying *we have determined that was a lie.* Yeah, okay. I admit it. I could handle the parents seeing me feed way more gracefully than if they caught me having sex.

"Sorry." I take a step back. "So, uhh… you might want to be a little more subtle about feeding… or go somewhere else for a while. People are talking about it not being safe around here at night."

"Is that you, or is there an actual serial killer running around this city?" Ashley bites her lip.

"Uhh, no idea. But I probably should move on. Starting to get a bit crowded around here." He shoots us a pointed stare.

I raise my hands. "Nope. We're just visiting. About to leave. Be careful. Hunters start showing up when the news cycle is full of random attacks."

He grumbles, turns away from us, and goes in for the bite.

"Let's get out of here," I whisper to Ashley while picking the bag up again.

Seems isolated enough here behind the Wendy's… so once I've got the technology cargo secured, I leap straight up into the sky.

Fingers crossed we don't encounter any pigeons.

14

GOING THROUGH THE MOTIONS

TUESDAY, OCTOBER 15

*I*t's almost four in the afternoon.

I'm sitting at my desk in Professor Guillermo's Art History class, for all the good it's doing me. Trying to be functional this early in the day isn't working out as well as I thought it would. Either that, or it's because today's content is super boring. Most of the time, Guillermo's voice turns into that wah-wah-wah sound from *Peanuts* whenever adults talk. I'm barely aware he's trying to compare and contrast the styles of Raphael with Degas. Something about chubby angelic figures and ballerinas.

Out of character for me, but I really am tempted to leave in the middle of class and just go home.

Speaking of home, Sierra was thrilled with the computer. I ended up grabbing a second computer desk for her to avoid having to disturb her existing setup. Between Ashley, Chloe, and myself, we managed to put the thing together in about thirty minutes in complete silence right next to her as she slept. It would've been too bulky to carry upstairs once assembled. I have a lot of respect for Dad now. Even with vampiric reflexes and speed, putting that desk together was a pain in the ass. I swear the people who design this 'build it yourself' furniture are at least half demons.

I have yet to see her reaction, since we were seriously asleep at the time Sierra would've gotten out of bed and I had to leave the house before she got home from school. My phone did blow up with a bunch of OMG texts and hearts. She obviously knows where the system came from.

But ugh, at the moment, I'm stuck here in class.

At least Dad was understanding about the idea of me putting college on hold after this semester. I only have to make it through a few more months of this and I can stop being jealous of Ashley for not having to go to school. For as much as she always talked about wanting to be a vet, she didn't hesitate at all to quit school for a 'medical emergency' once she took the vampire plunge.

Unlike me, she also had the added motivation of saving her mother money. Her college cost a bit more than SCC does. Not that this place is 'cheap,' just... closer to reasonable. Mrs. Carter makes an okay living, after all. However, she's only got one income. Both of my parents work and make good money. It's more of a burden on Mrs. Carter to pay for college that serves no purpose. Not that Mrs. C was going to pay for it anyway... thanks to the 'Leprechaun Incident,' I was taking care of her school charges. Either way, it's one less thing to worry about.

I'm settled. Gonna stop going after this semester. I don't need the theatrical set dressing of school to help me fake being normal anymore. Going to SCC was a psychological security blanket I tried to hide under in order to deny the reality of what happened to me. After all the craziness over these past two ish years, I'm well past trying to pretend everything is totally normal. Maybe I'm changing and 'growing up' as a vampire. So much for being stuck permanently the same.

Hmm. Wonder if because I got turned less than two weeks after graduating from high school into summer vacation, my brain is merely stuck in 'vacation' mode. Going to school feels crappy because my psyche still thinks we should be on break?

Who knows? I do know I've made up my mind. Family now, school later—maybe.

I'd only ever do it as a curiosity, like how Professor Heath keeps teaching. He enjoys doing it. Hey, vampires need hobbies. It's kinda hard to drift through eternity and keep from going insane without some sort of hobby. Teaching night college is a much more sustainable hobby than randomly impaling peasants outside your castle. That tends to rile people up and then they start reaching for the torches and pitchforks.

Of course, with that decision made, I have a new temptation to fight. It wouldn't be difficult to mind zap all of my professors so they believe I've been attending classes and doing the work. I could stop going to class right now and still get passing grades.

Nah. That's too much like cheating. Follows Rules Girl would never let me sleep again.

No rush. It's not like I have to get college done now while I'm young. I've literally got all the time in the world.

Out of nowhere, a noxious fart cloud rises up from below and punches me in the nose. It's horrid enough that my eyes water. This is one of those rare times I am happy to be offline. A butt-bomb this pungent would've knocked me out of my seat if my nose had been dialed up to eleven. Fortunately, even though it's daytime, I still do not need to breathe. Holding my breath infinitely is a minor power still available to me no matter how annoying the sky fireball is being.

Several people around me cough, cover their faces, and gasp for air. Everyone looks around for the source. I do too, but not because I really care where it came from. The person who is not looking around is the person everyone assumes to be responsible. A short, thin guy four seats back from me appears to be the guilty party. Good grief. How did something that foul come out of a guy so small? At least he seems embarrassed about it.

It's difficult to say what the best part about being a vampire is between flying, immortality, no more attacks from the red faerie, or the confidence it's given me. The worst part? That's easy. I could live without my nose being sensitive enough to tell what someone had for lunch two days ago every time they fart.

Really glad I'm offline right now.

A guy two seats to my left mutters a joke about this being 'fart history' class now.

"Well, on that note…" Professor Guillermo glances up at the wall clock. "Now seems like a good time for the break. See you all back in fifteen minutes. May I suggest that whoever is responsible for that… distraction make use of the restroom."

I get up and shuffle out of the room with everyone else. Don't mind me. I'm just a normal college student, being normal and doing normal things. A short walk down the hall brings me to the ladies' room. No, I don't have to use it. It's merely the most convenient place without windows to get a break from afternoon sunlight. Yes, I can tolerate sunlight pretty well these days. That doesn't mean it's not tiring to do so. Even a fifteen-minute break is wonderful. It's like stepping into an air-conditioned room after working outside in August for a few hours.

No matter how often I do this, it still feels weird to sit on a toilet with my pants up. Since I've started attempting these 3:00 p.m. classes twice a week, sitting in a stall relaxing in the relative dark has become routine. I just meditate here with my eyes closed until my phone nags me that it's time to go back to class.

A few minutes into the process of me enjoying the cool silence, the door of my stall rattles from someone trying to open it.

"Occupied."

The door rattles again.

Ugh. Really? What kind of idiot tries to open a locked bathroom stall door again after someone inside speaks?

I open my eyes and glare at the rattling door. "Occupied!"

Whoever it is doesn't stop trying to barge in on me. Grr.

Curious as to what kind of moron I'm dealing with, I gaze down at the gap under the door. Funky doesn't even begin to describe the boots and pants standing there. And I don't mean 'funky' in the sense of George Clinton. That fabric looks as if it spent a hundred years in a muddy grave.

Speaking of grave, the whole bathroom smells like rotting body.

Crap. Not again.

No sense trying to hide in a bathroom stall like a seventh-grader attempting to avoid social embarrassment. This thing isn't going to give up and walk away.

I jump to my feet, flick the lock, and yank the door open.

Yep. There's a ghoul standing out there. His coat is kinda cool in a period costume sort of way, or, rather, it *would* be if it didn't appear ready to disintegrate. Dude looks like a background extra from a movie set in the time of *Bram Stoker's Dracula*. The frilled collar's a nice touch despite all the holes and rips.

"What the hell do you want?" I blurt.

He grunts in annoyance while raising his right arm over his head, a wooden stake in his grasp.

"Seriously?" I shake my head. "Do you guys realize that stake thing is a myth?"

The ghoul groans and swings the stake at me.

Dude's not much faster than an ordinary mortal. I catch his wrist in my left hand while simultaneously thrusting my right arm out and grabbing him around the throat. Eww. His throat is cold, damp, and feels like a pot roast someone left sitting on the counter for an hour. We lock stares. Poor guy seems almost confused, as if this is quite far from how he expected his vampire slaying expedition to turn out.

He is beyond obviously dead already. This is not a living person. Not only is he 'wet farmland' brown, his skin's as brittle-hard as a drum from Ancient Egypt. He also stinks like corpse, and weighs about seventy pounds if that much.

"Nghhgn," mutters the ghoul.

I pivot my wrist, cracking his neck.

Blackish-teal gunk leaks from his nose and mouth for half a second before he falls apart into a cloud of dust. Even his clothing vanishes into the same uniform layer of greyish powder on the floor, except for his coat buttons. Some poor janitor is going to be highly confused later tonight. I'm still holding the wooden stake. That didn't disintegrate. Hmm. Weird. It did last time. Maybe because he hadn't been holding it when he 'died'? It resembles a rotten scrap of lumber taken from a sunken pirate ship. Smells like it, too.

Hmm.

For some stupid reason, looking at this large stake makes me think of Ashley's 'toy' collection. Both objects are meant for impaling, though stakes are considerably less fun. Come to think of it, I haven't seen any trace of those things for a while. It's almost like Ashley either got rid of them or hid them away really well. I can't even think of when she'd have had the chance to use them in the past few weeks. She's not been away from me for long enough. Oh, wait. I'm at school now. Maybe she dealing with that itch when we *can't* be hanging out.

But really, I don't think so. She's in the middle of an innocence phase. Maybe she didn't want to see them and break the illusion of pretending we're kids again. Not that she's consciously trying to act childish. It's the same weird brain crap I dealt with post-Transference. I dunno. Her psychology is really complicated at the moment. Honestly, apart from her increased ability to talk about sex topics without giggling or blushing, she didn't change too much from fourteen to eighteen. She couldn't even say the D-word without blushing in ninth grade. Wait, there's two D-words. One's plastic, one isn't. Well, she couldn't say either of them without snickering.

Question is, should I ask her if she's doing okay or just let things play out naturally?

While wobbling the stake around in my hand, I also ponder what the heck to do with it. Can't really flush it down the toilet. Someone will find it if I put it in the trash bin. I mean, it's not exactly a dangerous object, merely a hunk of wood with a sharpened point. Still, if someone found a 'vampire killing stake' in the trash bin here, rumors might start. This could end up on YouTube and attract a bunch of ghost hunters, or worse, vampire hunters. Finding a stake tossed aside would make them suspect a hunter got killed by a vampire.

Perhaps one did. I frown at the dust pile.

Nah. Ashley would totally talk to me if something was wrong. She's happy. For whatever reason, she wants to keep sexy stuff at arm's length. Maybe that's just her deciding that she doesn't need or want a boyfriend (or girlfriend) for now.

Gonna leave that to her.

Now—I pat the stake into my other hand a few times—where do I put this?

Meh. Might as well take it home if only so no one finds it and starts asking questions. Can always ask Max to incinerate it.

My phone beeps.

Dammit. So much for a relaxing break. Gotta get back to class.

15

TIME SUCKS

WEDNESDAY, THE USUAL OCCURRENCE AFTER TUESDAY

I really needed that.

Ever since that ghoul tried to stake me in the school bathroom... and I had the stake in my hand, I've been thinking about Hunter. Somehow, we managed to go almost two full weeks without making love. Tonight, we did our best to catch up on lost time.

He's asleep next to me. I kinda wore him out, I think.

Vampires don't get tired. Mortals do.

We went at it for a nice long time. Afterward, I borrowed the upstairs bathroom to clean up... then we cuddled while he put a movie on his bedroom TV. It's that philosophical Jim Carrey movie... *Spotless Mind* or something. I honestly haven't been paying too much attention to the movie. Mostly, I've been watching Hunter sleep and thinking about our potential future together.

There's something about lying here, both of us naked like some sort of Renaissance painting, that's totally romantic and totally awesome. Yeah, sure, his mother or Ronan could randomly walk in on us at any minute... but I'm not worried. It wouldn't embarrass me that much. That's got to be the vampire part of me taking over.

It's not like we're actively going at it right now. If someone walked in on us right in the middle of that... yes, I would be mortified. Simply lying here? Not so much. Besides, they wouldn't remember seeing us naked, anyway. That's a really easy mental fix.

Mrs. Lawrence has to know what happens up here. I have no idea if she approves of us or not. Whatever her opinions, she's kept them to herself or only told Hunter and he hasn't said anything to me about it.

Dad once told me he's uncomfortable at the idea of his daughter being old enough for sex, but he'd much rather it happened safe in our house than off somewhere sketchy where I could be in danger. It's become increasingly difficult to have Hunter over at my place for romance. With Chloe around and now Ashley living with us, privacy is in short supply.

I keep staring at Hunter, wanting this moment right now to stretch into infinity. The more I look at him, the more acutely aware I become that our time is really fleeting. Like every other mortal I love, he's going to grow old and go away. At least I'm still young. By that, I mean I'm still operating within a mortal's lifespan. I really am only nineteen. Time doesn't pass for me like it does for my parents. They blink and years go by. It's gotta be worse for a really old vampire. Blink and lose multiple decades, for example. I'm being melodramatic about Hunter. He's not going to get old and die in what feels like minutes. We'll have a reasonably normal feeling time together, then he'll be gone, and I'll still be around.

The real problem is how awkward it's going to be when he's older. If his mom walks in on us making love now, there's going to be a lot of blushing and awkwardness. If someone walks in on me and Hunter thirty years from now, they're going to call the police.

I love watching him sleep.

Not holding it against him that he passed out so soon after. Yeah, it's kinda a stereotypical guy thing to do, but he's working his ass off. Going to school, fixing up the house for his mother, waiting tables at the Mexican restaurant, then homework. He's got almost zero time to relax.

I lean against him like some fantasy princess with her wild barbarian lover. Taking some liberties there. He doesn't exactly have the physique of Conan—the barbarian, not the talk show host. Then again, few mortals do. He is, however, a bit more buff than the talk show host. Who needs a gym membership when you spend most of your free time doing construction on your own house?

Ooh. I am so tempted to put Sophia up to summoning an army of gremlins to fix this place once and for all. Really can't do that, though. Neighbors will notice the humungous four-family monstrosity change from a set piece for a haunted house movie to looking brand new overnight. Drawing attention is bad.

The movie on the TV's a barely noticeable sound in my left ear as I trace my fingers back and forth over his chest. I daydream about scooping him up and carrying him out the window, both of us still naked, and flying off to some remote Caribbean island where we'd live for a week or two of wild romance, not another person—or article of clothing anywhere in sight.

Fun to think about, but not practical. I doubt my flight range is long enough to make it to an abandoned tropical island before sunrise. He'd also miss so many classes that he'd fail the semester, get fired from his job, and probably be pretty upset with me.

Sigh. Daydream it remains.

Hunter… what shall I do with you?

Whoa, that sounded kinda vampiric. Like 'Petra vampiric.' No, I'm not going to keep him on a leash in my basement. Creepy bitch. I mean, how am I going to handle 'us.' We're stuck on a runaway train heading for a cliff. Things cannot keep going as they are right now without disaster following soon.

I've got a few options. My immediate knee-jerk reaction is 'turn him into a vampire, duh.' He's already said he wouldn't mind that. Just like Ashley, he'd happily give up his mortal future to stay with me. Sort of a reverse Arwen from *Lord of the Rings*. But how do we handle his mother or Ronan? Ro is in the know about the vampire stuff.

Kinda has to be what with him being Sam's best friend and knowing about the demons, too. Mrs. Lawrence is not. She has no idea her youngest son jumps into the bathroom mirror every day or that her older son is in love with a vampire girl.

It sounds really stupid, but the main reason I haven't pushed the vampire idea is it seems so cliché. Like, every story where the vampire has a mortal girlfriend always ends with her turning into a vampire. And sure, the vampire in those stories is always the too-cool-to-believe guy putting the moves on an innocent young mortal girl. Sometimes it feels okay, sometimes it's creepy… like the guy is clearly taking advantage of a helpless girl who can't resist him.

Hunter's not a helpless mortal. He's totally in love with me, all without the interference of any supernatural stuff. Is thinking like I'm a character in a vampire novel and not wanting to be cliché reason enough to doom our relationship to eventual separation? Hmm. Nah. Screw what people think.

Another option would be to keep dating him for a while more, then break up.

The mere thought of breaking up with him puts a lump in my throat and makes me want to go do unprintable things to an entire box of rocky road ice cream. I could try to make him forget me and pretend we never met. Doubt that would work for the same reason I didn't try to make Sierra forget the nightmare of a school shooter. I've been in his head. He really loves me too much to erase. Aurélie could probably make him forget me, but it wouldn't be perfect. His love is too strong. Some part of him would know a missing piece got cut out of his heart and he'd turn into this hollow, hopeless figure that stumbles through the rest of his life never feeling at peace.

Talk about a way to create an angry ghost.

I couldn't do that to him.

What's really and truly bothering me is that I've prepared myself to watch him grow old and die. I am pretty sure I could handle losing him—eventually. Does that mean I don't really love him if the idea of being without him doesn't make me want to throw myself at the sun?

Is that maturity? I understand it's possible to love, lose, and grieve... then find healing.

Hmm. Wanting to kill myself because my boyfriend dies seems super melodramatic. Total Romeo and Juliet stuff. Geez. Talk about trite. That's even cringier than turning him into a vampire.

So, I can't make him forget. That leaves only the third option of breaking up with him. Do we do that now or should I wait until he's so much older looking than I am that people freak out whenever we kissed in public? For that matter, if I'm stuck as a teenager mentally, will I lose romantic attraction to him as he ages? Someday, will he give me 'dad vibes?' My love for him could morph from romantic to platonic.

That sounds really confusing and awkward.

Do I really love him the way Mom loves Dad, or am I in the throes of a 'high school girl crush' here? Does that even matter? A high school girl crush is only a problem because it's as transient as being a teenager. My teen-ness is not transient. If I'm staying the same, it's not like I'd grow out of those feelings for him. Who cares?

Ugh. It might be like the way Mom loves Dad. Thinking about breaking up with Hunter makes me want to cry really hard... like when I found out they cancelled *Firefly*. Okay, that's a joke. I want to cry even worse... and that's gotta mean something.

Hey, 200 years ago, I'd have been married with at least one baby by this age. Did that count as love? Why would a girl my age in 1820 be a married mother in love but a girl my age nowadays is 'just a teenager who doesn't know what she wants from life yet'? Maybe it comes down to options. Girls in 1820 didn't have as many options as they do now. They basically went from being considered their father's property to their husband's property. Bleh. Society really sucks sometimes.

None of that really applies to me. I am not going to be chasing a career.

Can't make Hunter forget me. How would we explain that to Ronan? Hunter would still see me sometimes by virtue of our families being connected by the Sam-Ronan friendship. Even if I somehow managed to blank out his memory of feelings for me, seeing me over and over again would pop that loose. Then he'd be furious. And he should be. Blotting out that memory would be such a violation of our trust.

No, that's not happening.

He's got to become a vampire. That's the only way out that won't involve lots of crying and several metric tons of rocky road ice cream dying a horrible death.

I can't be the one to do it, though. Don't even want to watch it happen. I couldn't handle it. Besides, talk about a relationship killer... always hearing the other person's thoughts in your mind? It's cool with Dalton since, you know, we are not romantic and he only communicates to me occasionally. Usually, it's when he's gotten himself into a sticky situation and needs a bit of help.

I sense a scoff from across the ocean.

Heh. In fairness, for the most part when I've reached out to him, I've been in trouble, too.

That works, though. A sire-progeny mind link is perfect for the relationship I have with Dalton.

With Hunter, though? Someone I'd be around all the time? Constantly being able to listen in on each other's thoughts. Yeah... we wouldn't last three months.

Do I really love him? Is this real love or am I just afraid of time passing? Do I want to keep my life going around and around in some sort of *Groundhog Day* loop for eternity where nothing ever changes?

Yeah, kinda. I mean... I'd love it if my family stayed exactly as they are now forever. That's really selfish of me, though, and I wouldn't actually do it. No harm in daydreaming about it. I can't make my entire family immortal. At least I have Ash and Chloe.

Is there room for Hunter in there, too?

I stare at him for a long several minutes, still teasing at his chest hair.

Can't imagine being in love with anyone else. If I can't have Hunter, I'm not going to want anyone else. I'd just as soon stay single and pretend to be a high school kid forever. Much less complicated that way. But… here he is, and I love him.

Done.

Yes. I want him to join me in eternal undeath. I don't care what anyone thinks about us being a vampire cliché. Swear, I'll punch the teeth out of anyone who makes a *Twilight* joke… except Ashley. If she goes there, I'll just bonk her over the head with a plush unicorn.

The decision is not all mine, though. I can want him to become a vampire but he's got to make that choice for himself. I'm not going to force it on him or ask some other vampire to force it on him.

It's almost one in the morning now. As tempting as it is to talk to him about it, he needs to sleep because he's got early classes tomorrow. As much as I want to, it isn't practical for me to spend the night with him. His bedroom has large windows and they face east. The chance of me having a claw-tipped freakout when the sun rises is too great.

I push myself up onto my hands and knees, then lean down to kiss him on the lips. It's a long, sensuous kiss like something right out of a movie or a gender-flipped *Sleeping Beauty*. Despite being asleep, he kinda kisses me back. I think he's dreaming about me. That's fine. He's exhausted and needs to sleep.

Eventually, I force myself to disengage from the kiss and crawl backward, slipping off the bed to my feet. After pulling the blankets up to cover him, I take my time getting dressed, turn the TV off, and slip out the window, hovering outside and looking back in at him.

"Night, Hunter. See you soon."

He emits a faint murmur in his sleep.

Finally knowing what I want to do with *us* is such a weight off my mind, I come pretty damn close to flinging myself into the air and squealing with joy like some sort of giant, wingless Tinkerbell. Fear of roaming cell phone cameras keeps me from acting like a total idiot. I content myself with a mostly contained squee of delight before gliding up far enough to see over the roof. Gotta check the coast is clear before committing to takeoff and a flight home.

Thump.

The heck?

I pause.

Another heavy thud comes from the front of the house.

Ronan isn't old enough to stay out late drinking and stagger home after everyone's asleep. He's also far too small to make that heavy a thump from banging his fist on anything. What kind of jackass shows up at a house after one in the morning and hammers on the front door? Oh, shit. This might be Hunter's jerk of a dad. Yeah, I gave him a brain slap that should have left him inexplicably terrified of this place… but, enough beer might haze through that.

Grr.

I drop down to land in the dirt beside the house, then jog around the front, ready to get into an argument. That man did enough damage to Hunter and Ronan already. I won't let him do more. The instant I round the corner, I realize two things. One: it's not a drunk, violent crappy father trying to break into the house. Two: those ghouls are definitely coming after me.

Yeah, it's another ghoul.

This guy also looks like he walked off the set of a movie filmed a long time ago… and then got buried in mud for a century. Weird thing is… he kinda seems familiar. It's not the bathroom ambusher. Hang on. How the hell did that ghoul make it all the way into the SCC building without anyone noticing or having a panic attack?

Oh, maybe they thought he was with the drama club.

Right, anyway… got a ghoul here trying to break into Hunter's house.

This could be the guy I threw into a lamp post in the parking lot of Garibaldi's. Maybe. Kinda hard to recognize someone when their facial features resemble a whole turkey someone left in an air fryer for three hours.

Great. *Now* who did I piss off that's sending ghouls after me?

I whistle to get its attention.

He turns to face me. The instant his dry-rotted brain processes that he's looking at *me*, he forgets entirely about the door and charges.

Since I'm still a bit giddy over Hunter, I let my goofball flag fly and go full anime on this thing.

After doing a quick (and extremely fake) little martial arts bit of arm waving, I launch myself forward and punch my right fist completely through his chest. The ghoul stops rushing at me, emitting a bewildered grunt.

I stand there for a second or two, bicep deep in ghoul while the last bits of air in my lungs leak out my mouth in a cheesy Bruce Lee inspired war squeak. Once I'm empty of air, I yank my arm out all dramatically and stuff and drop into a fighting stance as if I'm a character in *Street Fighter*.

The ghoul bows his head, peering at the hole in his chest. He grunts again… then promptly collapses into a cloud of grey dust.

Well, at least these things—whatever they are—are super weak. It's not even dangerous enough to be annoying. This kinda reminds me of how Dad likes to throw packs of low-level goblins at us in D&D games for comic relief sometimes. A fight that's a complete non-challenge, but still hilarious.

I relax out of my video game martial arts stance and shake the dust off my sleeve.

Pretty sure this ghoul thing is going to build up to something more threatening at some point.

Question is… what?

With a sigh, I launch myself into the air and fly home.

16

A GLIMMER OF ADVICE

SAME WEDNESDAY, DIFFERENT HOUR

*O*r maybe I don't quite go home right away.

Hunter's place isn't *that* far away from home. However, the flight still takes long enough for my brain to do a couple backflips of insecurity. I need someone to talk to. Someone who knows about weird stuff. Someone like Glim.

So, I swing around toward Seattle, climb a bit higher, and pour on speed.

For no reason at all, I get a sudden mental image of another ghoul somewhere on the ground trying to chase me, spinning himself around in a 180 to follow my abrupt turn—and walking straight into a telephone pole.

The odds of that having really happened are worse than Dad winning the Lottery, but it's a hilarious thought.

I've mostly stopped laughing about it when Glim's apartment complex comes into view down below. Well, it's not really *his* complex. He doesn't rent an apartment there. His ex-wife and two sons do. She's only an ex because he officially died. Not like they divorced or even had trouble. When he's not needed to be doing anything else, he tends to sit there on the roof of a building and watch his former family.

Poor guy is trying to be there for them. Mostly, he wants to be close in case something crazy happens—like a fire or worse. It's gotta be rough on the guy to watch his sons from a distance without being able to talk to or hug them. For me, that's worse than playing dead and never seeing them again. I could never have lurked in the dark and watched my family from across the street for hours every night without having a complete breakdown.

Yeah, I'm pretty squishy like that. Glim is made of sterner stuff than I.

He's also a Shadow, which kinda complicates revealing himself to mortals. Most people don't react well to the whole grey skin, yellow eyes, pointy ears, and giant fangs deal. Dad found this old-as-hell movie called *Nosferatu*, which was about a vampire that kinda resembled Shadows. Kinda. The real ones are way scarier than the actor in the movie. Think of it this way. If that movie vampire was a Disney cartoon, real Shadows are theatrical quality Japanese animation. Somehow, Shadows manage to be both scary as hell and tragi-cool. Or maybe that's only me. Pretty much every other vampire I know tries to avoid being around them.

Well, except for Ashley. She doesn't mind Glim's appearance at all. When I randomly mentioned that, she said something flaky and esoteric about how the two of us are probably tuned into the nature of the person behind the frightful face, so we don't perceive him as quite as terrifying as some other people might. Makes sense. I mean, most non-Innocent vampires look smolderingly gorgeous, which is more of a mental thing than physical. Stands to reason that Shadows can make people see them as more frightening than any physical shape could convey.

Yeah, Ash got kinda out there talking about inner nature and us being tuned into the universal wavelength. Like... she was half a step away from buying a hoo-ha scented candle from Goop and communing with the stars at night while sitting beside a giant pink Himalayan salt crystal lamp.

I joke. Ash isn't that airheaded.

Shadows have this weird network of information. They just kinda know stuff. No clue how it works exactly, though he described it as whispers. Something about any Shadow anywhere in the world can whisper into the darkness and all the other ones know what was said, even if they didn't consciously hear the voice or speak the same language.

Hmm. That could be more of a reason the society vamps around here try to avoid Shadows. It's like inviting a spy to a White House dinner.

I land on the roof about ten steps away from him. No worry about startling him. His ears are even better than mine. And no, that's not a joke about them being huge. It's just how vampires work. Innocents give up some power to be as human-looking as possible. Shadows are the exact opposite. They lose any chance of pretending to be mortal, but they get the sweet powers—and more of them.

Pretty sure he could hear a flea fart from a hundred yards. Whether or not fleas actually do that is irrelevant to my tired metaphor.

"Sarah," says Glim without looking away from the direction of his family's apartment.

I can't see too much of what's going on in his wife's place from here unless I do the zooming-in trick with my vision. No reason to. I have no interest in spying on his family. Clearly, he's super focused on them at the moment.

"Hey." I sit on the roof next to him. "How goes?"

"Stefan's shut himself in his room alone," says Glim. "He's been crying for an hour."

"Ack. What happened?"

A pained, faint smile curls Glim's lip. "There's a girl at his school he's fond of. He's spent the past month trying to work up the courage to ask her out and finally did it."

"Ahh, she said no."

Glim nods.

"Poor kid. I'm sure he'll be fine."

"Yeah. I regret not being able to be there for him to talk to." Glim keeps staring into the distance. "Ana Maria's boyfriend isn't there right now. He's working. Also, I doubt Stefan is ready to confide in him."

I look down and fidget my fingernails at the roof material for a moment before an idea hits me. "You could do something strange... I could go there and pretend to be a crazy mystic hippie chick who gives him like a 'spirit phone' or something and you could call him on it."

Glim finally shifts his attention off the window to look at me. Eighty percent of the mortal population of Seattle probably would've fainted from that look. Somehow, I can tell he's not angry. It's just... pain. The emotion, subtle as it may be, in his eyes fades to sorrow soon after. "Tempting as that is, I couldn't do that to him. If the boy starts believing he can talk to the dead, it could screw up the rest of his life."

I bite my lower lip. Does that mean I've done a crapload of damage to my family by revealing myself? I mean... Sophia would never have unlocked magical abilities if I played dead and stayed away. Good chance Sam would not have discovered demons. Of course, Sierra couldn't have been enchanted if Sophia never had access to magic.

Of course, if I stayed 'dead' to them, things would have gone dark. Yeah. It's a nightmare I've had more than once since waking up in a morgue cooler. Mom can't handle the grief of losing me and turns into an alcoholic. Dad withdraws and just stays in his computer office. Sierra also can't handle losing her big sister that she secretly idolizes. She's also powerless to do anything about it so she gets furious, stops caring about anything, rebels, gets into drugs. Sophia ends up in a mental hospital for crippling depression and anxiety. Hmm. Yanno, that nightmare didn't really dwell too deeply on what became of Sam. Maybe he decided to get the hell away from the darkness and moved out of state for a normal life.

Sigh.

No, I did the right thing, even if my nightmare wouldn't have really happened. I'm not an oracle. All that bad stuff came from my imagination. No guarantee any of it would've happened for real.

Besides, tricking Glim's son into talking to a ghost on a telephone is a bit crazier than an Innocent vampire going home and pretending to be mortal. Other people can *see* me, whereas everyone around Stefan would think he's lost his grip on reality talking to ghosts.

"You're right," I say. "Sorry. Forget it. That was dumb."

Glim nods once, then looks down at his lap. His dark grey hands dangle limply over his knees, three-inch claws glinting in the moonlight. Yes, they're retracted. They get longer when he needs to use them.

"Want me to go grab some beer?" I ask.

He manages a smile. "Perhaps next time. You're already here."

"That I am." I smile. "Stefan will be fine. He'll find another girl someday. Hope it wasn't too public or embarrassing for him."

"No. Certainly not as serious as what happened to your sister."

I cringe. "You know about that?" The question makes me chuckle at myself. "Of course you know about that. You're a Shadow. That's what you do. You lurk and you know things."

Glim chuckles. "I hope Sierra is coping with that."

"Yeah. We're not going to move to the East Coast." I exhale.

"I was so happy to have two boys..." Glim waves in a 'no thank you' manner. "Was not looking forward to having to deal with girl stuff."

I narrow my eyes at him. "Oh?"

"Indeed. Boys are much simpler creatures." Glim holds up his hand, having pulled a thin book out of seeming nowhere. "The instruction manual for boy child is pretty light reading." He shakes his hand like a stage magician... and now he's holding a massive, ten-inch-thick encyclopedia dictionary type monstrosity. "The manual for girls is a bit more dense."

I laugh. "Would you have been one of those girl dads who tried to scare the hell out of any boy she brought home? Seems like a thing for military dads."

Glim dispels the illusionary book into a puff of smoke, then rubs his chin. "Possibly."

We sit there for a while talking about high school romance, first crushes, rejections, dates, and so on. He's totally trying to convince himself that Stefan will be fine. Shutting himself in his bedroom and crying is admittedly not the reaction I expected from a boy. However, that is a lot better than punching holes in his wall. Seems Stefan *really* liked this girl. Then again, he's only fourteen. Damn unlikely it's anything deeper than a passing crush.

Hmm. I wonder if this might have been Hunter if he had the nerve to talk to me when we first met in ninth grade. And by 'met' I mean happened to be in the same school. Yeah, I saw him on and off in the hallway or classrooms, but he never tried to talk to me. Could Stefan have the same kind of feelings for that girl Hunter did for me? At what point did Hunter's infatuation with me change from a childhood crush to true love? Is it possible for that whole 'love at first sight' thing to be real?

Speaking of Hunter...

"Glim?" I ask.

"Yes, Sarah?" He looks over at me.

"So, you know how I'm dating a mortal, right?"

He nods once, despite my question being beyond stupid. We've talked about Hunter—and my unlife in general—quite a lot.

"I've been arguing with myself for months about how to handle our relationship." I wipe both hands down my face, then sigh. "It's unsustainable as it is right now. We're either going to have to break up at some point when the age gap starts to look obvious... or he's gotta become a vampire."

Glim raises one eyebrow. "Have you considered asking Sophia to enchant him to stop aging?"

Uhh. I open my mouth and close it. Honestly, the idea never even occurred to me even though she may have done that exact thing to herself already. If so, I kinda hope the magic waits until she's eighteen (or closer to it) rather than freezing herself at eleven. Poor kid thinks if she never grows up, she'll never have to deal with all the evil and sad things in the world. She's also one of those rare individuals who does not mind being thought of as a 'cute kid'. Sierra hates being treated like a kid. She wants to be twenty years old tomorrow. Sophia has mastered the art of weaponizing cuteness to get what she wants.

Ugh.

"Nope. Never thought of that. She'd probably turn him into a giant purple mushroom. Or a talking crayon." I roll my eyes. "Her magic is not exactly predictable. I still don't believe Sierra trusted her to do a big enchantment on her."

"Desperation makes risk seem trivial." Glim exhales. "Sierra had been ready to beg Dalton to turn her, even if it meant being frozen in time as a child."

I nod. "Yeah. That's kinda my fault. She didn't feel safe with paranormal threats showing up so often."

Glim stares off into the sky. "Do you consider vampirism a bad thing?"

"Ooh, going for an easy question, aren't you?" I chuckle. "It's complicated."

"Girls usually only say 'it's complicated' when talking about relationships." Glim chuckles.

"Well." I hold my chin up. "I kind of am talking about a relationship here. Vampirism in general, though? I love it. But, like… when I think about Ashley, it's simultaneously awesome she's going to be my friend forever and sad at the same time. There's always a little bit of 'holy crap she died' in there, too."

Glim reaches over and rests his hand atop mine. "You think of becoming a vampire as a wonderful gift."

I look down at his hand, slate grey next to mine. "I do."

"Then why does it make you sad to think about Hunter having it as well?" Glim tilts his head like a curious dog. "Are you mourning his lost mortality or are you afraid to be stuck with him forever?"

I blink. "What? No. I'm not afraid to have him forever. I'm... I guess I'm just trying not to be selfish and *make* him do it. I do want him to stay with me for eternity. Finally made up my mind a little while ago. But I'm not going to force him to do it. It's got to be his choice. The only thing... I'm worried about is what if he'd be happier with a mortal girl, having kids of his own and stuff. I mean, we're both teenagers now and teenagers like to do stupid and impulsive things. Like, even if we know it's stupid and impulsive, we'll just shrug and do it anyway. What if we're both caught up in a teenage crush and he really would be happier with a mortal girl and kids and stuff?"

"Yolf," says Glim.

"What?"

"You only live forever." He winks.

I cackle. "Worst case scenario. A teenager who not only thinks they're immortal... they actually are."

He chuckles. "Look out, world."

Me striking a fake badass pose makes him chuckle. Yeah, I'm about as intimidating as a Toyota Prius with a shark-mouth paintjob.

"You are forgetting the other side of that coin." He smiles. "You will forever be a teenager, so you are spared the part where you grow older and come to regret all the impulsive decisions you made."

"Heh. True."

Glim pats my hand. "Ask him how he feels. You've got the advantage of him already knowing what you are. So, there's a crazy conversation you've already avoided." He tries to pull off a sugary teenage girl voice. "Oh, sweetie, you might not believe this, but vampires are real... and I am one."

His voice is hilarious. I'm in tears from laughing.

He waits for me to get control of my giggling. "If you're worrying about being impulsive, you could always wait a few years. See if his feelings change when he's in his early twenties."

Hmm. I let that thought roll back and forth in my head. Not too many people would make faces at a twenty-two-year-old dating an eighteen-year-old. "Worth considering, yeah. I also did ask him what he wants already. He always says what makes him happy is being with me. Like, he doesn't care about losing any future mortal life. He also doesn't seem to care about the idea of growing old with me while I stay the same."

Glim looks me over for a few seconds. "Why don't you believe him?"

"Huh?" I blink. "I believe him."

"You aren't acting like you do, Sarah. He says the only thing he wants is to be with you, yet you've tied yourself up in knots over what to do. Are you looking for an excuse to break up with him or not? What are you really afraid of?"

I stare at him for a while, feeling metaphorically slapped. Again and again, I open my mouth to defend myself... but can't. Is Glim right? Could I possibly not really believe Hunter? No, it's not exactly that. I don't think Hunter is lying to me. I think he might not be mature enough to really know what he wants and right now, he's saying whatever he thinks I want to hear.

Guilt. That's what I'm really afraid of. What would I do if Hunter changes after he's immortal and all that 'the only thing I want is to be with you' is no longer true? Yeah, it's true for him right now, but will it stay that way? He's so dutiful, hard-working, and loyal now. How much could he change once he's become a vampire with power? I kinda like him being the 'normal' part of my existence. Alas, it can't last forever that way. That's what I'm afraid of. Taking advantage of him. Of losing him.

I shrink in on myself, folding my arms, looking down. Oh, come on, Sarah. Don't cry in front of Glim. Nothing even happened. These are only thoughts.

"What are you truly afraid of?" asks Glim in a soft, comforting voice with more than a bit of gravel under it.

"Lots of things," I mutter. "I wanted to break up with Scott for months and never had the courage to do it. When I finally did, he killed me."

Glim puts an arm around me, snugging me against his side like a big brother being there when I need a hug. "Are you afraid he might come unglued if you leave him and run off to join the ranks of the vampire hunters to get revenge?"

"Hah!" I snicker. "Well, if he's turned, he will literally become a vampire Hunter."

"Oof." Glim groans.

I snap my fingers. "Oh, it's gotta happen now. Dad will totally adore that pun."

"So, you do not wish to break up with him?" Glim cocks his head at me.

"No. I know what wanting to break up feels like. That's not going on here. I love Hunter. It's just... well..." I sigh. "Ashley gave up her mortality to stay with me."

Glim reaches over and puts a finger under my chin, tugging my head around to make eye contact with him. "You keep saying 'gave up mortality.' That tells me you think it better than being a vampire."

"No." I exhale hard. "I mean, she had dreams and stuff she talked about for years. She gave that up. Losing mortality for vampirism isn't a 'giving up' situation. It's a massive upgrade."

"You feel guilty she walked way from all of her dreams just for you."

"Yeah. I do. A bit." I fidget at my hair. "I'm just me. I'm not a husband and kids and nice house and grandkids and a successful veterinary practice."

Glim pats me on the back. "That guilt is proof of the depth of your friendship. She made that choice. She valued your friendship more than any temporary prize a mortal life might've given her."

I manage a faint smile. "Yeah... I guess."

"You told me she was suicidal when she thought you'd died."

"Ouch. No... not exactly." I tilt my hand in a so-so gesture. "She wasn't suicidal. Ash would not have actively hurt herself. Just... like you know how they say some people can die of sadness? More like that. She shut down. Didn't want to do anything. No idea if she literally would've died of sadness, but she was in bad shape."

He nods, then sits there in silence, allowing the somberness of that thought hanging in the air to dissipate. "Talk to Hunter. Explain all of what you told me to him. See what he wants to do. It isn't like he can lie to you."

I stare at my foot and idly flick the laces of my sneaker for a moment.

"There you go being afraid again," says Glim in a comforting tone.

"I'm not afraid he's going to say yes." I lift my gaze up into the stars. "I'm afraid he'll say no."

17

A WHORL OF DARKNESS

YEP. STILL WEDNESDAY

*S*ilence can be therapy sometimes.

Since becoming a vampire, whenever I 'just can't even', it's been my habit to fly to the Space Needle and sit on top of it staring down at the city. Yeah, I know. Very Batman of me. Not doing it tonight since I'm already on a rooftop. Having Glim around makes me feel better. I love my family, but it's not like I can talk to them about vampire problems. Sure, Ashley's one of us now, but she's even newer than me. Not as if she's going to have any deep insight into sticky conundrums, like whether or not I should arrange my boyfriend's death.

That's also the part of it that's making me cringe.

Even though I think vampirism is amazing, the price of entry is steep: death. It's really stupid of me to fixate on it so much. We're not staying dead. Why does my stupid emotional overload brain attach such sadness and weight to the concept of death even if it's not a permanent state in our case?

Guess some things are too hard-coded into our DNA to easily set aside: death is a great big bad thing, love is a force of nature that can do amazing things, and it's impossible to resist saying 'how 'bout that heat' on a bad day in August.

Unlife is a great, amazing adventure. Every day that happens brings new oddities I never imagined possible… like ghouls.

"Oh, question." I lift my head and look over at him.

My sudden mood shift from somber to normal catches him off guard. He leans back and blinks. "Ask away."

"How much do you know about ghouls?"

Glim regards me with an expression of barely contained bewilderment for a few seconds. "Ghouls? Are you talking about personal injury lawyers or being more literal?"

"I don't know what these things really are. Just calling them ghouls because it kinda fit." I describe the attacks. "… wearing clothes that looked super old and rotted. They were kinda like zombies but faster and less robotic."

"That is certainly unusual. Can't say I've seen that before." He stares off to the side. "I will speak with the others. I am certain the secrets lie within the crypt somewhere."

"Awesome. Thanks." I start reaching out to hug him, but stop short.

Twin masses of inky blackness well up out of the roof, spinning about in a whorl of darkness before coalescing into the solid forms of two more Shadows. Oh, that was quick. I've only got the time to mentally process their bizarre outfits—they look like those desert warrior guys from the *Mummy* movies—before they pounce at Glim.

Straight out of the *Matrix*, Glim throws himself upward, spinning around and between the other Shadows' claws while simultaneously planting one foot on my chest and 'gently' shoving me out of harm's way. I slide across the roof for a couple seconds until managing to catch myself with flight and stop.

Three Shadows having a fight reminds me of how Looney Tunes used to depict brawls—a big cloud of smoke with random hands, faces, and feet appearing in places. Despite it looking like a cartoon, nothing about it is the least bit funny. Glim's ghastly appearance never bothered me. Those other two? Eek. They look like grey devils.

Vampire or not, the part of me that remains a teenage girl totally wants to scream and run away... but I don't.

The two attackers say stuff in some other language, probably Arabic or something along those lines. I have no idea what they're talking about. They also don't genuinely look much different from Glim. Their scariness isn't a thing of physical appearance at all. Like, the way some people can look at me and I feel like they're fantasizing about doing unspeakably evil things to me and leaving my body somewhere in a remote forest? Yeah, that's the vibe I'm getting from these two.

However, they seem content to ignore my presence right now.

I spin in place, following the wild action as the brawl hops around the giant roof in a series of micro-teleports and smears of solid darkness. Every so often, the flashing cloud of illusionary nonsense pauses to give me a clear look at Glim's fist making contact with one of the bad guys' chins or one of the bad guy's feet planting a painful kick into Glim's ribs.

The roof is starting to look like a Jackson Pollack painting, streaked with blood so dark it's essentially black. It's anyone's guess which vampire the blood's coming from. Probably all three of them.

Claws out, I widen my stance and get ready for badness to come my way. I can't run from this, even if it's scaring the hell out of me or if Glim would want me to. Couple times, I almost jump into the mess to help, but I can't even tell who is where.

All of a sudden, the 'cloud' stops to reveal three individual figures in clear detail. Glim's got one guy up off his feet by a chokehold with claws sunk into the man's neck. His amazing leather trench coat is in tatters. Both Arabic Shadows also look like they got into a fistfight with a lawnmower and didn't exactly win. It's not a problem that Glim seems to have gotten the upper hand against one of them. No, the problem is that there are *two* bad guys and one's about to eviscerate Glim from behind.

Only one thing for me to do... I Supergirl charge. Maybe I'm a chicken, but those guys have six-inch claws. In five-one-thousandths of a second, my brain forces a tactical change. Rather than attack the dude trying to ambush Glim from behind, I tackle Glim out of the way. We hit the roof twenty feet past where he'd been standing and go sliding.

Our slide abruptly ends as Glim does something bizarre. One second, I'm riding him like a toboggan across the roof. The next thing I know, we're standing beside each other with a cyclone of darkness fading away from around us.

Bad Guy number one—who Glim had by the throat—now also has ten more giant claws stuck into his chest. Black blood gurgles out from both sides of his neck as well as bubbles between his teeth to dribble down his chin. The dude who tried to ambush Glim from behind pounced anyway, not expecting me to fly in from the side and body-check his target out of the way. He shredded his buddy.

The two foreign Shadows exchange a brief glance, then both stare at me.

Uh oh. I'm in trouble.

Ambusher dude disappears into thin air.

Pain rips across my stomach. He just freakin' appeared right in front of me. I'm hit before I can even react.

Glim elbows that guy in the face, knocking him away from me and almost sending him flying off the building. He doesn't get the chance to follow up, having to spin around and use a micro-teleport to stop the other one from grabbing at me from behind.

I do my best to put up a defense, but… there's literally no way for me to defend against bad guys who can appear anywhere they want to be at any time. Glim blurs around, his body half immaterial darkness, blocking, diverting, or eating every attack coming my way. I have never felt so helpless in my life.

It's not that they're so much faster than me. Yes, they are faster than me, but that alone wouldn't make me defenseless. It's the damn teleportation. They appear behind or beside me and swing so fast there's little chance of me escaping without Glim also teleporting to block them and protect me. Maybe I could hang on against one of them, but two? Nope. That's not happening. I'm screwed.

Never once have I really claimed to be a total badass. I'm so scared right now I'm about to scream and beg them not to kill me. All I want to do is go home to my family. I'm sorry for interfering in whatever Shadow business was going on. But you guys wanted to kill my friend!

Glim flips around and jumps on me, wrapping his arms around my body. A thick column of inky blackness bursts up to surround us, blotting out sight of anything. My stomach does a triple backflip with a twist, springs upward to punch me in the vocal cords, then crashes down against my pelvis.

Or at least it felt like that.

The column of darkness surrounding us like a circular curtain falls to the floor.

We're no longer on the roof of an apartment building. We're inside a massive gothic chamber with big stone columns. Dozens of suits of medieval plate armor line both walls, mounted on pedestals in little arched alcoves. Not sure if this is a castle, a cathedral, or a museum.

The room has no windows at all, nor any sources of light. I get the distinct feeling we are underground.

Glim lets go of me, then falls over sideways like a mannequin.

His blood smells strong and unpleasant. It's nowhere near as stinky as the ghouls' fetid ooze. The scent is more along the lines of what I imagine normal blood would smell like after sitting out in the air for a while.

My blood has an odor, too. Can't say it *stinks*, but it's certainly not appetizing. Smells like fresh blood.

Realizing I'm smelling my own blood makes me look down.

Four slashes run across my stomach horizontally. The cuts are pretty deep, the sort of wound that likely would have caused a mortal's intestines to come tumbling out. Let's just say that if I'd been pregnant, I could've reached in and pulled the infant out without too much fuss. Thankfully, I'm not mortal. All my inner bits stayed pretty much where they belong. Blood isn't even really seeping out of me, merely welling up in the wounds. My belly looks like a wooden statue someone gouged before covering the grooves in dark red paint.

And holy shit, it hurts.

Vampire claws suck. So much.

I clench my jaw and try not to scream. Four hot curling irons pressed across my stomach would be less painful than this. The burn isn't stopping. I know it won't. Not for at least an hour or so. This is hell, but I got off light. Glim probably has claw wounds all over him.

"Sorry," I rasp. "I know you wanted me to run, but I couldn't just leave you there."

He grunts.

"Stupid. I know. I wasn't any help." I close my jaw hard to stifle a scream when the pain flares momentarily. "Made it worse. You might've been okay if you didn't have to protect me."

He grunts again in a tone like he's trying to tell me it's okay.

Maybe ten minutes later, the searing pain in my stomach has a momentary weakening that allows me to finally move. I sit down and fold my arms over my gut. Things get significantly worse soon after that. The stinging returns along with serious itching. All my sliced up inside bits are putting themselves back together. A wrath of ten-thousand crawling fleas has a dance party inside my guts.

It's all I can do not to scream.

Eventually, I manage to pull my phone out and send a 'home soon, WSA' text to Ashley. WSA is 'weird shit alert.' It's a code that means paranormal stuff I can't talk about anywhere the NSA might be watching... or whoever might be snooping on text messages. It's a good idea not to leave a paper trail, even a digital one... and my phone has no signal here. Great. Modern vampire problems.

I'm in too much pain to put the phone back in my pocket, so I just set it on the stone floor next to me and keep holding my stomach.

Glim hasn't made a sound. He's just kinda lying there staring at the vaulted ceiling.

After another some number of minutes, the angry stinging fades from 'someone's pressing red hot irons to my skin' to 'it only hurts when I move.' I look around at this strange place. An unmistakable sense of being watched comes from everywhere, almost as if every suit of plate armor has a person inside it. That's unlikely. Chances are, a bunch of other Shadows are lurking out of sight. Or just standing around us out in the open but not allowing me to see them.

This chamber, whatever it is, is pretty cool. Looks like how I'd imagine the master vampire's lair or underworld vampire king's throne room might be—back in like 1650. Only, there's no throne... just three hallways leading off in different directions. I'm going to guess that Glim shadow-ported us to the place he sleeps during the day. The Conclave or something like that I think he called it, a place where those two jackasses wouldn't dare chase us, assuming they could even find it.

I look over at him. "What was that?"

"Nothing you need to worry about."

"That guy tried to give me a C-section and I'm not even pregnant." I gasp at a sudden pain spike. "I am worried about why someone tried to kill my friend."

He takes a deep breath and lets it out slow. "Syed sent them."

"Your sire?"

"Yes."

I blink, scrunching my nose in confusion. "Why?"

"He is unhappy with my decision to return to the US."

"Little melodramatic, huh?"

The two Arab Shadows appear in black puffs of smoke, standing maybe thirty feet away from us. Oh, I know what happened. The fight advanced to the next stage. Scenery shift from rooftop to enormous gothic chamber. Dammit. I am not stuck inside a *Mortal Kombat* game!

Glim shoves himself to his feet with a pained grunt, then calls out in Arabic.

At least, I think it's Arabic. Yeah, it probably is if those two work for Syed.

The two glare at him for a long moment before one briefly shifts his gaze to me and back to Glim.

He says something stern and ominous sounding.

Glim bows his head, seems to be thinking, then says a short phrase in Arabic before switching to English. "Sarah, go. Run. Get out of here. They only want me."

There's a finality in his tone that scares the shit out of me. I don't need to understand Arabic to figure out that he just asked them to spare me in exchange for allowing them to finish him off. Somewhere deep inside my mind, mini-Sophia and mini-Sierra arrive in the emotion processing center at the same time. Sophia wants to cry. Sierra's furious.

Sierra wins.

I mean, she'd want to cry about this, too. But she saves the crying for later.

Glim's going to let them destroy him in order to protect me.

Remember that whole stupid teenage impulsiveness crap? Yeah. I embody that to the tee right now. I spring to my feet, careful to grab my phone as I get up (hey I am still a teenage girl, right). I beeline for the nearest plate armor statue and grab the broadsword out of its gauntlet. This is a lot closer to the sort of weapon Dalton's used to swinging than a katana. It's comically large in my hand, but thanks to my being a vampire, the weapon isn't heavy.

"I'm not gonna leave you to die!" I yell.

"Sarah, get out of here!" Glim spins to glare at me. "That's not a request."

I hold the broadsword up. Inside, I'm freaking out and terrified. Maybe the tip of my sword is shaking. Those two Shadows are going to rip me apart. I'd basically need to predict the future and start swinging at empty air where they're about to appear to have any chance. Images of my family flickers through my consciousness. I don't want to lose them, but I just can't walk away and leave him here alone.

"I can't. You're going to die."

"Sarah… go." Glim bows his head. "I'm already dead."

I rush over to stand beside him. Both bad Shadows make faces at me like I'm some little kid who thinks they're going to be a challenge. The guy who sliced me on the gut half-smiles. I'm sure he wouldn't mind an excuse to ignore their agreement and kill me anyway.

Ugh. Shit. We are so screwed. Why aren't the other Shadows in here getting involved? Is there some messed up honor code at work?

Or maybe I'm imagining them. This place could be completely empty except for us, the two bastards, and a bunch of ghosts. Dammit. I thought the Sefil was an unstoppable evil that would devour me. Now I'm going to be destroyed by a pair of…

Wait a second.

I grab onto Glim and whisper, "Jump us to my backyard!"

"What? Are you insane?" He gasps.

"Just do it!" I yell. "Now!"

Another wave of black vapors rush up from the floor and surround us. My guts bottom out worse than going on the Free Fall ride. I'm too freaked out and scared to care about the pain from the claw wound at the moment. Up is down. Left is right. Inside is outside. Well, not literally. The shadowy Puke-A-Tron 9000 zooms through a tunnel of undulating images that fly by too fast to recognize as anything more than random shapes. We roll side to side, zip upward, fall into a hard downward curve…

It all stops in an instant.

No sense of deceleration happens; I go straight from flying at hundreds of miles an hour through an undulating spirit tunnel to a dead standstill faster than the blink of an eye.

We're in my backyard.

The two enemy Shadows appear a short distance away, seconds later. They do not seem pleased. Dude who really seems to want me dead has this cocky expression of disbelief, like a cop who just re-caught a 400-pound shoplifter who tried rather feebly to run away from him.

"What good did this do other than put your family in danger?" asks Glim.

"I was thinking about that sefil…" I shift my gaze to the bad Shadows.

They start walking toward us. Sure, they could teleport the twenty feet in an instant and be done with me, though they seem to want to be melodramatic and draw out the fear.

A giant flamethrower stream of dark crimson fire appears out of thin air, engulfing both of Syed's men in a conflagration so vicious they disintegrate to screaming ashes in four seconds. The heat is intense enough to force me and Glim to back up several steps.

"What the..." Glim blinks, then seems to realize what happened. "Your hellhound..."

"Max isn't *my* hellhound. He's Sam's friend." I look at the seemingly empty backyard. "Thank you, Max."

A deep growly, snort answers. I think that's demonic dog for 'no problem.'

"So, yeah. I was thinking about the sefil, and how it was an impossible problem until Mel blew him up." I start to set my hands on my hips in triumph, but it hurts too much so I end up cradling my stomach again. "Like they said on *Saturday Night Live*, FIRE BAD."

Glim chuckles, though it sounds pained. "How the heck do you know that?"

"Dad watches old TV all the time." I gingerly stuff my phone in my pocket, then look at the broadsword, which I offer to him. "Sorry. I didn't mean to steal this."

He takes it. "I don't know what to say, Sarah. You know they would've killed us both."

"Nah. If you didn't have to protect me, you had a fighting chance." I nudge him. "If they thought they could kill you easily, they wouldn't have accepted your offer to surrender for sparing me."

"I wouldn't let them kill you."

"Thanks. I wouldn't let them kill you, either." My smile is a little cheesy. I know I couldn't really have done much to help him there. Having a sword would've given me more of a chance, but that fight was way over my pay grade. "Umm, is this going to be a problem?"

"What?"

"Destroying those two minions of evil." I gesture at the ash cloud.

"Hopefully not... Losing them should send an appropriate message." Glim grumbles. "Syed might be an evil bastard, but he's no fool. It wouldn't be like him to get so caught up in pettiness that he would waste resources trying to get revenge on me after he's already lost two progeny."

"Revenge?" I raise an eyebrow. "What did you do to him?"

"I left the Middle East and refused to be his protégé."

"Oh, is that all?" I roll my eyes. "Seriously? That guy sent two goons to kill you because you didn't want to work for him?"

Glim nods, then exhales. "Thank you."

"No worries." I squeeze his hand. "That's what friends are for. Besides… Max did the heavy lifting here."

Glim looks at the empty yard. "You have my thanks, Max."

Another deep canine snort answers.

"Never would I have imagined having a demon close by would offer security." Glim chuckles.

I grin. "Yeah. He's really good at keeping away vampire hunters, evil vampires, various other monsters, and Jehovah Witnesses."

"Urgh." Glim bows his head. "Don't make me laugh right now, please. Too many claw marks."

"Thanks for saving my ass."

"That's what friends are for." He gives me a toothy smile. "I need to feed… and rest."

Yeah. Same. I glance over at the Perry's house next door. This is breaking major rule number one, but I'm in a lot of pain and lack the willpower to fly all the way back to Seattle. Mr. Perry will do for a quick nibble. The first and only time I will feed from anyone close to where I live.

"Goodnight, Glim." I hug him.

"Night, Sarah." He salutes me with the broadsword, stark silver against the deep black of his coat, then disappears in a cloud of smoke.

That really is a neat trick.

18

RAIN CHECK

THURSDAY, AT LAST!

*C*law wounds are a good enough excuse to miss my chemistry class.

It's not like I'm being lazy or unmotivated. I didn't wake up until 5:29 p.m. Way too late to even bother going in, since the class runs from three to six. Sent Professor Markov an email apologizing for missing and blamed 'excessive bleeding' and 'pain so bad I couldn't move without screaming'. I'm sure she did not think of a vampire claw wound in response to that description. Yeah, I deliberately made it sound like a red faerie attack.

This is crazy of me to say, but I'd rather deal with a bad period than another claw hit.

Yes, claws hurt *that* much. Cuts of the same depth from a steel blade wouldn't have been a fraction of the agony. They also would have completely healed in about an hour. I'll be dealing with soreness for a week at least.

I still haven't gotten out of bed.

Chloe's playing with dolls on the floor. Ashley's watching *Naruto*.

I'm kinda half-listening to it, not really paying much attention to anything other than trying not to move. If I hold perfectly still, the soreness is not all consuming.

Sierra walks into my room. The formless mass of a huge oversized purple sweatshirt makes her already scrawny body look even thinner. A little bit of her black bike shorts are visible poking out from under the bottom of the sweatshirt. She's barefoot. A few black cord bracelets dangle from her right wrist and she's wearing a purple fabric anklet on her left leg. Her expression is neutral-curious.

The girl's also carrying two rattan longswords.

"Hey, Sare," says Sierra. "Wanna spar a bit?"

"Ugh. I would… but I'm a bit too sore right now. Can we schedule sparring a couple days from now?"

She gives me a wicked little smile. "What did he do to you?"

Ashley ignores the question, not going for the easy joke. Surprising.

"It wasn't Hunter." I smirk at her. "Got a nasty scratch."

She gets a little whiter in the face, eyes wide. "Ack! What happened?"

I gingerly pat my stomach. "Couple idiots tried to attack Glim when I happened to be there talking to him. One of them tagged me with claws."

"Stupid." She mutters. "Who's dumb enough to attack him?"

It's cute she thinks he's like the Superman of vampires. Honestly, he's not that old yet. I give her a basic explanation of the attack, though I don't go into any details about how close I came to ending up as a pile of cat food.

"Eep!" Ashley pauses the video and runs over. "Let me look."

Little awkward. I don't generally wear anything under my giant sleep shirts, but we're all girls in here. Besides, blankets exist. Ash and I have also shared showers on occasion. Not like she hasn't seen everything before. Sierra turns away, not wanting to see the wound. She's not squeamish about blood. I think she just doesn't want to see her big sister hurt. I lift my shirt out of the way so Dr. Ashley can examine me. The unicorn knit into her pink sweater stares judgmentally at me while she traces her fingers over the wound.

The cuts have sealed enough to be red lines across my skin. I look like I pissed off a huge housecat. Despite its outward tameness, my entire gut region is sore as hell. Having a bunch of three-inch nails stuck into my belly would be more comfortable.

"That doesn't look too bad." Ashley smiles.

"Yeah. It's healing. Just takes time to stop hurting." I flip my shirt down.

Sierra sighs, risks a quick peek, then turns back to look at me once she's sure the angry claw marks are no longer exposed. "No problem. It can wait. Just wanted to test if the stupid red faerie was messing with the enchantment at all."

"I could spar if you want," says Ashley.

"Thanks, but... you don't know how to use a sword. And you're too cute." Sierra winces. "It would feel too much like clubbing a baby seal."

Ashley gives her a raspberry.

I laugh.

Ouch. I should not have laughed.

Hmm. Is Sierra really worried about her enchantment weakening? Usually when she asks to spar, she needs to vent and work off excess angst. Though, she doesn't look upset. Still, I'm kinda concerned.

"You okay?" I ask.

"Yeah, fine." Sierra's face reddens. "I'm actually less worried about an attack at school now than I am about everyone making fun of me for what happened at the fitness center."

Whoa. Progress. "That's... good."

"Yeah. Sophia warded the school." Sierra twists some hair around her fingers.

"Oh no." I fake gasp. "What now? Where did the stray magic shoot off to?"

Sierra grinds her toes into the carpet. "Umm, no idea if stray magic went anywhere. She, umm, basically enchanted the school so like if anyone brings a gun into the building, they get massive explosive diarrhea that won't stop until they go outside."

"Eww." I squirm. "Why?"

Sierra lifts her arms a bit and lets them flap against her sides. "I dunno. This is Sophia. She didn't want to do anything that would hurt someone, and I guess uncontrollable pooping was the first, most crippling thing she could think of that didn't involve serious injuries. I mean, it's not a bad idea. Kinda difficult to go on a murder spree when you're exploding from the butt."

Ashley waffles back and forth between laughing and looking ready to throw up.

"It's not going to hurt anyone and it's effective. I like it." Sierra grins. "Course, those cops who came to the school to talk about drugs didn't really like it." She bites her lip. "The janitors liked it even less."

Oh no. I cover my face in both hands, trying my best not to imagine what that looked, sounded… or smelled like. "Please tell me you're teasing."

"Nope. Serious." Sierra gives a nervous laugh. "She's fixing it, modifying the spell so it only goes off if the person has a gun, *and* bad intentions."

"Ack. We've created a monster." I shiver.

"Yeah, but she's an adorable monster." Ashley snickers.

Chloe's head rises into view past the side of my bed. Her eyes are glowing red, fangs extended. "I'm a 'dorable monster, too."

I pull her up into a hug. "Yep. You sure are."

When Dad yells about dinner being ready, I make my way upstairs.

Yeah, it's a waste of food for the three of us to eat. However, it feels normal and the 'rents insist. I think having us never eat dinner would bother them more than me putting college on hold. It's a small thing that lets them both pretend not that much has changed with me. Since they insist, and it helps them cope, I don't complain. And maybe we aren't wasting food after all. Mortal bodies absorb nutrients from food before it comes out the other end. I absorb peace of mind and a sense of sanity from it.

Mom's in the kitchen when I make it to the top of the stairs. She's scooping something out of a pot into a serving bowl. "Hi, Sare. You okay? Slept a bit late today. I hope you didn't get into a fight again."

"Not by choice. Random attack." Since I now have pants on, there's no awkwardness in flashing my stomach at her. "Claw swipe. I'll be fine in a couple days. Nothing major."

She winces at the sight of the red lines. Thankfully it *does* look tame now.

Sophia wanders in carrying a big, but thin, burgundy book. "Mom?"

"Yes, dear?" Mom hands me the serving bowl. Ahh. Mashed potatoes. "Bring that to the table, hon?"

I nod at her and start making my way to the dining room.

"What happened?" Sophia points at a page.

Looks like she found one of Mom's high school yearbooks. She's pointing at a girl's picture that's been scribbled out with permanent marker.

"Oh." Mom looks away, reaching for another pot on the stove, seeming a tad aloof. "Just a bitch I never got along with back then. That's how we used to unfriend people in the ancient times before Facebook."

I walk into the dining room while singsonging, "Draaaaamaaaa."

Dad stares at me from across the big table. He looks like the grim reaper without a robe, or a scythe. This is the sort of glower from him I'd expect if I'd been a 'handful' as a kid and did something like stealing his car without permission to go to a party I'd already been told not to go to. Thankfully, Follows Rules Girl is not panicking because my conscience is clean.

"Umm... Dad?" I set the potatoes down and stop where I stand. "What's wrong?"

"I'm disappointed in you." Dad bows his head.

Sam, already seated at the table and waiting for food, perks up with 'uh oh' all over his face.

Sophia creeps in from the kitchen like a mouse making sure no cats are in sight before breaking cover. Sierra, also in a chair already, gives him side eye. Chloe's flying around in circles above the table near the ceiling. She's making a 'what the heck is wrong with you' face at Dad.

Mom sighs, so I suspect Dad is being silly.

"What's wrong, Dad?" I ask.

He lets off this huge sigh of disappointment. "I expected so much better from you."

"I'm not wearing socks with sandals." I raise a leg and wiggle my toes at him. "See?"

"No, dear." Dad grabs his heart. Good grief, you'd think I robbed a bank or something and he's being forced to turn me into the police. "I can't believe a child I raised could do such a thing."

Sam gives me a 'what the hell did you do?' look.

Sophia's getting ready to cry.

Sierra looks baffled.

Mom walks in with the serving tray of chicken. "Jonathan, what are you going on about?"

"Allie…" Dad fake sniffles, then gestures at me. "Our daughter has brought a Macintosh into this house."

Sierra sighs at the ceiling.

A few seconds of silence hang between us.

Mom rolls her eyes and continues forward, setting the chicken down in the middle of the table. Sophia wipes her eyes, blushes a little, and quietly takes her seat. Sam laughs, as does Sierra. Ashley shakes her head at him.

"Apples are bleh," says Chloe.

"See?" Dad points up at her. "She understands."

"The child is talking about fruit," says Ashley.

"What?" Dad folds his arms, looking around at everyone's non-reaction. "This is serious. I thought I raised you better than that."

I take my seat. "Really?"

Dad fake swoons.

"Oh, come on." I laugh. "It's just a computer. Stop being a drama queen."

"A Macintosh. In this house." Dad waves his hands about in random nonsensical gestures. "I'm going to have to perform a cleansing ritual now. Maybe a sage scrubbing."

I lean an elbow on the table, chin on palm. "Dad. I got it cheap, used. Already with a bunch of software and a drawing tablet. It's something for Sierra to practice on."

"Almost all the professional artists are using Macs," says Sierra in an uncharacteristically timid voice.

Yes, she's acting to go along with Dad's silliness.

Dad grimaces as if wounded. "There are perfectly viable art programs available for PC as well."

"I really think she's going to go long term with it." I smile at Sierra. "She might as well get used to what she'll be using later on when she's a professional."

"Tragic." Dad shakes his head. "I weep for the future of this nation if they trust their future to Apple."

Mom plops herself down in her chair and rolls her eyes at him.

"What's wrong with Dad?" whispers Sophia.

"He's being melodramatic," I say.

Dad drops the gloom and doom act, breaking into a chuckle. "Just never thought I'd have one of *those* in the house."

"Demon?" asks Sophia.

"No." Dad looks down. "Worse."

"Stop already." Mom nudges him. "It's only a computer."

"It's not a computer. It's a Mac," says Dad as if he's making total sense.

Somehow, this is an Eighties reference. I just know it. Not sure how, but it's got to be.

"Whatever it is, it's hardly worth this level of drama." Mom starts serving out chicken to everyone's plate. "Go on and eat before it gets cold. Young lady, please stop flying around the dinner table."

"Sorry!" Chloe flips around and floats down into her seat, then hits mom with this super adorable fanged smile.

Yeah. Grandkids really can get away with bloody murder. I just hope that phrase never turns literal.

19

THE MONTHLY SOCIAL

THURSDAY NIGHT, LATE

I am grateful that vampire parties, at least among the society crowd in Seattle, don't involve dancing. There is a lot of standing around, not really moving much. Perfect for me. My stomach feels like someone hung me from a chain and let Mike Tyson use me as a punching bag for a few hours.

Aurélie and Ashley helped me into the gown, and by 'helped' I mean basically dressed me like a giant doll while I just stood there trying not to move. My vampire patroness did give me a sip or two of her blood, which she said will help me heal faster. So far, it hasn't had too much of an effect on me other than making me feel like I've had *all the coffee*. I'm still sore, but holy crap, am I awake.

If we were characters in a Japanese anime cartoon, I'd have lightning and stuff crackling all around me. I'm so full of energy it doesn't seem out of the realm of possibility that if I shouted at someone, they'd go flying across the room as if hit by a speeding bus.

Ashley made a joke about it being similar to a level two character drinking a healing potion meant for level fifty characters. That's probably not a bad way to look at it. So, yeah, it's time for the monthly.

The soiree, I mean. Not *that* monthly.

Generally, the society vamps have a gathering once a month. I don't mind going, even if it does tend to eat the entire night. It's only once a month and any mortals I'd rather be spending time with are asleep now, anyway.

As usual, we are all dolled up in ridiculously elaborate gowns as though we've stepped out of a French royal court from 1644. Mine's white and sorta yellow. I feel like a lemon chiffon elemental. Ashley's gone full strawberry shortcake. Her dress is rose pink where mine's yellow. Chloe's gown is sky blue with white frills. I don't exactly know what this material is, but it's plush and really lustrous. Traipsing around wearing seventy pounds of fabric (or so it feels) isn't something I want to do all the time, but I'm used to it enough that I no longer feel ridiculous. The first few parties, I felt as embarrassed in this getup as Sierra did wearing the Girl Scout uniform. I think she would've been less mortified going out in public in full clown makeup. About the only thing likely worse for her would be a dress like this. She's not a fan of super girly stuff.

Ashley loves cute. These dresses aren't really 'cute' as much as 'elegant.' Despite how she is, playing with dolls is a bit past her. Kinda weird, honestly. Hugging plushies is just fine but playing dolls is 'for kids.' She only does it to entertain Chloe. *Becoming* the doll is a bit much, though. Still, she doesn't seem to mind being the anachronism. Every other vampire, even some old-as-dirt ones are wearing modern clothing… except for this one guy off the corner who, I guess, still hasn't gotten it through his skull that the Revolutionary War is over. He's not in uniform or anything, but the outfit is like something you'd see George Washington depicted in.

The usual crowd of super pretty vampiresses who often get into catty arguments with Aurélie are all gathered around Chloe tonight. Definitely a welcome change from them standing around sniping at each other over who's the prettiest. It's like the hot girls from high school taken to another level. I suppose if you've got eternity to be alive and nothing better to do, obsessing over your looks is one possible pastime.

Chloe's perched on a sofa, surrounded by all these women. It's as if I brought the cutest grandchild in the universe into a grandma convention, except none of the women are old and no one's pinching any cheeks. They're having this weird little tea party with her, only instead of imaginary tea, the little cups have blood in them. It's creepdorable, especially with Aurélie dolling her up in the miniature elaborate dress.

Kiddo looks like a larger version of one of those haunted porcelain dolls.

I suppose in an odd sort of way she *is* one—a spirit trapped forever in a small body that's never going to change. At least she can move under her own power. Ugh. How much would it suck to be a haunted doll? Gotta be similar to someone who's totally paralyzed. No wonder those dolls can get angry so easily and/or keep trying to possess people.

Since I don't really want to move, I hover by the wall and watch. Ashley's mingling and talking, which is good to see. Not jealous whatsoever she is mingling randomly instead of hanging out with me by the wall. She hangs out with me *all the time* now. Being Aurélie's progeny, she's something of a minor celebrity here. Most of the society vamps try to be overly nice to her, likely in hopes of gaining favor from Aurélie—or they could simply be afraid of angering her by treating her 'vampire offspring' poorly.

Hmm. That makes me think about Hunter.

I start looking over the vampires in attendance, wondering how it would work for each one of them to give the Transference to him. Right off the bat, I don't even consider Wolent, Stefano, or Paolo. I'd never have the nerve to ask the big guy... and no way would I approach the two elders who distrust me the most. Vanessa Prentice has been nice to me, though for some reason, I'm nervous that she'd try to steal him. Not sure Hunter would be interested in getting the bite from a man, though I think Henry Arnold would be willing to do it. His husband Ashton might object, though.

Sigh.

It's a big thing to ask. Not only does making a new vampire leave the sire fatigued for a while until their power returns, it's giving them a permanent mind link to another person. Making that request is a serious imposition, basically like asking someone you don't know that well for a ride to the airport.

I end up going back to watching Chloe play tea party again. Vanessa, Jennifer Ruiz, and like five other women I don't really know hover around her, all absorbed by her presence. I think they're going through the mental motions of what it might have been like had they remained mortal and had children. Or perhaps they simply find her endearing and fascinating. Vampire children are super rare, after all. It's a testament to kiddo's powers of cuteness that she's kept them enthralled rather than throwing barbs at each other over who's got the prettiest dress or whatever.

This is not what I expected at all.

The traditionalists have warmed up to Chloe a lot faster than they warmed up to the idea of me living at home with my mortal family. It got to the point Mr. Wolent had to issue an official edict prohibiting anyone from turning other small children into vampires. He's concerned about people getting used to Chloe's presence, 'wanting one of their own' and having Easter Rabbit syndrome. Meaning, they make a kid vampire because they think it will be awesome... then get tired of the kid or realize they're a lot of work, and abandon them somewhere down the line.

Heh. I wonder if Dad would have loved to be turned into a vampire somewhere between age ten and thirteen. He always talks about missing his childhood. Honestly, I'm sure he's only venting about wanting a break from having to be a responsible adult. He looks back fondly on a time when he didn't have any real worries. Dad doesn't want to be a literal child again. He's trying to get us to enjoy being young and not want to rush through it with the whole 'I can't wait until I can drive' thing.

Dad's fantasies are totally ignoring all the inconvenient parts of being a kid. The past is, after all, viewed through rose-colored lenses.

I smile at nothing in particular. Fate got me just about perfectly. I'm old enough to fake it at adulting when I have to and young enough to goof off like a child most of the time. Alas, I only get a few minutes of feeling happy and content with the Universe before motion coming toward me snaps me back to reality.

Mr. Wolent, Stefano, and their associated hangers-on are heading in my direction. George Washington is with them, too. No, it's not really George Washington. That guy didn't get turned into a vampire... at least I don't think he did. Pretty sure someone by now would have told me that. The man in the fancy getup (that is way more modern than my gown while still looking antiquated) is much younger than George Washington. This guy's gotta be somewhere between eighteen and twenty-two. He's carrying himself with a posture that doesn't belong in the modern era. Head slightly raised, right arm at his chest, poise and so on. He's kinda dashing, to be honest. Light brown hair, chiseled jawline. Not the most muscular critter in the world, but he's Hollywood handsome.

I can't help myself thanks to this gown. When the group finally reaches me, I curtsey at them.

Ouch. That hurt.

Stefano sort of rolls his eyes at me.

Wolent seems amused. The four other hanger-on vampires don't react.

"Sorry. It's the dress. Just kinda felt like I should do that." I force a smile past the raging ache in my belly.

Mr. Wolent gives me a brief look of sympathy. He's absolutely aware of my injury. The guy totally saw something unusual in my expression and looked into my thoughts out of concern. At least it's minor enough not to deserve mention.

"Sarah." Mr. Wolent gestures at the hot guy. "This is Eldon Whittmore."

I'm not sure if I'm being a wiseass or just tripping into character because of this silly gown. Without even thinking, I offer my hand like some woman in an Elizabethan court. "A pleasure to meet you, Mr. Whittmore." Oh, good grief, I damn near called him 'Lord Whittmore.'

Not missing a beat, Eldon offers a bow and kisses my knuckles. "The pleasure is mine, lass."

Ooh. He's got a British accent.

Stefano doesn't look impressed. He kinda reminds me of a teacher whose students just cracked a joke at his expense, but he didn't quite get the meaning. He thinks I'm somehow making fun of him, but isn't sure enough of intentional mockery to call me on it. Honestly, I'm not trying to make fun of anyone here.

Mr. Wolent picks up on that and forces himself not to smile. "I'd like for you to do us a favor, Sarah."

This is him giving me a job. Okay. No worries. I signed up for this. "Of course. Should I go talk to the usual guy for the firebomb?"

Everyone except Eldon—yes, Stefano as well—chuckles.

I think Mr. Wolent found that funny because I was mostly serious. Most of the time I get asked to do a favor for the 'organization,' it's them wanting to leverage my sun tolerance to FedEx a boom boom somewhere. And wow, 'Fedex a Boom Boom' sounds like it ought to be a Gwar song. Yes, I know of Gwar. A boy I dated briefly before Scott was really into them.

"Not this time, my dear." Mr. Wolent chuckles. "I think you'll find this favor much less stressful. Eldon has recently joined us in Seattle. Unfortunately, he's been out of the loop for a while and could use a guide for the modern world."

"Oh." I blink. "Umm. Okay."

Mr. Wolent pats Eldon on the arm. "Since you're both about the same age, insofar as you appear to be, I figured you would be the best person to help him acclimate. Spend some time in each other's company, maybe show him around the city, get him used to how things have changed and how the younger people of today should act."

"I can do that." I nod at him, then at Eldon. "You can basically just call me whenever you want to get started."

Eldon nods, then hesitates, head cocked. "What shall I call you?"

"No, I mean like with a phone."

"Phone?" Eldon's eyes flutter in a rapid blink of confusion.

"Oh boy," says Ashley, swooping up beside me. "This is going to be a project."

"Madame…" Eldon bows and kisses Ashley's knuckles.

She makes a 'is this guy for real' face at me, eyes bulging from the urge to laugh—though she holds it in.

"I should thank you two fine young ladies, by the by." Eldon flashes a knowing smile.

"Thank us?" I blink. "Showing you around town isn't exactly that big a deal."

"Ahh." He chuckles. "Of course you wouldn't recognize me. The two of you freed me from that crypt a few nights prior."

I stare, jaw open.

Ashley squeaks.

This drop-dead handsome movie star looking guy is the same withered 'overcooked fried chicken' head we found in the mine? Are you serious?

"Seriously?" I blurt.

"Verily," says Eldon.

"Huh?" Ashley blinks.

"That means yes," adds Stefano.

Eldon dusts at his coat. "Allow me to apologize for frightening you. I was not feeling very put together that night."

Oof. Dad would love this guy.

"It's all right." I wave dismissively. "I have the hell scared out of me at least once a week these days."

Mr. Wolent smiles at us, then pats Eldon on the shoulder again before wandering off to do big important vampire things—and leaving Eldon with Ashley and me.

Yeah, he's really damn pretty but, I'm only admiring the view. He's so damn handsome I feel like a tween again having romantic daydreams about a movie poster with Orlando Bloom's Legolas on it. Pure fantasy that will never be possible. No, I'm in love with Hunter, and this man's perfect-as-hell face isn't going to change that.

All I have to do is play tour guide for a bit.

I can do that.

ANOTHER ORBIT 'ROUND
THE SUN

FRIDAY, OCTOBER 18, 2019

I woke up a few minutes after three today.

That's improvement. Aurélie's remedy seems to be working to speed up the healing process. I'm still sore, but it's more of a nagging annoyance rather than making me not want to move. I've been thinking about the conversation with Ashley over birthdays and how, past a certain age, people don't generally have parties.

It will probably be a while before Sierra ever willingly attends a birthday pool party again. At least until she gets used to the whole cycle thing. I am somewhat concerned for her. Not sure how a tampon is going to handle a supernaturally excessive amount of blood. Hope it doesn't like, build up pressure and fire the tampon out of her like a champagne cork. Also, who knows if her next time will be as bad. Guess it's a case of crossing that bridge when we get to it.

So, yeah. Birthday parties.

Today is Mom's birthday. We don't usually have a party for her. Dad usually takes her out to dinner, just the two of them, on her birthday. That is happening today, too. Ashley and I took care of feeding the Littles. Before I was old enough to be left unsupervised near a stove, we'd end up at the grandparents' house for dinner.

So, yeah. We're going to surprise Mom with a mini-party and cake when she gets home. Sure, I could go overboard, tracking down and kidnapping her high school friends. Seems a bit excessive and would more than likely result in a big mess. So, nah. Not inviting friends over for her party like she's still a kid.

While Mom's still at work, Ashley and I conspire with the Littles for Operation Mom Cake. The name was Sam's idea. Sophia went to Mrs. Carter's house to hijack the kitchen so Dad doesn't know a cake is on the way. She and Mrs. C have the baking part covered. Ashley's on decorations and games. I'm dealing with the gifts. Since we're kinda doing this 'have a birthday party like a kid, adulting sucks' theme, the gifts are all going to be stuff one might give a high school-aged girl for her birthday. Within reason, I mean. No iPhones, for example.

I got a list of input from the Littles and Ashley, then went shopping. It's fun stuff. A boy-band album, a Bratz doll, a music box, stuff like that. Each item is going to be 'from' one of the Littles, Me, or Ashley. We're trying to make her smile, not lavish her with expensive stuff.

It all comes together once she gets home from work. Doesn't take her too long to get all fancied up and go out with Dad for dinner. How messed up would it be if they ended up going to Garibaldi's? I haven't mentioned to them it's part of Wolent's empire. Doesn't really matter.

Once the 'rents are out of the house, Ashley and I go into high gear, decorating the dining room with Happy Birthday stuff. Somewhere, an elder vampire is rolling in his crypt at us using our accelerated reflexes to do this. Gotta get everything ready before they're home.

Ash got a 'pin the tail on a donkey' game for the party. She's also pulled a stack of board games from the closet so Mom can pick one. Not sure if my mother's going to be a good sport and play pin the tail.

That really is more for little kids. But hey, Ashley thought it would be cute even if it's only scenery and we don't play it.

Chloe flies across the cul-de-sac to tell Mrs. Carter it's time and she should bring the cake over.

She's left the front door open. I start toward it, shaking my head, and spot Mr. Niedermeyer on his porch. He's in a wheelchair and rubbing his eyes after having seen Chloe literally fly past him. Oh boy. That's not good.

Mr. Neidermeyer stops rubbing his eyes and looks around. He doesn't seem angry, mostly confused. I get the feeling he thinks he hallucinated a flying child. Whew. Close call. Remind me to tell her to be more careful. Hey, maybe Sophia's spell will make him forget seeing her in a little while. Speaking of which, she hasn't said anything yet about having caught the stray magic that ran off. Wonder if she got it or if it's still hiding somewhere like a magical land mine?

Hmm. I'm kinda tempted to go check on Neidermeyer later. See if he's okay, needs anything done around the house. At least he's home and acting pretty normal. From a distance, it doesn't look like he's got dementia or anything. Had to be the bonk to the head that left him loopy.

A rectangle of light from Ashley's house brightens as the front door opens. Eep!

I stare at Neidermeyer and poke him with a mild compulsion to go inside. He turns the wheelchair half a second before Chloe comes flying back to the house. She'd have gone right past him.

"Chloe!" I grab her as she zooms in the door. "You have to be more careful."

"I didn't crash." She hugs me.

"Not that. Neidermeyer was right there on his porch. He saw you flying."

Kiddo's expression goes from smiling to 'oh crap' in an instant. "Oops!"

"We got lucky this time." I set her on her feet. "Just before you take off outside, look around to make sure there's no one watching."

"Okay," says Chloe in a somewhat sheepish tone.

I pat her on the head. "It's okay. I know you're just excited for Mom's birthday party."

She offers an apologetic smile, then nods, then hugs me.

Blix babbles in demonic from the stairs. I glace over at him.

He's wearing a headset and staring into the screen of Sam's laptop.

"They're on the way back," calls Sam. "ETA eleven minutes."

I blink at the imp. "You guys bugged Mom's Yukon?"

Blix pokes at the laptop keyboard, acting all serious.

"Nah. The computer's not even on. He's being a goof," says Sam.

We all hide in the dining room, waiting in silence while trying to contain our nervous excitement. Really, I'm the only one who's nervous. Really hope Mom doesn't freak out.

Eventually, a wash of headlights pans across the front of the house, getting close. Yep. The 'rents are back. Of course, now that everyone is trying extra hard to remain quiet, we're making more noise than before.

The engine cuts off. Doors open and slam. Mom's high heels click on the driveway, then the sidewalk, then the small concrete slab pretending to be a front porch. Dad's keys jingle.

"That was wonderful," says Mom.

"I'm glad you enjoyed it."

They kiss.

Ugh. I could really have done without hearing that.

The crunch of a key going into the lock follows. Squeaking hinges announce the door opening. The 'rents come inside. Front door closes. Rustling tells me they're taking their shoes off. I give Chloe the 'now' signal.

She darts out of hiding into the archway separating dining room from living room. "Gran'ma, c'mere."

"Just a moment, sweetie. We just got in the door." Mom chuckles.

"It's important. You gotta see this!" Chloe bounces on her toes.

Mom gives a faint sigh. Kiddo really is irresistible. "What is it?"

Chloe waves for her to come over and backs into the dining room.

The instant Mom walks into view, we all yell. Mrs. Carter, Ashley, and I shout 'Happy birthday,' while everyone else goes for the more predictable call of 'surprise.'

"What on Earth?" Mom looks around at the decorations.

Dad appears behind Mom. He looks surprised for a half second, then fixates on the cake. "Ooh. There's cake."

Mom sets her fists against her hips, seemingly working hard not to laugh. "Whose idea was this?"

Everyone points at me.

Mom shifts her gaze my way. "You guys didn't have to do this."

"I know, but I wanted to." I grin. "Ash and I were talking the other day about how weird it is that adults don't really have birthday parties anymore, so we wanted to have one for you."

She approaches the table, slightly shaking her head. "After twenty-one, there's not really much left to celebrate. And even twenty-one's only a big deal if you like drinking."

"There's presents!" Sam gestures at the cluster of gift-wrapped boxes.

Much to my relief, Mom tolerates being a birthday girl. We all watch her open the gifts, laughing at the assortment of stuff no one in their right mind would give an adult woman for her birthday.

"Thank you, everyone." Mom looks over her loot. "Not really sure what to say."

Somehow, I think she's going to treasure this stuff. The way she's gazing at all the gifts makes me think they're going to occupy an honored place on a shelf in her room. Hey, if grown men can collect Star Wars toys, why can't Mom have a Bratz doll?

Sam looks up at Dad. "What did you get Mom for her birthday?"

"Well…" He rocks back on his heels. "I was going to whisk her off to a beach resort in Cancun for a weekend of unbridled passion…"

The Littles (and I) cringe.

"However, your mother had a much less grandiose request. She wanted to spend time with the family. Movie night?"

"After cake?" asks Sam.

"Of course."

The glass patio door in the kitchen shudders, then slides open all by itself. A heavy wind blasts through the house along with a pungent sulfur smell. Deep breathing drifts toward us along with the sense of a heavy dread presence.

Mom and Sophia freeze like mice in the highway staring at an oncoming car. Sierra tenses.

"It's just Max," says Sam. "He wants to be part of the birthday party."

"Oh. Umm." Mom looks at the nothingness in the hallway. "All right, I suppose. He's not going to shed on the couch, is he?"

"No." Sam chuckles.

A happy canine grunt accompanies a blast of warm, moist air that throws Chloe's hair back like a flag for a few seconds.

We have cake and play pin-the-tail. Yes, Mom participates. Chloe has a blast. And yes, it's child safe. The tails are magnetized, not literal pins.

One large piece of cake gradually disappears nibble by nibble from a plate on the floor.

Sophia runs around collecting empty plates and ferrying them to the kitchen.

"All right then." Dad claps his hands together in anticipatory glee. "Movie time."

Sierra folds her arms. "Movie night? But we do that all the time. We should do something special for Mom's birthday."

"Having you all here *is* something special," says Mom.

"Cheese alert," deadpans Sierra.

Sophia and Sam chuckle.

"That's fine." Mom drifts over and hugs Sierra. "I love cheese." She gives Dad side eye. "I also wouldn't mind a weekend in Cancun sometime."

Dad wags his eyebrows. "I don't remember where I put my swimsuit. It's been a while."

"Who said anything about us needing swimsuits?" Mom winks at him.

The Littles squirm and rapidly nope out of the dining room, heading for the sofa.

Chloe remains, head tilted. "Why would you go to Cancun if you aren't going to go swimming?"

Mom and Dad crack up.

I take Chloe's hand. "C'mon. It's movie time."

21

AT LONG LAST

FRIDAY (LATER)

onight, we watch *The Ice Pirates.*

Okay, it's funny. I mean, sure it looks dated. Not a big deal. For the year they made it, the effects are pretty good. And obviously, it's a comedy, so the studio didn't go massive with the budget. Not terribly bad for kids either, though the 'space herpie' joke went right over the Littles' heads. The way the little slimy thing zoomed off down the corridor totally reminds me of the stray magic carpet lump. Sophia laughs, since she got that reference now. She still doesn't understand what herpes is for real. The Littles all think herpes is a nasty little space slug thing. I'm glad none of them asked for more information.

Given Mom and Ashley's reactions, I think Sierra suspects an adults-only joke happened.

After the movie ends, it's late enough that Mom sends the Littles off to bed, mostly Sam. Sierra can stay up for maybe another thirty minutes—in her room—before going to bed. I do the uncool thing of hanging out with my parents for a while. Never once have I claimed to be one of the cool kids, though.

The parents get 'tired' a few minutes after ten. This is unusual. They almost always stay up until eleven. Sometimes, Dad even stays up until midnight. Them being 'tired' this early means only one thing: I'm going to have a fourth sibling… or at least they're going to go through the motions of trying to make one.

Ack.

La la la la la. I don't need to think about this.

With my fingers metaphorically in my ears so I don't hear them talking cute, I hurry down to the basement. Chloe occupies herself with a PlayStation portable. Ash resumes watching anime. I decide to call Hunter. He should still be awake. It's only like 10:13 p.m. now. Hunter's usually up until at least midnight finishing homework.

I would've called him earlier, except for it being Mom's birthday and her wanting the family together. Now that everyone is on the way to bed and my parents are… yeah, not going there.

"Hey," says Hunter. "I was just thinking about you."

"Weird coincidence. I was thinking about you, too." I idly scratch my fingernails over my stomach. Ack! Crap. Ouch. Stupid habit. I need to not do that for a few more days.

"You okay? What was that gasp?"

"War wound." I grumble. "Nothing serious. I'll be fine. So, I was wondering if you were going to be up for a little while. Kinda wanted to talk to you a—" Beep.

Argh. Call waiting. I don't recognize the number, so I ignore it.

"What?" asks Hunter.

"Sorry. Stupid call waiting. Don't freak out. We need to talk. It's not bad."

He's quiet for like twenty seconds. "Umm, sure. When do you want—?"

Beep.

Argh!

"I was thinking of popping over now, if you're—"

Beep.

Someone's getting their face ripped off.

"Sarah? Are you still there?" asks Hunter.

"Yeah. Stupid call waiting. Hang on. Whoever this is keeps calling back. I'm going to tear them a new butthole."

He chuckles. "Hope you're not being literal."

"Hah. No."

Beep.

"Argh!" I fume. "Be right back." I tap the button to swap lines. "Hello?"

No one says anything. I wait like twenty seconds and repeat, "Hello."

Something clanks in the background. Then my eardrum explodes under the blare of button tone.

"Gah!" I jump, yanking the iPhone away from my head.

Whoever is on the other end stops holding down the button. They hit a few more buttons. Sounds like a cat walking over a telephone.

"Hello?" I yell. "Who is this?"

"Where is the… how does this infernal thing work?" asks Eldon.

Ugh. I sigh at the ceiling. "Eldon? You don't have to do anything. We're already connected. Just talk into the phone. I can hear you."

"Sarah?"

"Yep. That's meee."

"Excellent. Sorry to bother you." Eldon clears his throat. "I was hoping that perchance you might have the time and inclination to begin tonight?"

Ashley pauses the anime to look over at me.

Eldon sounds far away.

"You have to hold the phone closer to your face. No, uhh, ordinary person would be able to hear you."

Lots of clattering and bumping come over the line. What the hell? Is he trying to juggle the phone?

Dammit. I really wanted to have 'the talk' with Hunter tonight. No, I'm not looking for sex. Still too sore. Bleh. Crap. It's late anyway. Hunter needs his sleep. Can't leave him hanging though.

"Is this an improvement?" asks Eldon, sounding much more normal for a telephone conversation.

"Yes. Okay, sure. I'm a little involved with something at the moment. How does midnight sound?"

"Quite amenable, lass." He pauses. "Shall we meet at Mr. Wolent's estate?"

"Yeah, that'll work. See you there."

"All right then."

We sit there listening to silence for a moment.

"Sarah? What am I supposed to do with this phone now?"

"Is it an Android or an iPhone? Or something else?"

More fumbling thunders in my ear. "I've not the bloodiest idea. How can I tell?"

"Is there a little apple shaped drawing on the back of it?"

Banging, clattering. "If there is, I am unable to locate it."

"Honey," says Vanessa Prentice in the background. "What are you doing?"

"Looking for the apple," replies Eldon.

"What?" Vanessa laughs. More rattling. "Hello? Who is this?"

"Hi, Vanessa. It's Sarah. Eldon didn't know how to end the call. Was trying to figure out what kind of phone he's using."

She cackles. Wicked Witch of the West, anyone? That's not fair. She's really not that bad a person. Just gets a bit catty around Aurélie (or any woman hot enough to be a threat). She likes me and Ashley. I'm girl next door and Ash is too cute. Neither one of us are smoking hot supermodels, so we're not a threat to her superiority.

"Oh, hilarious." Vanessa snickers. "He's on one of the desk phones. I'll help him figure it out."

"Thanks."

The line goes dead.

Wow. This guy is really out of touch.

I flick back to the call with Hunter. "I'm coming over right now."

"Okay. Can't wait to see you."

Ash perks up. "Mind if I go with you when you're taking Eldon out?"

I fake grumble. "We're not 'going out.' I'm just showing him around."

"Uh huh." She winks.

"Seriously. I'm not horny for him." I smile at my phone.

"Whoa." Chloe looks up from her PSP. "We have horns, too?"

I'M STILL LAUGHING WHEN I REACH HUNTER'S WINDOW.

Maybe it's wrong of me to lie to Chloe but I'm not going to talk about sex with an eternal seven-year-old. So, yeah. She thinks vampires sprout devil horns when we get really super mega angry. Hopefully, she forgets that before it becomes an issue.

Hunter opens his window. I fly into an embrace, kiss him, and stand there for a moment, enjoying having his scent wash all over me.

"Is something wrong, Sarah?" he asks after the silence becomes intolerable.

"No. Just not the kind of conversation to have over a phone." I keep holding his hand and guide him over to the bed, then sit on the edge of the mattress.

"You're not pregnant, are you?"

The total sincerity in his eyes when he asks that is too much for me. I flop over backward and laugh until I'm crying.

"Oh, wow, uhh." Hunter rakes a hand up through his hair. "Suppose that was a really stupid thing to ask, wasn't it?"

"Just a bit." I cover my mouth, my hand half lost in the long sleeve of my sweatshirt.

"Oh, ouch." He leans over me, pushes the sweatshirt up, and ever so gently traces his fingers over the red marks. "What happened?"

"Someone tried to assassinate Glim. I happened to be too close."

"Want me to kiss it and make it better?" He smiles.

"Yes, but if you do that, I'm going to start thinking certain things and then wanting to do stuff I'm too sore to do right now."

Hunter plants the most innocent little kiss on my belly, then pulls the sweatshirt down to cover the red marks. "I hope whoever did that to you paid for it."

"Yep. They're dog chow."

"Good." He sits next to me, then stretches back beside me with his head propped up in one hand. "What did you want to talk about?"

"Eternity."

"Oh, is that all?" He chuckles.

I grin. "Yeah. That's all. I want you to be with me forever. Don't want to watch you get old and go away. Really don't want to have people call the cops on us in forty years if they catch us kissing."

He laughs. "You don't look like a little kid."

"Ugh." I sigh at the ceiling. "You're the only one in Washington State who thinks that."

"You do it on purpose."

"What?" I lift my head to look at him.

"When you're trying to be sneaky or unnoticed or avoid conflict, you do kinda look a bit childish." He plays with my hair. "When you're with me, you don't. It's almost like you can control how other people see you."

Huh. I've never noticed that... then again, how would I? If I'm mind-tweaking people subconsciously, there would be no way for me to even realize. Still even if I legit look nineteen, people would not be comfortable watching me make out with a sixty-year-old man. That's all kinds of icky, even if it *is* Hunter.

I reach over and brush my hand down his cheek, savoring the texture of his stubble. "I know you've said you don't care about the normal life, having kids with a mortal woman and all that stuff."

"You want me to become a vampire, too."

"Only if it's what you want, and you're absolutely sure you want it. I have this weird hangup about the whole death thing. That's why I've been acting so weird. Makes no sense. I want you to be with me forever, but the thought that you'll have to technically die first is freaking me out."

His heart rate picks up. "It kinda freaks me out, too, but I'd do it without hesitation if it means I can spend the rest of forever with you."

I roll into his arms. "Are you sure it's what you want? Is there any chance we're being stupid teenagers and you're going to end up hating me in twenty years for doing that to you?"

He kisses me on the forehead. "I thought you didn't want to be the one to do it."

"I don't. I can't." A shiver runs down my body. "Not sure I'm even going to be able to watch it happen if we get there. I meant doing it to you like talking you into it."

"I'm sure."

We lay there, nose to nose, talking about a potential future in which we're both vampires. As soon as the opportunity presents itself, I slip in Glim's suggestion of waiting a few years.

"Where did that come from?" asks Hunter. "Thought you wanted to do this?"

"I do. But... think about it." I kiss him. "Age is a bit different for guys than girls, right? A boy at nineteen is still a punk kid."

He laughs.

"People might take you more seriously if you're like twenty-two when we do it. And that's not too old to be with a girl my age. Also gives you a chance to finish school and stuff."

"Not like I'm going into the workforce if I'm a vampire."

"True, but if you still feel this way in a couple years, then we'll both know it's not some crazy out of control teenage hormone crush thing and what we have is real."

He traces a finger across my jawline. "I can tell you what we have is real. If it makes you feel better, I'm happy to wait. Why hurry when we have eternity ahead of us?"

"Yeah." I hug him tight. "Maybe I won't be able to wait three whole years. Still feels like a long time."

He brushes a hand over my head. "What's three years compared to forever?"

"A long time." I playfully frown. "I'm stuck at eighteen, remember? Time is weird."

"I'm okay with waiting a little if it will help you not feel guilty about stealing my mortal future." He winks. "Besides, when I'm twenty-three or whatever, maybe I'll be as mature as you are now."

"Hah. That's not really true. Boys don't mature more slowly than girls. We just get judged more harshly for acting immature."

Hunter purses his lips. "That part is true, but I still think girls mature faster. You don't usually see girls trying to jump off the roof of a two-story house into a pool or lighting their farts on fire."

That makes me snort laugh.

I lay there in his arms for a far-too-fleeting twenty-ish minutes. We talk about the future. I'm sure Ashley won't mind having him around as a vampire. Our little family grows by one. Hunter's house is massive. His basement's practically a catacomb. A whole coven of vampires could live down there. Not that I want to leave home, but he's definitely got a place to sleep after he commits to the Transference.

Now the big question remains: who the heck is going to sire him? I'm going to have to do a bit of research and probably a whole lot of butt kissing. I can worry about all of that later.

"Ugh. I need to go. Work calls. Don't be jealous."

"Of the immortality?" He grins. "Why would I be?"

Sigh. "No, not that. I've gotta play tour guide for this other vampire. He's Hollywood cute, but I am not interested in him."

Hunter goes blank. There it is. A little jealousy. The boy does have functional emotions. It's not distrust, though. He believes me.

"Seriously. It's just a job. Like I'm the low-level secretary who got asked to show the new guy around the office. Just escorting him around Seattle."

"Escort?"

"Hah. No, not like that. Literally only showing him the city and helping him figure out how to behave like a, umm… young adult."

"How old is this dude?" Hunter raises an eyebrow.

"Dunno. Looks like he's maybe twenty. Anyone's guess how old he really is. He's not used to modern times."

He leans forward and kisses me on the lips. "I hate that you have to go, but I understand. Wish we could have more time together. Stupid job, stupid school…"

I kiss him back. "We'll have all the time in the world… eventually."

He smiles, then gets this almost worried look. "What about Ro or Mom?"

"Well…" I sit up and drape my arms across my knees. "Ro already knows about vampires, so it's not like you'll have to hide anything from him. He'll probably think it's cool. Your mother? Umm. She doesn't know. We don't have to tell her anything. You also don't have to fake your death to her. We can just make her not think it's unusual that you're not getting any older."

"Will that work?"

"Yeah. Not too hard. I mean, look at Keanu Reeves." I laugh. "Some celebrities never seem to get any older… at least not in a few decades before it, uhh… won't be a big deal."

He looks down. "Yeah."

"Are you sure you don't want to give her grandkids?" I bite my lip, suddenly terrified he might change his mind. "It would be okay if you wanted to do that."

"Mom will understand." He squeezes my hand. "I'll make sure Ronan knows he needs to take care of that. Even if I have to mind control his little ass to settle down."

Anxiety bursts out into laughter.

My iPhone alarm beeps at me.

"Ugh! Shit. I really need to get going." I kiss him a third time. "I love you, Hunter Lawrence."

He stares deep into my eyes. "I love you, Sarah Wright. Enough to die for you."

"Lay it on a little thicker, why don't you." I poke him in the side.

He chuckles. "Kinda being literal there."

"I know. I know…" I head for the window. "That's the one part of this that still makes me feel all weird. See you soon."

"Be careful out there." He gets up and walks with me to the window.

"I will. Oh, keep an eye out for ghouls," I whisper.

"Ghouls?"

"Rickety undead. They've been coming after me lately for some stupid reason." I grumble. "They're really weak. Even a mortal should be able to take them out. Break their neck and they disintegrate. I doubt they'll bother you, though. But they might end up around here looking for me."

He glances at the baseball bat leaning on the wall by the nightstand. "Okay."

One more time, I sneak a quick kiss, then leap out the window.

How is it possible I can be this relieved, worried, excited, nervous, and happy all at the same time?

Something's going to blow up in my face soon. I just hope whatever it is, it's a manageable catastrophe.

22

A CREDIT CARD AND
LEPRECHAUN GOLD

FRIDAY (EVEN LATER)

On tonight's episode of 'Sarah probably shouldn't have done that,' I've decided to bring Chloe with us. It's maybe twenty minutes to eleven at night. The 'rents are sleeping already—or still doing things I'd rather not picture. Not going to risk going up there ask if they'll watch kiddo only to see something that will send me straight to Aurélie for a memory wipe.

I can't say it's completely unheard of for seven-year-olds to be outside at this hour. That happens sometimes, though there are usually some sort of complicating circumstances. Road trip gone wrong, getting lost looking for a hotel, or coming home late from a relative's house after some major holiday. That sort of thing. People don't generally let little kids run around outside playing at night.

Good thing we're not running around and playing.

We're just going to Wolent's manor to meet Eldon.

Oh, yeah, then running around Seattle for a while. Sigh. At least that's the plan. Oh, I suppose Vanessa or someone at the manor might be willing to watch her for a few hours. That's less of a problem than dragging the kid around outside where people might see her. Okay, maybe this isn't totally stupid of me. I'm sure Ashley would have caved in and stayed home with her if it really came down to it, but she really wanted to go with me tonight.

She hasn't been talking at all about wanting to try hooking up with Eldon or anything of that nature. Her mood reminds me of how she used to get when we were like fifteen and about to go to a One Direction concert or something. Can't really call it fangirling because this guy isn't famous.

Whatever.

Ash and I get dressed in our usual normal outfits. I'm doing the T-shirt and jeans thing with sneakers. My shirt is black with red Japanese writing on it spelling out 'Akira.' Her outfit is similar but ever so slightly different enough to be 'Ashley': pink T-shirt and a denim skirt instead of jeans. She's presently carrying her shoes. Those ballet flat style things fall off all the time while flying. Chloe's having one of the uncommon days where she's doing a Sierra, as in *not* wearing a dress. Kiddo's also in a T-shirt and jeans today, with *Sponge Bob* sneakers. Her shirt's lavender with a cute anime samurai girl on it trying to look menacing.

It's about as threatening as a hamster.

We go upstairs to the kitchen and slip out the patio door. The backyard smells like rotting flesh and sulphur. Either hellhounds fart after eating birthday cake or another ghoul made the mistake of trying to get to the house from behind. I should probably be more alarmed than I am at the thought a ghoul or two showed up at the house. They found me at Hunter's, so it's pretty obviously impossible to keep my home a secret from them. Somehow, these creatures can just find me. At least they're only a minor nuisance. Honestly, the ghouls are *less* annoying than those people on the street at SCC who keep trying to hand out spiritual literature. The only reason the 'pamphlet commandos' are more annoying is that it's not socially acceptable to kill them where they stand.

Yes, I am kidding. Not going to kill a mortal randomly just for being annoying. Also, I'm pretty sure they wouldn't disintegrate into a nice tidy cloud of pale grey dust. I'd have to hide the body afterward, and that's a real pain.

Seriously, though. I should probably do something about this ghoul problem eventually.

We take a quick look around for spectators, then leap into the air.

Chloe can't help but give off a little squeal of delight every time we start flying. It's almost as if every time is the first time for her. While her mind is frozen forever as a child her age, she isn't like a goldfish. Kiddo doesn't forget everything she learns every time she goes to sleep at sunrise. It's more that her thinking process, attitude, and perception of time are never going to change. Forever an innocent child, so to speak. Some people might think this is sad. I don't. Yeah, she'll always need a caretaker, but it isn't like her mind will develop into an adult woman trapped inside a child's body. Having an adult attitude and desires in a body that couldn't manage them would suck.

She'd basically be Sierra.

Though in my sister's case, I don't mean romantic stuff. More like Sierra wants to be a grown up with the freedoms that go along with that, plus be a big, tough ass-kicker who keeps the Forces of Evil™ away from our family despite having the body of a scrawny preteen. At least in her case, she will eventually grow up—unlike a vampire.

My mind wanders around somber thoughts as we fly, in total disregard to the gleeful expression on Chloe's face. Watching her so happy while the wind whips her jet-black hair around her pale face gets me all sorts of angry at the Universe again. How is it even remotely fair that such a cute, lovable, innocent kid like her ended up with such cruel, sadistic parents? Or worse, the world has a lot of innocent kids who endure horrors as bad or worse than what she went through.

The surge of joy that comes from her every time we leap into the sky makes me think she's somehow aware that she's free, able to zoom away from all the bad memories and evil down on the ground.

Or, maybe she simply finds flying awesome.

It really is.

Okay, Sarah. Enough with the depressing thoughts. Kiddo is not thinking about her past life. She's gleefully adoring the fact we can flagrantly violate the law of gravity.

Going to Wolent's manor isn't an incredibly long flight. Takes us a couple minutes before the property comes into view. Talk about hard to miss from the air. His giant reflecting pool is impressive. I've never bothered to ask or go researching, though I wonder what the mortal world thinks of this place. Like, who do they believe lives here? It's probably a form of the 800-pound gorilla joke.

As in, what does an 800-pound gorilla eat for breakfast? Anything it wants.

Who do the mortals believe lives here? Anything Mr. Wolent wants.

And yes, Dad told me that joke years ago. Crazy how we remember the dumbest things forever, right?

We dive out of the air and swoop in for a landing in the little courtyard by the house's main entrance among a handful of nice black Cadillacs parked in the pavement circle. This place is the size of a hotel. It doesn't really have a porch, per se. As always, Aziz stands sentinel by the front door. I almost feel sorry for him. That's got to be a seriously boring job.

Eldon's already outside, having a conversation with Aziz. The big guy is what some people might call a 'man of few words,' though he doesn't seem annoyed by Eldon's attempts to make small talk. He's probably being so quiet because Eldon's going on about weird things like sailing ships and trade goods prices. I'm sure discussing the price of tea is, to Eldon, like guys today talking about football.

And yeah, he's still dressed like he just walked off the stage from a production of *Hancock*.

"Oof," I mutter to myself. "First thing we're going to need to do is get him some clothes."

"Are you sure?" Ashley grins. "His outfit is pretty revolutionary."

"Ugh." I hang my head.

Chloe peers up at us, confused. It takes her a second, but she eventually senses a pun happened even if she didn't get it. "Boo."

That's her standard reaction to a pun. I can tell she didn't understand it because she didn't groan, roll her eyes, or laugh.

"Ahh, excellent." Eldon spots us and waves in greeting before walking down the four steps from the porch to the pavement.

Ashley and I get hand kisses. Eldon pats Chloe on the head. She gives him a 'really' stare, but doesn't complain.

"I do appreciate your willingness to assist me on such short notice," says Eldon.

"It's all right." Ashley fidgets.

Yeah, she's staring at him kinda like how I'd imagine she'd have stared at the One Direction guys if they walked right up to us to say hello.

"Where shall we begin? It seems there is much for me to learn." Eldon gazes around at the distant city lights.

"First thing we need to do is get you some less antiquated clothes." I bat at the frills hanging from his collar. "If you go outside like this, people are going to stare."

Ashley nods. "Yeah. And take pictures."

"I dare say if I see someone setting up a photography apparatus, I should be able to distance myself before they are able to employ it." Eldon peers at me confused.

"Oh wow." I chuckle. "You're thinking of those big old wooden camera things with the black cape on them or something?"

He quirks an eyebrow at me, making a face as if I just tried to describe a car to a modern person as 'one of those things with wheels'.

"Umm." I pull out my iPhone. "This is a phone."

Eldon blinks. "Was not the device upon the desk a telephone?"

"Yeah." Ashley nods. "They're both phones, but the desk one is an older style. Everyone... well, almost everyone today has these."

"Where is the wire?" Eldon leans closer, peering at my phone.

"It doesn't have a wire. It's like radio, basically," I say.

"Radio?"

Ashley slaps herself in the forehead. "Wow. What year are you from?"

"I met my mortal demise in 1852." Eldon grimaces, making me think the process hadn't been pleasant.

"Uhh." Ashley pulls out her phone. Her thumbs blur. "Google says radios weren't really popular until the 1920s."

"Right…" I exhale, then give Eldon a super basic explanation of the idea of radio waves.

He nods. "I believe I am following you. What does a telephone have to do with your worry about photography?"

That's an easy explanation. I show him my phone, then snap a close-up of Ashley's face, then show him the image. "Every phone like this has a camera in it."

Eldon gawks at me as though I'd just grabbed a live baby, pulled on it really hard, and cartoonishly produced two separate fully intact babies. I'm sure he's wondering how one of those old, massive Wild West era cameras got squeezed down into an iPhone.

"That's in color…" He stares in awe at my phone, looking back and forth between the screen and Ashley. "Do people mount these phones on their walls after taking the photograph?"

Ashley and I chuckle.

Chloe leans close to me and whispers, "Did someone drop this guy on his head?"

That makes Eldon laugh.

I nudge her. "No, kiddo. He's just really old. Eldon dealing with smartphones is like the time Dad asked me if I knew what the relationship was between a tape cassette and a pencil."

"Ooh." Ashley grumbles. "He wouldn't even tell us. Just kept laughing."

"Google to the rescue." I smirk, then look back to Eldon. "No, people don't put their phones into picture frames…"

I spend a few minutes explaining the concept of digital images, email, the internet, and printers.

"… so basically," adds Ashley. "If one person snaps our picture with one of these"—she wags her phone at him—"that image can be all over the world in five minutes."

Eldon stares at us. The sound of rusty gears grinding is almost audible.

"The point is… if you're going to do something that is obviously supernatural, try to make sure no one is around to take video of it."

"Video?" Eldon tilts his head. "Were we not just discussing photography? What is a video?"

"Ugh. Video is basically a whole ton of pictures put together so it moves." I demonstrate by taking a video of Ashley making goofy faces, then play it back for him.

Eldon points at the phone. "Oh, like a rather small television."

"Yes!" I exhale in relief. Clearly, someone in the manor already showed him TV. "So, first order of business is to get you some less conspicuous clothing. We should go to the Gap."

"Which gap?" asks Eldon.

"*The* Gap," I say.

He ponders for a moment. "There is a canyon nearby significant enough for everyone to understand your meaning?"

"The Grand Canyon is a big-ass hole." Chloe grins, fully aware that what she said could easily have been mis-heard.

Ashley sputters into a laugh.

I'm not going to make a big deal out of it. Don't want to encourage her.

"No, not a literal gap. It's the name of a store." I shift my weight onto one leg. "There's also Marshall's No, not a lawman. It's also the name of a store. Do you have money?"

He lets out a wistful sigh. "I used to. It is likely all gone now."

"All right. No problem. I can spot you for some clothes." I glance at my phone, 10:56 p.m. Dammit. We are really cutting it close. Something might be open later tonight since it's a Friday. "Stuff might be closed now. If we can't find an open store, we could go back home and you can borrow some stuff from my dad until you have your own wardrobe."

Eldon starts to nod, then seems confused. "Your father? Is he like us?"

"No. It's a complicated situation, but it's totally fine." I smile.

He snaps his fingers. "Ahh, yes. Mr. Wolent did mention something about you staying with your family still, who are all mortals."

Call me crazy, but I swear a note of sadness and envy washes over his face for a few seconds. Not the first time another vampire reacted to my story in such a manner. I think a lot more than are willing to admit would have rather allowed their mortal families to know they hadn't really died. Still, it's probably for the best I'm an anomaly. Like the CIA says, the more moving parts, the more the chances of a leak.

No, I have no idea if they really say that. Just being a goof.

"Can you fly?" I ask.

"Fly." Eldon's eyes flutter. "Are you being serious now?"

I levitate a few inches off the ground. "Yes. Totally serious."

"How the devil are you doing that?" Eldon walks around me, waving his hand as if he's searching for invisible wires.

"Not sure exactly how it works. I want to fly and it just happens." I settle back down on my feet. "Not every vampire can do it."

"Seems about three in ten or something like that." Ashley taps a finger to her chin. "It's more common in some bloodlines than others."

Eldon stands there for a few minutes, making faces like a high school nerd attempting to do the Jedi thing and make a pen fly off the desk into his hand. Alas, it seems he is not gifted with flight. Should've figured that. Can't go letting a guy be *too* perfect. When Eldon was making his vampire character up, he put all his development points into being handsome. Didn't have any left for flying.

I chuckle to myself. Dammit, Dad. Why do I keep thinking of life as a game?

"Guess that's a no on the flying." Ashley sighs, patting his arm like she's trying to console him for the loss of a beloved pet.

"Sounds like we Uber back home," I say.

"Hold on." Aziz raises a hand. "A ride is simple."

I smile at him. "Thank you, Aziz."

He smirks at me.

Dammit. I said it like the movie again, didn't I. Yeah, he gets *Fifth*

Element jokes all the time from the younger vamps. As soon as I wince, he stops looking annoyed. Nope, did not say that on purpose.

We stand there talking to Eldon for a few minutes about phones and pictures and some basic differences between the 1850s and the modern era. Finally, one of Wolent's mortal employees comes jogging out the door and heads over to a seemingly random black Cadillac. He waves for us to follow him.

"Ooh, the limo treatment." I wag my eyebrows at Ashley, who laughs.

The four of us head over to the car and get in. Ash scoots ahead, clearly trying to race me for the back seat so she can sit next to Eldon. No worries. She can have it. I go for the front passenger seat. Eldon, Ashley, and Chloe climb in back. The car's fairly big. All four of us could have squeezed together back there.

"Oh no," says Chloe in a dry tone. "There's no child safety seat."

Ashley and I chuckle. Eldon seems confused. The driver looks back at her, concerned.

"Don't worry about it. She's exempt." I chuckle, then like an idiot, put on my seat belt.

Not that it's stupid to use a seat belt. But... yeah. Habit. I don't exactly need them anymore. Getting catapulted through the windshield would not be comfortable. Wouldn't kill me, though.

Eldon examines the interior. "An interesting coach. Is someone going to be bringing the horses around soon?"

"You're not for real." Ashley snickers. "Please tell me you're kidding."

The driver starts the engine and backs away from the decorative brick wall surrounding the circular courtyard.

"Oh. We are moving!" Eldon peers out the window in genuine shock.

Ashley's not being terribly subtle in her fangirling at him. She's also not being sexy, either. So, either her brain's truly reset itself to early teens or she's attempting to be polite. Yeah, she's probably being polite. She didn't really go full 'sex kitten' until after her encounter with Aurélie, and it only got worse after she went vamp. Before that, she never acted inappropriate around people we didn't know very well. She is dialing back the childishness tonight, though… and she isn't wearing anything with unicorns on it.

Uh oh. She definitely has a crush on Eldon.

Not sure he's my type. What kind of guy gives a girl head the first time they meet? Okay, that was awful. Hey, if Ashley wasn't going to go for the cheap innuendo, I might as well fill it in mentally. No, I am not saying it out loud. Especially not where Eldon can hear me.

"This is magical." Eldon continues looking out the window, making faces like a small boy getting a ride on a fire truck for the first time. "This coach is moving on its own. How does it do this?"

"I'm not a mechanic. I can't really explain the physics behind the workings of an internal combustion engine." I point at the front. "There's a machine in the front end that burns, umm, fuel oil, and it converts it into rotating motion that makes the wheels go."

"Ingenious," whispers Eldon. "You are saying this is not literal magic."

"I'm saying it is not literal magic." I chuckle. "What *will* be literal magic is if we can find a store still open."

The driver heads toward downtown.

"So, you said you used to have money?" asks Ashley.

"Indeed." Eldon tugs at his lapels. "My family was rather wealthy. Father took over a shipping enterprise from his father, and we were doing rather well, moving commodities around the globe. I expect by this time, our family fortune has long since evaporated. Even if it hasn't, there is no practical way for me to lay claim to it. Do either of you recognize the name Whittmore, or the Eastbourne Company?"

Ashley and I shake our heads.

"Nope," says Chloe. "But I'm only seven, so I wouldn't."

Eldon sighs. "Seems the company did not survive my father's madness."

"Your dad went nuts?" I ask.

"Not that manner of madness." Eldon fusses at his frilled cuffs. "He found himself involved in something of a tiff with a vampire. I've not the foggiest idea of how it began. This vampire had some connection to the Duch East India Company, and evidently decided we were a threat too great to leave alone."

Ashley fake cringes. "Oof. Getting into a pissing contest with a vampire isn't the smartest thing a mortal can do. They're going to lose."

Eldon blinks at her. "They weren't simply teasing each other."

"Huh?" Ashley blinks.

"He's thinking of 'pissing contest' in a British sense," I say. "As in to take the piss."

"Eww," says Chloe.

I laugh. "Hah. No, it means to tease someone."

"This phrase no longer means thus?" asks Eldon.

"Wow." I collect my thoughts and then explain all possible uses for the word. "… does not mean a literal contest involving urination. It's a way to say they were fighting."

"Ahh. I see." Eldon nods at me. "Yes, father and the vampire set about the task of destroying each other. It was rather like two businesses in competition resorting to unsavory means to harm the other. Burning warehouses, that sort of thing. Quite ugly business."

"Wow." I whistle. "Hard to imagine something like that going on today… being so open and all."

"Even then, the citizenry did not know of vampires. They thought it all a labor dispute or some such trifle—insofar as a trifle can be men running around while lit on fire."

"Ouch," says Ashley.

"Fire… BAD!" I wave my arm sideways.

Ashley cackles.

"My father fell into a particular kind of madness. He thought it his duty to rid the world of abominations."

"Oh, one of those." I roll my eyes. "Sorry."

"Mind if I ask what made you join team vampire?" Ashley smiles.

Eldon chuckles. "It was not my decision, unfortunately. Benjamin Jacobs—that's the vampire with whom my father decided to quarrel— turned me to torment my father."

"Oof." I grimace. "He sent you to kill him?"

"No. Nothing like that." Eldon chuckles. "He merely turned me into that which my father considered an abomination. In truth, I believe the man was curious to see if my father would destroy me or change his position."

"Did he?" I ask.

"No." Eldon frowns. "To either."

"Umm." Ashley kneads her hands together, building up the courage to ask an awkward question. "How did you end up in a stone box at the bottom of a mine?"

Eldon doesn't seem bothered, merely a little sad. "My father *attempted* to destroy me. He believed separating my body into several pieces and interring them apart from each other would free my soul to rejoin the afterlife it belonged to."

"My daddy was a piece of shit, too." Chloe looks down, idly tapping her sneakers together.

Eldon gawks at her.

"I'm sorry." I resist the urge to climb into the back seat and squish-hug her, beyond grateful the Universe gave me a Dad who didn't try to destroy me when he found out I'd turned into a vampire.

"I can't even imagine what that was like for you." Ashley whistles. "That's so messed up."

Eldon offers a weak smile of thanks for our condolence. "At that point, I was no longer his son. Rather, an abomination that merely looked like Eldon Whittmore and pretended to be him. He thought my 'heavenly soul' was trapped within a corpse and needed to be cut free."

Wow. People really do believe some dumb things when they don't have accurate information and simply start guessing and making stuff up. This is like one step up from trusting a Nigerian prince email asking for money.

"Sorry that happened," says Ashley in a quiet semi-whisper.

"It's all right, dear." Eldon pats her hand. "Father believed he was doing something noble to 'save' me."

Ashley glances at him. "Do you mind if I ask why he did that instead of simply leaving you out in the sun?"

"I can only assume…" Eldon pauses, perhaps to keep his emotions on an even keel. "I believe he did not want to run the risk of entirely destroying me in hopes he might someday find a cure."

"Oh." Ashley fidgets her hands in her lap. "I guess that was nice of him."

"Speaking of which…" I twist around in the seat to look at Eldon. "You recovered from being dead for like 150 years pretty fast."

"I can't even imagine how awful that must've been for you." Ashley shivers.

Eldon offers a blasé shrug. "I do not remember the time. Only a momentary awareness here and there whenever someone got close to my crypts. I lost consciousness soon after my father took my head off. It is as though that happened only hours ago. My body has been essentially asleep since."

"The big pause button," says Ashley.

"Again, let me express my gratitude for putting me back together." Eldon smiles broadly at us. "It is grand to be awake once more."

I cringe a little. "Umm. How many people did you kill when you came to?"

Eldon rubs his chin. "Everything is a bit fuzzy, to be honest. I remember these small, cylindrical containers with blood in them. I awoke, drank from them, and likely returned to sleep. Then I found myself in the woods, drinking hot blood. It might have even been a bear. In truth, the only solid recollection I have is walking among the trees and following the two of you until I reached the city. Soon after, some of Wolent's people found me."

Relief spreads over me. Yay. My Thermos idea worked. He probably didn't murder any hikers.

"The outfit is pretty obvious." Ashley grins. "Hey, question. Where did you get that?"

"Get what?" He tilts his head at her.

"Your clothes. Did you raid the wardrobe room of a theater?" Ashley covers her mouth to hold in a giggle.

"These are my clothes."

I blink. "When we found you… you didn't have anything. Looked like you'd been roasted over an open flame. Where did the clothing come from?"

"Oh. I suppose it reconstituted along with my body... somehow."

"That makes no sense." I scratch my head.

"Neither does it make sense that vampires can fly." He tugs at his sleeve. "But you can."

Ashley pokes the back of my seat. "Stop trying to be all sciency about vampires. We're magical."

Umm. Hang on. My brain bounces over a logic speed bump. "Eldon? How did you follow us? When we left the mine, you were seriously out."

"I did not literally follow you. By my best estimation, I regained consciousness—and sanity—two nights later." Eldon waves randomly, as if he's trying to grab words out of the air. "It seemed more a bit of intuition that I ought to travel in a particular direction. I found my way to the city you refer to as Seattle and soon thereafter happened upon contact with some of Mr. Wolent's associates."

Our driver takes a corner a little fast, which makes me spin around to look out the windshield. We're zooming across the parking lot toward a Marshall's. Lights are still on inside. Good sign, though we are cutting it super close.

We come to a stop by the curb at the front of the store. I stare at the entrance trying to find the posted hours. They close at 11:00 p.m. on Fridays. It's 10:52 p.m. according to my phone. A woman who looks an awful lot like an employee is approaching the door from inside. I think she's spotted us and is rushing to lock the door before we can get inside.

Normally, I would feel a little bad about making employees stay a few minutes late. Something about the 'hah, got you' expression on this woman's face pisses me off, like she's taking extreme satisfaction in locking the door in our proverbial faces. Smugness annoys me.

I blur out of the Cadillac, abusing my superhuman reflexes to reach the door before she can lock it. Her fingertips are an inch away from the deadbolt when I yank the door open. She flicks her hand around as if locking the door and gives me this irritatingly smug 'oh, so sorry, we're closed' smile.

Her brain takes a second or two to catch up to my speed. Once she realizes I got the door open before she could lock it, she goes blank-faced, then flushes. Her mood is exactly like someone who said something rude about a classmate not realizing said classmate was right next to her. She doesn't have the luxury of retreating back into the store with a locked door between us.

Of course, she could kick us out if she wanted to. Legally, anyway.

I don't give her the chance to say anything, instead diving into her thoughts. "We'll be fast. I promise. Don't mind us."

Ashley and Eldon get out of the car and walk over to the store at a normal speed. Looks like Chloe is staying in the car with the driver. Good idea, Ash. Weird enough our shopping trip is going to be on video. Smart not to have a child involved.

Trying to be as quick as possible—I do know what it's like to get stuck late at work because of a pushy customer—we head right for the men's section. Ashley drags Eldon over to the shoe area while I grab a couple of T-shirts, a couple pairs of jeans, a button-down shirt and one pair of khakis. We're not going to make the employees stand around while Eldon tries everything on. I'm fairly good at eyeballing his size. If I make an error, it's going to be on the side of too big for him. That's easy enough to hem at home.

A few minutes later, Eldon and Ashley meet me as I'm exiting the men's clothing area to head for the registers. He's carrying a box with a New Balance logo on it. Hey, this isn't about fancy. It's about not looking like an artifact from the 1800s.

"Are we planning to steal this merchandise?" whispers Eldon.

"Of course not." I blink at him. "What makes you say that?"

"*You* are going to pay for it?" He blinks in disbelief.

"Well, yeah. That's kind of how a person gets stuff without stealing it." I chuckle.

"You're a lass, though. You… have money of your own?" He scratches idly at his chest. "Oh, I suppose your father allots you something of an allowance, then?"

Ashley and I stare at him.

"No, it's not an allowance. I have money of my own. We can even go outside the house without a male chaperone." I shake my head.

"They even let us have jobs now." Ashley fake gasps.

"I did not mean offense." He flashes a wan smile. "Merely not accustomed to such things. I have quite a bit to learn, it seems."

Okay, to be fair, he doesn't sound offended or shocked that a girl can have money of her own... merely caught off guard. I'll let it slide this time.

"Are you certain this is not an imposition?" Eldon looks over the stuff in my arms. "These garments seem rather extravagant."

I can't help but laugh. "Extravagant? This is as ordinary as it gets."

"They're pre-made in a size that you think will fit? Where is the tailor?" Eldon brushes a hand over one of the pairs of jeans. "This is a most exotic fabric, indeed. Did it come from India?"

"It's a polyester-cotton blend." Ashley chuckles. "Suuuper exotic."

"No. I'll explain once we're out of here. The employees are already staying late for us." I hurry over to the only open register and give the exhausted looking woman there an apologetic smile. "Sorry. Emergency. Thanks for putting up with us." I dump the armload of stuff on the conveyor.

"It's all right, hon." The woman smiles at me, then goes bug-eyed at the sight of Eldon.

"Stupid prank." I mutter. "We're in the drama club. A bunch of jocks stole all his clothes out of the locker room."

Not the best excuse I could've come up with. I mean, why wouldn't he simply just go home in costume? Luckily, the woman doesn't question us more. Dumb teenagers doing impulsive things, I suppose. It's a stretch for Eldon to pass as a teenager, but not a big one. After all, some guys do get mistaken for being twenty-one while they're still seniors in high school.

Eldon watches the process of items being rung up and bagged.

"Okay, dear," says 'Ann,' the checkout woman. "The total is $146.32."

"Dear Lord," rasps Eldon. "I cannot in good conscience ask you to proffer such a fortune on my behalf."

Ashley whispers at the cashier behind her hand, "He's a method actor. Stuck in character."

I pat him on the arm. "It's not that much. I'm just a girl with a debit card and a bunch of leprechaun gold. If it bothers you, consider it a loan."

Ann chuckles at my 'joke,' not realizing the actual truth of it.

Not gonna sweat $146.32, though I suspect it'll get back to Wolent somehow and I'll be receiving a reimbursement check. Or cash. Vampires aren't too fond of paper trails.

Considering the amount of money Aurélie got from the gold—which she put into a bank account for me—I feel kinda weird for not having gone crazy at the mall. Haven't even spree shopped for shoes or so much as bought one really nice handbag.

Might have to surrender my 'teenage girl' card.

Or maybe just my 'teenager' card. If my dad got his hands on this much money at my age, he'd have installed a Cray supercomputer in his bedroom and bought every video game available at the time. Honestly, I've never been one of those girls who cared about expensive designer purses. Seems stupid to spend thousands of dollars on a bag to carry crap around in. I don't need a $6,000 Gucci to do the same thing a $50 Walmart bag can do just fine. Really, I don't even carry a purse often. It's more of an annoyance. Just another thing to put down somewhere and forget where I left it.

Anyway…

I'm probably just being way too pragmatic for anyone my age. Sure, that gold turned into a staggering amount of money… but I also have to make it last for a really long time. Maybe the bizarre manner in which I obtained it is so crazy it's easy to kinda set it aside and pretend it's not real.

I thank Ann for her help, then hurry for the way out. That smug woman is still standing there, not having moved since we entered. It's only been about twelve minutes. I scramble her memory a little so she hopefully won't remember exactly what we look like beyond a brown-haired girl, a redheaded girl, and a cute guy with light brown hair dressed in a theater costume.

We hop back in the car, which is still waiting by the curb.

Chloe's engrossed in a movie playing on a tablet-sized screen that folds down from the middle of the ceiling. Looks like a Disney cartoon, but I can't place which one. Gotta be one I haven't seen since being her age.

"Ooh, *Black Cauldron*," chirps Ashley. "I love that movie!"

Yep. Haven't seen that since I was like eight. I remember it being scary. Chloe doesn't look bothered.

"Where would you like to go now, miss?" asks the driver.

Hmm. I'm 'miss' now. Makes me feel important. "Let's start off with a dark, secluded spot Eldon can get changed."

The driver nods and pulls away from the curb.

Ashley and Eldon get to talking about his family. Sounds like they owned a medium-sized shipping company back when 'shipping' literally involved sailing ships. It wouldn't surprise me if Benjamin Jacobs kinda owned Dutch East India the same way Arthur Wolent 'owns' various companies here. It would certainly explain the rivalry between the vampire and the Whittmore family, especially if Eldon's shipping company did well enough to be a serious competitor.

We stop on a street somewhere in the outskirts of Seattle downtown where one of the lamps is only barely on, creating a rather dark swath between a small hardware store and a Burger King.

"This will work," I say. "C'mon. Pick a shirt, pants, and grab the sneakers."

"What?" Eldon blinks. "You are suggesting I disrobe outdoors?"

"You're a vampire, Eldon. Ending up naked outside is going to happen, eventually." I grumble.

"Are you serious?" He tilts his head at me.

I flap my arms. "Yeah. Happens to me all the time."

"Might I inquire as to how? Do your garments simply evaporate?"

"No. It's usually an idiot with claws. Or a sword. Or something that blows up." I wrap my arms protectively around my shirt. "Our bodies are a lot tougher than fabric. We survive stuff clothing can't."

Ashley grimaces. "And if we get knocked out and the mortal authorities find us, we end up in a morgue cooler with no clothes on."

Eldon somewhat reluctantly slips out of the car, holding a bundle of new clothes. "I am not terribly inclined to go around inciting hostilities."

"Neither is Sarah." Ashley heaves an exasperated sigh. "Trouble's gonna find us."

"It's expedient and the more we can do to avoid leaving a record of our passage, the better." I gesture at the dumpster alcove behind the Burger King. "Besides, if anyone spots us, we can make them forget."

"I see." Eldon's expression says 'there are questions'. He sets them aside for the time being and scurries into the dumpster alcove.

I wouldn't mind enjoying the scenery, but I'm not tempted to sneak over there. Ashley stares at the cinderblock wall, no doubt fantasizing. Chloe, who thus far hasn't seemed terribly impressed with Eldon's existence, remains fixated on the movie in the car.

A few minutes go by. Eldon pokes his head out into view around the wall. He appears to be shirtless. "Sarah, would you mind terribly explaining how these garments work? For example, what the devil is this for?" He holds out a packet of underwear.

"Those are your smalls," I say, using Dalton's term for them.

"Oh." He blinks and looks at the plastic packet. "How is it supposed to go on?"

"It's in a package. Tear open the plastic. The clear stuff is not part of the garment."

Ashley leans against me. "Why are the really cute guys always so airheaded?"

She's teasing. He's not dumb, merely out of his time.

Eldon disappears back into the alcove. A few seconds later, the sound of plastic tearing echoes out from within. "Aha! I see now. Am I supposed to wear all of them?"

"No, just one. The pack has three. Those, you change every day… or every night." I fidget. "Maybe not so important now to go a couple days in the same skivvies."

"Ick." Ashley shivers.

"What? He's not an Innocent. Not like they'll get funky."

"Still ick." She chuckles.

A few minutes later, Eldon emerges, having changed. Seems he figured out the modern clothing just fine except for not tying his sneaker laces. I walk over, crouch, and do it for him like he's a four-year-old. Reminds me of when Sam was tiny.

"This is… light." He looks himself over. "Almost feels as if I am undressed."

"Yeah. I can kinda understand that." I chuckle. "The gowns Aurélie loans me to wear for the soirees are so damn heavy. Changing back into normal clothing is freeing."

Eldon nods once. "I suppose I shall endeavor to acclimate myself then."

"Old clothing isn't the only thing that will make you stand out as weird." I poke him in the side. "We have to work on your language skills."

"I adore the way he talks." Ashley gives him this starry-eyed smile.

"Yeah, but it's not normal. Our job is to help him learn how to blend in." I face Eldon. "When you're out in society, it will help if you talk like someone from modern day. You said 'you shall endeavor to acclimate.' People today would say something like 'I'll try to get used to it.'"

He nods. "Try to get used to… Interesting. When you said something about claws earlier, did you imply there are creatures out there who pose a threat to us?"

"Yep. Other vampires."

"Have claws?" He raises both eyebrows.

"Some do. Some don't." I hold up my right hand and extend mine. "Like this. They're magical. Really sharp. Way tougher than fingernails should be. And finally—and the worst part—being scratched by vamp claws hurts like heck."

"They're also different from vamp to vamp." Ashley makes a clawing gesture at the air despite not having claws herself. "Sarah's look like a nail extension nightmare. Glim's are tiny swords."

I examine my claws, brush them on my shirt, then look at them again. "Yeah, these 'nail extensions' can definitely be a nightmare for someone if I want them to be."

"Do you have claws?" Ashley smiles.

She's not exactly making goo-eyes at him. She's also not exactly *not* making goo-eyes at him.

He stares down at his hands. "I've not the foggiest notion."

I take a few minutes trying to coach him through the process of sprouting claws. No dice. Eldon Whittmore does not have pointy fingernails. He cannot fly. Not sure who his sire was or what the guy was like, but he's certainly got to have *something* lurking in there. I got the ability to sweet-talk locks open from Dalton. Ashley's charm is supercharged thanks to being Aurélie's progeny. I know little about Chloe's sire. However, she seems to have the ability to sense the intentions of people. Like, she doesn't know the specifics of what they're planning—at least not without reading their minds. However, knowing in an instant someone's a danger is pretty handy. Kiddo's also really sneaky. Like abnormally sneaky for a child. She can almost do that Shadow thing where people can only see her if she lets them. So far, it only works on mortals. The guy who turned her was probably a Lost One like Dalton.

Anyway...

"Well, I'm sure you've got some tricks up your sleeve." I usher him and his wadded up ancient clothing back to the Caddy. "They'll come to the surface sooner or later. Let's go tour Seattle."

"Brilliant." He smiles. "That shall give me the opportunity to *get used to* this curious outfit."

23

INTO THE COOKIE JAR

SATURDAY

*I*t's been a while since I had to race home to beat sunrise.

No damn idea what the hell a bug was doing outside in October, but let me say that having an insect hit me in the face while flying at top speed stung like a bastard. I swear it hurt more than being shot. Stings. Isn't it crazy how the superficial stuff hurts more? Like skinning a knee after falling off a bike makes kids cry but they can run full speed into a wall and be like no big deal.

We made it home in time to get inside before the Sun knocked us out. Had to fight to stay conscious long enough to get across the basement. Slept in our clothes. Like I said to Eldon, it's not quite as bad as it would've been as mortals. He's Old Guard, so his body doesn't even attempt to pretend to be alive without him consciously trying to think about it. There is no sweat, no secretions, no body odor. He legit could wear the same clothing every day for ten years and not stink. Ash, Chloe, and I, not so much. I won't call it a 'downside' of being an Innocent. Our bodies are really good at pretending to be mortal and alive.

So, we have to change clothes frequently and still even shower and stuff.

This is, again, not me complaining. I love feeling normal, and really, sleeping in my clothes for one morning isn't a big deal. Not like I'm planning to wear the same outfit all night again.

My stomach wound is mostly healed. A few faint red lines remain, but it doesn't hurt at all anymore. I even wake up at my usual time around 2:30 in the afternoon. Ash and Chloe are still sleeping, so I strip right there, wrap myself in a towel, and jog to the downstairs bathroom for a quick shower.

Ash and Chloe are still sleeping when I return and change into sweat pants and a T-shirt. Barring Eldon wanting to go out *again* tonight, I have no plans to leave the house. After flopping in my computer chair, it's time to decide between wasting time on games or doing some schoolwork. Staring into the blank screen doesn't help me decide what to do. The quiet of my room lets me hear the goings on upstairs. Something's afoot. Nothing alarming, merely a lot of talking. I pause to listen. Oh, Dad's got the itch to run a Dungeons & Dragons game, sounds like. Everyone seems to be in the dining room. Aww, why not. This is some prime quality time to spend with the fam.

I head upstairs.

Dad's sitting behind a gamemaster's screen at one end of the dining room table. All three Littles plus Ronan are poring over various books, including Sierra who appears to be there of her own free will. Dice and character sheets are scattered everywhere. Mom's standing nearby watching the proceedings. She doesn't really play too often. I'm not exactly super into D&D, but I can't resist the opportunity for a whole-family event. The last time we all got together to do something, we ended up in the outer planes of the Abyss. This is a lot safer.

Blix is seated next to Sam, twiddling his tiny thumbs. Looks like he's got a character sheet in front of him—and he's ready to start.

"Hey, all." I approach the table. "You guys start yet?"

"Just making characters now," says Sam, his tone distant since he's trying to read.

230 | ETERNITY AND YOU: TIPS FOR THE YOUNG VAMPIRE

"Cool. Got room for one more?" I help myself to the only unclaimed chair.

Dad beams. "Of course." He does weasel hands and emits a Disney-evil laugh. "My plans are complete. I could not have done it without you, Allie."

Mom is unimpressed. "What are you going on about now?"

"The reason we had so many kids was to rebuild a D&D group after my friends all grew up and moved away." Dad does the 'mua-ha-ha' laugh again.

The Littles don't seem to care or react to the joke. Mom shakes her head, chuckling. Yeah, that's my Dad. He's still a kid at heart... not that D&D is really a 'kids' game, per se. Sophia passes me a blank character sheet, then shoves a pile of dice at me.

Might as well start with the stats. "Usual stat rules?"

Dad nods.

Okay, that means I just generate a pile of numbers and can put them in whatever stat I want. That's the best option. Being stuck using them in order kinda limits what type of character you can play. No one wants a wizard with high strength and horrid intelligence.

I start rolling up stats.

Ash and Chloe emerge from the kitchen. Kiddo's got one of my T-shirts on. Ashley's wearing one of my oversized tees, bright red with the symbol for *The Greatest American Hero* on it. Dad loved that show.

"You guys are in reverse world. Went to bed in clothes, changed into sleep stuff when you woke up." I chuckle.

"We're not going anywhere today, right?" Ashley leans against the table beside me.

Chloe meanders over as well. She plants her left foot in a square of sunlight on the floor, jumps back, then hisses at the window. It's not a real vampire hiss. Just a kid pretending to be a cat.

The 'rents chuckle at her.

"Aww, are you okay?" I ask.

Chloe sticks her foot up so I can see it. No burns. "Ow."

"Looks fine." I pat her foot. "You're getting pretty good at fighting the Sun."

Kiddo grins from ear to ear. "Are you playing a game?"

"We're *about to be* playing a game." I drop dice again. Ugh... a five. Ruined a good stat set. Time to start over.

Chloe climbs into my lap. "Can I play, too?"

"I dunno." Sam scratches his head. "I'm not sure if she can play."

"Girls can play D&D just fine," snaps Sierra. "Did you forget all *three* of your sisters are here?"

"Chill." Sam holds up a hand like a crossing guard stopping traffic at her. "It's not a girl question. It's a seven-year-old question. She might be a little young for this."

"Says the ten-year-old," mutters Siera.

Sam is unfazed. "Three years is a major difference at this age. You were still watching *My Little Pony* at seven. You wouldn't watch it now."

Sierra blushes.

"What's wrong with *My Little Pony?*" asks Ashley in an overacted innocent voice.

"I rest my case." Sam looks back down at the sourcebook on the table in front of him.

"No harm in letting her try," says Dad. "If she loses interest, that's fine, too."

Ashley has played D&D with us before. She's a bit more into it than I am, and wastes no time grabbing a sheet, dice and a player's handbook. Of course, she almost always makes weird offbeat characters like a were-panther ranger or a tiefling paladin (which isn't supposed to be allowed). Dad told us about his friend Brian, who would have lost his mind at her characters. Brian, who almost always played wizards, insisted on games being serious. Ashley's characters would have driven him crazy.

Dad has this adage: D&D groups always start off trying to be *Lord of the Rings* and invariably end up as Monty Python. The more serious Brian tried to be, the more things unraveled.

We're all working on our characters while Dad sits there grinning with anticipation. He's clearly got a campaign ready to go. Odd that he didn't spend the past two weeks talking about it while he worked on it. Wonder if he downloaded a pre-made module online on the spur of the moment. It's not like him to use 'canned' games other people wrote. Meh, whatever. He looks like he's going to have fun.

Sam finishes his character first. Well, second. Blix was done before I came upstairs. From the chatter around the table, Blix made a barbarian. He wants to smash things with a giant axe. In the game, I mean. Not for real. Sam's made a warlock, which is really just a sorcerer that's focused on spells around demon summoning and stuff like that. Gee. He's basically playing himself. Heh. Soph's making up a healer. Sierra's stuck trying to decide between a warrior or ranger. Ronan's working intently on his character without talking to anyone. Sierra glances at his character sheet, and seems to make a choice. She, too, starts scribbling things down furiously. Chloe ends up fixating on a picture in the book of the druid turning into a big fluffy bear. She wants to do that.

My brother scurries off to the kitchen.

Come on dice, work with me here. Good grief. That's six sets of stats, all of which got ruined by one extremely low roll. It's almost tempting to accelerate myself to change one of the dice before anyone sees… except it's daylight out and I can't. Don't look at me like that. I'm not 'cheating' for uber stats—merely wanting to change an awful roll to a low roll.

Sam walks back in carrying the cookie jar.

"Little hungry?" asks Mom.

"No. I only want one cookie, but the lid won't open." He hands it to her.

Mom takes the cookie jar and tugs at the lid, which doesn't budge.

This is unusual since it's a ceramic pottery thing where the lid is only held in place by its own weight. Unless someone is pranking us with glue, it should not be stuck. Mom tugs at it for a while before getting frustrated and handing the jar to Dad.

"Ahh yes. The sacred time-honored duty of a husband, opening stuck jars." Dad takes the cookie jar from her as if he's accepting an ancient holy relic from a high priest.

Mom rolls her eyes.

Dad wraps his left arm around the urn and grabs the nub atop the lid in his other hand, pulling with all his strength. I can practically hear the Rocky music building up in the background. His eyebrows go up as if to say 'holy cow, this is really stuck on there.'

A tiny blue spark runs around the top of the cookie jar.

"Wait!" yells Sophia.

Too late. The lid pops off with so much force I expect a shower of cookies to fly all over the table. There are no cookies. Like something straight out of *Ghostbusters*, streams of bright light burst into the dining room, wavering around and flashing. Half a second later, a concussive blast wave goes off that hurls me out of my chair.

I land flat on my back—in grass, staring up at a picture-perfect blue sky and fluffy white clouds. Somewhere, way off in the sky overhead, a dragon lazily cruises by.

"Toto, I don't think we're in Washington State anymore," says Sophia.

I sigh. That narrator guy who does like all the movie trailers starts speaking in my head: And, several days later, the Wright Family would finally learn where the burst of stray magic went.

24

ABNORMALLY INTO CHARACTER

SATURDAY (MAYBE)

I sit up.

My T-shirt and sweat pants are gone. No, I'm not in my birthday suit. I'm dressed up in leather armor, knee-high boots, studded leather bracers, and a cape. My belt's holding a ton of little pouches. There's a shortsword in a scabbard on my left side, three daggers on my right hip, and an assortment of small throwing knives across my chest in a bandolier.

Aww, come on. I wasn't totally settled on playing a rogue.

Ashley's sitting on the meadow beside me. She's kinda almost in the same outfit I am. That is to say, she seems to be wearing leather armor. I'm using 'seems' here because the armor shows off a lot of cleavage. Anyone trying to kill Ashley could easily stab her bare, unprotected flesh and pierce her heart. Instead of roguish pants like me, she's got a fluffy, multilayered microskirt and thigh-high laced boots. Her other accessories include a longsword on her belt and a mandolin in her hands. She's also got horns, pointy ears, and bubblegum-pink skin. Her eyes are entirely black. Her hair is also pink, like cotton candy. And yes, she's got a cute little tail. Reminds me a bit of Mel's tail, only smaller and with a much less scary blade-barb at the end.

"Bard? Really?" I blink at her.

"Cute, happy, and of questionable usefulness," says Sam.

"What?" she snaps, defensively, her voice slightly lispy thanks to nonretractable fangs. "They're perfectly viable."

Sierra groans. "What the hell just happened?"

I look over at her. Ever see a skinny twelve-year-old in plate armor? I haven't either until right now. She looks pretty much the same as normal other than the outfit. It's not full plate (some bits are covered in chain mail), so I think she's gone warrior instead of knight. Sam's standing not far from us in a black-and-purple wizard type robe with a dark leather armor breastplate. The black triple-headed flail hanging from his belt has spiked skulls instead of plain metal balls. He might be smart and mature for his age, but he's still a little boy. Skulls are cool.

Sophia's somewhere between Disney princess and sorceress in a bright blue mage robe. She's holding a staff tipped with a pinkish-white crystal. A fluffy grey panther sits beside her with glowing cyan eyes. Is that Klepto? Wow.

Next to Soph stands this towering mountain of man meat. He's like a cartoon version of a WWE wrestler crossed with a Viking warrior who ate *all* the steroids. 'Knuckle-dragger' is supposed to be a metaphor, not literal. Despite being human (I think), the barbarian's face has a strong resemblance to Blix's face, only without the big ears and pointy nose.

Ronan is adorable. He's all decked out in leather-and-chain armor with green tights, green cloak, and a longbow. His blond hair hangs down to the middle of his back (which is pretty much how it looks for real) only he doesn't have pointy ears usually. Poor kid looks freaked out.

Chloe's twirling around nearby. She's dolled up in a fancy white-red-and-black gown and laced-up corset deal. Her gown sports a dangerously plunging neckline completely inappropriate for a seven-year-old. Her dress has a fancy, tall collar in back that totally screams 'evil vampire countess.' The ruby amulet and elbow-length fingerless gloves only add to the 'I am a vampire' theme. No idea where she got black lipstick from.

The real shock is Mom. She's wearing shiny white armor with gold trim and big shoulder pads. In one hand, she's carrying a golden mace, a giant book in the other. That's totally cleric. Fits, I suppose. The one time she tried playing with us, she took the healer role because no one else had done it yet. I'm not sure she intended to play today, rather just wanted to watch.

"Holy shit." Sierra gasps at herself.

"Yeah, this is pretty messed up." I glance down at my 'rogue costume'.

"No." Sierra turns to face me. "My armor! It's like… *normal*. I'm not stuck in a stupid chain mail bikini! This doesn't look like 'girl armor.' There's no boobs on it. I mean, if I had a helmet on, no one could tell if I was a girl or a boy."

"That's true in real life, too." Sam laughs.

"Mom, can I hit him?" asks Sierra.

"Yes, dear. Once."

"Aaaah!" Sam runs while Sierra chases him. "Mom!? You said yes?!"

Our mother turns in place, watching them run around. "This is not really happening, so it won't matter."

"Stop and face justice, turdling!" yells Sierra.

After going around us three times, Sam finally seems to give up and stops running. Sierra storms over and, instead of punching him, simply grabs him by the collar of his armored robes and throttles him a little.

"Not funny," growls Sierra. "But you're not exactly wrong, either. I'm too damn skinny."

"We all are," says Sam.

"Thanks, Dad," chorus the Littles together.

Sierra looks down at her armor again. "This is either coming from

Dad's imagination or mine. So, we're not getting the Hollywood treatment."

"I'm not so sure." I gesture at Chloe.

Kiddo stops twirling to look up at me. "Some of my dress is missing. There's no front."

Take that same dress and scale it up to adult size, put it on a woman with a bosom, and you'd have serious cleavage. On a kid, it just looks incomplete.

"I guess vampires are required to be sexy," deadpans Ashley. "Oops. We fail."

Mom looks around like she's trying to find a shawl or sweater or something to wrap around Chloe. "I don't think this is coming from your father's imagination. He wouldn't dress her like that."

"I wouldn't either." Sierra folds her arms, making her armor clank.

"So, whose imagination are we in?" asks Sam.

Sophia gazes up at the clouds. "Are we even in someone's imagination, or did we get portaled into an alternate dimension?"

Blix-barbarian makes a face like 'don't ask me. I just want to smash things.'

"How should I know?" Ashley scratches her head.

"Maybe you can sing a song and get the answer." Sam cackles.

"Bards are not useless!" Ashley huffs.

I glance at her. "Do you even know how to play a mandolin?"

"No. Umm. Well. I mean. Ashley doesn't." She flicks her unicorn-pink hair back over her shoulders and holds her chin up high. "Pixie's been playing for years."

"You're not a pixie." Sam shakes his head. "You're a full grown adult tiefling... though I don't think they're supposed to be pink."

Ashley sighs. "No, I'm not a pixie. My *name* is Pixie. It's like a rogue nickname, you know? My stage name."

"Try to play something." I nudge her.

"Stop making fun of me." She whines.

"I'm not. This is a legitimate experiment." I hold up a finger. "If you can play that thing, then we're obviously not in reality."

"Oh." Ashley adjusts her grip on the mandolin into a playing stance, then begins to pluck away. No one looks more shocked than her that she's not committing a crime against eardrums. No idea what the song is, but it sounds like it belongs in a fantasy world. "Holy crap! I can play the mandolin!"

Sophia holds her staff up to the sky. The pale crystal at the top glows, then emits a camera flash of light. A tiny glob of magical energy rockets up and away from her into the heavens. A moment later, she lowers her gaze from the sky. "This is happening within an instant of reality. We're all still at home, sitting around the table, frozen in time. This is basically a shared daydream."

Sierra reaches out and touches the big crystal on top of Sophia's staff. "Wow. This is like the first time in recorded history that a Himalayan salt crystal lamp actually did something useful."

Sophia sticks her tongue out.

Mom chuckles.

Blix wallops himself in the face with the flat of his battle axe, grumbling in his own language.

"What did he say?" asks Sierra.

"Barbarian not like smart talk. No understand. Give headache," says Sam.

"Or… maybe we've been astrally projected somewhere." Sophia bites her lip. "We're either daydreaming or our consciousness has left our body and been pulled elsewhere."

"What's the difference?" asks Mom.

"Well, if this is a daydream, then all we have to do is find a way to wake up. No big deal." Sophia scurries over to stand beside me, looking scared. "If we've been astrally projected, then if we mess up here, we could really die… and our souls will be trapped forever while our bodies become soulless husks in the real world."

Ashley eeps, then snickers. "So, we have to be careful about escaping or we turn into politicians."

"No." Sophia stomps one foot. "I mean soulless husks. Just a body with nothing inside it that lays there staring into space and drooling on itself."

"Oh." I nod. "Television network executives."

"Sarah!" Mom shakes her head.

"Like the ones who cancelled *Firefly*." I sniffle.

Mom blinks. "Never mind. I apologize. You're perfectly right."

Sierra, Sophia, and Sam get into a debate about the silliness of 'chainmail bikinis' in fantasy and film. Mostly, they're trying to figure out why Sierra, Sophia, Mom, and my outfits are reasonable and realistic but Ashley's 'armor' is all sexed up and Chloe's dress is straight out of *Vampiress of Slutville*. Well it kind of is. At least her super-gothy skirt is floor-length. As far as I am aware, there is no such movie. If it exists, I don't want to know about it. It's possible that Ashley chose her own outfit because it fit the character. She's ballsy enough to wear something like that risqué for real, like on Halloween. There is no way in hell Chloe dressed herself. She has no concept of cleavage or slutty vampires or anything like that.

"Question." I do a slow turn, scanning the area. "Where is Dad?"

Everyone gets quiet at the same time.

There's no sign of him anywhere.

"He's the GM." Sierra says after a long pause. "He has become the world."

"Or maybe he's still holding the cookie jar and we all got sucked into it," whispers Ronan.

"Are you sure?" Ashley swishes her little demon tail back and forth in the manner of a wary cat. "If Sophia is right about us astrally projecting, the world couldn't be him. Maybe we're having a shared dream and this is his imagination."

"Can't be," says Sam in a flat tone. "We've existed here for about ten minutes and haven't experienced a cripplingly bad pun."

Everyone murmurs in agreement.

"What about Chloe's dress?" Mom gestures at her. "That didn't come from Jonathan."

Sierra examines her two-handed sword, not entirely disappointed in it. "Maybe the costume department didn't have 'vampiress gown' in a kid size."

"That doesn't make any sense." Mom goes to rake her hand up through her hair but stops herself upon realizing she's holding a mace.

"Like any of this does." Sierra fake glares at Sophia. "Her magic went haywire again."

"Sorry," says Sophia in a mousy voice. "I didn't mean to."

"Can you fix it?" I ask.

"Umm." Sophia looks around. "Probably. Just need to do a little scrying. Can we find a mirror or water? Something reflective?"

A loud roar comes from not too far away on our left.

The ground trembles.

Uh oh.

I spin toward the approaching commotion. A musclebound, green-skinned orc riding a massive, hairy war elephant has evidently seen us and decided to attack by charging at us at a full gallop—or whatever it is that impossibly big elephants do. We have no time to plan anything. Everyone scrambles to one side or the other. Choe and Sophia scream at the same time. Chloe disintegrates into a cloud of bats, blurs across the meadow, and reforms a football field's distance away. Sophia just runs. Giant panther-sized Klepto ducks between Soph's legs and tosses her up to ride on her back like a furry horse. She scrambles to keep hold of her mage staff and not fall off.

Sam and Ronan run left. Ashley and I go right.

Blix the Barbarian stands his ground and tries to 'parry' a charging war elephant.

It works about as well as I expect. The big guy spends a few seconds plastered onto the elephant's face until the creature stops charging. He falls off, lands flat on his back, and says, "Ow" in a super deep voice.

Sam thrusts a hand out. Two fiery dogs about the size and shape of ordinary Dobermans appear out of thin air and start spitting little fireballs at the orc. Ashley strums away at her mandolin. In response to the music, a tingling sensation washes over me. Feels almost like the supercharging I got from that sip of Aurélie's blood the other night.

Sierra raises her two-handed sword over her head, roars, and charges at the orc rider. Not sure what she's hoping to accomplish. At her size, that sword isn't much bigger than a broadsword. She can't reach the orc while he's up on top of that creature.

The orc wails, raising his arm in a futile effort to shield himself from the pelting fireballs. They look more annoying than deadly. Each flaming projectile is only about as big as a tennis ball and poof away in a blast of fire upon impact, not leaving much of a mark on him. Hmm. I should probably do something. I scurry off looking for a good hiding place. Hey, I'm a rogue, right? Might as well try for a backstab modifier.

Sophia points her staff at the orc, raises her left hand up toward the sky, and chants, *"Zhar dorun ka loramet!"*

A bolt of lightning crackles down from the sky, hits her raised hand, then flies out the tip of her staff into the giant elephant, nailing it right between the eyes.

The creature belts out a trumpeting screech, then careens over sideways, sending the orc diving for his life.

"Oh, no!" Sophia gasps. "I wasn't trying to hit the elephant!"

"It's kind of difficult to miss," says Mom in a flat tone.

Once it becomes clear the creature did not survive the lightning strike, my little sister bursts into tears.

Mr. Orc is about to have a bad day.

After taking cover behind a tuft of tall grass that seemingly appeared out of nowhere as soon as I thought to search for a hiding spot, I nock an arrow in my little shortbow and aim before letting it fly. My shot whistles across the meadow about the same instant Sierra gets close enough to attack. Her blade scores a decent stroke across his chest, sending a flap of his fur armor flying off amid a spurt of green blood. My arrow gets him in the lower back, causing him to howl in pain.

Damn. I don't think I got a critical hit, since he didn't stagger too much. Still, backstab bonus damage hurts.

The orc swats at Sierra. Twice, his curved one-handed sword bounces away from her blade as she expertly parries. The third time he swings, he clobbers her across the chest, knocking her back a step. Armor's dented slightly. Don't see any blood at least.

A cloud of bats forms in front of the orc. He's baffled for only half a second before Chloe solidifies out of the swarm. Her arms blur in a frenzy of claw swipes. Somewhere between her woodchipper claw frenzy at his face and Sierra running him through while he's distracted, the orc is doomed. I'm sure the poison from my arrow helped out. It's just not terribly visual.

The dead orc falls over.

Mom sprints to Sierra. "What the hell are you doing!?"

"Fighting the orc," says Sierra, sounding a bit pained.

"Are you okay?" Mom starts checking her over.

"Yeah. I've taken worse slaps at the sword class." She coughs. "Maybe not. Spitting up some blood. I think it critted me."

Mom starts to panic.

I run over and grab her arm. "Mom. Relax. You're a healer. Heal her."

My mother blinks a few times, looks at me, looks at Sierra—who does not seem worried at all—then seems to finally calm down.

Yeah, a little blood is dripping down Sierra's chin.

Mom looks at me as if she's about to ask how the heck she's supposed to do anything here. Then, as if some strange implanted memory takes over, she hangs her mace on her belt, places her hand on Sierra's head, and invokes a prayer to Tymoni, the Goddess of Light.

It's something Dad made up. The world's kind of custom.

A golden flash surrounds them both. The blood on my sister's chin vanishes.

"Whoa, Mom. Overkill." Sierra laughs. "That was probably only like an eighteen-point hit. You didn't need to use the big heal."

Sam, meanwhile, has an arm around Sophia, trying to comfort her. "It's not a real elephant. This is imaginary."

"I don't like hurting animals." Sophia sniffles. "Why did it have to hit the elephant? I was aiming for the orc!"

"It wasn't a real animal." Sam keeps patting her back. "And it would've totally trampled us to death. It was an evil elephant."

Chloe runs over to me, all smiles, her hands covered in green blood. "I ripped its face off! We won!"

"That's only a *little* creepy," whispers Ashley.

"Go wash your hands," I say. "Remember what I told you about killing orcs. They're dirty."

"Okay." Chloe spins around. "Umm, where's the bathroom?"

Sierra kicks the dead war elephant. "How do we loot this?"

"It doesn't have loot." Ashley laughs. "It's just a mount."

"What the heck are we going to do with two tons of dead elephant?" asks Mom.

"Wow. Yeah. It's going to be a major project." I shake my head. "Proper burial of a dead, hairy elephant is truly a mammoth undertaking."

Sam bursts out laughing.

Sierra stares at me in an 'I can't believe you' manner.

Mom facepalms.

Sophia appears to be caught between wanting to laugh and disown me.

Chloe didn't get it.

Ashley starts giggling. One of those giggle fits that's probably going to keep coming back randomly for the rest of the day whenever she thinks about that pun.

"Ooogh," says Blix.

"Mom?" Sam tugs on her arm. "Can you please heal Blix? He got trampled."

Sophia shakes her head. "Why did he just stand there?"

"He attempted to 'parry' the charge," I say.

"Is he stupid or something?" Sophia gawks.

"Yeah." Sam laughs. "He put a two in intelligence."

Mom walks over to the giant barbarian. "Is this healing magic going to work on Blix? He's a demon."

"Not here he isn't." Sam points at Ashley. "Technically, Ash is more of a demon than he is right now. This is his character."

"Okay." Mom invokes another prayer to Tymoni.

Golden light washes over Blix. He moans in relief.

"Soph, you can figure out how to get us home?" I ask.

"We *are* home. This is…" She waves her staff around at the world. "Some sort of collective dream. We're not really here."

Mom stands up away from Blix, evidently having done all she can do for him. "How do we wake up?"

"We realize that our society is built upon an infrastructure that marginalizes and disenfranchises certain segments of the population, and work to change that to a more equitable state," says Sam.

I chuckle. "Not the kind of waking up she means."

Mom tromps over to Sophia, her white and gold armor clanking. "Soph, you lost control of this magic. You know I expect you to clean up your messes."

"Yes, Mom. I'm working on it." Sophia leans on her staff. "I just need something reflective to scry in."

"We might as well play in the game world while we have the chance." Sam holds his arms out to either side. "If everything that we're experiencing now is taking place in the span of one second of real time, why not have fun. This is like the ultimate VR video game."

Sierra purses her lips. "Are you forgetting the part where there's a chance we could actually die for real if we die here?"

"Nah." Sam shakes his head. "That's not going to happen. This is comic relief laced with a bunch of nerdy gamer references, not drama."

Ashley and I laugh.

"He's got a point." I snap my fingers. "If this is all Sophia's doing, it's probably going to be tame."

"This place isn't real." Sierra nods.

"I'm scared," says a tiny voice in the grass.

Ronan emerges from where he'd been hiding. He's a little smaller than usual. And, okay, he's not the most masculine critter out there to begin with but here? It really is impossible to tell by looking at him if he's a girl or a boy. Right! Pointed ears. He's an elf. No wonder. Elf features plus long blonde hair. That'll do it. If his outfit is any clue, he's a ranger with a focus on archery.

"You're always scared." Sophia shakes her head.

"I'm small." He frowns at her. "And I don't have cool powers like everyone else."

"That doesn't matter here." Ashely ruffles his hair. "In this place, we have whatever powers our characters do. Except Chloe."

"Huh?" Kiddo looks up at us.

"You turned into a cloud of bats." Ashley makes a flapping gesture.

Chloe grins. "That was cool!"

"Vampireth can't do that for real," says Ashley. "That'h something from thith game world."

"Are you sure?" I wink at her. "We've never seen a really, really old vampire from Europe. Who knows what the heck they can do."

Ashley folds her arms. "Thtill. Chloe ith not a really old vampire."

"Thtill?" I snicker. "Why are you talking like that?"

"Fangth." Ashley shows off her half-demon teeth. "They're a bit fatter than the fangth I'm used to."

"Bollocks," says Sam, doing a reasonable impression of Dalton. "She can talk just fine. She's doing it to act cute."

Ashley's pink face darkens somewhat.

"It is cute." Mom smiles at her.

"This place isn't safe." Ashley swishes her tail around.

"This place isn't real," repeats Sierra.

"Can we die here?" Ronan leans against Mom.

Ashley, Mom, Sam, Sierra, and I exchange glances. Do we take a guess that might terrify Ronan or do we or just tell him we'll be fine?

"If Dad's running the game," says Sierra. "No. He won't kill our characters. He's all about the story, not combat."

"He likes combat, too." Sam cracks his knuckles.

"Yeah, but he doesn't overwhelm us." Sierra rests her sword across her shoulder. "He wants to see us win. It's not like he's running the games for his buddies. Back then, he didn't really care so much if characters died. He's more mature now. Plus, we're his kids. He doesn't want us to get hurt."

"Okay, but what if he's not in control?" I fidget.

"Then I suppose if we die, we'll just make a new character." Sierra starts walking away in the direction the orc came from.

"Will dying hurt?" Ronan swallows hard.

"No clue." Sierra shrugs. "Never died before."

"Only hurts briefly." I pick at my chest. "Then you wake up and don't remember anything."

Everyone stares at me.

"What?" I flail my arms. "Just kidding."

25

COLORFUL LANGUAGE

*W*e walk, mostly because Sierra picked a direction and went.

Sam and Ronan chatter about how cool it is to be 'in the game.' Ro is still kinda nervous about getting hurt. Oddly, Sophia isn't showing any signs of fear whatsoever. It's unusual for her not to be the most skittish, fearful person in any given situation. Mom's just kinda going with the flow, more or less acting like a parental chaperone on a Renaissance Faire trip from hell. I think she's kinda feeling like a badass in that cleric armor. Carrying a big ol' golden mace around is new for her, though she has prior experience engaging in combat with a blunt weapon. There are certain similarities between a mace and a giant iron frying pan, after all.

Did I mention Dad added an enchanted frying pan mace into his game world named Impslayer? Blix wasn't terribly fond of that, though he does understand. Imps are kind of like fish: herd mentality most of the time, but no real loyalty to each other. So, he found it hilarious watching Mom wallop other imps with the pan.

Ashley is prancing along. Yes. I said prancing. That's because it's the best word to describe whatever it is she's doing. That outfit. The tail. Making her chest bounce. She's gotten totally into character. Chloe is merely walking along beside me like a kid being led around Macy's, waiting for Mom to finish looking at clothes, so the 'fun thing we're going to do after shopping' can start. She wants to find a town so we can buy 'the rest of her dress.'

Really, it's not *that* bad. Ash is showing way more skin. Just, yeah. No one her age should have such a plunging neckline. It looks wrong. Hoping Sophia can figure out a way for us to escape this—whatever it is—before too long.

"Hey, guys?" calls Ashley. "Does anyone have any idea where we're going?"

"Soph needed something reflective." Sierra waves around at the landscape, still marching on. "So, I'm looking for water."

"Right, but do you have any idea where to go?" Ashley scurries forward, catching up to the Littles.

"Forward," says Sierra in a dry tone.

Ash grabs Ronan, one hand under each arm, and lifts him off his feet, holding him out to Sierra as if showing off a giant doll. "We have a ranger. Shouldn't he be leading?"

"W-what?" blurts Ronan, who doesn't particularly seem to mind being held by Ashley. He just kinda hangs there, tolerating it like a big housecat who doesn't seem thrilled about cuddles but is also too lazy to protest.

"She's right, Ro." Sam nods. "You're a ranger. Use your navigation proficiency and guide us to somewhere we can find a mirror or something."

Ronan glances around at us. "Umm. I can't do that. How am I supposed to do that?"

"The same way Ashley played mandolin," I say. "Just... I dunno. Try to do it."

Ash sets him back down.

Sierra stops walking and pivots around to look expectantly at our miniature elf.

"C'mon, Link." Sam nudges him.

"Not funny." Ronan grumbles.

Sophia and Sierra laugh. Yeah, me too. Poor little guy really does kinda look like Link in that outfit.

Ronan sighs, then looks around. He takes a knee, studies the grass, then stands and faces left. "That way."

If Sierra had been walking directly west, Ronan's indicating we should go more or less to the south. No one seems to object, so we start going that way. A moment or two later, Ashley begins to pick at her mandolin. She's not singing this time. The music she's playing sounds like the medieval equivalent of what you might hear in a supermarket or an elevator, if either one of those things existed in this setting.

Next thing I know, we're on a road approaching the outskirts of a town. An enormous three-story rectangular building stands off to the left of the road up head. Two horses stand hitched to posts out front. Looks like a roadside inn.

"Whoa." Sierra stops short. "What the heck just happened?"

"Hmm." Sam taps a finger to his chin. "Either we just skipped a bunch of boring travel where no random encounters happened, or Ashley played a rapid travel song."

I move up to the front of our group, gesturing at the inn. "Let's go in there. If all Sophia needs is a bowl of water, we can find that inside. Better that than going into town and running into more complications."

Murmurs of agreement come from everyone, even Mom.

"Ooh. I'm going to have an ale," says Sam.

"No, you are not." Mom pats him on the head. "Not for another eleven years."

"Aww." He snaps his fingers. "But this isn't real. And there's no drinking age in… wherever we are."

Mom shakes her head. "Nice try, Sam. No dice."

He's not really disappointed.

"You're not missing much," I whisper. "Beer tastes horrible."

Mom gives me that look. Yeah, she knows about the time I ended up passed out in Tiffany's hamper. She also knows I puked so bad the mere thought of drinking again made me sick. I didn't get in *too* much trouble because the 'rents considered it an object lesson. Stupid teenager thinks she's cool. Drinks so much she throws up, and now doesn't want anything to do with alcohol. Admittedly, I got drunk on wine coolers—not beer—at Tiffany's. However, I have had beer before. Didn't get drunk on it since I only tolerated like four sips. Bleh. I have no idea how anyone can *like* that taste.

I am over my alcohol issue, by the way. Ironic, right? I literally cannot get drunk now, and the smell of wine coolers no longer makes me queasy.

Oh well. I never really wanted to drink; it was more of just trying to fit in with everyone else at the party.

We make our way into the tavern and look around. It's reasonably normal as fantasy inn/taverns go. A long wooden bar runs along the wall on the left. The back end of the room has a giant stone fireplace with several chairs facing it and a white fur rug. Tables fill the majority of the remainder of the floor space. On the right, stairs lead up to guest rooms like a hotel.

Sierra clanks over to the bar and peers up at the man behind it. "You've got rats in your cellar and need to hire some adventurers to clean them out."

The man gawks at her in the manner of a medieval peasant seeing a witch. "By the gods... how did you know that?"

"Because we're level one." Sierra sighs. "Every inn has the giant rat quest."

"Quest?" asks the bartender.

"Noooo." Sophia whines. "I don't wanna kill cute little ratties."

Sierra glances back at us. "They are neither cute nor little. Probably going to be the size of golden retrievers, with red glowing eyes and teeth as big as daggers."

Mom squirms.

Ronan scoots back and hides behind her.

"Yeah, sure." Sierra looks back at the bartender. "We'll clear it out for you. We could use the experience."

"In a minute!" Sophia darts over to the bar. "Can I have a cup of water, please?"

"Of course, milady." The man sets about filling a big wooden cup with water.

Weird. This guy is talking to my sisters like they're adults. I wonder if all the NPCs here see us as our characters? Eek. That could get kinda creepy if someone starts trying to flirt with one of the Littles because, to them, they appear to be fully adult. I really hope Dad is somehow in control here, so that won't happen. I mean, technically, everyone's character is at least seventeen years old even if I'm not seeing them at that age. Ronan's probably like 200 years old. Well, his elf is anyway. So weird.

Sophia takes the cup of water and runs with it to a table. She flops in a chair and begins staring into the liquid as if the stein holds the deepest, darkest, most delicate secrets of the universe. Klepto-panther sits beside her like a guard dog.

"That's going to take her a while," Sierra pats her sword. "Shall we go get some rat xp?"

Mom grasps Sierra's armored shoulder and pulls her closer. "Let's just give your sister a moment to see if she can work some magic first, okay?"

Whoa. Mom is afraid of giant rats? Or maybe she doesn't want to watch her kids fight such creatures. Can't say I'm terribly interested in getting bitten by a rat the size of a dog. We sit at the table and wait. A generic looking barmaid brings us water to drink and some mini breads to snack on. Sam hands her a few coins.

The front door slams open.

This dude in dark leather armor, a flowing black cape, long semi-curly black hair, and a 'douche mustache' parades in. Six nearly identical men in chain mail armor follow him. Something about this guy causes an immediate sense of dislike in me. Also, worry. If that's the local town guard and we are only level one, they could wipe the floor with us. Ugh. I really don't want to end up in prison in a fantasy world where my vampire stuff doesn't work.

Act casual. We haven't done anything wrong.

Pretending not to care about the guards being there doesn't last too long.

The Sherrif of Douchingham thrusts his arm out, pointing at Chloe. "There's the fiend!"

Chloe points at him. "There's the cocksucker!"

Mom spits water all over the table, then begins to choke and cough.

Everyone in the room falls silent, staring at us.

The guy in black tilts his head at her. He doesn't look the least bit offended, merely confused.

"Sorry," says Sierra a hair louder than a whisper. "She's from New Jersey."

Sophia leans forward, looking at Sierra. She's blushing like crazy. "They won't understand that word. It's out of character."

"I really hope *you* don't understand that word," I mutter.

The look Soph gives me says she doesn't *fully* understand it, just knows it's something dirty.

Mom bangs a hand into her chest a few times and clears her throat.

"Yeah." Sam looks over at the guards. "Any modern cuss word would be out of character. Chloe should have said"—He stands and points at the guy with the curly hair—"There's the puking, plume-plucked pustule!"

All the NPCs in the room gasp and make faces like he's just said the rudest thing imaginable, such as claiming pineapple on pizza tastes good.

Fancy guy glares at Sam.

Chloe leans over to me and whispers, "Why would anyone suck on a rooster?"

Whew. I smile at her. "Because they are very, very silly."

"Oh," says Chloe.

Mom makes an urgent face at us.

"Chloe? Sweetie?" I ask.

"Hmm?" She grins up at me.

"Can you maybe try not to use that particular word around Mom?"

Mom clears her throat.

I cringe. "Or at all… like ever again?"

"Okay. Sorry." Chloe gives Mom an apologetic glance before glaring at the guard captain guy. "There's the asshat!" She looks back at me. "Is that better?"

"Marginally," mutters Mom.

"Chloe… try to say it in character." Sam rolls his eyes. "Like, call him a milk-livered maggot-pie or something."

Again, every NPC in the room gasps.

The guard captain's face reddens.

"Are we supposed to fight them?" whispers Ashley. "They look like cops. Err, I mean… guards."

Blix-barbarian grunts, grins, and stands up out of his chair, bouncing in eagerness. "Fight? Someone say fight?"

Sam folds his arms. "How the heck did they show up here so fast? Doesn't make any sense."

"Oh no," I fake gasp. "We've been pulled into Skyrim! The guards just materialize out of thin air as soon as we do something wrong!"

My brother and Ronan crack up laughing.

"We didn't do anything wrong, though?" Ashley flails her arms.

I frown. "A vampire walked into a town and got spotted. That's even worse than getting caught picking a lock. The guards usually go right to kill on sight."

"They do that for everything in that game." Ashley rolls her eyes.

"This isn't Skyrim, though!" Ronan bangs his fist on the table. "It's D&D."

"Seriously, though…" Sam shakes his head. "We shouldn't fight them. If we're getting the rats in the cellar quest, we're definitely only level one. Those guards will stomp us."

"We are not giving them Chloe," says Mom.

"No. Absolutely not." I grab her hand and hold on.

"We can't fight them." Ronan shrinks down in his chair. "Can't she turn into bats again and go out the window?"

"Good idea." Sierra grins. "That might work."

"Only problem is, I think the guy is more upset with Sam right now than Chloe." I bite my lip. "Not sure what the heck you called him, but he looks angry."

Sophia grabs the stein of water in both hands. "I got this. Need a minute or two. Try to stall them."

The six clone guards all draw longswords. Fancy guy in black whips a rapier out of a scabbard. Oh, figures. He's a duelist or something, a Three Musketeers type swordfighter. That's pretty close to Dalton's style. I wonder if I could keep up with him because I actually know how to sword fight and wouldn't need to rely on my 'character' to do it? How much does this place override our real selves? Not sure I should take that risk.

Fancy guy swishes his rapier sideways at us like an old school college professor with an antenna pointer. "Slay the fiend and all its minions."

"I'm not an *it*, you butthead!" yells Chloe.

Blix roars a war cry and charges at the guards, knocking five tables aside on his way across the inn.

Oh, no. You dumb, stupid, meathead of a barbarian...

The one guard he swings at ducks the giant axe, then he and the others proceed to beat the ever-loving snot out of him.

Ashley springs out of her chair, then leaps up to stand on our table —and begins playing her mandolin while singing about the faerie king's court.

The beatdown rapidly slows to the point where the guards are merely tapping Blix-Barbarian with their swords while staring at Ashley, mouths agape. He's lying on the floor in an almost cartoonish tangle of limbs. One by one, the guards begin tapping their feet, then twitching like marionettes on strings.

Guard captain guy closes his eyes. "No. No. No. Must... resist..."

"Dance, bitch!" yells Chloe while thrusting both arms toward the guy, claws extended. Her eyes glow red.

He convulses, shudders, then convulses again before whipping his head back like something out of Michael Jackson's *Thriller.* His facial expression is pure fear, as if he's lost control of his body. All six guards, the captain, the bartender, three barmaids, and eight or nine random tavern patrons all fling themselves into a wild, exhausting dance.

Ashley whips herself around and around atop the table, spinning and dancing as she plays.

Ronan and Sam exchange a look of disbelief.

Sierra seems unhappy. I'm guessing she would rather have gotten into a sword fight. She knows they would've trounced us, otherwise she would be complaining about not fighting.

Mom quietly tosses a healing spell at Blix.

Chloe begins to dance, but only because she wants to.

"Yeaaargh! Stop this at once!" shouts the guard captain. "Fiend, get out of my mind!"

Sophia waves her arms around in a series of mystical gestures. Trails of sparkling blue glowing magic hang in the air in the wake of her fingers. In seconds, a tiny star of intense white light appears between her hands and sinks down toward the water in the stein.

At the instant the tiny glowing star makes contact with the water, a blinding flash floods the room. A mild blast wave makes me rock back in my chair. I teeter for half a second, unsure if the chair's going to tip over backward. Thankfully, it lurches forward. As soon as it crashes down on all four legs, I can see again.

We're back home around the dining room table.

Everyone looks fine—except for Blix, who's face down on top of his character sheet, tongue sticking out. He's fine, just being a goof.

There we sit in stunned silence for a few seconds, giving our brains a chance to process what happened.

Dad's back. He's still holding the cookie jar. His face is blackened, hair blasted up and to his left like a Wile E. Coyote bomb went off in his face. Faint wisps of smoke rise out of the cookie jar. The whole living room smells like burnt chocolate chip cookies.

I glance down at my phone, which is sitting on the table next to the paper I used to scratch down stat rolls. "Whoa. Only forty-two seconds passed."

"Forty two... you know what this means." Dad solemnly sets the smoking jar on the table. "We have to watch *Hitchhiker's Guide* now."

"Now?" I raise both eyebrows.

"Not right this second, but soon." Dad places the lid on the jar, the clatter of ceramic simultaneously delicate and loud. "We have a game to start."

Chloe looks up at me. "Do I *have* to play a vampire character? That seems kinda silly."

"Of course not." I smile at her. "Play whatever you want."

Blix perks up and grabs a pencil, rapidly erasing something on his character sheet while babbling.

"Is it okay if he rerolls his stats?" asks Sam. "He wants more intelligence."

"So." Ashley folds her arms. "Tell me again how useless bards are!"

26

AN INCOMPREHENSIBLE MILIEU
OF NONSENSE

SATURDAY (DEFINITELY)

*I*t's about twenty minutes to eleven at night.

Eldon's come over. One of Wolent's people gave him a ride.

Chloe's stretched out on my bedroom floor beside me, fussing around with a Smurf jigsaw puzzle I got down from the attic. Haven't opened this box since I was like nine. Yeah, Dad showed me the cartoon when I was a kid. I remember thinking it was okay back then. As an (almost) adult, I look at the Smurfs and wonder what kind of drugs were involved in the creation of that show. Probably 'shrooms.

I'm at the computer, trying to help acclimate Eldon to technology, specifically the internet and social media. Ashley's flopped on the bed, her face aglow in the light from her laptop screen. She's an hour deep into researching Eldon's family.

"Oh, Sarah. Yes... I have been attempting to learn this... Facebook." Eldon pulls a phone off a belt holder. "I have obtained one of these devices."

The sight of it shocks me, not because it's a phone, but because he had one on his belt the whole time he's been here tonight and it hadn't occurred to me to consider it strange. He's still wearing a Seahawks T-shirt and jeans from our trip to Marshall's the other night.

"Where did you get that from?" I ask.

"Thought you didn't have any money," Ashley chuckles.

"I do not." Eldon eyes the phone. "Upon finding an establishment that appeared to be a purveyor of phones, I simply asked the man to give me one."

I gawk at him. "You stole a phone?"

He leans back, mildly offended. "I did no such thing. The man gave it to me."

"Did you pay for it?" I swish my computer chair side to side.

"Well, no. It was a gift." Eldon fidgets. "He did not ask for money."

Ashley and I look at each other. She facepalms first.

"You mind controlled the guy." I can't decide if I should laugh or feel guilty.

Eldon purses his lips. "It had not been my intention to do so."

"What other explanation is there? People don't just walk into Verizon stores and get free cell phones." I chuckle, then face him. Lesson time. "Okay, so as vampires, we can affect the minds of mortals..."

A short while later, Eldon's got a beginner's grasp on how our mental powers work. We're both now convinced he charmed the store employee without meaning to. Follows Rules Girl is ten spoonfuls into a box of imaginary rocky road out of anxiety. Is hanging out with someone who stole something a crime? Knowing about a crime like stealing a cell phone and not reporting it probably is a crime. But... he's a vampire. Our need for secrecy crashes headlong into my mortal goody-two-shoes brain.

Undeath has to supersede mortal law here. I don't like it, but making waves over something so lame is only going to cause problems for me down the road. Stefano would absolutely lose his mind if I called the cops on a vampire for yoinking an iPhone.

Ugh.

"So, I've been trying to familiarize myself with this device." Eldon swipes the screen active and shows me his Facebook. "It is rather surprising that so many young, partially dressed ladies want to be my friend."

"No, it isn't," whispers Ashley.

"Let me see that…" I reach for his phone.

He hands it over.

I scroll through his notifications list. Yeah. That's what I thought. He did not post a profile picture of himself, so 'the ladies' aren't fawning over his movie star looks. The profiles of the 'pretty underwear-clad women' requesting friendship with him are faker than vegetarian ham.

"Scammers," I say. "Those aren't real women."

"They look real." He leans close, peering at the screen.

"There is no law or rule saying that the photo of a person attached to an account has to be the person." I rapidly make my way through the list and hit decline on all of them. "They're all probably dudes in some foreign country."

Eldon blinks. "Why would they do this? Pretend to be women?"

"Scammers," I say. "They're either trying to steal your personal information, get money, hack your account, or perhaps they're only trolls."

"Are you serious? I did not believe such creatures existed." Eldon blinks.

"Oh, they do." I frown. "Not in this reality as far as I know, but if you go into the wrong cave somewhere…" I shiver. "Troll is not literal here… It's what they call people who do annoying things for no reason other than to make someone angry."

"Like trolling for fish?" adds Ashley. "They're trolling for people dumb enough to engage them."

"Ahh. Now the word makes sense." Eldon frowns at his phone.

Ashley emits a cute growl. "Sucks that we can't read people's minds over the internet."

"Read people's minds?" Eldon twists around to look at her.

Ugh. This guy. I sigh at the ceiling. "Didn't we just spend like half an hour going over how to compel mortals to do things? Mind reading is in there, too. Aren't you, like, over 150 years old?"

"Yes, but… I'd only been a vampire for a few days before my father cut my head off." Eldon sighs at his phone. "Pity they were not genuine solicitations of friendship. Though, I suppose it would not be wise to make friends with too many mortals."

I'm one to talk, but I nod at him. "Yeah. It's a bit of work, but worth it. Easier for me, though."

"How so?" He raises an eyebrow.

"You are so pale you look like you've stepped out of historical French nobility." I chuckle. "I can't forget to turn the warmth up."

"Oh." Eldon makes a face of concentration. His skin color shifts from clearly dead to merely British.

"Sorry again about your dad." Ashley grumbles at her computer. "I'm not seeing anything online about Mr. Whittmore's ultimate fate. Can't find what happened to the shipping company at all. There's no mention of it anywhere. I did find one thing about how the former estate has become a gimmick hotel."

Eldon and I both turn to look at her.

"A hotel?" He pauses, then exhales. "Well, I suppose that means my family is gone."

"What do you mean gimmick hotel?" I ask.

"Umm. They claim to be super haunted, so they do ghost tours." Ashley twirls her hair around her fingers. "Most of the people who rent rooms there are probably going there to have a paranormal experience."

That's a little too much coincidence for me. "Gonna take a leap of logic and say there probably is something funky going on there."

"Yeah." Ashley rolls off her stomach, then scoots forward to sit on the edge of the bed. "Do you have any idea what happened after the night your dad put you in boxes?"

Eldon meanders around in a circle, then sits on the second computer chair off to one side against the wall. It's my older one that usually pulls duty as a clothing storage device now. "I imagine he kept going at his war with Benjamin. My father appointed himself the agent of the light or some hogwash of that nature. Before I ended up among the undead myself, father announced he would dedicate his life to hunting them. To answer your question, no. I do not know for certain. My awareness during that time was limited to a handful of moments where mortals ventured close to the crypts. I suspect my father got himself killed rather soon after interring me in that cave."

Eldon gets up, crosses the room, and sits on the bed beside Ashley, interested in what's on the laptop. "Show me more of this... social media."

I slide off my chair and flop on the floor beside Chloe, helping her work the puzzle.

The room is so quiet for several minutes that the clicks and taps of laptop buttons seem deafening over the scrape of cardboard jigsaw bits. Sam's still awake, playing video games with Blix in his bedroom. Creaks above are probably Sierra's desk chair. She's still up, too, trying to learn the drawing software with the help of YouTube videos. Sophia is suspiciously quiet. Maybe she's asleep or perhaps reading. I think some squirrels outside are fighting.

"And this is TikTok," says Ashley.

"How does that nearly naked woman waving herself about relate to clocks?" Eldon might have blushed if his body was capable of it as a subconscious reaction.

Ashley snickers. "She's not naked. That's a sports bra and bike shorts. And she's posting a dance video. Lots of people do that."

Poor guy is still trying to wrap his brain around women being allowed to show themselves in outfits so scandalous their knees are bare in public. He doesn't object to this, merely finds it every bit as much of a drastic a change to his reality as horseless cars.

They spend a few minutes looking at videos before moving on to Pinterest.

"This is an incomprehensible milieu of nonsense," says Eldon.

Ash bursts out laughing. "Yeah, that about sums up social media. Hey, let's introduce you to some music."

She goes to YouTube and starts playing an assortment of music videos. The look on Eldon's face is absolutely hilarious. It's almost as if we barged into Uncle Hank's room at the home and blasted him with Limp Bizkit. Though, Eldon doesn't seem to hate it as much as find it alarmingly loud and 'busy' as he calls it. Not like Ashley's starting off with heavy metal. Taylor Swift is quite tame. Then again, this guy is used to like pianos and harpsichords or some crap like that —whatever passed for music in the 1850s.

Eventually, he seems to adjust and winds up grooving to some Billie Eilish.

Soft thumping comes down the stairs from the second floor, then goes across to the kitchen. Sounds like Sophia. The icemaker in the fridge chugs and grinds. She must be thirsty.

Wow, this is getting weird. Out of nowhere, I feel as if Ash and I are sophomores in high school and we've snuck a senior boy into our bedroom after the 'rents went to sleep. I lay there on the floor, staring at the two of them while Chloe hunts among jigsaw puzzle bits. Oh, not again. I'm past that nostalgia crap. This has to be Ashley's charm affecting me. It *has* to be. Why does she feel awkward with a boy in the room like we're going to get in trouble?

The doorbell rings.

What the hell? It's like 11:30 at night. No big deal to me, but people don't generally ring doorbells at this hour without there being something wrong.

Rapid soft thumping goes overhead from kitchen to living room.

Sophia lets out an ear-destroying shriek of terror. Glass shatters.

Without even thinking, I launch myself off the floor with so much force, my sweat pants end up around my ankles. It's like the 'yanking a tablecloth out from under plates' thing. Since I'm flying rather than running, I don't have to stop or slow down to pull them back into place while rocketing across the basement to the stairs.

I fly up to the ground floor and burst through the door into the kitchen.

Sophia's stuck in a slow motion run toward me, both hands thrust forward, grabbing at nothing. One bare foot makes contact with the carpet. Her other leg is out behind her. Blonde hair trails after her like a streamer in the wind. Her pink nightgown's pressed tight to her body from the pressure of air as she runs. My littlest sister's eyes are wide with terror, mouth equally huge to release a continuous scream.

Now I know where the people who draw anime get their inspiration.

Behind her, a ghoul arm sticks into the house, having smashed the narrow, tall window beside the door. He's fumbling around at the knob, but doesn't have a chance to find it before the door breaks inward. By the way, our door is supposed to open *out*. Three ghouls spill into the house, falling in slow motion.

No, time isn't weird. I'm in combat mode. Everyone else is normal. I am *fast*.

I swerve around Sophia, who still hasn't reacted to seeing me, and throw myself at the ghouls, punching the closest one square in the chest. Exactly like the last time, I end up bicep-deep in awfulness. Its brittle skin and equally brittle bones offer such little resistance to my attack, my arm pierces it like an arrow. Gloops of teal-black muck fall from the hole onto the carpet. Ugh. Mom is going to be mad.

"Yaaaaaah!" screams Sierra.

She leaps off the stairway at the midpoint and falls on the next nearest ghoul with her sword, pulling a full-on *Voltron* chop that cuts it in half completely from head through the crotch.

Yes, I know what *Voltron* is. No one could honestly believe I could grow up without being exposed to my father's absolute most favorite cartoon from his childhood, did they?

The bisected ghoul explodes in a blast of grey dust, covering Sierra and me so it looks like we stood too close to a bag of flour getting dynamited. My ghoul groans and raises a stake. I lazily catch his wrist in my left hand before he can stab me. Since my right arm is still stuck through him, I reach up behind him and grab his neck, cracking it with a quick hand motion.

He collapses in a cascade of dust.

Sierra grabs her sword in both hands, then rams it forward in an upward thrust. The blade pierces under the chin of the third ghoul—who is still out on the stoop—before breaking out the top rear portion of the skull. A fourth one, a couple steps back on the walkway, levels off a flintlock pistol at me. I notice it right as he pulls the trigger.

Click.

The hammer falls. Nothing happens.

I'd say my heart stopped, but it did that a while ago. Okay, to be fair, it does fake beating quite well. If I randomly bumped into a doctor with one of those listening things, they'd hear complete normality going on in my chest. Guess that means it didn't stay stopped.

The ghoul Sierra head-stabbed falls into dust cloud.

Mr. Flintlock shifts his eyeballs downward to gaze at the gun in his outstretched hand like he can't quite figure out why it didn't go off. Oh, I dunno, pal. Maybe trying to fire a 150-year-old pistol that's been buried in wet mud for most of that time isn't the smartest tactic?

Sierra glances up at me. "I got two, you only got one. You want the last?"

"They're ghouls, not cookies. But, sure. Might as well." I rush out the front door into a field goal worthy kick. My foot hits him in the crotch and stops moving somewhere around the base of his ribcage. I do not have the words to describe how *nasty* it feels to have my bare foot stuck *inside* a ghoul's torso.

"Oh, man." Sierra groans. "I don't even have balls and that hurt to watch."

"Neither does he." I hop once, then pull my foot out of his body.

He collapses into a cloud of grey powder.

"Not anymore." She wince-chuckles.

We spend a moment swatting dust off our clothes. De-gunking my arm and foot will require a shower.

"I'll get the vacuum," says Sierra.

"Not now. It's too late to run the vacuum." I lean out the front door and check the front yard. No sign of any more ghouls—or witnesses.

Mom appears at the top of the stairs in her nightgown. She notices the broken-in front door, smashed window, dark glorp stains on the carpet, and ash piles—plus a few stray ghoul fingers, then gasps. "What the devil is going on?"

"The Jehovah Witnesses are getting a tad pushy," I say in a flat tone.

Sierra shakes her T-shirt out, making a haze of dust. "I don't think these were Witnesses, Sare."

"No, you're right. Whatever they are, they had a little more higher brain function than that."

"Ouch," deadpans Ashley in the dining room behind us.

I turn to look at her. Eldon's trailing a step or two behind. "Is Sophia okay?"

"Yeah, she's under the bed." Ashley grins.

Mom creeps the rest of the way down the stairs, staring in horror at the smashed front door.

"No idea." I shrug. "They rang the doorbell, then tried to... I dunno... attack us."

"Max just incinerated something in the yard," calls Dad from upstairs.

I rake my hand up through my hair in frustration. "Probably more ghouls. Sorry."

"What did you do, Sarah?" asks Mom.

"No clue." I gesture at the mess on the floor. "They just started coming after me out of the blue. If it's something *I* did, I'm clueless what it could be. Sorry about the undeath goo on the carpet."

"Maybe they're just trying to reach you about your car's extended warranty." Sierra smirks.

I laugh.

Mom meeps at the rug. "That's not going to come out, is it? Gah. It smells so bad."

"I think it'll scrub out." I wince. "After a few minutes, the slimy parts will dry out and become dust."

"Looks like someone dropped a cremation urn." Sierra traces her sword across one dust pile.

Sophia peers out of the door leading to the basement stairs. "I-I can c-clean it."

She steps out into view, shaking like a chihuahua that drank two triple espressos as she pads down the hall to us, one hand over her face in a futile attempt to shield her senses from the odor of rotting corpse.

I put an arm around her. "Are you okay? Those things look a lot scarier than they are dangerous."

"I expect nightmares." Sophia gestures in an 'away with you' manner at the floor. The ghoul mess levitates into a floating mass, which promptly flies out to land in the cul-de-sac. "But I'm okay." She stares at the front door until it wobbles up off the floor and zooms back into place, a whole mess of splinters, screws, and plaster bits rapidly coalescing back together as if we're watching reversed video of it being broken in. Even the window knits back into a spotless pane of unbroken glass.

"You make that look so easy." Mom squeezes her shoulder.

"It's a lot easier to do when paranormal stuff happened." Sophia fidgets. "It's like I'm *supposed* to clean up those messes."

Eldon's jaw is hanging open.

Uh oh. He didn't know about the magic.

"Don't mind Sophia." I grimace-smile at him. "It would be easier for everyone if you didn't talk about her."

He continues staring at the floor where the dust had been, looking as shocked as if he'd just seen a vampire.

Yeah, it might be a little tricky to explain the whole magic thing

27

SWORD OF VENTING

OH NOES. ANOTHER MONDAY

*E*ldon didn't really question the magical repairs to the front door at all.

Soon after the attack, he thanked us for our efforts tonight helping him get used to the modern era and left. By 'left,' I mean Ashley ended up driving him to Wolent's while I stayed home to watch over Sophia.

Sunday went by without anything unusual happening... which, these days, probably counts as unusual.

It's a little after eight at night. Sierra wanted to cash in that rain check. Considering it is raining outside fairly hard, we are using the basement for a sword-sparring arena. The outer basement is big and open, only a few columns holding up the ceiling in the way. Dad really wanted to get a pool table at some point, though he's never followed through with it. Apparently, he's always wanted one ever since he was a teenager, but didn't live anywhere with enough room for one until he and Mom got this house.

Alas, Mom pointed out that he'd get the table, be all over it for a week or three, then it would just sit here under a protective cover and collect whatever junk we piled on top of it. Folding cafeteria-style tables are a much cheaper (and far more portable) place to store random stuff than a pool table. So, Dad still hasn't gotten one.

Works for us. Plenty of room for Sierra and I to chase each other around with rattan swords. Hey, it's just practice. We aren't actually trying to hurt each other. All things considered, she could probably use a real sword without too much of a problem. Worst case scenario, she stabs me in the brain and I sleep for a couple days. In all seriousness, we're not doing that because an accident would mess her up mentally and Mom would *freak* the hell out.

Speaking of 'trying to kill,' Sierra is going a little harder than usual. I'm having to actually work to fend her off. After a few intense minutes of us trading strikes, parries, and counterstrikes, she finally makes a small mistake and commits too much to a risky overhead chop. She's definitely angry about something and letting her emotion take over rather than being tactical.

I don't punish her for the mistake, even though I could've whacked her across the chest hard enough to leave her gasping for breath. Instead, I sidestep and smack the top edge of her wooden sword, adding my strength to her momentum. That causes her to overextend, lose her balance, and land on her chest.

A reprieve for us both. I back up a couple paces. "Sierra? Are you okay?"

She shoves at the floor in a push-up motion that flings her back into her feet. Ahh, the joys of superhuman strength on a skinny tween body. "Fine. Just getting my anger out. I'm not angry with you."

"I can tell you're angry." I point my sword at her. "Do you know why you ended up on the floor?"

She grumbles. "Yeah. Yeah. I know. Went barbarian mode there."

"Yep. You really wanted to hammer something." I stick the tip of the training sword into the carpet and lean on it like a cane. "Wanna talk about it?"

"The pool thing." She looks off to the side.

"Ahh. Okay." I ready up. "Swing away, then. Get it out."

Sierra re-engages without a war cry. She's being more cautious now, tactical, and not swinging as hard. This feels like we're doing Olympic fencing, trying to score point hits rather than kill each other.

"Good. Stay calm." I knock her next attack aside, then go for a thrust.

She spins in a blur, bringing her rattan sword around in time to deflect my attack. Oh, we're doing that, are we? I speed myself up, too. We keep going at it, trading strikes and parries. Feels normal to me, as if we're both ordinary mortals. Anyone watching us would probably get dizzy and throw up.

"Dammit." Sierra ducks a love-tap heading for her forehead. "When did you get so freaking good at this?"

"I've had centuries of practice..." I swing again. She jumps over the sword, spinning in an arc over my head to land behind me. "All pumped into my brain in a matter of like twenty minutes." Expecting her next move, I swing my blade up and around behind me to block the strike going for my back.

Wood hits wood with a sharp *crack*.

Then, I leap forward and spin to face her.

"Hah. Seriously, you're getting better." Sierra circles left.

"I'm just not holding back at all anymore. You caught up to me." I smile.

She gives a playful growl and lunges.

We cross swords, nose to nose, for a few seconds before I shove her flying.

"No fair!" she wails while in midair before crashing down on her back. "You cheated."

"I did not cheat. You weigh like fifty pounds."

"Grr!" She sits up.

I point the sword at her. "I'm not making fun of you. You really are light as hell. Any vampire or supernatural whatever you get into a fight with is not going to hesitate to take advantage of that. Don't stay still long enough to cross swords. You will not win a contest of brute force, if only because you are so light."

Sierra heaves a big sigh. "I think that's enough. I'm kinda tired."

"No problem." I walk over and offer a hand, then pull her to her feet.

She groans. "Am I going to be stuck like this forever?"

"I don't think so. Well. Definitely not *forever*." It's only been a few months since the enchantment, so I'm not too concerned that she doesn't look any different. Time to change the subject. "Are the kids at school leaving you alone?"

"Mostly." She shrugs. "A few boys teased me, but they stopped."

"That's good." I pause. "Or... did you make them stop?"

She examines her fingernails. "I just said they can make fun of me all they want after *they* lose three pints of blood and can still walk without help. Boys aren't tough enough to do that."

"Neither are most girls." I chuckle. "At least ones who don't have magical healing powers."

"Heh." Sierra laughs. "Yeah, but they don't need to know that. Anyway, they left me alone after Parker called them out for being jerks."

"Parker?" I ask. "Who's that?"

"A boy from school," says Sierra in a far too casual manner. "He gave me a towel at the pool when it happened."

"Guess he's got an older sister."

"Yeah. He said that." Sierra shifts her jaw to one side.

"Sounds like a nice kid."

Sierra narrows her eyes at me. "I do not have a crush on Parker Williams."

"Okay." I nod.

She growls and takes a swipe at me.

I just barely manage to get my sword up in time to block. "I'm not trying to make fun of you. You're getting angry anyway."

Sierra stops pushing into my defense and lets her weapon down. "Shit. Dammit."

"What?" I ask, still wary of a potential surprise attack.

"You're right. I got angry when you said 'okay' like that." She growls. "I might have a crush on him. Don't tell anyone."

I raise a hand. "Swear. Total secrecy."

She's quiet for a moment. "Sare?"

"Hmm?"

"Do you think Mom and Dad will freak if I went out with a black kid?"

No idea where that came from. It's gotta be more society in general than anything the 'rents have said or done. Maybe she's worried because Mom's related to Uncle Hank and he would *totally* lose his mind over that. Mom and Dad though? I don't see them having any problem with it... especially at this age. 'Boyfriends' in sixth grade are measured in weeks.

"Nah. Wouldn't be an issue." I chuckle. "Look at me. I'm dating a mortal and they don't mind."

Sierra laughs.

"You know Uncle Hank would have something to say if he manages to blurt before I can whack him with the derp hammer."

She frowns. "Yeah. I don't care what he thinks."

"Good. You shouldn't." I gather the rattan swords and walk them over to the shelf. "The world is full of Uncle Hanks. There's always some jackass out there who thinks they have the right to tell other people how to live."

Sierra wanders along behind me, arms folded. "Is he gonna die soon?"

Oof. I set the swords on the shelf, then turn toward her. "Umm. Well, he is really old. So, it's a safe bet he's probably not going to be around for much longer. Kinda morbid."

"Sorry." She looks down. "I just hate the way he shows up here for Thanksgiving every year and just ruins it for everyone."

I ruffle her hair. "Don't worry about it. If he shows up this year, I'll make sure he stays polite."

Sierra grins.

"Another subject change." I squeeze her bicep. "You've still got it. Not slowing down."

"Soph did say her magic was permanent. I don't have to keep getting more like when I was on vampire juice."

I squirm. "That sounds so wrong."

She stretches, then grins at me. "Yeah, it kinda does. Okay. Gonna go draw some… or maybe play a game."

"Cool. Have fun." I watch her run across the basement to the stairs, smiling again.

Sierra pauses at the bottom of the stairs to point at me. "Do not tell anyone what we spoke of."

"Promise." I trace an X over my heart.

She gives me this fake 'good, otherwise I'd have to kill you' nod, then darts upstairs.

Ugh. Uncle Hank. The guy is such a piece of work that even thinking about him can put me in a bad mood. Speaking of crotchety old men, I'm going to go check on Mr. Neidermeyer. It's about that time. Ever since he's come back from the hospital, Ashley and I have been visiting him a couple times a week to see if he needs anything and help out around the place. Obviously, since he's stuck in a wheelchair with a broken hip, he's not too mobile and can't exactly clean his house.

That's us. Vampire Maid Service, Inc.

Even crazier, Sophia and Sierra sometimes pop over there during the day. The crazy part isn't that they're doing that, it's how he doesn't seem to mind. Maybe the guy really was just lonely. Kind of a weird way to go about hating loneliness—acting like a dick to everyone. It seems ending up basically helpless caused him to reevaluate things. Granted, Sophia is abnormally sweet. There are a lot of kids out there who can be jerks, too. I'm sure some of those baseballs in his collection got thrown through his windows on purpose.

Oh well. Doesn't cost me anything to be nice to the guy. Maybe someday, he'll even apologize for being mean to me when I was little.

AN UNEXPECTEDLY HAIRY
COMPLICATION

a little after three in the morning, Ashley and I return home once we're done running messages around Wolent's various operations. The night was quiet and pretty boring except for one weirdo downtown. Dude rode a motorized skateboard down the middle of the street wearing nothing but a lime green speedo and a huge foam cheese wedge hat. That's the kind of unexplainable weird crap I'd expect to see in Portland. Not around here.

Cops dragged him off.

Just in case anyone happened to be wondering, it is *not* a good idea to scream 'Behold, the power of cheese' and punch a police officer. They *really* don't like that. Ash and I didn't get involved. The guy wasn't exactly in the greatest shape and had no weapons on him, so he didn't seem like much threat to the cops. We did not need to play superheroes.

That happened over an hour ago and we're still chuckling about it when our sneakers touch down on the deck. A sight waiting for us on the other side of the sliding glass door is bizarre enough to make me forget entirely about cheese guy.

Sophia's standing in the middle of the kitchen with her arms wrapped around a giant grey wolf. I mean this thing is sitting, as canines tend to do, and it's tall enough that she's hugging it around the neck while standing. Granted, Sophia is not the biggest critter in the world, but still. That is a *large* dog.

I step inside, eyebrow raised. "Soph? Everything okay?"

"Yeah," she says in a quiet voice as if trying not to wake the 'rents.

"What are you doing up at this hour?" asks Ashley.

"Heard noises. Klepto said there's a doggie in the kitchen, so I got out of bed." Sophia yawns.

The wolf looks at me, then Ashley, almost pleadingly. I can't help but get the sense it wants something from us. Perhaps it's had enough of Sophia's clinginess and wants her surgically removed.

"Wow. Big doggo," says Ashley before going full on goofy voice. "Who's a good boy? Aww, yes you are."

The wolf flattens its ears. If our life was a comic panel, there'd be a speech bubble over the wolf's head with 'really? Are you serious?'

"I think that's a wolf, Ash." I nudge her. "Not a dog. And it might not be a boy."

"Yeah. I know." She folds her arms. "Wolves are still doggos, all cute and fluffy and stuff."

I glance at her. "And they'll eat your face off."

"Aww, no they won't." Ashley offers her hand for the wolf to sniff. "That's a misconception. Wolves are not inherently dangerous to humans."

"Are you sure?" I ask.

"Well, I mean, as long as they're not starving or rabid." Ashley seems confused at the wolf not sniffing her hand. Still, she reaches forward and skritches its cheek.

Again, the wolf stares at me as if asking for help.

"Does he look hungry?" I ask.

"He looks fluffy!" chirps Sophia. "And he's not *that* big."

I blink at her. "You could ride that wolf like a horse... not that big, hah."

Someone comes down the stairs and heads for the kitchen. My guess is Mom based on the way the stairs creak without the thud of a footfall.

"Naw, he's not quite big enough for that." Sophia finally releases her hug, takes a step back, and looks the wolf over. "Maybe if I was only eight. Then I could ride him like a horse."

Mom appears in the archway connecting the kitchen to the dining room, looking bleary eyed in a nightgown. I can practically see the words 'what the heck are you doing out of bed' form in her mind and start drifting toward her mouth, but then her eyes register the wolf and she lets out a startled yelp.

This makes Sophia jump-scream. She did not hear Mom coming. In turn, her scream startles Mom, who screams again.

Sophia drops in place, sitting on the floor, and starts crying. Nothing weird there. That's her usual response to being snuck up on and startled. It takes her a few seconds to process that no one scared her intentionally to be mean, at which point she stops crying and sits there making a pathetic face. After a moment, she wraps her arms around the wolf again.

Mom collects herself, hand pressed to her heart. "Sophia! We are not adding an enormous dog to the family."

"That's not a dog. It's a wolf," whispers Ashley.

Mom stares at us. "Even worse. What the heck are you doing, Soph?"

Sierra arrives, ready for battle with a sword, tank top, and her blue pajama pants. "What's all the screaming? Do you guys know what time it—whoa. Big dog."

"That's not a dog. It's a wolf," whispers Ashley.

"What are you doing, Soph?" asks Mom in an 'I'm too old and tired for this' voice.

"I'm hugging him." Sophia sniffles. "Because he is fluffy."

Mom's gaze falls on me. "What is a wolf doing in our kitchen?"

"He just flew in from Alaska, and a typo online ended up listing our house on Air B&B," says Ashley with a totally straight face.

For a second, Mom seems to think she's being serious.

"Umm." I scratch idly at my arm. "Not a damn clue. Ash and I just got back from, uhh, work, and here he is."

"Can none of you tell me what a wolf is doing in my kitchen?" Mom pinches the bridge of her nose.

"Being hugged," whispers Sophia.

Mom sighs.

"Apologies for the disturbance," says the wolf in Eldon's voice. "Tonight has been... strange. I am not entirely sure what has happened."

Mom lowers her hand from its nose-bridge-pinching duty and stares blankly over it at the wolf.

Sierra steps farther into the kitchen, giving me a whimsical half grin. "This is like a dialogue option in an adventure game. You have just discovered that the giant wolf in your kitchen can talk. Do you: One, scream and run. Two, faint. Or three, have a glass of wine."

Ashley and I stifle laughter.

Mom sets her hands on her hips. "I am not a wine mom stereotype." She pauses. "Am I? You girls keep making jokes about that. Are you trying to tell me something?"

"Nah." Sierra leans her sword against the wall, then hugs Mom. "If you were a wine mom stereotype, we wouldn't dare joke about it."

"And," chirps Sophia, "if you were that stereotype, you'd get really angry if we joked about it. Like asking if someone's got a crush and they get really mad."

"What's that supposed to mean?!" snaps Sierra while glaring at me.

Sophia also points at me. "Remember when Sare wanted to kiss that boy in eighth grade and we kept teasing her about liking him, so she stuffed us in the closet?"

"Oh." Sierra stands there, seeming conspicuous. "Right. Yeah. I remember that."

"Oh, gawd." I cackle. "Evan Lee. Wow, I haven't thought about him in forever."

Ashley bats her eyes at me. "Didn't you go around calling him Heaven Lee?"

"Ugh." I blush. "Don't remind me. I am trying to forget I was ever that cringey."

"Eww." Sophia scrunches her nose.

Mom regards the wolf. "Well, I'm not going to scream, run, or faint, so I suppose it's choice three. A small glass might settle my nerves and help me get back to sleep. Speaking of which, why are you girls awake at this awful hour?"

"Because we're vampires?" I ask in a sheepish tone.

"Not you two." Mom rolls her eyes at me and Ashley. "The ones who still have bedtimes."

"Giant wolf broke into the kitchen." Sophia squeezes Eldon again, then takes a step back to stand by Mom. "Sorry. I thought we might be under attack again, so I was investigating."

Eldon-Wolf scoots a little closer to me, still sitting. "I don't know how this happened."

"Soph? Did you do this to him?" I ask.

"No. I swear. If it's me, it had to be stray magic." She rubs her chin. "But I don't think there are any active strays running around now. The last one was in the cookie jar and it's spent."

Ashley is unable to resist petting him. "Can't really old vampires turn into wolves and stuff?"

"He's only been a vampire for a few days." I shift my gaze to her, then back at him.

"A few days 150 years ago." Ashley chuckles. "Maybe that sort of thing doesn't really care about being conscious, merely being old."

I raise my arms and let them fall against my sides. "I have no idea. Shapeshifting is not something I can do, nor will it ever be something I can do. Wouldn't even begin to know how to describe thinking about it."

"Maybe that's just it?" Ashley keeps skritching him. "Think about wanting to change back to human."

"Think about it." Eldon tilts his head. "Well, I suppose there's nothing to lose—"

The giant grey wolf abruptly transforms into Eldon... who is rather naked. At least, he's still sitting on the kitchen floor, which affords him a bit of modesty. He also hastily covers his unmentionables in both hands.

Mom grabs the girls, clamping her hands over their eyes. Face flushed, she stares at me. "I'd cover you girls' eyes, too, but I only have two hands."

"Oh, this is quite mortifying," says Eldon. "My sincerest apologies."

Ashley's face almost matches her hair for color. She averts her stare off to the side—after a few seconds.

Sophia does not seem to mind having her eyes covered and stands there holding still.

Sierra doesn't try to squirm way, though she does sigh. "Come on, Mom. It's nothing I'm not going to eventually see someday."

"Not on my watch, young lady." Mom tries her best not to look at Eldon.

The view is not unpleasant if I do say so. I don't stare nor do I shy away. It's usually me who ends up unexpectedly naked thanks to vampire weirdness. Glad it's *not* me this time. Suppose it's kinda hypocritical of me to check him out. This is pure admiration of a work of art, mind you. I'm not tempted to do anything. "What happened to your clothes?"

"They are likely somewhere back in the woods." Eldon looks like he really wants to scratch his head but doesn't dare move his hands. "I do not recall. Some ruffians attempted to accost me. I endeavored to distance myself from them as rapidly as possible... and the wolf happened quite unexpectedly."

"Bummer." Ashley bites her bottom lip. "Vampires who shapeshift in movies always keep their clothes."

"There's Hollywood for you." I shake my head. "Americans can't handle nakedness. Guess real vampire powers are from a more feral, primal creation that doesn't give a crap about social mores and clothing." I nibble on my lower lip. Leaping out of my clothes is the main thing keeping me from being jealous about vampires who can turn into animals. Neat ability but I'd rather not go streaking if I can help it. Vampirism hasn't quite turned me that primal.

Ashley snickers. "Are you saying vampires are kinda like wolves that allowed themselves to become doggos for the easy food? Giving up the freedom of a primal, feral existence to fit into society?"

"When you put it that way, it does kinda make sense." I chuckle.

"Hey." Ashley snaps her fingers at me. "Didn't that Ladonna person turn into a raven? Do you remember if her clothing went with her or fell off?"

"Umm." I try to remember. My mind is telling me her clothes seemed to vanish, not falling off her. "I think they somehow did. Huh. Or maybe I'm remembering it wrong."

"Oblivare could be weird." Ashley shrugs.

"Or her clothing wasn't real. Just illusions," says Sophia.

I scratch idly at my arm. "Or keeping your clothes with you is like another thing about shapeshifting that a vampire has to learn how to do." Damn, now if that's a possibility, maybe I will start being jealous of shapeshifters.

"Could be." Ashley randomly decides to help herself to a cupcake from the box on the table. "He got his clothes back when he reassembled himself. You could be right. The same effect that did that could carry them for him when he's a doggo."

Mom, her hands still over Sophia and Sierra's eyes, tries to angle her head to look at me without catching too much of Eldon in her view. "Will you please bring him down to your room? I'll go get some of your Dad's things for him to put on."

"Okay. Huh? Wait." I smile at her. "Mom? Did you just tell me to bring a naked man to my bedroom?"

Mom sputters.

Sophia and Sierra snicker.

"I'm teasing." It's hard not to snort-laugh at Mom's reaction. "Problem, though. Chloe is down there. Not sure we should bring him to the basement where she could see him."

"Damn." Mom fidgets. "Right."

Eldon scoots across the kitchen floor in a series of hops until he's close enough to the counter to swipe the dishtowel from where it hangs on the dishwasher's door handle with his teeth. He drops it on his lap, then sorta wraps it around his waist into something of a skirt, though it's not big enough to go all the way around him. He has to keep holding it.

Mom nods at him. "That towel is never again to touch any dishes. You may keep it. I will be right back with something he can put on." She pivots and tugs the girls along, escorting them out of the kitchen by her grip around their heads, still covering their eyes.

Eldon backs into the corner of the counter, holding the towel in front of himself. "Truly sorry about this. I had no idea."

"It's all right." I sigh. "Nothing I haven't seen—or experienced —already."

Ashley snickers. "No one warned me being a vampire would be just like high school."

I blink at her. "What?"

She thrusts her arms out to either side, grinning broadly. "An endless series of awkwardly embarrassing moments!"

"Right?" I roll my eyes.

"And that's so damn cool!" Ashley beams at him. "You can turn into a freakin' wolf!"

METAL STORM

YAY! MADE IT TO WEDNESDAY

A whole week has gone by, and things have been fairly normal. Haven't seen or heard from Eldon since Monday of last week when the whole wolf thing happened. Poor guy has to be embarrassed to hell and back. One day, he's a twenty-year-old with a rich family and high society influence, then he's stuck naked on the floor of a suburban kitchen in front of three women and two tween girls. I'm counting myself and Ashley as women for purposes of that statement. I think we handled the situation maturely, thank you very much.

I said it's been a normal nine days, and it has—more or less. Ghoul attacks have continued at random intervals. They're almost getting funny now. Like, I walk outside with a trash bag, open the lid on the giant outdoor bin, a ghoul pops out of it, and I casually destroy it before dropping the trash bag on top of the dust pile. Had one try to get me today when I left the house for school. He came running across the cul-de-sac.

Since I was already in my car, I just ran him over.

It couldn't have been these ghouls who attacked Eldon. As old as he is, he can make himself stronger than me. There's no way he'd be afraid of them and need to flee. Then again, he did seem kinda freaked out the other night when they kicked in my door. Maybe it hadn't been Sophia's magic that shocked him. Could the guy be phobic of ghouls for some reason? Hmm. The shock on his face fit that whole 'looked like he'd seen a ghost' idiom. Eldon first showed up in old clothes kinda similar to what the ghouls are wearing. I wonder if he maybe knew them or something. Heh. Funny to think about. What are the odds of that?

I'm sitting in my Rise of Modernity class while Professor Meredith Ross lectures… and I'm thinking more about ghouls than taking notes. After Mom came back downstairs sans Littles and with some clothes for Eldon, he talked about the attack a little. He didn't remember too much, only that he'd turned into a wolf to get away from them. However, what he did say about the two men who tried to rough him up made me think vampires more than ghouls. Could be some random anarchists looking for a new guy to mess with for kicks.

Ugh, if I'm going to bother finishing off the semester, I should at least try to pay attention.

My phone vibrates at an incoming text a little after eight. I ignore it until the mid-session break at 8:30. Hey, I'm trying to respect the teacher here. Sorry. Can't help it.

Once the fifteen-minute break is upon us, I pull the phone out and look. It's a text from Eldon requesting that I go with him to a concert tonight. It's not a date. He's in need of me to stand between his 1850 mentality and the modern world. In effect, I'm an interpreter. For once, the Universe is aligning with me. Wednesday nights are bad for Hunter. They are when he does the bulk of his homework, since he is usually off work. I've offered to help him out financially so he doesn't have to wait tables, but he insists. Grr. What is it about guys? When we talk about immortality and the future, he's all like 'whatever you want. I'll do anything for you.' But the idea of him letting me pay for his tuition and books and food and such, that's an issue. Whatever. It wasn't worth arguing over. He can't be perfect.

I send a text back to Eldon, accepting the request. He sends me the time and location for the show he's picked. Never heard of the band 'Tempest of Storms' before. Figure they're local. The link promises the 'ultimate heavy metal experience.' Ugh. This is going to be loud. The show starts at 10:00 p.m. at a small concert hall downtown. It's not that far from the campus, which helps. Feeling like I won a major victory—since Eldon has learned how to text—I reply again informing him to just meet me there since I'll zip right over from class.

Wouldn't be right of me not to mention this to Ashley, so I text her with the plans.

She replies in a few minutes with 'see you there!'

Yeah, I figured she'd want to hang out with Eldon again.

Great. *Two* of my sisters are in crushville.

Should I investigate this Parker kid?

Nah. At this point, Sierra's only having thoughts. It's not like they're going on dates or anything. I'll just content myself to worry about Ashley. It's entirely possible that Eldon won't have any interest in her—or any woman. Some vampires have no sex drive whatsoever. Not sure how that works. I mean, we are dead, so one would think there's nothing going on down there. Then again, one would also think it impossible for a person to fly.

The only thing that makes sense about vampirism is that nothing is going to make sense.

Ash has been dropping subtle hints and Eldon's been oblivious. Could be he's from olden days high society and is simply over polite. Oh, that's got to be it. Modern flirting is a little different than the kind of flirting he'd have been accustomed to among rich people in the 1850s. You know, she's making cute faces at him or being close. She's not saying stuff like, 'well *my* father owns an entire railroad.'

I chuckle. Okay, back to class.

TAKES ME LESS THAN TWO MINUTES TO FLY FROM THE PARKING GARAGE at SCC to the concert place.

I left a little early, using a bit of vampire-fu to conceal myself from everyone's perception. Hey, if I can streak bare-ass naked through downtown Woodinville and not end up going viral on the internet, it's easy to walk out of class undetected while fully clothed.

Eldon and Ashley are together, hanging out on the sidewalk about half a block from the place. Looks like he's finally gotten himself some new clothes. Now, he looks more like a modern rich kid about to go bar hopping and less like a gamer geek in a cheap T-shirt.

I land and approach them. Ashley hugs me.

From the outside, it's a fairly unassuming square building with a dedicated parking lot. Signs announce various other shows as well as indoor paintball. Huh. Weird. Guess it's one of those modular deals where they can change the interior around.

I'm assuming Wolent (or his organization) covered the ticket fees since Eldon says it's been handled. We make our way inside. He shows his phone at the counter. There's a teenage girl in the booth with a short, white pixie cut and about forty earrings, two nose studs, and a gold star embedded in her right eyebrow. Without a word, she scans a QR code from his email. Three tickets burp out of a machine. She hands them over to us, looking entirely *done* with the whole process. This girl totally wants to go home.

We follow—well, not the crowd. There aren't *that* many people here. Before long, we end up in a big, open room with a few hundred other people. No chairs anywhere in sight. The walls are black. The ceiling is black. The stage is black. Ugh. Standing room only. I hate this crap. This is why I am mostly an introvert. Being in a place like this would've scared me as a mortal.

Eldon gazes around, seemingly confused. His bewilderment grows when four guys and a girl not too much older than me rush out on stage. They're all dressed in black stuff: jeans, T-shirts, studded forearm guards, and so on. The girl's like five foot nothing with long, Smurf-blue hair, way too much eye shadow, and a spiked black dog collar around her neck. I'm assuming she's the vocalist since she went straight to the center microphone stand.

I lean toward him. "Not what you were expecting?"

"This was supposed to be about heavy metal." Eldon glances around the audience. "Is that not a meeting of shipping concerns for mining?"

"Uhh, are you serious?" I gawk at him.

"What else would it be?" He practically jumps out of his clothes when the band suddenly kicks in with an explosive drum smash and guitar chug.

Welp, there goes any chance of talking...

The music isn't super fast, though it's heavy and deep. I think they call this 'doom metal,' though I'm hardly an expert on this sort of music. Smurfy (as I'm mentally calling the singer) alternates between an operatic, melodic voice and deep growling vocals. I'm not the biggest fan of growl-singing. However, this is not entirely intolerable.

My brain is pulsating in my skull from the volume. Sound waves reverberate in my body fluids, making it feel as if my entire skeleton is vibrating. I think Eldon is screaming. Ashley's headbanging, a giant floof of red hair flailing around.

As best I can tell, this song has something to do with a goddess of lightning wreaking havoc on a kingdom because they turned their back on her and started worshiping some demon instead. Okay, fantasy metal. I can get into that. I'd get into it more if half of the lyrics weren't incomprehensibly growled. Sounds like someone took a D&D campaign and turned it into music.

Eldon appears to be trying to speak to me. Can't hear him at all over the music. His expression is hilarious. My imaginary speech bubble over his head fills in the words 'I have made a tactical mistake.'

He's not gesturing like he wants to leave, so I don't. Everyone in the audience is grooving in varying degrees from headbanging like Ashley to jumping around. Minutes later, the song smoothly changes into the next one without a break. This one's a little faster tempo and has more growl vocals. Ugh. I can't make out what she's singing except for the chorus being something about 'endless torment'.

Someone not too far away from me on the right lurches forward and crashes into another guy from behind, knocking them both to the floor. A third guy near them picks up the guy who initiated the tackle and throws him into the crowd.

Another man farther to the left hammers his forearm into the face of a random person close enough. The violence begins to spread around us.

Oh, crap. This is turning into a mosh pit. Now, I do kinda want to get the hell out of here.

A man starts to lunge at me. I lean back, raising my arms defensively. I must be surprised enough to look like a frightened kid or something. The guy aborts his attack and jumps on Eldon instead. Oh crap. That's right. I kinda remember someone at school (that's high school, not SCC) saying mosh pits aren't mindlessly violent and they don't just attack people who aren't into it. I didn't really believe that. Guess I was wrong—or this is a tamer show than some.

Eldon staggers to the side from the force of the guy plowing into him. When he recovers his balance, he glares indignantly at the man and shoves him away—launching the poor dude twenty feet into the crowd. The 'oops' look on Eldon's face at that is priceless.

A scream nearby briefly overpowers the music. I recognize Ashley's voice. She's not screaming in terror-no, that was a war cry. I spin to look. She's moshing around into people, sending dudes and women flying off their feet. Can't tell if she's mad because someone hit her or just vibing to the music and letting out some pent-up rage. Kinda weird for her to pummel random strangers out of nowhere. Gotta be retaliation.

Eldon gets pulled into the crowd. He eventually shoves the guy who grabbed him off, but not before he's like fifteen feet away from me. We make eye contact. He points and seems to say 'behind you!'

I spin around and catch a wooden stake right in the chest. My reflexes kick in, dragging reality around me into slow motion. Having nothing else to do and a mere hundredth of a second to come up with *something* to do, I fling myself over backward. The old wood point pokes me in the sternum, failing to break skin as I am moving away from it faster than the arm wielding it thrusts it at me. Of course, the maneuver leaves me flat on my back in the middle of a mosh pit. Not the best place to be.

… and there's a damn ghoul standing over me.

Some random concertgoer with spiked hair hammers the ghoul from the side, oblivious to the fact it's an undead monstrosity. The ghoul crumples into a heap, bones snapping and breaking as this guy crushes it into an unrecognizable mass of dried out flesh. It's gone in seconds, becoming dust.

Someone stomp kicks me in the stomach.

Grr. I grab the leg at the ankle in both hands, and swing the guy like a giant baseball bat to the floor. Yeah, I got a little angry there, but what kind of dick stomps on a girl who's fallen in a mosh pit? He should consider himself lucky to walk away with a sprained knee and broken nose.

I leap back to my feet and get body checked by a mortal woman. She's not too much older than me and seems to be caught up in the mosh energy. Annoying, but there's no reason to hammer her back. I bounce off her into another guy who tries to forearm-smash me in the nose. I duck his arm, resist the temptation to slam my knee into his balls, and settle for shoving him into the crowd hard enough to knock five people over.

Ashley's pale hands rise out of the crowd holding a severed head she's apparently just torn off someone.

I'm about to freak the hell out until she throws the head toward the stage and it disintegrates into dust before making it halfway across the room.

Oh, just a ghoul.

Another one comes out of the crowd and gets in my face. I think— no, I'm pretty damn sure it's the same guy who pointed a flintlock at me last week. He doesn't try that again. This time he's got a stake.

The sneer he's giving me makes it totally clear he thinks I'm an abomination that needs to be destroyed. Yeah, same to you, butthead. I swipe the stake out of his hand before he can swing it at me, and ram it into his right eye.

He moans, flails, and falls over. Another ghoul trying to get to me doesn't make it. A big mortal with a giant beer gut trying to stage dive falls out of the crowd and crushes the ghoul before he's within reach of me. The blast pattern of dust on the black floor looks like the big dude dropped a WWE flying elbow on a bag of flour.

A severed arm goes sailing up out of the crowd about twenty feet to my left. It also breaks apart into dust. Can't tell if Ashley or Eldon did that. Some random jerk drives his knee into the middle of my back. I lurch forward from the hit and crash into another guy who tries to mash me in the nose after I bounce off him. I jump back to duck his punch. Taken by a sudden upwelling of rage, I whirl around on the dude who kneed me and return the favor. He goes down. Maybe a doctor will be able to find his nuts somewhere up near his stomach. Once he's on the floor howling in pain, I try to grab my back while doing this awkward little shimmy around in a circle waiting for the pain to stop. Damn, that hurt. My freakin' spine...

Ghoul number—I lost track—rushes out of the crowd at me. This dude's got a small sword. Oh, we're escalating, are we? I sprout claws and whack him across the face, ripping off the entire front of his skull. His eyeballs fly to my left. One splats into the side of a woman's head like a rotten egg. The other one takes a higher trajectory and is lost to the darkness. Sword ghoul drops to his knees, twitches once, and collapses into a heap of dust. Eyeball-splat girl thinks the dude behind her hocked a snot-ball into her hair, so she goes off and starts beating the crap out of him.

Ashley zips up beside me, giving me an urgent stare.

I nod to her and mouth, 'where's Eldon?'

We turn together to scan the crowd.

A moment later, I spot him up near the stage where the moshing is at its heaviest. He's trying to batter his way through the crowd without overdoing it and killing anyone. Three ghouls emerge from the undulating mass of mortals almost simultaneously, going after him. Eldon screams—not that I can hear him—and looks an awful lot like a kid having a nightmare. He flails in a mostly uncoordinated attempt to defend himself that reminds me of Sophia getting into a fight with a giant spider. Purely because of how fast he can move, he ends up dusting all three ghouls without too much difficulty. He also unfortunately clobbers a random mortal in the shoulder hard enough to swat him to the floor. Oof. I hope that didn't break his arm. Can't tell. The music is so loud, it's impossible to hear anything else.

Some people near us have finally started to notice the rotting dead body smell from the ghoul dust and are looking around making WTF faces. Crazy thing is no one appears to be freaking out or even really noticed the undead creatures. It's kinda dark and chaotic in here.

We force our way through the crowd to Eldon, being slightly less than gentle in moving people aside. Don't want to break anyone else's bones; however, I'm not tolerating delay.

Ashley grabs one of Eldon's arms while I grab his other. Then, we fight our way out of the mosh area to where the rear part of the audience is still calmly standing there grooving to the music. Without having to worry about random fists, forearms, or knees flying at my anatomy, it's much easier to slip through the crowd to the exit.

The farther we get from the concert room, the less oppressive the music becomes.

Once we make it outside to the parking lot, the band is pretty much inaudible beyond a thrumming noise coming from the building, making the entire structure seem to vibrate.

"Bloody hell." Eldon huffs. "What was that?"

"Are you talking about the music, the mosh pit, or the ghouls?" I ask.

He stares at me. "What is a mosh pit? I don't recall seeing a pit in there."

"It's just what they call the part of an audience where people start slamming into each other and stuff." I brush dust off my arms. "That is kinda normal for a show like this."

"Unpleasant…" Eldon also swats dust off his shirt. "I am to understand that this 'heavy metal' has nothing to do with iron ore?"

Ashley laughs. "Nope. It's a type of music."

"Why the devil do they call music 'heavy metal'?" He stares at her.

"No clue. They just do." I shrug. "Maybe because guitar strings are metal? Who knows?"

"Makes as much sense as anything." Ashley shrugs.

I face Eldon. "Okay, what's up with those ghouls?"

He somewhat sheepishly looks over at me. "Ghouls?"

"The undead creatures that threw themselves at us in there." I keep batting dust off my sleeves. "Those stupid things have been coming after me for a few weeks now. You had a reaction to them. First at my house and now here. Like you're unusually scared of them."

Eldon's quiet for a moment, then sighs. "I just thought they looked familiar. Reminded me of people I knew."

"Maybe you did. Their clothes look kinda old." Ashley folds her arms. "Are they after you, too?"

"It is possible." Eldon shifts his jaw back and forth. "There have been a few minor disturbances on the grounds of Mr. Wolent's manor, though no one has spoken to me about them. Can't even begin to guess what's going on."

"There she is," says a man before adding something in Spanish.

I look toward the voice. Two twentysomething guys in tank tops and bright track pants jump out of an older Camaro. One points at me.

Not entirely sure what he called me. Got a feeling 'puta' isn't a nice word, though.

"You guys are making a mistake," I say. "I'm not who you think I am."

The one on the right pulls a handgun while yelling at me in Spanish. The only word I catch is 'Dalton.' Oh, shit. These guys must be from LA.

I dive for cover behind the nearest car as he starts shooting. Side mirrors and windows burst apart into showers of glass fragments.

Eldon runs after me as I scramble forward, trying to keep my head down while windows continue to explode above me. When I run out of car, I leap forward and fly, skimming inches off the pavement to dart behind the next row of cars.

Both LA vampires continue shooting, probably hoping to get lucky and put a bullet through a car into me, anyway. It's not going to do much more than hurt unless they tag me in the head or heart. I'm sure that's what they're trying to do. A shot like that is lights out, then I wake up chained to a tree for sunrise again... if I wake up. Yeah, these guys are probably pretty pissed off that Dalton and I arranged a sun bath for their gang leader.

Another gap in cars forces me to fly-jump to keep ahead of the bullets. I roll over in midair, cringing as several slow-motion projectiles Matrix right past my face. I look between the creeping bullets at the shooters. Ashley's standing behind them as if they haven't even realized she exists... and she looks pissed.

I disappear behind a big red SUV.

Two men scream in pain. That's my cue.

Pushing off the ground, I launch myself straight up, flying in an arc toward the two LA vamps. Ashley's grabbed the guns away from them both, breaking one guy's wrist and ripping the other one's index finger off in the process. She looks triumphant for a few seconds until they realize she's there and start beating the snot out of her.

Ashley's a fighter, even if she's not very good at it. She growls and tries to give as much as she gets in the half second it takes me to reach the fray. Unlike her, I have claws... and I'm going to use them. Ashley's bleeding from the face. I am furious.

I land behind the two LA vamps, slapping my hands into their backs at the base of their necks and shredding my claws all the way down their spines to their butts. They howl in agony, their bodies lapsing into involuntary convulsions at the extreme pain. I may as well have shoved a taser down their throats and turned it on.

Ashley backpedals. She's battered and roughed up. Not too bad. Looks no worse than a fairly standard fistfight.

"You okay?" I ask.

"Yeah. I'm good." She points both handguns at the guys on the ground. "Losers."

The weapons only click when she tries to shoot.

Out of ammo.

Eldon rushes over to us right as the two LA vamps get back up. My claws destroyed the waists of their track pants and shredded their briefs. Didn't leave much of their tank tops, either. Being naked from the waist down does not appear to have sapped their desire to kick my ass. If anything, the afterglow of claw pain has made them even more determined to end me.

I hold my arms out to the sides, claws extended. "Wow. You guys should be ashamed bringing such small guns to a street fight." They're average. I'm trying to insult them so they forget about Ashley.

Eldon holds his fists up like some old timey boxer.

The LA vamps both come after me. Eldon lunges at the one on the right, punching him in the jaw. His speed catches the guy—and me— way off guard. The idiot flies into a Toyota thirty feet away like a human missile, punching right through the window of the passenger side door.

I duck and weave around a few fast punches, angling for an opening to land a good shot. This guy is pretty quick. He's getting his arms up to block everything I throw at him. Yeah, I'm shredding the crap out of his forearms. It's slowing him down, though. I fake an attempt to claw Mr. Winkie. He panics and leaps ass-first in reverse like a matador evading a bull. Too bad for him I wasn't really trying to grab his junk. While he's distracted protecting that thing—and obligingly leaning his head toward me—I catch him with a fast left-handed swipe across the throat.

He staggers away, clutching his neck and gargling in agony.

Other dude's already pulled himself out of the Toyota and re-engaged with Eldon, who hammers him in the chest with a one-two punch combo that knocks him over on his back. The dull *whud-whud* of the hits are so loud it makes *my* lungs hurt. LA vamp two coughs up blood. Eldon's 'boxing' stance is so janky and weird I don't know how the heck he's landing any hits other than being crazy fast.

"Oh, hells bells," says Eldon. "This mafficking is rather exhilarating. Not my usual pastime, but I dare say it is mildly entertaining."

"Umm, what?" asks Ashley.

Eldon, fists still up, waves in a taunting manner at the man he knocked down. "Come, ye quarrelsome roustabouts, let us engage in fisticuffs."

The LA vamps pause, exchanging a WTF glance while trying to pull their mangled track pants back up. The garments aren't totally obliterated, merely the elastic in the waistband. They won't stay up without being held in place.

I gesture a clawed hand at Eldon. "He's been out of the loop for a while. I'm trying to coach him."

He glances sideways at me, fists still poised in his weird stance. He kinda resembles that 'fighting Irish' logo, other than not wearing green. "How would a more contemporary person say that?"

I blink. "What the hell is mafficking?"

"Uhh, something of a brawl out in the streets." He again gestures for his opponent to come closer. "Rather feeling foolish for fleeing from these louts the other night."

"These are the guys that made you turn into a wolf?" Ashley laughs. "They're not dangerous at all."

Both LA vamps give her the finger.

Ashley frowns, then throws something at one of them.

A severed index finger bounces off his chest and hits the parking lot.

"Heh. Now *that's* giving someone the finger." I chuckle. "Come on, let's wrap this up fast. The cops will be here any minute. Will you guys just like go away? You have a problem with Dalton, discuss it with him."

"They're too chickenshit to fight him. They're gonna pick on his baby." Ashley scowls.

"Sarah, what is the modern translation, please?" asks Eldon.

"Umm. Come, ye quarrelsome roustabouts?" I purse my lips. "Uhh, probably something like 'come at me, bro.'"

Eldon clears his throat. "Come at me, bro."

The LA vamp darts in, holding his track pants up with his left hand, and punches him in the face. Ooh, that's a *meaty* thud.

Eldon takes a step back, seeming unbothered. "Impressive."

The LA vamp hits him again the same way. That time, Eldon didn't move backward. The genius in lime green track pants begins to look a bit worried.

"Allow me to retort." Eldon punches him back. The guy tries to dodge, but isn't fast enough.

Ashley, I, and the other LA vamp all turn our heads, tracking the guy as he flies across the parking lot and slams into the front of a dumpster almost sixty yards away with a dull, echoing *whoomp*.

"Holy crap," whispers Ashley. "That's a broken neck."

The guy picks himself up.

"Or not." Ash blinks. "Wow, these guys are tough."

Apparently, claw wounds down the spine plus across his throat aren't enough to convince the other one to leave me alone. He fumbles a folding knife from his pocket, snaps the blade out, then staggers toward me with murder in his eyes.

I pull my phone out and shoot a text to Sophia: ‹need sword, send kitten›.

There's barely enough time to hit send before I have to jump away from the knife. Eldon stands there, waiting like a gentleman for the other LA vamp to stumble back across the parking lot. My guy tries to stab me three or four times. Yeah, okay, maybe this is a little bit of PTSD, but I'm totally on the defensive. I have a thing about knives and angry jackasses.

A flash of violet light erupts in front of me. My katana's hanging in midair with a fuzzy grey kitten wrapped around the handle.

"You are awesome!" I grab the sword.

"Mew!" says Klepto before disappearing.

I point my sword at the guy, tapping the end of his knife and almost knocking it right out of his grip. "Once again, you're coming up a bit small."

He growls.

The other LA vamp stops advancing on Eldon to look at me. He babbles in Spanish. Pretty sure it's something like 'where the eff did that bitch get a sword from'.

"Are you two jackasses going to leave me alone now or am I going to get stuck cleaning up a serious freaking mess?" I glare at them.

There's a certain confidence in knowing how to actually use a sword. I don't look like some punk teenage brat attempting to be all cool and edgy. These two can sense the seriousness in my voice, my body language, and my glare. I'm absolutely confident that if these two don't go away right now, I'm going to hack them up like a sushi chef on cocaine.

Sirens rise in the distance. Yeah. Nice going dumbasses. Fire guns in the city. That always works out.

Maybe it's not my sword that scares them. Maybe it is. As soon as the sirens are noticeable, the two LA vamps limp run for their Camaro, struggling not to lose their pants. Speaking of guns, Ashley grabbed their weapons away from them and just tossed them aside. There's a chance she left fingerprints on them thanks to our bodies trying so hard to be lifelike. Can't let the cops find those weapons. I zoom over and pick them up.

"We have to get out of here right now." I look at Eldon. "Turn into a wolf and put as much distance between you and this place as you can. No time to argue. Do it!"

Eldon looks down at himself, cracks his neck side to side, then leaps forward onto his hands. His body blurs into the shape of a big grey wolf that runs straight out of his clothes and flows like a ghost off into the night.

Wow, he really is majestic.

Ash gathers up his clothes and shoes. The two of us leap into the night sky mere seconds before the flashing lights of police cars are visible on the street leading to the concert hall. Eek! Too close.

We land a few miles away, meeting Eldon in a small park near the water.

Ash and I politely look away while he shapeshifts and changes.

"Why did you keep the guns?" Ashley raises an eyebrow at me, seeming worried as if I might actually want to hang onto them and, like, start carrying a firearm.

No way. Mom would kill me. She wouldn't be happy I'm even holding guns someone else tried to shoot me with so the cops don't go after Ashley. Not that she wants Ash in trouble. Mom just has this thing about guns. I used to, as well—before I had to use them. Still don't really want to be around them but they don't *scare* me anymore. Maybe that's because I can't die to a gunshot. Yeah, that's probably why I'm not too scared of them anymore.

"Fingerprints." I wag the weapons at her. "I think we still leave them."

Her worried-slash-accusing expression shifts in an instant to worry. "Oh, crap!"

From a girl who's taken to using 'unicorn sparkles' as a curse word, saying 'oh crap' is about as bad as an F bomb coming from a normal person. Just a phase. She'll get over it once her brain finishes descrambling itself.

"Fingerprints?" asks Eldon. "What are you talking about?"

"Nothing you have to worry about." I chuckle. "It's an Innocent problem."

Ashley laughs. "He doesn't know what fingerprints even are. They didn't have forensics in his time."

"Oh, duh. Right." I exhale. "Well, like… every time a living person touches an object, the oils on their skin leave an imprint of their fingers. The pattern in the skin is unique or something. The police can use it to identify who touched a weapon, for example."

He makes a pondering sort of 'hmm' noise. "I have not once ever seen these prints of fingers… unless of course someone's got mud on their hands."

"We can watch *CSI Miami* or *Law & Order* sometime," says Ashley. "It'll take too long to explain. They're invisible unless you put stuff on the thing to make them show up."

"Interesting. Sounds like magic." Eldon chuckles. "So, what shall you do with those pistols?"

"Umm." I glance down at them. "Probably just hand them to Aziz and ask him to deal with it."

"All right." Eldon, once again dressed, walks up to us. "Would you mind explaining to me what that fracas was about?"

I exhale hard. "My sire and I got involved in a turf war in California. Dalton's a bit of a mercenary sometimes. That was just a revenge attack. It's a long story... hopefully, there won't be a sequel."

"I see. Well, now what shall we do?" Eldon rubs his chin.

"Not sure about you guys, but I'm hungry." Ashley scratches at her stomach. "Chinese or Italian?"

I groan. "Ash, come on. That joke is so old."

She laughs.

"Anything but vegans," I mutter. "They taste like kale."

SCRY HAVOC

THURSDAY

*M*y chemistry class ends early at twenty minutes to six. No, I did not misuse my power. Big test today with nothing else on the agenda, so we can leave whenever we feel done— or when the time runs out. This class seems to be going well for me. Who'd have figured having crazy amplified senses—especially smell— would come in so handy for mixing stuff in practical labs. Takes much of the guesswork out of 'did I mix it well' or 'has this been on heat long enough.' I can smell the changes in the chemicals and know when to kill the flame.

The early out works for me since I'm responsible for transporting Sophia to her dance class tonight. Mom is stuck late at the office doing prep work for an upcoming hearing. It's nothing exciting like a lawsuit or whatever. Some sort of Congressional oversight board is just 'rubber gloving'—as Mom put it—the budgetary details of some military project Boeing's working on. Gotta love politics. One side wants to make sure they're not spending frivolously while the other is looking for any excuse to shut the whole project down.

No idea what 'the project' even is. I don't think Mom does, either. At least not beyond its name and some rudimentary descriptions. The government should look into stealth attack kittens instead of whatever super plane they're trying to get made. Much less expensive —and cuter.

Being that it is still daylight out, there's not much choice for me but to drive myself home.

Dad's old Sentra—now mine—isn't a bad car other than feeling ponderously slow compared to flying. I must be getting comfortable in my unlife since *not* being able to mentally compel idiots out of my way is frustrating.

No, I am not driving like a maniac. When I say 'idiot,' I'm talking about this moron in a green Saab doing forty in the middle lane. Cars zoom past us on either side well past sixty-five, not leaving me any opportunity to get around this guy. I'm too much of a 'grandma' behind the wheel to make a risky maneuver to escape, so there I sit for at least eight minutes before a guy in a big blue pickup truck takes pity on me and lets me in.

I wave thanks and pull around the Saab. As tempting as it is to flip him off, that's not who I am. He'll have to settle for a 'what the hell is wrong with you' stare as I cruise past him. Dude is oblivious. Argh.

Two big reasons keep me from speeding. One: I don't want to cause an accident that would hurt someone who can't pick themselves back up from most injuries. Two: it's daylight out and I cannot mind-wank a cop to leave me alone. Not sure I could handle the shame of admitting to the 'rents that I've gotten my first traffic ticket—so I'm doing everything I can not to get one.

Sophia is waiting for me outside, standing at the end of our driveway by the sidewalk. Looks like a 'white dress with pink sneakers' day. She's got her backpack (that holds her dance clothes) over one shoulder.

I pull up sideways to the curb, putting the passenger side door right in front of her.

She hops in. "Hey, Sare. Little close today?"

"Sorry. Got stuck behind a slow SAAB."

Klepto jumps from her shoulder to the seatback, then leaps to my seatback before grinding her little fuzzy head against mine and mewling a greeting.

"Hi there." I reach up and give the kitten a skritch before she teleports to Sophia's lap and curls up.

Now I have a third reason to drive responsibly: one of my siblings' lives is literally in my hands.

Okay, maybe that's a bit melodramatic, but I'm mentally scarred from that driver's ed movie they made us watch in junior year. I think someone made that film back in 1972. Stupid thing made driving sound as dangerous as flying a B42 into Berlin at night in the middle of World War II. Like if anyone got where they wanted to go without losing limbs, it counted as a miracle. I will never forget that derpy cross-eyed guy driving the cement mixer truck… or the two teenagers who 'drowned' in cement pouring into their car because the jock driving didn't think stop signs were worth his time.

Obviously, it was staged and no one got hurt but good grief. They overdid it.

We end up chatting about random 'how was your day' stuff on the ride to the dance studio. The conversation is pretty light and fun until Sophia whips out a zinger.

"Any idea what you're going to do with Hunter?"

"Do with him?" I chuckle.

She waves a hand around in a 'you know what I mean' gesture. "Like, he's getting older. Are you gonna *do it*?"

I wag my eyebrows. We've already done it… many times. Not making that joke to Sophia, though. She'd miss it. Or worse, she wouldn't. The world is going to corrupt her innocence, eventually. It's not my job to hurry that along.

"It?" I ask.

"You know." She makes a biting gesture. "So you can keep him forever."

"Hah." I chuckle. "Boys aren't pets."

Sophia sighs. "That's not what I mean, either. You wanna stay with him forever or not?"

"I do." I smile out the windshield and get this extremely silly mental image of him, me, and Ashley hanging out in a night club somewhen in the year 2200 that's all *Star Trek* and whatnot. Who cares if I'm not really a 'night club girl'? How can I say what I'll be like *that* far in the future? I mean, I don't imagine Aurélie started off being a master of the Kama Sutra in all possible ways. Boredom stretched over centuries can do strange things to a mind. I really hope if I get eccentric, it doesn't turn *weird*.

"Are you gonna bite him?" She grins.

"No. Not me." I explain our plan to let him get a little older and then find some vamp around here that I trust to do the Transference.

Sophia nods along with my explanation of why it's probably going to be better for him to grow up a little more. Society doesn't take eighteen-year-old boys too seriously.

"Umm." Sophia scratches under Klepto's chin. "That's good. If he changes his mind before he's twenty-five, are you going to be okay?"

Oof, going for a heavy one, huh? I squeeze and relax my grip the steering wheel. "I hope so. That would make me sad for a while. Probably a long time. I'm not going to force him to go vamp if he doesn't want to."

She lets her head lean back against the seat and closes her eyes. "I think he's going to do it. The guy's really in love with you."

"Yeah, he is." I let a long slow sigh leak silently out of my nose. "Not looking forward to the process of trying to figure out which vampire to ask to do it."

"You're not going to?"

I shake my head. "No way. It would feel too weird, almost like I'd become his mother. And there's the mind link thing."

"Cool." She opens her eyes and grins at me. "Maybe becoming a vampire will make him a little more interesting."

I sigh into a chuckle. "Stop..."

"Oh, come on. You know it's true. He's a bit... well..." She shrugs. "Ordinary."

"I like ordinary. I need ordinary." I shake my head. "I tried dating the 'fun guy' once and he ended up stabbing me."

Sophia grimaces. "I don't like thinking about that."

"Neither do I."

We're quiet for a moment.

"Are you dating Hunter because you don't think he's going to stab you?" she asks a tiny bit louder than a whisper.

Can't help but chuckle. "Not specifically, though that is a definite plus. I really do love him."

"But?" Sophia peers at me.

"But?" I raise an eyebrow.

"You said that like there's a silent but."

Suppose I could make a Sam stealth fart joke there. Nah. I'll be the bigger person. "If there is a 'but' to that statement, I guess I'm a little worried my feelings for him might be a teenage high school crush thing. I don't think they are. Figure we will both know the answer to that by the time he's in his mid-twenties."

"Cool." She nods. "It's much less complicated not to grow up."

I give her side eye.

"Chill, Sare." Sophia runs her hand repetitively over Klepto's fur. "I'm talking about you being eighteen forever."

"You're not planning to stay eleven for eternity, are you?"

Sophia stares into the dashboard. Wow, that's an 'I've thought about it' face if ever there was one. "To be fair, Dad seems to think staying a kid forever would be the greatest thing. No responsibilities, no job, no taxes."

"Sophia... did you enchant yourself to stay a kid forever?"

She fidgets.

"Oh, good grief, Soph. Mom is going to freak."

"I didn't..." She pauses a second, then huffs. "At least, I don't *think* I did."

"What did you do, Ray?"

She turns her head toward me. "Ray?"

I let her think for a few seconds.

"Oh, duh. *Ghostbusters.*" She giggles. "Well, I didn't summon the destroyer of worlds."

"Good. Fuzzydoom needs to stay in his box."

She laughs nervously. "Hah. You know, I probably really could make a giant marshmallow man."

"You probably shouldn't."

"Yeah." She nods.

"The PIBs would go nuts." I raise and lower my eyebrows.

Sophia whistles. "Totally."

"Okay, so what did you mean by 'probably' there?"

"Umm." She looks down. "I did cast a spell on myself. You remember, going into the woods, the water…"

"Right…" I turn onto the street where the dance studio is. "Something about soul goo from the demons."

"Uh huh." She squirms. "I wanted to enchant myself to stop getting older when I was your age."

That tracks. My kid sister hero-worships me. Everything I do, she wants to do—except turn into a vampire. Pretty sure she's not interested in that. At least, she's not because she might have the ability to make herself an immortal teenager in other ways.

"You wanted to."

"Yeah." She bites her lip. "You know how my magic sometimes doesn't always quite work exactly the way I want it to?"

"Oh no. Again, what did you do, Ray?"

She sighs. "I don't know. I'm kinda sure I'm going to stop growing older when I'm your age. After what happened to Sierra, I tried to scry when *my* first period is going to be so I can make sure I'm not in public when it happens."

"Reasonable." I chuckle. "In a completely unreasonable scenario."

She laughs, then looks worried.

"That part you're not telling me? Please tell me." I pull into the strip mall parking area and navigate to an open spot near the studio.

"Umm. I kept seeing smoke. Like, nothing coming through. The scrying mirror remained blank."

"That's weird?"

"Yeah, it is." She fidgets. "Never did that before."

"What do you think that means?"

"Oh…." She sways her head side to side, drawing out the word 'oh'.

"It could mean a lot of different things. I might die before ever having a period. I might be stuck at this age and never get one. Might also be that I fail at scrying."

"Wow." I stare into space, not sure how to process that. If Sophia messed up the enchantment and froze herself at age eleven, what are we going to tell the 'rents? Should she try to fix that if she did screw up? What if she makes it worse and turns herself into an old lady overnight?

Sophia grasps the door handle, but doesn't open it. "It might also mean that the Universe doesn't consider a first period significant enough to show up during a scry."

"Clearly," I deadpan, "The Universe has never had a first period."

She winces. "Is it really that bad?"

"It's different for everyone." I chuckle. "Ash always said if it happened to her in public, she'd smear blood on her face like war paint and roar at everyone."

Sophia gags.

"She didn't." I cut the engine.

"Chickened out?" asks Sophia.

"Nope. It hit her when she was at home. Only her mom witnessed it. Total non-issue."

"Ugh." Sophia shoves the door open. "Something else for me to be anxious about. I should probably stop attending dance recitals until I know what my schedule is going to be. A pool was horrible, but if it happened to me on stage? I'd just drop dead."

"No, you wouldn't." I open my door and get out. "You'd reverse time and run off stage before it happened."

She laughs, jumps out, and shoves her door closed. "True. I'm sure something *that* embarrassing would give me the emotional power for a localized time warp."

"Mom saying you couldn't keep Klepto was enough for you to rewind time... pretty sure having a bleed in front of a theater audience would be worse."

"No." Sophia hugs Klepto possessively to her chest. "Kittens are special!"

"Mew," says Klepto.

"Suppose I shouldn't scry over spilled milk." Sophia starts walking toward the studio. "Or spilled blood."

I groan.

We reach the curb by the studio.

Sophia pauses. "You're right. If I am sufficiently mortified, I can back time up a few seconds and avoid the problem entirely. The problem is, if it's only a small embarrassment, I might not have the power to wield time magic."

"Then it's only a mild embarrassment you can deal with." I take two steps forward and open the door for her.

"Maybe I don't have to be anxious." Sophia shrugs. "The first visit from the red faerie is probably not significant enough... or maybe it'll be a non-issue like with Ashley. That's why I can't see it. The event is going to be minor. This doesn't necessarily mean I'm going to be eleven forever. I might stop at fourteen, eighteen, or even twenty-five. Not sure."

"Your magic is so predictable." I laugh. "Scry havoc and let loose the plush unicorns of war."

"Rawr," says Sophia.

31

THE OLD HANGOUT

FRIDAY

*S*pontaneous plans coalesced out of thin air.

It's almost a miracle for everyone's schedules to align, except for Ashley who isn't in school anymore. It's a few minutes after five in the afternoon. Ash and I meet Michelle at Frosty Buns ice cream and hamburgers. We used to go to this place three or four times a week after high school. Sounds unhealthy as heck, but we went there more to hang out than eat, considering we all would be having dinner later on at home. Besides, teenagers can tolerate a steady diet of junk much better than adults.

We hop in a booth seat the way we used to and order the cheese fries platter. If we didn't opt for ice cream, the three of us would always get one cheese fries plate and split it. No reason to change, especially not now. In fact, Ashley orders a medium chocolate milkshake, too. Ack. That's going to feel funky later.

Ash is managing the daytime fairly well, helped along right now by a grey hoodie and sunglasses. Chloe, who's still at home with Dad, tolerates sunlight incredibly well. I'm honestly a bit jealous how easy a time she has with it. Although she still doesn't wake up as early as me (yet), her tolerance for sunlight is basically as good as mine without having been tied to a tree for sunrise. I mean, I'm quite glad no one has done that to her. Still a bit jealous. Not too much, really. One does not have three smaller siblings without getting used to the idea that the little ones get away with things I couldn't. My theory is she's a little kid so operates on cartoon logic. As in, the coyote sails off a cliff and doesn't realize he should be falling until he looks down and notices he's floating in midair. Kiddo doesn't really understand the sun should incinerate vampires, so it leaves her alone.

Or at least, that's my working theory.

Yeah, I do wonder if it has something to do with innocence. There has to be a reason ancient vampires named my bloodline 'Innocent.' The implication that the less 'nice' a vampire is, the more the sun messes them up is also a bit weird to me. Why would the sun care if a vampire's a jerk?

Whatever. It's got to be a coincidence.

A nice gloomy Seattle Friday is perfect for me. I'm just at ease outside during the day at the moment as mortal me would've been. Ash will catch up sooner or later. She's newer than me and also didn't go through the shock training of forced sunrise exposure. Gah, that sucked. I never would have done that if given the choice. However, it ended up kicking my sun tolerance into high gear so, not totally a negative experience.

Frosty Buns might be a vampire too, despite it being a building. It hasn't changed at all since the first time the three of us decided to hang out and get ice cream. We all had a bit of spare change on us and decided to walk all the way here since none of us could drive at thirteen—or however old we were. That might have been one of the first times I spent my own money on something. Coming in here to order a treat and pay for it myself made me feel all grown up.

The place isn't exactly hopping like it probably was when the 'rents were in high school. The internet, social media, and video games make staying home a lot more fun than it had been for them as kids. Still, there are a few people here: one family of four, a single guy with two small kids, and two separate groups of high school kids. The older of those groups, probably seniors, gave us weird looks for a while but stopped. It's the kind of weird look you give someone you're pretty sure you know but can't remember why or how you know them. They'd have been sophomores when we were seniors. Maybe they saw us at the school and kinda remember us... then think Ash and I look like we're still sixteen so we couldn't possibly be who they think we are.

I'm being mildly sarcastic there. I don't think I look sixteen. Ashley definitely does look like she's sixteen. So what if people tell me I look like I'm sixteen? It doesn't mean I do, merely that they think so.

Sigh. I am the reverse Bree Swanson. She got mistaken for twenty-one while still being seventeen. No. I'm not jealous of a girl who peaked in high school. Actually, I kinda feel sorry for her after what happened with Scott. Wonder whatever happened to her? Maybe I'll ask Glim if he can find out.

We easily fall into talking about everything and nothing like we used to do here. Today, it's less about school and boys and movies and bands and more about internships, jobs, and idiots. Ash still sometimes 'works' at the veterinary place since she loves helping animals. Yeah, she's still basically a glorified janitor, but they let her do some really basic care type stuff too. She's even helped out lifting huge dogs sometimes—once the sun was down.

Conversation swells and ebbs, drifts around corners, and flows freely among us for a while. At one point, Michelle and Ashley get to talking about their respective 'jobs.' This leaves me sitting there watching them without having much to contribute.

One of those annoying nostalgia moods comes over me. Frosty Buns, the scenery, the background noise, the smells, the way the fading afternoon daylight stretches into skewed rectangles on the blue-and-white tile floor, me dreading homework waiting for me... this moment could be any of a thousand similar moments we've shared here.

Somehow, sitting in this booth table with my friends feels simultaneously like a time travel to the past and completely different than it used to be. It's an indefinable difference I can't really put into words.

My dad said something kinda sad-profound a while ago when we'd had one of our afternoon chats in the kitchen by the fridge after I woke up from vampire sleep. Don't remember the exact way he phrased it, but it kinda went like: one day, you go out to play with your friends for the last time and none of you know it's the last time.

He wasn't being super morbid. Not 'last time' in any dark sense, just a nostalgic sense of growing up, moving on, friends going in separate directions. When Dad was nine or ten, he used to play outside in the yard all the time with his friends and their *Star Wars* or GI JOE toys or Transformers. One day that he and the boys played out there together happened to be the last time they ever did so before stuff changed. None of them had been aware in the moment of that day it would be the last time all of them got together to play imagination with their toys.

I don't think they even noticed or cared the 'last day of playing together' had even occurred for several years. Kids don't think about that sort of thing. They just want to rush on to the next great adventure. They want to grow up in a hurry so they can have later bedtimes, watch the cooler movies, learn to drive… that sort of thing. No, it's only the introspective mind of a forty-seven-year-old father of four that looks back on a fleeting moment of carefree childhood happiness with a somber curtain hanging over the lens. Dad doesn't regret his life, or his age. Just… sometimes he likes to daydream about a world without deadlines or taxes.

That kind of midlife longing for simpler times isn't supposed to happen at my age. Then again, not too many teenagers are literally immortal.

Damn vampire brain.

If this feeling isn't coming from my mind still being in the process of coming to terms with eternity, then it's gotta be some sort of psychic or intuitive read I'm getting. Maybe there is something going on with Michelle. She's talking so much about being so damn busy with school and her internship job. Got the same vibe from her at Ashley's birthday party.

Yeah, Dad. One day we go outside to play with our friends—or hang out at Frosty Buns—for the last time and none of us know it. Except, I kinda have a feeling something is over now. Grr. I think it's kinder not to be aware that I'm hanging out with my friends for the last time right in the moment. Come on, Universe. Give me a couple months of blithe obliviousness before it hits me it's been months or years since the last time we did something as a group.

Throw a girl a bone here.

I let out a long, somber sigh, careful to keep it inaudible. This would have happened anyway, vampire or not. Only difference is I wouldn't have been thinking about it in the moment. The last time Chelle, Ash, and I hung out together would have come and gone like no big deal. We'd all have gone down whatever paths life had in store for us as the 'yeah, we'll get together soon' thing never quite happened. What is the phrase Mom's friends always use when they're on the phone? 'We'll do lunch sometime.' Yeah. That's it. Only, none of them are serious about actually getting together for lunch. The phrase is merely a polite acknowledgement of a status quo that no longer reigns, a tacit nod to friendships once strong that are now only the equivalent of an honorary degree.

Oh, another difference… if nothing supernatural happened to me, it wouldn't have just been Michelle drifting away. Ashley, too. Life. Careers. Kids maybe. More bonus points for vampirism: Ash isn't going anywhere, at least not anytime soon.

Good. A happy thought.

I force the maudlin aside and reinsert myself in the here and now.

"… getting good with the daylight tolerance pretty fast." Michelle reaches across the table to touch Ashley's hand. "Were you always this pale, or is that a side effect?"

Ash and I laugh. Of course the question isn't serious. Ashley's always been this color. We used to joke that we had to warn the FAA whenever we went to the beach because Ash in a bikini could knock planes out of the sky from the glare.

"Trying…" Ashley swipes her hair out of her eyes. "Sare got a crash course in sun management when those lunks tied her to a tree and roasted her."

I shudder non-seriously. "Don't remind me."

"I'm not *that* much of a tree-hugger." Ashley sticks two fingers into a patch of sunlight on the table and stares at them. Nothing visible happens. "I just have the power of an abnormally clingy friendship steeped in desperation."

Michelle raises an eyebrow. "I'm not sure if I should laugh at that or suggest you see a therapist."

"It's fine." Ashley grins like a goof and leans against me. "I own my neediness."

I put an arm around her. She's kind of kidding but also kind of not. We couldn't be closer if we'd been actual twins.

"Gonna be so weird." Michelle leans back in the bench seat, gazing down at the small plate in front of her holding French fry crumbs, cheese bits, and little fragments of bacon.

"What is?" asks Ashley.

"When I'm like forty and hanging out with you guys." Michelle idly picks at her beige angora sweater.

"You look like someone who's about to surrender their dog because they can't afford the surgery." Ashley takes a long sip of her milkshake. "Like, you don't really want to but you think it's best for the dog."

Michelle keeps staring at the plate, perhaps intentionally to avoid eye contact. "Yeah. Look, it's not like I'm trying to get rid of you guys or anything. Just so busy lately and… really, I'm gonna outgrow you. Don't really want to be thought of as your babysitter or mom."

"Chelle." Ashley, acting over serious, holds her hand out next to Michelle's. "Look at me. No one will ever mistake you for my mother."

"There's adoption." Michelle laughs. "Just because the great inkjet in the sky ran out of ink before it made you doesn't mean I couldn't be your momma."

We all crack up laughing.

The happy mood fades to somberness in only a few short minutes.

"At some point, life's going to pull us in different directions." Michelle sits up straight again. "I hate it, but it is what it is. And no, I'm not interested in getting a set of fangs."

I'm really glad undeath has given me permanent protection from the red faerie. If that little bitch was punching the walls of my uterus right now, I'd be a weeping mess. I'm still feeling pretty morose. Still, it's not bad enough to leak out of my eyes. Stupid, I know. It's not like she's dying. Maybe *this* is why vampires allow the world to think they died: they're cowards. They don't want to deal with the emotional load of having to spend the next several decades gradually losing everyone they loved while knowing they don't really have to. Michelle refusing to be turned vampire is kinda like a cancer patient refusing treatment and just letting the disease kill them.

No, not really.

Damn. I guess that's kind of a clumsy metaphor. Michelle isn't sick. Her life isn't being cut short—it's only 'short' compared to immortality. That's all on me.

"Yeah," I say eventually. "I know. Time marches on and whatnot, even if Ash and I aren't walking in the parade anymore. I'll always be in the shadows to help you if you need it."

"Me, too." Ashley makes a goofy face. "As much as any shadows can exist near my pale moonlight-reflecting butt."

We all laugh again.

"Thanks guys." Michelle stretches forward, takes our hands, and squeezes. "Now, this is not me saying I never want to see you again, only recognizing it's going to be weird hanging out in public."

Ashley sets her elbows on the table and rests her chin on both hands, eyes downcast. "Yeah." Her mood shifts on a dime. She snaps her gaze up to Michelle. "Oh, you should see this guy we're showing around the city. He's unbelievably hot."

"Ooh, tell me more." Michelle leans closer.

"He used to live around here. Spent a while away, now he's back." Ashley lifts her head off her hands, leans back and finishes off her milkshake. "Crazy gorgeous, and nice. He's a bit of a dweeb though."

I snicker. "He's not a dweeb. He's just... not used to modern times."

"How old is this dude?" asks Michelle.

"Like twenty." I shrug, then whisper, "1852."

We spend a while talking about Eldon and giving Michelle all the deets. Well, most of the deets. Lot of mortals around, so we omit most of the supernatural parts. Ashley gets the bright idea to say he's ex-Amish so we can talk openly about helping him adjust to technology. Naturally, Michelle wants to see a picture of him, which we don't have. Ashley thinks he looks like Chris Evans, younger. I think he's got more Cary Elwes in him with a bit of a Christopher Reeve chin. He's somewhere in between them, dashing yet humble and a bit clueless. He wouldn't have come off as clueless back in 1850. I imagine him being in command of his destiny there. Confident, self-assured, rich…

No, I'm not daydreaming about him like that. I am legitimately happy with Hunter. Eldon is more like the hot romantic lead in a book I'm reading that I daydream about in idle fantasies. Ashley's kinda doing the same thing. Oddly, I can't tell if she actually wants to try getting romantic with him or if it's a more innocent crush. It's not like she's been flirting with him or parading herself around him in alluring outfits. No, she's still wrapped up in anime geek couture most of the time.

"And how does Hunter feel about this job of yours?" Michelle wags her eyebrows.

"He's okay with it because he knows I am not going to break his heart." I pluck the last cheese fry off my little plate and devour it.

Michelle flashes a sly grin.

"Seriously. I'm not even tempted," I say while chewing. "Eldon's *too* handsome to be real. Besides, he's too old for me."

Ashley sputters into a laugh.

Our conversation pauses as the waitress comes by to give 'Chelle and me a refill of our iced tea. Those are bottomless here. Milkshakes are not. Each one is like six bucks. "Need something to drink, hon?"

"I'm okay, thanks." Ashley smiles at her.

"Okay, hon." The waitress looks us over, then grabs the empty serving platter plus the three small places. "Let me know if you girls need anything else."

All three of us murmur some form of thanks and agreement.

When the waitress walks away, Michelle leans in conspiratorially. "Since Hunter is in the know, you ought to let him show this new guy around for a 'boy's perspective.'"

Hmm. I grab a napkin and wipe fry grease off my fingers. "That's not entirely an awful idea. Eldon wanted to go to a sports game, and I'm not really into sports."

"It's our job, though." Ashley nudges me. "And you know Hunter's almost as busy as 'Chelle."

"Yeah. True." I sigh. Bad enough Hunter doesn't really have the time to spend on going to some sort of game, he would insist on paying for his own ticket.

We chat for a little while more, sipping our ice teas, until Michelle's phone chirps at her.

"Oh, crap. It's getting late. I have a ton of homework to do." Michelle groans. "Someday, all this will be worth it."

"That's the dream, right?" Ashley scoots out of the seat and stands.

"Sure is." Michelle gets up, then hugs us both.

As we always used to do, we all chip in cash for the bill, dividing it evenly. Ashley insists on standing 'guard' by the table until the waitress comes by to get the money. She's paranoid about someone randomly swiping it and then the place thinking we left without paying. Once the waitress shows back up, we thank her again and head outside.

The sun's starting to get dark orange, on its way down over the ocean in the distance.

"That was fun." Michelle grins at us. "We should meet here again next month."

"Every month." Ash thrusts her arms out to either side. "Make a routine."

It's the sort of thing people do as they get older. Make plans and then something comes up, so they're delayed... then something else comes up, and the people never quite get around to doing the thing before decades pass.

We all say 'yeah, good idea, next month, definitely' as if it's actually going to happen.

Being a vampire is really amazing, though it does have its downsides. I stand there with Ashley, watching Michelle walk away from us to her mother's car and try not to think about it being a metaphor. It's not like we will never see her again. We're just never quite going to ever hang out at Frosty Buns like a pack of goofy teenagers anymore. 'Chelle always was the most mature of us.

Guess she's finally grown up.

32

GUY STUFF

LATER THAT SAME FRIDAY

*H*iding my mood from the world is something I'm fairly good at.

After leaving Frosty Buns, I fell into a real somber funk. It makes no sense being as sad as if we'd just watched Michelle die. Really, it's not her that's dying but my childhood. Yeah, been around that rollercoaster already and I'm sick of riding it. Come on, brain. Settle down. It's not entirely irrational. Michelle is a strong part of that time of my life. Realizing she's on a different course than us is like picking a mental scab open.

Thankfully, Chloe exists.

She is so damn adorable. Also, I get to constantly think about how she is not going to grow up, get a career, and flit off to a life of her own that doesn't have much time for hanging out with me anymore. It takes only twenty minutes of being back home in her company for my stupid depressing mood to die.

As luck would have it, Eldon calls.

Plans hastily coalesce. The Seahawks don't usually play games on

Friday nights, but yesterday's game got rained out. Yeah, Eldon wants to understand sportsball. Or at least, he is curious to go view the spectacle as he put it.

No one in my immediate family is into sports. Sure, we have some Seahawks sweatshirts and other stuff because state pride or something... and Grandpa Sheridan is a massive fan. In addition to our 'real' presents, he always gives us Seahawks merch every Christmas, and on our birthdays—usually sweatshirts, sweat pants, hats, mugs, that sorta thing. It's kinda all over the house.

So... yeah. Eldon, me, Ashley, and Chloe are attending a Seahawks game. I think they're playing the Rams tonight. Good thing it's not the 49'ers or it might be too dangerous in here for Chloe. Heh. Seriously, though, it's kind of misty out. One of those weather oddities one can't really call 'rain' but also can't *not* call 'rain.' Whoever is in charge of the football stuff has apparently decided it's not bad enough to cancel two nights in a row.

This is my third time attending a football game in person. I don't remember the first; I'd been way too little. Dad brought me along when his company took his entire programming team out as a bonus for some major project being completed. He worked in the office back then. I think I was two. Not sure who thought an entire office full of computer nerds would have any interest in football, but evidently some did.

Second game had to be around when I was Chloe's age. Not sure why we went. Grandpa Sheridan had something to do with it, I'm sure. Maybe he was trying to see if he could turn one of his grandkids into a football head. Didn't work.

Since we arrived at the stadium, Eldon's been gawking around like a little Amish boy who's been brought to Los Angeles for the first time. Even now that we're in our seats looking down over rows and rows of other seats, he's still gawking. Yeah, the seats aren't great. They don't *suck* either. Let's just say if I cared about football, I'd be really happy I can zoom my vision in.

"You're going to catch flies," says Ashley.

Eldon glances at her. "What?"

"Your mouth has been hanging open." She chuckles. "You're making faces like you just heard the network changed its mind and they're bringing *Firefly* back."

"Too soon." I overact being grief stricken.

"I do not understand..." Eldon quirks an eyebrow at me.

"Don't get her started." Ashley leans against me.

"Me? Don't get *you* started. You love that show as much as I do." I laugh.

"True."

"I am still confused." Eldon blinks.

We explain about television shows, and how networks seem to have the bizarre habit of always cancelling the shows that people really adore while nonsense like *Duck Dynasty* or that thing with the Kardashians go on forever.

"Networks don't care about fun, smart, engaging, and witty storytelling." Ashley scowls. "They want money. They keep the shows that don't take too much power to think about or too much energy to keep up with, so they get the widest possible audience for the advertising money."

Eldon purses his lips. "Is it not the goal of a business to make a profit?"

"Yeah. It is... but." I stop, trying to think of how to explain to him in a way he'd understand. "If your shipping company could get the same money for moving cargo by loading it in a giant catapult and flinging it across the sea—even if it ended up being mostly smashed when it landed—would you have done that?"

"Of course not." He makes a face at me like I'm an idiot. "What good would it do to our reputation if everything we transported ended up destroyed? No one would hire us again."

"Okay." Ashley laughs. "Now imagine everyone in the world got three times dumber and they're willing to accept smashed-up goods because they got there *faster*."

Eldon shakes his head. "Then I would say the world has gone mad. Lost any sense of reality."

"I think they call it reality TV to be ironic." Ashley nibbles on her fingernail. "Or do you think they're trying to fool people? Like if they simply *call* it reality some people are dumb enough to believe it actually *is* reality."

I hold up a finger. "The second option. If some big corporate entity has to directly *tell* us something is true, or fair, or reality, it almost certainly isn't."

Chloe removes her mouth from the straw sticking up out of her soda. "Are you telling me Barney isn't a real dinosaur?"

Ash and I laugh.

Kiddo's expression is only serious for a few seconds before she also laughs.

"This is an astonishing number of people." Eldon whistles. "When are the games going to start?"

Ashley makes an 'are you dumb' face at him. "It's been going on for at least half an hour already."

"It has?" Eldon gazes down at the players lining up for another... whatever they call that. Scrooge? Scrimshaw? Scrimmage! That's the word. "They've just been running around and crashing into each other."

"That kind of is the game." I chuckle. "What are you expecting?"

"When do the swords come out?" Eldon's head moves as he follows the path of a football being thrown on a long pass. "You're saying all they're going to do is toss that pointy lump around?"

"That pointy lump is called a football," says Ashley.

Eldon blinks. "Why? I have not yet seen them use their feet on the ball once yet. All they're doing is tossing it about or cradling it like a rather unfortunate infant and attempting to run."

I laugh. "I dunno. They just call it football for some reason."

"Wow. Swords?" I whistle. "This isn't Ancient Rome. We're not at the Coliseum."

Ashley peers at him. "How old did you say you were again?"

He loses his straight face and can't stop from grinning. "I am teasing you about the swords. However, I am genuinely befuddled why this is referred to as *foot*ball."

Ash and I sigh in relief.

The crowd erupts in cheers; the Rams receiver lost the ball half a second after he caught it. Popped right out of his hands when a defensive player plowed into him. Once the roar dies down, I try my best to explain a general overview of how football works to Eldon, given my little knowledge of the game. Don't ask me for specific rules, though.

"I see. Interesting. I suppose it does make for an occasionally entertaining diversion." Eldon rests an elbow on the armrest, chin in his hand. He looks far more like a rich guy watching opera than an ordinary person at a sports stadium.

Halftime happens. There's not much of a show considering it's only an ordinary season game. The team band comes out along with the mascot. Lots of people around us get up to go use the bathroom or visit the vendors. Ashley and I take Chloe with us and go to the bathroom as well. Fries, milkshake, and iced tea want out.

The three of us take adjacent stalls and 'do the nasty.' Chloe's had a bunch of snack food she needs to be rid of as well. When we're done, we wash our hands and make our way back out past several women at the sinks looking around like they aren't quite sure why it smells like a fast-food place in there.

Eldon's still in his seat.

He doesn't do the food thing. If he ate anything other than blood, he'd vomit pretty harshly soon after. Thankfully, he's already figured that part of vampire existence out. I didn't have to witness him learning it.

We sit again and resume talking about football. It doesn't take him long to ask some questions about the game I am unable to answer, like why the referees let some things happen and then throw a flag on another situation that kinda seems like the same thing they just let slide moments earlier. I'm sure there is a subtle variation that makes something a rules violation. I merely do not understand the specifics.

"No idea." I chuckle. "If you want, maybe it wouldn't be a bad idea to hang out with Hunter at some point. Have a guy night."

"You associate with a hunter?" Eldon raises both eyebrows.

"No. My boyfriend's name *is* Hunter."

"Ahh. Did I see him at the party?"

"Nope. He's uhh, not part of that social club... yet." I examine my fingernails.

For some reason, I expect him to blurt 'you're dating a mortal' like a man from his time period might react to me dating a guy who wasn't white. Surprisingly, he doesn't.

"You're seeing a mortal?" he asks in a rather ordinary tone.

"Yeah. It's complicated."

Eldon peers at me for a moment in silence. "He knows?"

"He does." Ashley nods.

I twirl a lock of my hair around my finger. "Yeah. He's aware of some basics. He doesn't know anything about society or who's who and so on."

"He knows enough to be able to hang out with you and try to give you a guy's perspective on the modern world." Ashley stretches, thrusting both arms straight up and making this little squeaking noise for a second. "Problem is, Hunter doesn't really do 'guy stuff'. He's either working, studying, or fixing his house. I've never seen him go hang out with friends. Does he have any?"

I sigh. "Yeah, he has friends... or had. He doesn't get to see them much anymore since high school. I think one joined the Navy, another moved out of state for college. He said something about another guy named Charlie who ended up getting his girl preggo by accident. They got married in a hurry and now he's working two jobs to try and support them."

"Is that romantic or tragic?" asks Ashley.

"Romantic here. Tragic if it happened in Florida." I chuckle.

Ashley blinks. "What's the difference?"

"Crystal meth." I examine my fingernails.

"That's awful." She laughs. "And there's plenty of that around here, too. Well, maybe not *here*, but not too far outside the city."

"I'm being a dork." I sigh up at the massive lights ringing the stadium. "I guess it's romantic if they really love each other and tragic if they don't."

"You could check." Ashley nudges me.

"I'm not that nosey."

Ashley perks up. "Okay. I'll do it."

"You will not." I chuckle.

"For the baby. If they hate each other and are only married for social pressure reasons, it's not going to be good for the kid." Ashley bops side to side in her seat.

Not sure if she's teasing or serious.

"Heck. Guy stuff." Ashley laughs. "*We* could show Eldon how to sit at home and play video games. That used to be considered 'guy stuff', except we try to be quiet about farting and don't have balls to scratch."

I can't look at her *or* Eldon right now. I bury my face in my hands and laugh.

"Video games?" Chloe grabs my arm. "Let's go play video games. I don't really like football." She leans up and whispers in my ear, "Bad daddy always watched it."

Oof. Crap. Why didn't she say something before? Could have let her stay home with the 'rents. I guess football isn't that traumatic for her, merely a little worse than normal boredom. Either that or she's saying it to get me to do what she wants—which is to go home. I can sympathize. Still remember being about her age at Grandpa's on New Year's Day. All the adults had football on the TV all damn day. Being the only kid present and not at all into football made for an incredibly boring time.

"It's all right." I put an arm around her. "We don't have to stay the whole time if you hate it here."

Not like we're wasting money. We just kinda walked in unnoticed thanks to Ash's charm.

"Right, then." Eldon nods at me. "If the little one is not feeling well, I've certainly seen more than enough to sate my curiosity. We may take our leave whenever you desire to."

"Shall we?" I ask.

"Up to you guys." Ashley leans forward to peer past me at Chloe. "Sorry, kiddo. We didn't know football bothered you so much."

Chloe snuggles against my arm. "It doesn't *bother* me. Just makes me think about him and I don't wanna. He got mean and angry whenever his team lost, and he liked the Jets."

"Aww." I hug her.

Ashley makes sad faces at her.

"The Jets?" Chloe waits, as if expecting us to understand some joke we are totally missing. Finally, she sighs. "He was *always* angry whenever he watched football."

"Oh." I wince. "Sorry. I don't know football very much."

"Good." She grins.

We shuffle out of the seating area and head up into the stadium. This place is a bit of a labyrinth; however, we eventually find our way to a usable entrance and go outside into the parking area. Since Eldon is a flightless bird, I drove us here. Slow and annoying, but it does eliminate the need to worry about coming in for a landing somewhere without having anyone see us.

While walking across the massive parking lot and trying to remember where the heck we left the Sentra, Ashley asks, "Eldon? What did you do for fun when you were alive?"

"I mostly assisted my father with the shipping company." Eldon gazes off to the side, seeming sad. "Always so much work. One crisis or another cropping up."

"So, you didn't do anything for fun?" Ashley overacts a pouty face. "Like you had theaters back then, right? Plays?"

"Yes. They existed. I did not have time for such diversions." Eldon lets out a somber sigh. "We were in the midst of an exquisitely busy period. And father had become increasingly obsessed with his conflict against the vampires. Managing the company fell almost entirely upon me."

I wince. "Ugh. That sounds unfun. What about when you were younger?"

A wistful smile plays across his face. "As a lad? We'd go exploring the wilds, imagining that we fought back Indians or found lost treasures. Chased hoops down the street. Listened to stories. Rode horses. Of course, as my father was moneyed, I spent long hours with the tutor while my less fortunate friends got to enjoy the outdoors.

Alas, that trend would continue. Father always made sure responsibility and the future of our shipping enterprise came before fun."

"Sounds like your dad was the life of a party." Ashley sighs. "That's kinda sad."

"Well, it's not 1850-whatever now." I finally spot the Sentra in the sea of cars and point at it. "There! So, yeah. Like I was saying. It's not the 1800s anymore and your shipping company is gone. Allow me to introduce you to… the PlayStation!"

"Yay!" cheers Chloe.

We get into the car. I start the engine and look up at the rearview mirror. Three ghouls rush up behind us. Oh, dammit. This is getting old. Grr. I drop the shifter into reverse and stomp on the gas.

Chloe and Ashley scream at the sudden, hard acceleration. Eldon, who is still rather unaccustomed to cars, is totally unprepared for this. His face bounces off the dashboard.

It's quite obvious the ghouls have no idea what a car is either, by the fleeting expressions of utter shock on their faces in the half second before I run them over.

I slam on the brakes to avoid crashing into the next row of cars behind us and cut the wheel hard to the left. Eldon bounces back into his seat, giving me a 'why the devil did you do that?' stare.

"Buttheads!" calls Chloe, having spotted the ghouls out the window.

Before I can accelerate, the rear door on the right opens. A rotting guy in shredded, muddy 1850s clothes reaches in and grabs Chloe by the neck, yanking on her as though he's trying to throw her out of the way so he can get at Ashley. Oh wow. These ghouls have figured out how to work car doors. Hmm. Apparently, they either can't tell kiddo is a vampire, too, or something else is at work focusing their attention on me, Eldon, and Ashley specifically.

A fifth ghoul in a fancy outfit with a frilled collar yanks my door open. Yeah, this car isn't quite new enough for the doors to automatically lock when I put it into drive. Who'd have thought such a minor feature could've been so damn helpful?

"Get offa me!" shouts Chloe before hammering a punch into the face of the ghoul with a hand around her neck. Her tiny fist disappears inside his mouth midway up her forearm. She yanks her hand out of him, yells, "Eww!" then punches him again in the forehead, mashing in most of his face.

My ghoul throws water on me from a small silver container while hissing, 'fiend.' Other than smelling like it shared a morgue tray with a dead body for ninety years, the water doesn't do anything but piss me off.

Ashley sees a ghoul coming for her. She shoves her door open before the dead guy gets close enough to reach it. He lunges at her chest, swinging a stake. Geez, these things do not learn, do they? Ash grabs his wrist and does this jiu-jitsu style spin flip, hammering him face first into the pavement. I haven't heard a crunch like that since Sam jumped butt-first into our sofa and landed on a whole bag of Doritos he didn't see.

Sierra was pissed, by the way.

Ash darts back into the car and slams her door.

My ghoul stares at me as if he's expecting the fetid water to dissolve me away to nothing.

"Really, dude?" I grab his hand, including the small silver bottle in his grasp, and ram it upward, embedding the flask deep in his right eye socket. He teeters over backward, his body as rigid as a board. The instant he strikes the ground, he explodes into a pile of grey dust, clothes, flask, and all. "Holy water doesn't do a damn thing."

Ashley gags. "That smells more like *unholy* water."

It's disgusting. If Eldon wasn't here, I'd be sorely tempted to pull my sweatshirt and tee off and drive home topless—just to stop touching this nastiness.

"Butthead exploded." Chloe yanks her door shut.

"Yeah… they do that." I close my door and step on the gas, perhaps squealing the tires a bit. "Great. Now I need to take a shower."

ALTERNATE REALITY CHECK

SATURDAY

Other than being spattered with disgusting, fetid water, the rest of my Friday night was fun.

Eldon seems to have been born in the wrong century. He took to video games quite readily. I know it's all in my head, but I can *still* smell that 'holy water.' Ugh. How do stupid rumors start? Like why do people think holy water matters to vampires? Or stakes, or running water, or any of that folkloric stuff? Ehh, people are superstitious and like to make stuff up to explain things they can't understand.

Could be coincidence, too. Like, long ago, some idiot rammed a stake through a vampire's heart at the same time something else happened to him that knocked the vampire out—like a sword through the head. For whatever reason, the stake got the credit. Meh. Who cares? It's a good thing the Forces of Derp™ are misinformed.

Gotta be some of that 'unholy water' lingering in my sinus cavities. The smell is not going away.

After waking up Saturday afternoon, I take a quick shower more for the mental peace of mind to *feel* clean, then throw on a shirt and pair of sweat pants before making my way upstairs into the kitchen.

Mom's in the hallway, in the little space between dining room and living room where the little door leads to our downstairs toilet closet on one side and an actual closet on the other side. She gives me a quick 'oh good morning' smile before opening the closet door. She freezes in place, staring into the closet as if she's just caught Sierra and that boy she seems to like making out.

A thick black tentacle whips out of the darkness inside the closet, coiling around her face with a gloopy *smack* like someone slamming a six-pound slab of roast beef onto a wet marble countertop. In an instant, Mom's gone, yoinked into the void, the closet door slamming behind her.

It's too daylightey here to fly, so I am forced to run like a normal person over to the closet. My brain tries to shout 'Mom' and a bad word at the same time, so I end up yelling, "Muck!"

The door swings open by itself before I can get to it. Mom slides out into the hall, flat on her back. The door slams again. Except for having jet black goo all over her face, she doesn't appear hurt. I stand there staring at her for a few seconds. Mom doesn't move, simply stares straight up at the ceiling while lying on the floor. I half expect her to whip out a cigarette like that scene where Samuel Jackson gets thrown out of a moving car in *Long Kiss Goodnight*. Fortunately, Mom doesn't smoke. The house is eerily still and quiet for a minute.

"*Sophiaaaaaa!*" yells Mom, startling me.

"Uh oh," says Sierra somewhere upstairs.

Rapid soft thumping goes overhead. Sophia comes running down the stairs, grabs the banister pole at the bottom to swing around, then jumps down to the ground floor. She spots Mom on the floor and stops short.

Among the animal kingdom, it's not uncommon for creatures to evolve patterns and colorations that help them defend against predators and survive the dangers of the wild. Sophia adapts this evolutionary process by means of having chosen to wear a somewhat frilly white doll dress with pink ribbons and a narrow pink lace choker. If she didn't expect to get in trouble today, she got lucky. Mom is a sucker for adorable.

Sophia pads over to us and stops next to Mom, her toes gripping the carpet in confused anxiety. "Umm... sorry?"

"Young lady," says Mom, her tone neutral. "What did I tell you about closet tentacles?"

"Umm." Sophia fidgets. "I don't summon them on purpose."

"Then why is there one in the hall closet?" Mom shifts her gaze to me. "Sarah, would you mind grabbing a paper towel, please?"

"Sure." I run to the kitchen.

"I have no idea," says Sophia, all innocence. "I never use this closet for magic. What happened?"

After snagging a paper towel, I run back to them, handing the towel over.

Mom sits up and wipes the goop off her face. "I opened the door to grab the vacuum and... there's nothing but existential void in there. Next thing I know, this slimy thing is wrapped around my face."

"Oops." Sophia clasps her hands behind her back and twists side to side.

"Don't oops me, young lady."

Wow. Soph got called 'young lady' twice. Mom's really upset.

"Umm. I didn't do it on purpose." Sophia's face reddens. She shivers. Tears are seconds away. "I think the house has absorbed some energy and, like maybe sometimes, things on the other side are attracted to portals when they open. As soon as it realized you weren't what it was looking for, it put you back. Kinda like us reaching into the cabinet for the cinnamon without looking and we grab the nutmeg by accident."

Mom wipes her face again, then stares blankly at Soph.

"Think of it like a void octopus wrong number." Sophia glances at the closet door. "If you open the door again, it should be fine."

Mom turns her gaze to the door, sighs, then stands up. After a moment's hesitation, she gingerly reaches out to take the knob. Sophia and I step back.

"You two aren't helping." Mom chuckles. "Are you sure this is going to be normal?"

"There's always a .033 repeating chance of something crazy happening." Sophia smiles innocently. "But it should be fine."

Mom turns the knob, pauses a second to steel herself, then pulls the door open—to reveal an ordinary closet. A heavy, relieved breath comes out of her nose.

"Sorry." Sophia looks down.

"It's all right, honey." Mom hugs her. "I was only a bit startled. If you did not just do something now that made that happen, it's fine. You're not in trouble."

Soph slouches in relief. She no longer looks like she's about to start crying any second. "No. It's kinda become an operational closet hazard."

Mom drags the vacuum out of the closet. "Does this have anything to do with you flushing the essence of pure evil down the toilet?"

My sister makes 'eek' face. "Umm, no... that might have caused a whole host of different problems. The closet portal thing is different."

I try not to laugh. "Yeah, there are probably half a dozen sewer service employees in therapy now."

They stare at me in horror.

"Seriously guys... Sam dealt with it already." I scratch at my arm. "Stop panicking about every little case of misplaced ancient evil."

Mom sighs.

"Sare!" Sophia zips over to me. "I have info for you."

"You do?"

She nods rapidly, making her hair fly all over the place like one of those old troll pens Mom used to collect in high school. "Those ghouls that have been annoying you?"

"What about them?" I gather the vacuum hoses and help Mom put it together.

Sophia clasps her hands in front of herself like she's about to give a presentation in class. "Those ghouls are the remains of an old family coming back to finish a job they started a long time ago."

"Remains of an old family?" I sigh. "Who did I piss off this time?"

"Does the name Whittmore mean anything?" Sophia tilts her head.

"Crap." I facepalm. "That's Eldon. Are you telling me the ghouls are his family?"

"I think so." Sophia taps her foot. "Coralie only said the last name. She didn't give me any first names."

I nod. "Oh, cool. Thank her for helping us again. Umm. Don't s'pose she has any idea how much longer those stupid ghouls are going to be pestering us?"

"She said they're gonna keep coming after us until they resolve their unfinished business or the curse is broken." Sophia scratches at the base of her neck. "The curse is on you and Ash for breaking something. I saw like these strange rune marks."

Ugh. Cursed? Really? Well, that would explain why they ignored Chloe the other night. I pull my phone out of my pocket and open the photos app, flipping to the pictures I took of the weird 'witch's cross' things from the mine where we found Eldon. "These?"

Sophia leans forward to look, then sets her weight back on her heels while nodding. "Yes. That symbol is called a Leviathan Cross, only it's upside down. The infinity symbol should be at the bottom. It represents the element of brimstone and is usually used by satanists in modern times."

Mom stares at her. "I'm not sure how I feel about you knowing this stuff."

"It's okay, Mom." Sophia smiles at her. "It's not really evil. Some people long ago were scared of magic, so they made up a bunch of stuff about it. Pretty much an 'everything I don't like is Satan' situation."

"Brimstone invokes thoughts of Hell and demons," I say. "How is that not evil?"

"It's just a symbol." Sophia makes 'writing' gestures in the air. "By itself, it's no different from like a Chinese word symbol thing. I think you saw it in that mine because the people who put Eldon in there thought they were creating a magical ward to hold back evil. They put stuff like that all the time on the gravestones of suspected witches, thinking the symbol would prevent the witch from coming back as an undead monster for revenge."

I stuff my phone back in my pocket. "Are you saying that was real magic? We set off a curse?"

"I doubt it." Sophia taps her big toe into the rug repetitively while making thinking faces. "Those guys didn't know what they were doing. If they made a real ward, you would totally have noticed something weird happen when you smashed the crypt."

"I suppose that's good news." I chuckle. "Okay, so if the ward failed... where did the ghouls come from?"

Sophia stops tapping her toe into the rug, giving me this totally straight-faced look. "Someone who was a total jerk died super angry. He was so furious, his spirit stayed around and didn't let all the other spirits go off to wherever they wanted. I didn't say there's no curse, only that those symbols didn't cause it."

Mom looks at us the way she usually looks at Dad and Sam when they go off talking about comic book stuff. She shakes her head and lugs the vacuum into the living room.

"Hmm." I think back on the various ghoul encounters. "Seems like it's the same five or six guys every time. Any idea if it is or if they all just look similar? Are the same specific ghouls putting themselves back together or does our movie budget require us to use the same six character actors for the ghouls?"

Sophia scratches her head. "I don't know exactly. Probably the same exact ones getting back up. The way Coralie explained it, they're all part of the curse."

I wander to the kitchen. This is going to require coffee.

Sophia follows so we can keep talking while the vacuum roars in the living room.

While dumping coffee and water into the machine, I ponder this information. Seems like the unfinished business on these ghouls' minds is destroying Eldon. I mean, they kinda look like vampire hunters. The guy told me his father basically declared himself the destroyer of vampires. Kinda makes sense these ghouls are probably Mr. Whittmore's employees, friends, or whoever else he conscripted into helping him fight Benjamin Jacobs. Could even be Eldon's brothers, uncles, or whatever if he had any. Yeah, that could completely explain why Eldon had such a strong reaction to seeing the ghouls. Suppose they could be relatives… or, at the very least, men he knew in life.

The vacuum stops, allowing the sound of the burbling coffee maker to take over.

Given the complete lack of anything left regarding the Whittmore family, at least as far as Ashley's powers of Google Fu are able to locate, my guess is Mr. Whittmore's fight against the vampires of his day did not go terribly well for him.

"They're going to keep coming after us until Eldon is destroyed or the curse is broken," I say.

"If you think Eldon is the business they have to finish, yeah." Sophia leans on the counter next to me.

"Any idea how one might break the curse?" I ask.

"Good question." She folds her arms. "Coralie didn't know. We should probably start by looking at his old house if it's still around, or maybe the family grave."

Dad wanders into the kitchen. "Did someone suggest a Saturday afternoon family adventure?"

Mom groans from the living room. "Jonathan, we went to hell once. Isn't that enough?"

He laughs. "I suppose. Happy to help if you need the backup, hon. Still have that giant Nerf cannon ready to go."

I hug him. "Thanks, Dad. I don't think this is going to be as epic of a project as that. The ghouls are pretty weak. Sounds like Eldon's father got his vampire hunter license from a cereal box. Only thing I'm really worried about is telling Mom that Sophia's gotta come with me."

"What?" yells Mom. She rushes into the kitchen a few seconds later. "Didn't we talk about you not bringing your siblings along on crazy vampire stuff again? Sierra almost got killed."

She's overstating things a little bit. Yes, Sierra wound up in a dangerous situation I never should have exposed her to… but we had no idea it would go there.

Sophia makes a face like she wouldn't necessarily mind being told to stay home.

"This is a curse at work, Mom." I pour myself a cup of coffee. "Even if I had magical potential, which I do not, it would take me months or years to learn enough to maybe dispel it. Sophia can break the curse already."

"Umm. I can?" Sophia swipes at her hair, tucking a strand behind her right ear. "I mean… yeah, I probably can. Won't know for sure until we find the focus."

I pat her on the shoulder. "You've done a bunch of things a bit bigger than breaking a curse. I'm sure you got it."

Mom facepalms. "I don't like the idea of you taking Sophia somewhere that could be dangerous."

The other night with Eldon-wolf in the kitchen, Sierra made a joke about adventure game dialogue options. I see text floating in front of me now with choices for a dialogue response. Option 1) Say something comforting and apologetic. Option 2) 'you don't have to *like* it, Mom.'

Sometimes, in those adventure games, choosing the wrong dialogue option leads immediately to death and a game over screen. Option 2 is one of those choices. Selecting that response would be Bad™.

"I don't like it, either, but what else can I do here?" I sip coffee again. "Maybe call Darren Anderson and see if they can do something about it. Do you really want me owing them a favor if it's something stupid and trivial Soph can just snap her fingers and be rid of?"

Mom pinches the bridge of her nose. "What is this going to involve, Sarah?"

"I don't know yet." I blink. "Oh, wait. Ashley found online that Eldon's old manor house has become a hotel that does ghost tour stuff. Maybe we could just go there and it would be like a day trip. No more dangerous than visiting a small local museum."

"Sounds fun." Dad smiles.

"Sarah…" Mom exhales. "That seems tolerable. I can live with a day trip. I don't want you bringing her anywhere near fighting or restless dead, and absolutely no vampiric territory wars."

I hold up a hand. "Promise."

"If you need any help, hon, just ask." Dad pats me on the shoulder.

"Cool. Umm, any chance you could watch Chloe while we're out?" I grin at him. "Even if we might be a bit late coming home?"

"I want Sophia in bed by ten," says Mom.

Sophia bites her lip. "It is a hotel… they have beds there. You aren't specifying *which* bed I have to be in by ten."

Mom wanders off back to the living room, still pinching the bridge of her nose. "I'm being lawyered by my own daughter."

Sierra scurries into the kitchen. She ducks around Mom and looks at us. "Are you in trouble?"

"No." Sophia shakes her head. "It was an accident."

"What was?" Sierra opens the fridge.

I glance at the hall closet. "Mom got tentacled."

Sierra grabs an apple. "Ugh. I hate it when that happens."

WHITTMORE INN

*W*ell, it's happening.

I'm bringing children on a mission again. Or something like that. Things are not quite the same as last time. Mr. Wolent isn't sending me to do business with vampires. There shouldn't be any vampires involved here other than us. We are not doing anything more dangerous than taking a quirky day trip to a haunted house-turned-hotel. Well, more of a 'night trip.' Eldon can't fly, nor can he go out during the daytime.

He didn't answer his phone until after sunset.

Anyway... I've got both Sophia and Sierra with me. Sam was having dinner over at Darryl's house tonight. The boys are doing this 'camping' adventure thing in the backyard. Basically, they are getting to stay up late and watch movies, hang out, and generally just be boys having fun for the weekend. I wasn't about to go drag him away from that just so I could have all three Littles in the same place.

Sierra insisted on going with us to help protect Sophia. I'm sure she's also pretty curious about the haunted hotel thing, too. She's adventurous and wants to participate with me in the 'weird stuff' whenever possible. Since Mom reluctantly allowed Sophia to go along, she saw her chance and took it.

Ashley and Eldon are here as well.

Yep. That's right. *Both* sisters.

Mom is Not Happy™ with this, and only agreed on the condition that I bring the girls home at the first sign of anything more dangerous than a ghost tour in a haunted hotel. She relaxed a bit on requiring they be in bed by ten. Not only is Sam getting to stay up late tonight, Mom figured the girls will probably fall asleep in the car on the ride home. Also, Ashley pointed out that the first ghost tour doesn't start until nine. The next one starts at midnight. Pretty much guaranteed the girls are going to get to stay up past their bedtime tonight. They are both thrilled. Mom, not so much.

The Whittmore Hotel is in Port Angeles, roughly sixty miles northwest from Seattle as the vampire flies. Not *too* far. Also, not a fast drive. Honestly, if we weren't bringing the girls along, I might have suggested Ashley and I carry Eldon and fly there no matter how awkward it would have been. The two of us together probably would've been fine supporting his weight in the air. Him plus Littles? Not happening—at least not safely enough for me.

The ride takes us about an hour and a half ish. Basically, we cut across Seattle through Tacoma, Gig Harbor, then take Route 16 up to Route 3, then follow Interstate 101 all the way west to Port Angeles.

At this hour, it's not a very scenic ride for the girls. They can't see in the dark. Well, okay, Sierra can... sorta. Sophia did model the enchantment off vampires after all. Sierra's eyes are essentially like a military starlight scope. She needs a tiny bit of light to see, whereas any vampire can see perfectly even in an absolute void of darkness (like an underground cave). This just means she'd have to use a cell phone to navigate if we end up stuck somewhere moonlight cannot reach.

Yeah, so... we arrive at the hotel a few minutes to nine. Since they run ghost tours well into the night, it's not uncommon for people to arrive at this hour. Some guests show up for the paranormal entertainment, then go home the same night. Others get rooms and use the place like an actual hotel.

Eldon gets out of the car, gazing around at the modest parking lot while making a face like someone kicked his dog. "A parking lot…"

"Yeah." Sierra shuts the door after Sophia gets out. "Most hotels have them."

"This used to be a field. I spent many days learning to ride a horse here." He sighs.

Sierra bites her lip. "Oops. Sorry. Forgot you lived here."

Hooray for useless skills, I suppose. Eldon's not going to get much value out of knowing how to ride anymore. Hmm. I wonder how that will feel someday when the idea of driving a car is as anachronistic to the average person as riding a horse is to me? I have skills that are probably going to end up being obsolete, eventually. Kinda like how Dad is one of the seven people on Planet Earth who knows how to set the time on a VCR. The future is scary and exciting.

I lock the car doors and walk around the front end to join everyone. We're standing in a line facing the building as if posing for the opening shot of an action movie, only we don't exactly look like a high-adventure crew. Sierra and I are rocking the T-shirt and jeans thing. I went for the heavy boots in case I have to stomp a ghoul. Sierra's content with her canvas sneakers. We're both wearing denim jackets. Sophia's still in the same white doll dress. Since we're not in the house anymore, she's no longer barefoot. I think she expects some stuff to happen since she didn't opt for her usual ballet flats. Pink frill socks and pink sneakers, while quite girly, are not going to go flying off her if she needs to run away from something.

Klepto sits like a parrot on her left shoulder. The kitten's wearing a tiny pair of white plastic sunglasses, the lenses of which are pink hearts. I think they came with one of Sophia's dolls, but they fit kitty perfectly.

Ash went girly, too. Pink sweatshirt and a white skirt over black yoga pants and thick fuzzy purple socks. Standard sneakers.

Eldon's outfit makes him look like he should've driven here in a Porsche or something. Dark polo shirt, pale slacks, nice shoes. People will probably give him weird looks for not having a coat on. He doesn't notice the cold. We also still have to remind him to 'warm up' so he's not paler than Ashley. And mind you, being paler than Ashley is not an easy thing to do.

Yeah, look at us. We're only slightly more serious than the Griswold family from those National Lampoons movies.

I send Mom a text to let her know we have arrived at the place okay and are on our way inside.

Eldon makes faces at the building, grumbling about new siding, or additions… things that weren't there before. Ashley and I do our best to be comforting. After all, 150 years have passed since he last saw the place. There is no easy way for him to re-exert ownership of the property, so he's got to deal with it. I mean, if he *really* wanted it, he could mind control the current owners to sell it to him for two bucks. It's not a wise thing to do. Not only is it mean, certain mortal agencies get rather curious when people do crazy things like selling million-dollar properties for pocket change.

He's not morose or sad, really. It's more like someone who used to own an expensive classic car sold it to another person who promised to take care of it… and years later, they see it's been modernized with all new parts so it's no longer worth anything as a classic.

We go inside. What I imagine used to be the main foyer and living room area is now a lobby with a hotel desk. Various passageways lead out of here. Left is an arch to a small restaurant. To the right, past a small sitting area with cushioned seats and a few sofas, corridors lead to what appears to be sitting rooms or some such thing.

Eldon continues making faces while looking around. "This is beyond strange. The place is at once familiar and alien. If there are spirits here, no wonder they are restless."

"I'm kinda hungry," says Sophia. "Can we eat?"

"Me too." Sierra scratches at her stomach. "I also really gotta pee. Long car ride."

Like a highly coordinated pit crew, we leap into action. Ashley and Eldon head to the restaurant area to get us a table while I escort the girls to the nearest bathroom. It's nice and fairly modern inside, even if there are only three stalls.

I sit on the small cushioned bench by the sinks, waiting for the girls to finish.

"Do you mind?" Sophia's voice echoes from one of the stalls. "I'm trying to pee."

"Not at all." Sierra laughs.

"I'm not talking to you. A ghost just stuck her head through the wall."

Sierra exhales. "I am so glad I can't see them."

"Ask her if she knows anything about the curse," I say.

"She's gone already." Sophia pauses. "Sorry. I kinda chased her away."

I stand again. Been sitting too long already. "It's fine. She shouldn't have invaded your space."

Soon, the girls are done, and we head back to the table. Yes, Mom, I made sure they washed their hands.

This restaurant doesn't exactly have the biggest menu. Lots of seafood, go figure. Port Angeles is right on the water. In order to avoid standing out as suspicious, Eldon orders a basic fish dinner. He doesn't eat a bite of it. Bit by bit, while no one is paying attention, we all 'sneak' food off his plate. Sophia gets his salad to herself. I end up being overly full. Becoming a vampire didn't magically give my stomach more capacity or anything. In fact, I think it shrank. At least the portions here aren't crazy. We all manage to finish eating enough to where it doesn't make me feel guilty to refuse having the remains boxed. Can't do it, anyway. We're not going straight home. Any food we doggie-bagged would spoil before anyone would want it.

Dinner is normal (other than there being three vampires at the table). Another mild oddity is coming from our waitress, Rachel. She keeps looking at us. Every time she walks through the room, she always spends a few seconds staring. Seems as if she's focused on Eldon. Understandable. The guy really is hot. Rachel's demeanor isn't fawning, though. It's more of a 'have we met before' kind of inquiring, lingering gaze.

Just to be safe, I listen in on her thoughts. Yeah, that's exactly it. She thinks he's familiar but can't place why he's familiar. At the moment, she's wondering if he's a celebrity. Ashley thinks he looks like Chris Evans. He's obviously not, being both too young and, well, *not* Chris Evans. Besides, Eldon isn't anywhere near muscular enough to put on a Captain America costume. I suppose it's possible someone in his family went on to be related to the guy, but that's a stretch. They don't really look *that* similar.

"What's the plan?" whispers Sierra.

"Find the curse's focus." Sophia sips her iced tea. "It's got to be here somewhere."

Ashley sucks something out of her teeth—so ladylike. "What does a curse focus look like?"

Sophia rips open the little sanitizer napkin packet that came with her crab legs, and proceeds to wipe her hands. "It could be anything. Just… nothing that is currently alive."

"Well, that narrows it down for us," Eldon chuckles.

I wouldn't mind just sitting here for another half an hour and letting my stomach deflate before moving. "Figure we'd do their ghost tour and look around."

"What if the focus isn't anywhere the tour goes?" Sierra stretches.

"Then we take the *special* tour." Ashley grins.

By that, she means using her charm abilities to make us functionally invisible so we can wander the house wherever we please without a guide.

Rachel approaches the table. "Can I get anyone dessert?"

We all politely decline, even the girls. Yeah, they're full. It takes a lot to make Sierra pass up a chance for chocolate cake.

"All right then. I'll be back in a moment with the check. Thank you guys so much! You were great." Rachel grins at us and whisks off.

Sierra leans forward over the table. "Why is she staring at us?"

"She thinks Eldon looks familiar." I glance at him. "You don't know her, do you?"

"Not in the slightest." He pretends to wipe his mouth on the napkin. "She's mortal. Couldn't possibly know her. I have not been in this area since the... disagreement with my father."

Getting chopped into pieces and put in stone crypts at the bottom of a small prospector's mine is a disagreement? I don't want to know what he would consider a 'violent attack.'

Sophia closes her eyes and appears to be meditating. She's either attempting to use magic to sense the location of the curse focus—or she's trying not to burp out loud. It really embarrasses her.

Sierra doesn't care. She'll rip them as loud as she can. Sam, too. In fact, on family road trips, the two of them usually get into contests to see who can burp the loudest. Mom is not usually pleased with this.

"There's definitely something here." Sophia opens her eyes. "I don't see any ghosts in the room with us now. Energy is all over this place."

Rachel returns, making a strange face at Eldon. "Excuse me. Have you been here before? Do you live nearby?"

"It's been a while," says Eldon. "The last time I visited this area I was much younger."

Technically, not a lie.

Rachel sets the check on the table, closest to him. "That's so crazy. You look just like someone in one of the paintings in the lobby."

If that painting was an original to this manor house, there's a good reason for the resemblance. It's almost certainly a portrait of him as he was in life.

"Crazy coincidence," says Ashley. "Like that art meme going around where people find paintings that look like them in museums and stuff. Guess there's only so many possible combinations of DNA before people start looking like each other."

"Or reincarnation is a thing." Sierra grins.

Ashley points at her. "That, too. I mean, if souls are energy and energy cannot be destroyed, only transformed... reincarnation makes way more sense than that whole heaven and hell thing. An endless conveyor belt of souls ending up in one trash bin or another doesn't make sense from a physics perspective."

Neither does vampire flight, but hey, who's going to argue logic when magic is involved? Still, I'm inclined to agree with her.

Reincarnation is almost definitely a thing. Maybe it isn't the *only* option. But for our purposes right now, making Rachel think Eldon looks like the painting thanks to reincarnation is a good distraction.

I grab the check and put my credit card in the leather thingee.

Rachel seems surprised but doesn't question it. She thanks me and takes the check before zooming off to process the charge. Dinner wasn't exactly cheap, though it's far from exorbitant. It costs Dad more to take us to the hibachi place.

When Rachel comes back, three more wait staff are following her in a none-too-subtle attempt to check Eldon out. It's obvious to me what they're doing since it shows clearly in their expressions when they look at him. The words 'oh, yeah, wow. He *does* look like the guy in the painting' is practically tattooed on their foreheads.

I make sure they all think it's just a crazy coincidence. Seems they're so used to crazy paranormal stuff happening here, they're wondering if Eldon is a ghost powerful enough to appear solid.

A woman at a table nearby with her family—three kids younger than my sisters and a husband who's not taken his eyes off his phone the entire time they've been in here—gives me a weird disapproving glower. I don't care enough to look into her head. Maybe she thinks I'm not dressed nice enough for this place, even though most of the people in here are wearing jeans, too. This is not a 'fancy' place.

Once the check is paid, we make our way out of the restaurant area to the lobby and hotel desk. And yep. There it is. An enormous oil panting on the wall by the fireplace shows Eldon standing next to a big green wingback chair. In the painting, he looks a bit younger, maybe sixteen or seventeen. The woman in the chair is probably his mom. I'm guessing the man standing on the other side of the chair with the bits of grey in his beard is Mr. Whittmore. Not getting any dark vibes from the painting, merely a 'we are rich and better than you' vibe—mostly from the dad. The man doesn't look scary or evil, merely stuffy and superior.

"Oh, wow, that guy in the painting really does look like you," says Sophia.

"Dork." Sierra nudges her and whispers, "It *is* him."

"I know that." Sophia rolls her eyes then whispers, "I'm acting. I might be blonde, but I'm not stupid."

We approach the counter. I talk to the clerk, a guy named Tim, for a few minutes and sign us up for the next ghost tour, which starts at midnight. We've got a little more than two hours to kill first. "Also, I'd like to book a room for one night. Whichever one is your most haunted."

He hesitates. "Are you sure about that, miss?"

"Totally." I smile. "Not scared."

Tim chuckles. "Well, all right, but don't say I didn't warn you. I should advise you that we don't issue refunds if guests run away screaming in the middle of the night."

"If something is in this building that can make *me* run away screaming in the middle of the night, you guys have bigger problems than refunding my room charge."

Ashley, Sophia, and Sierra laugh.

Tim gives me a 'we'll see about that' stare. Yeah, he's overacting. Mostly. I think he expects me to be scared by something, even if I don't go sprinting off in terror. Can't blame him. I don't exactly look like a badass.

That same woman who gave me the dirty look in the restaurant, and her family, wander up behind us, waiting in line for the desk clerk. Seems they're interested in the tour, too.

"Why is that man letting his kid sister pay for their rooms?" whispers the woman to her husband, thinking she's inaudible to me. "How does that kid have a credit card? Where are their parents?"

"I don't know, dear," says the husband in a distracted, unconcerned tone.

"Look at them." The woman huffs to herself. "That man doesn't look old enough to be the father of those two little girls."

"He's probably not their father, dear," says the husband, most certainly not even lifting his gaze off the phone to look at us. "Leave it alone."

While Tim, the clerk, processes the modest charge for the ghost tour and room, the woman walks over to us. She's decided, evidently, that it's her business to know exactly what we are doing here without parents.

"Excuse me," says the woman while getting in Eldon's face.

He raises an eyebrow at her.

The husband finally looks up from his phone, giving his wife a stare like 'don't… please don't.'

I grab the woman's arm, not too roughly, merely enough to get her to look at me. "You are excused."

Her three kids crack up laughing.

A light tap of the derp hammer leaves her out of sorts for a few seconds, enough for me to insert a mental compulsion to not pay any attention to our group. Yeah, she just thought we looked too young to be out here on our own and convinced herself something suspicious must be going on.

"All set," says Tim, handing me a receipt. "Thank you. The tour will be starting from right here in the lobby. Please be here by 11:45 to make sure you don't miss it. Look for Lisa. She'll be the guide. She's the short girl with the black ponytail."

I turn away from the busybody to smile at him. "Thanks."

We make our way over to the right side of the lobby, past an alcove full of sofas and cushioned chairs—some of which look like they're original to the property. An archway leads to a huge hallway going deeper into the place past sitting rooms and other such things. I follow a sign with an arrow (that is not original to the property) pointing left to a stairwell up to the second floor. Another set of signs point right for rooms 21-40, left for rooms 1-20, and up again for rooms higher than 41. The 'most haunted' room according to Tim is number 40. So, I turn right.

We walk down a nice, carpeted hallway. It doesn't really feel like we're in a hotel despite all the rooms. I'm used to hotels being extremely uniform. Every door is identical, the distance between the doors is the same, and so on. This place is the exact opposite. Some doors are close together, some spaced wide. They're not even all the same kind of door. I haven't spent that much time visiting expensive manors in my lifetime. I imagine this place still looks more like a manor house than a hotel... at least a modern one.

Eldon mutters to himself about how different it looks now. He doesn't sound terribly happy that the rooms up here all have numbers on the doors or electronic keycard locks.

Part of me sympathizes with the guy for having his childhood home converted into a public building and modified. Another part of me also thinks it's kinda crazy for one family to occupy a 'house' so huge it literally could be a hotel.

I stop at the door to Room 40, which is at the end of the hall on the left. To no one's surprise, the keycard works, and we go in.

This space is a lot bigger than I expected for a hotel room. Seems like we're at the corner of the house. Two of the walls have windows. A huge four-poster bed is positioned at the middle of the windowless wall on the right, against the adjacent room. In the corner between the outside-facing walls, stands a vase as tall as Sophia. It looks expensive, which immediately makes me nervous even though it makes zero sense for a hotel to put a priceless, breakable thing like that in a room they rent to random people. A massive wooden wardrobe cabinet stands in the corner opposite the bed. Crushed velvet wallpaper creates a swirling kaleidoscope of gold and dark rose pink.

The decor in here... it totally feels like we just jumped back to 1844.

"Are we going to spend the night?" asks Sophia, sounding worried.

She can't fall asleep easily in new surroundings. It takes her being at a place for two or three days before she doesn't end up staring at the ceiling for hours.

"Maybe." I shrug. "Depends on how late this goes. It's almost a two-hour ride home."

"It's super creepy in here." Sophia shivers. "I think that guy at the desk was right. Something doesn't want us being here."

"It won't take that long to drive when it's late." Sierra folds her arms. "We're not that far from home. It's just traffic."

"It's like sixty miles." I wander over and sit on the edge of the bed.

"Even if I could drive at sixty the entire time without slowing down or stopping, that's an hour."

"So what? We can sleep in the car. Not like you get tired." Sierra tosses her hair behind her shoulders, grinning.

I glance at her. "You sound like you really don't want to sleep here."

"We didn't bring any pajamas or any other clothes." Sierra swipes a hand down her T-shirt. "What are we supposed to sleep in?"

"Who said anything about sleeping?" Ashley laughs. "Stay up all night."

Sophia goes wide-eyed. "Mom would kill us! We'd be grounded until Sarah gets old."

"I'm not going to get old, Soph."

"That's exactly what I mean!" She thrusts her arms out to either side.

We all chuckle.

"Sare, are you forgetting that we told Mom we'd be home tonight?" Sierra shifts her weight onto one leg. "She's going to flip."

"Yeah." Sophia nods rapidly. "She won't let us sleep over at a creepy haunted inn."

"Haunted inn," says Eldon.

"Didn't you see all the signs advertising the ghost tours?" Ashley snickers.

He waves dismissively at her while gazing around the room. "No, I am not asking. Merely saying it to better understand what has become of my former home. I believe this room used to belong to Bethany."

"Who's Bethany?" I ask.

"My sister." Eldon wanders past the table holding a small television, frowning at it as if he doesn't want it there. "Her bookshelves used to be here. She was only a year older than me. We were quite close."

Sierra furrows her brow. "Why wasn't she in the painting?"

"That one was supposed to be a portrait of me. Mother had them made for all of us. I cannot say why the people here now only left my portrait up." He gestures off to one side. "There are several paintings of Bethany posing with them at different ages. Or... there used to be."

"Oh." Sierra exhales, sounding like she's trying to calm down.

I'm sure she was ready for him to say something like his father didn't think girls were worth being included or something like that.

"Yes. Second floor, back left corner." Eldon strides over to the window and peers outside. "This is definitely her room."

Sophia kneads her hands in front of herself. "Do you know what happened to her?"

"Alas, I do not." Eldon keeps staring outside. "The last I saw of her, she had been pleading with Father not to attack me, trying to convince him I was no threat to them."

"Eep." Sophia jumps, then scoots sideways, staring at the wall beside the bed. "There she is. I think..."

"What?" Eldon turns to look at her.

Sierra, Ashley, and I all look around. Nothing weird catches my eye. Oh, wait... there it is. A faint white haze hangs by the head of the bed, as though a person stood beside it near the wall.

"There is an older lady there." Sophia gestures at the mist. "She's watching us."

"I see nothing." Eldon takes a few steps closer to the misty cloud.

Sierra squeezes her hands into fists. "That will never stop being creepy."

"Sophia can see spirits all the time," I say. "We can only see them when they want us to."

"Yeah." Ashley nods at Eldon. "It takes them less energy to appear to vampires than it does for mortals to see them."

A faint whisper emanates from the white mist. I can't make out what the heck is being said, only that something spoke. Vampire ears are kind of like those EVP things where people say they've picked up ghostly voices on digital recorders. Sometimes, I can make sense of them. This time, it's garbled.

"Yes," says Sophia to nothing. "We are." She stands still for a few seconds. "No! I promise. We don't want to hurt him. Uh huh. Oh, I'm so sorry... we'll totally help."

"What's she saying?" asks Sierra.

At least Sophia doesn't have to worry about us not believing she can see ghosts or thinking she's nuts.

Soph still seems scared of the room, though not quite as much. She appears to listen to the ghost speak a little while longer, then faces Eldon. "Bethany wants me to tell you she's happy you are okay."

"What became of her?" asks Eldon, his voice heavy with sorrow.

The misty form drifts away from the wall, gliding forward until it's right beside him. A disembodied voice spits a handful of unintelligible warbles. It sounds like three separate words or short phrases with a few seconds in between them.

Sophia nods at the ghost. "After your father was killed, she and your mother lived here. She married three times, but had no children. Her first husband lost his mind due to the darkness trapped within this house. The second left her after a year to escape the madness. The third grew old with her and died only three months before she did."

"I am so sorry, Beth." Eldon reaches a hand out. The look of pained longing and apology in his eyes makes me sure she's appeared to him.

The misty shape shifts form slightly. I can't see much, though I'm guessing she's taken his hand.

"It's not your fault," says Sophia. "You didn't ask Benjamin to make you like him. Nor could you have stopped him. I know you are still my brother, even as one of them. Not a monster like Father believed."

"What's trapping her here?" whispers Sierra. "Can she tell us how to get rid of this curse?"

Sophia peers upward, as if making eye contact with a woman standing right next to her. "She says her own guilt at what happened to Eldon kept her here. For years, she believed she should have done more to stop their father from trying to destroy him. She is free now."

"What about the curse?" asks Ashley.

Sophia listens patiently to the ghost. "She says it's in the mausoleum."

"This house has a mausoleum?" I blink.

"No, silly." Sophia shakes her head. "It's in the cemetery on the other side of town. The Whittmore family is all in there. Bethany says the curse focus is probably inside Father's crypt."

Sierra folds her arms. "It probably *is* the father."

"Wait, didn't Soph say a curse focus couldn't be alive?" Ashley scratches her head.

"Umm, Ash?" Sierra blinks at her. "I am pretty sure Eldon's dad is no longer alive."

Ashley stares into space. "No kidding. I mean, she said can't be alive. I figured that meant people in general. Does a formerly alive body work as a curse focus?"

Sophia nods. "Yeah. But don't worry. Vampires don't count. It would have to be *dead* dead."

"Well, that's good." Ash rubs her hands together as if cold. "If the father is the curse focus, that means he can't be a vampire, or undead, right? Just a body?"

"We're making too many assumptions." I pace around. "It could be an object buried with him. Doesn't necessarily have to be the guy. The curse could even be infused into the tomb itself."

Sophia twists around as if the ghost spoke again from another part of the room. "Bethany's saying when the curse is broken, she and the rest of the family who are trapped here will be released."

"Cool." Sierra grins. "Bummer for the people who run this place, though. Won't be haunted anymore."

"Umm, there are other ghosts than the family. And, I could always try to summon some more once she's gone." Sophia swishes back and forth, flaring the skirt of her dress.

I lightly clap my hands and rock back on my heels. "That's probably not a great idea."

"Right?" Sierra snickers. "With her luck, she'd call a bunch of Fuzzydooms."

Sophia rolls her eyes. "Nothing that bad. I'd only make a ghostly lighthouse or something to attract some here."

I hold up a 'wait' hand. "If you do anything like that, don't do it until we're going to leave."

"So, what do we do now?" Ashley tilts her head at me.

Out comes my iPhone for a navigation app. "Now, we go to the graveyard."

"Oh, joy!" chimes Sierra in a sarcastic tone. "Just what I've always wanted to do in the middle of the freaking night."

Ashley chuckles. "Are you scared? Really?"

"No." Sierra rolls her eyes. "I just don't have earplugs on me."

Ash and I exchange a glance.

"What the heck do you need earplugs for?" I ask.

Sierra gestures at Sophia. "We're bringing *Soph* to a graveyard at night? There will be screaming."

Sophia fidgets. "I will try my best not to be a scaredy-cat, but I cannot make promises."

"We should get going then. Ghost tour starts in a little over an hour." Ashley puts her phone away. "Don't want to miss it."

GHOULS' NIGHT OUT

SATURDAY

I pull over and park on the street by the old cemetery.

Thanks to Ashleypedia, we all know this is a historic site no longer accepting new 'residents'. It's also generally not open to the public because there are no living relatives around who would want or need to visit any of the graves. The bureau or whatever responsible for the property sometimes hosts tours for historical societies or whatnot. So, either way, we're effectively breaking into a place we're not supposed to be in.

This is a recurring theme of my unlife, apparently.

Question being, is fate doing this to me because Dalton's my sire and I have some tools that make breaking into places easier? Or would things have been like this anyway, and I got lucky by inheriting talents that get me into places? Meh. No sense wasting time wondering about such a pointless question. It's not like I'm a character in a game and I have the option to reroll and pick different stats or abilities.

Almost the exact instant I cut the engine, my phone rings.

Sophia screams. It's short, merely a startled, 'Aaaah!' rather than a cry of existential terror.

Sierra clamps her hands on her ears, overacting as if she'd been blasted at point blank range with an airhorn. "Told you. And we're not even inside the graveyard yet."

"Sorry," whispers Sophia. "The phone scared me."

The caller ID says 'Mom,' so there's no possible way of ignoring it. If I don't answer, not only will things become exponentially worse, I will feel guilty. Follows Rules Girl is already tied up in the closet so she doesn't have to watch me breaking into a closed graveyard.

"Hey, Mom," I say after holding the phone to my ear.

"It's getting late and you're not home yet."

"Yeah. I know. Didn't I say this might turn into a sleepover project? The place is a hotel, after all."

Mom sighs. "So, you're spending the night now?"

"Umm, maybe. I'll be able to answer that question more accurately soon." I smile innocently, even though my mother can't see my face right now.

"Why is that?"

"Sophia saved us a whole bunch of time. We didn't have to go roaming around the entire manor house looking. A ghost told her exactly where to find the curse focus." I give Soph a thumbs-up.

She grins.

"Can she dispel the curse?" asks Mom.

"Probably. We're at the graveyard now. About to go in."

"What?" blurts Mom. "When did your little vacation trip involve a graveyard? You were supposed to go to a haunted hotel."

"We did… and now we're at a graveyard."

Mom's quiet for a few seconds. "You took the girls to a cemetery at midnight? What are they still doing awake?"

"It's not midnight yet, Mom." I fight the urge to sigh. "It's only a couple minutes to eleven."

"What time are you bringing them home?" asks Mom.

"As soon as possible. Maybe right after the ghost tour we bought tickets for. That runs from midnight to one. Though, they'll probably want to sleep then. Unless the tour is too scary."

"Dooooubt iiiiit," singsongs Sierra.

"We'll definitely be tired at one in the morning." Sophia blinks at her.

"No, I mean, it's not going to be scary." Sierra fusses at her hair.

"Oh." Sophia turns to look out the window at the overgrown wrought iron fence. She shivers. Yeah, somehow the girl who can see and speak to ghosts is still scared here.

Mom mumbles 'unbelievable' as if I can't hear her. "Can you do this without the girls there? I don't feel safe with them in harm's way."

"*I* don't feel safe with them in harm's way, either. At the moment, we're just scoping out an old graveyard. Nothing's moving in there."

"Yet," says Ashley.

"Staaaahp!" whines Sophia.

"Can you do it without them?" asks Mom.

"No idea." I glance into the back seat at Sophia. "Soph, can I destroy this curse alone?"

"Doubtful." She bites her lower lip. "You can kill the ghouls, but they'll just keep coming back over and over again."

"Nope," I say into the phone. "Gotta fight magic with magic."

"How dangerous is dispelling this curse going to be? I don't want Sophia to handle unstable intraplanar breaches yet. She's far too young."

I blink, entirely unprepared for something like that coming out of my mother's mouth.

"Sarah?" asks Mom after a few seconds of silence.

"Uhh, sec." I face Sophia again. "How dangerous is it going to be to destroy this curse?"

She shrugs one shoulder. "I dunno. Umm, anywhere from fizzling out in a puff of smoke to some big, giant boss monster appearing."

Sierra cackles. "This isn't a video game. Boss monsters aren't a real thing."

Sophia narrows her eyes. "Five-headed tarantula-wasp-nopeasaurus."

For a second, Sierra looks defeated, then her expression lights up. "Not a boss. That was a random encounter. It wasn't at the end of a stage or anything. Just attacked us out of nowhere."

"Bosses aren't always at the ends of stages. Sometimes they're hidden bosses or special random spawns." Sophia folds her arms.

"Forget it," says Mom in that tone of voice she uses right before she leaves opposing counsel halfway into a bottle of Jack, seriously contemplating a new career. "I'm coming there. Don't do anything more until I'm with you."

"Uhh." I know better than to say 'no' to that voice. But I can ask questions. "Mom, we're almost two hours away from home. It would be one in the morning before you even got here. And… what are you going to do once you get here?"

"I… I…" Mom pauses. "Have no idea. Just… I will feel better not having the girls assaulting a ghoul nest in the middle of the night without parental supervision."

Sigh. "We're not assaulting a nest of ghouls, just looking for the source of a curse."

"And what, exactly, do you think you're going to find in a creepy, remote, abandoned old cemetery that houses the mausoleum of the family responsible for the ghouls that have been attacking you on and off for two weeks?"

"She's got a point." Ashley examines her fingernails.

Yes, Ash can hear her just fine. Our ears are pretty sharp at night.

"Okay, fine." I give up. It takes a far better lawyer than me to win an argument with my mother. "Ask Blix to mirror you to the Whittmore Inn in Port Angeles. That's the only way you'll get here in time unless you want us to just spend the night and do it tomorrow."

"Sixty miles is pretty dangerous for a mirror trip." Sophia taps her sneakers together repetitively. "Make sure Mom knows that. We should be fine."

"Soph says the mirror could be risky," I say into the phone.

"I'm on the way," replies Mom with zero hesitation. "Stay put until I get there."

"Okay." We hang up.

"Wow…" Sierra whistles. "Mom is really coming here?"

"Seems that way." I stuff the phone back in my pocket.

Sophia wobbles her head side to side. "Yanno, it's kinda silly considering Mom can't really do anything about supernatural stuff… but having her here is going to make me feel better."

"That's good." Ashley pats her on the head. "Your magic works much better when you're not scared."

I wipe both hands down my face. "Mom's not coming here to help us. She's coming here to help herself. Ugh. I really shouldn't keep bringing the Littles on dangerous missions."

Ashley leans forward, sticking herself halfway into the front between the seats, grinning at me. "This isn't a Wolent job. I mean, it's technically related, but it isn't."

Eldon peers over her head at me. "Your mother is certainly an interesting woman."

"You say 'bring the Littles' like we aren't right here." Sierra rolls her eyes.

"For the record?" Sophia raises a hand as if in class. "As soon as you learn how to disenchant ancient curses, I would be happy to stay home and safe."

I start the car. "Might as well go wait for Mom back at the hotel."

36

THE WHITTMORE CRYPT

YEP, STILL SATURDAY

a few minutes after we return to the Whittmore Hotel lobby, Mom marches out of the ladies' room.

She's carrying her big iron frying pan like a mace. The look in her eyes is definitely, 'I have seen some things you would not believe.'

Sophia and Sierra run over and hug her.

This seems to relax her.

"Hey, Mom." I join the hug. "How was the trip?"

"Surreal," she says, sounding distant. "I suspect I now know what it would be like to be insane."

"That bad?" asks Ashley.

"Sixty miles," whispers Sophia. "I told you…"

Blix, standing a few paces behind Mom, waves dismissively like 'no big deal, I had everything under control' before saluting us and darting back into the bathroom.

Mom shakes her head. "It felt as if I walked through *Alice in Wonderland* if it had been directed by the guy who did that *Twin Peaks* movie—after he'd dropped a bunch of acid and suffered a nonfatal gunshot wound to the head." She rubs her face. "It's going to take me a while to process that."

"Are you okay, Mom?" asks Sierra.

"Yes. I'm fine now." She hefts the frying pan. "Shall we get on with it?"

I laugh.

We head out to the Sentra. Once again, I drive to the little cemetery a few miles away. Due to the small size of the car, child-stacking must occur. Mom and Ashley sit in back with the girls squished on top of each other between them. Not exactly safe. There's also no one else driving around out here and I have incredible reflexes if anything unexpected happens.

Fortunately, we make it back to the graveyard without seeing a single other car on the road.

"Hope this is fast. The ghost tour is starting in twenty minutes." Ashley fake grumbles.

"There aren't going to be any ghosts there by the time we get back." Sierra makes a goofy face. "A tour of an old house is going to be super boring."

Sophia twiddles her thumbs. "Don't be so sure."

"You did?" Sierra chuckles.

"Umm. I got bored while we were waiting for Mom." Sophia fusses at her hair. "Don't worry. I made it so only nice ghosts would be attracted to the place."

I facepalm.

"I had to, Sare!" Sophia reaches forward and grabs my arm. "I would've felt guilty if what we're gonna do here ruined the hotel and put all those people out of work. It's bad for ghosts to be trapped against their will somewhere, but now it's gonna be a bunch of ghosts who want to haunt a place and have fun. Think of them like, I dunno, like the hired actors at a fake haunted house. They wanna be here."

"This could be bad." Ashley covers her mouth and giggles. "They're going to be off the wall."

I open the door. "Well, you guys heard Ash. Ghost tour is starting soon."

Mom hops out and approaches the old wrought-iron fence, shaking her head. "The things I do for my kids."

"Trunk please." Sierra points at Eldon. "And technically, we're not involved. The ghouls are after him. Sarah's helping him."

"It's kinda my job." I reach back into the Sentra and pull the trunk release. "And the ghouls are very much after me, too."

Sierra runs around to the trunk. She grabs her sword and my katana.

Probably won't need them, but it never hurts to be prepared.

Ashley nods. "Me, too. We broke the crypt open, so they're kinda upset with us."

"You don't have to help *everyone* you run into, Sarah." Mom gives me side eye.

"I know. But I basically work for Mr. Wolent and it's literally my job to play tour guide for Eldon."

Sierra rushes over and hands me the katana. She then takes a few steps away from everyone and goes through a few stretching exercises to limber up.

Mom blinks. "Since when do tour guide duties involve ghoul removal services?"

"Umm, what career path *does* include ghoul removal?" I chuckle.

"Cops, usually." Sierra pulls out a scrunchie and gathers her hair up into a ponytail. "But that's taking 'ghoul' metaphorically."

I approach the gate, which is secured with a heavy padlock and chain. At least the lock is in good shape, more modern than the fence. A light tug gets it to pop right open. Heh. Thanks Dalton. This is super handy. I pull the gate open enough to slip in. Mom comes in right behind me, then Eldon, then the girls and Ashley. We kinda end up standing there in a vee formation with Mom at the head, two-handed iron frying pan at the ready. We're either going to film one crazy music video, or this is the action sequence from a Michael Bey movie. Alas, I don't see any lens flares *or* musical instruments around here… so it's going to be option three: the usual crazy weirdness of my unlife.

"Hurry," whispers Sophia. "We're not supposed to be in here. We broke in."

Sierra leans her head side to side as if cracking her neck. Nothing cracks. "Damn, it feels good to be a gangster."

"You are not a gangster, young lady," says Mom.

Sierra rolls her eyes. "I know. It's just a quote."

"Since when do you listen to rap?" asks Ashley.

"I don't." Sierra peers back at her. "Ever see *Office Space*?"

"Oh, right." I chuckle. "When the guys were smashing the printer."

Dad loves that movie. He says it depicts exactly how his job was before they let him work from home all the time.

We walk up the path from the gate. It's paved, but not with modern blacktop, cobblestones or something. I bet the last time a vehicle drove here, it had horses pulling it. Much of the graveyard is overgrown with trees and weeds. Doesn't seem like anyone makes much of an effort to keep it neat. The city probably sends in a bunch of guys with weed eaters right before any historical society tours or whatever. I get the feeling that hasn't happened in quite a few years.

Snaps and crunches come from everywhere.

Sophia clamps both hands over her mouth to hold back a scream.

"I believe it is this way." Eldon points and takes lead. "Shameful that this cemetery has been left unprotected from the machinations of nature for so long. Despite the rampant foliage, I believe I remember the way."

Mom lets Ashley and I go by, then takes up a protective spot near the girls.

Two ghouls come rushing toward us out of the dense tree cover.

Ashley, Eldon, and Sierra turn their heads, easily seeing them. It's too dark for Mom and Sophia to see, only hear.

"Incoming ghouls," I say in a quiet tone. "Don't freak out."

"I told you. You never listen to me." Mom sighs and gestures around. "Go into a graveyard at this hour, there are going to be ghouls."

She's not serious. She can't be. Ghouls aren't common.

"I think I've seen these guys before." I raise my sword and widen my stance.

"Aye." Eldon heaves a somber sigh. "Rory and Ian. They used to work for my father. Sorry, gentleman. Your services are no longer required."

As soon as the ghouls are close enough, I lunge forward and neatly decapitate the one on the left. The severed head flies over me, heading straight for Mom, who takes a baseball swing at it. Iron skillet meets severed ghoul head with a dull clank, sending it sailing off into the weeds.

Eldon punches the other ghoul in the face, though it doesn't seem to have much of an effect other than stopping the creature's charge. "Oh, bother. Forgot…" He tilts his head in concentration for half a second, then punches the ghoul again as it simultaneously rams a wooden stake into his chest. This time, he hits it so hard the head explodes in a shower of dust and fragments.

The rest of the ghoul disintegrates soon after, as does the stake. His shirt isn't even ripped. Seems he's working on toughness as well as strength.

Mom coughs, covering her mouth. "Holy cow, Sarah."

"Yeah, they stink." I step over the dust pile and keep walking.

Eleven seconds later, more ghouls come racing toward us, leaping headstones and ducking around the larger monuments.

"I would rather have had a family reunion under different circumstances." Eldon lets a somber sigh out.

"Your brothers?" asks Sierra.

"Three of them, yes. The other two were some of father's compatriots in the 'righteous cleansing' business."

I'd say it's chaotic but it's kinda slow to me, really. It's like I'm under attack from a bunch of riled up elderly people the night after the care home let some of that Resident Evil juice leak into the cafeteria. I cover our front left flank, whirling about and slicing my way through ghoul after ghoul. Having my sword makes this *so* much easier.

It helps that they are drawn to Eldon, Ashley, and me. Mom and the girls are pretty safe. The ghouls don't bother with them at all except to try shoving them out of the way so they can get to us. That's mostly why I felt reasonably safe in taking the chance of bringing Sophia here. Guessing it's also got much to do with why she agreed to come. She knows how this works. That curse is compelling the former associates of Eldon's father to attack Ashley and me specifically because we broke the crypts—and Eldon because, well, he's the direct focus of this entire family mess.

Ashley didn't bring a weapon *or* claws. She does, however, have a warrior's spirit. Cute as she can be at times, whenever she thinks I'm in danger, out comes 'Red Sonja.' Ghoul after ghoul runs at us and promptly disintegrates on contact with either my katana, Eldon's fist, or one of Ashley's sneakers. She's kicking more than punching mostly because they stink, kind of like how most people flush public toilets with their foot.

Sierra goes out of her way to get involved, scoring a few kills. She may even be trying to show off for Mom in hopes of making her feel less worried about her being in situations like this.

"The mausoleum is right over there." Eldon points—by thrusting his entire arm and extended finger through the chest of a ghoul, then flinging the collapsing body off to one side.

A dull, crunching thud tells me Mom smashed the skull of a ghoul trying to sneak us from behind.

Sophia emits this continuous uneasy whine while clinging to Mom. She sounds more disgusted than frightened.

I stab a ghoul in the chest, yank the katana out, then spin into a downward slash at another one going for Ashley, almost cutting him completely in half from left shoulder to right hip. Wow, these guys are brittle.

"That guy looks familiar. I think I've killed him before." I whirl around to face forward, ready for the next wave.

"You probably did," says Sophia. "The curse keeps bringing them back."

"No, I mean like twenty seconds ago." I lock my focus onto another ghoul in the distance pointing a black powder pistol at me. Reflexively, I duck.

He tries to fire. A tiny wisp of smoke rises from the hammer, then a tubular glop of grey mud oozes from the barrel and plops to the ground.

"They do not have to walk sixty miles to find you again." Eldon grabs another ghoul's head in both hands, then rips it off the creature's shoulders as casually as if he's lifting a vase off a desk. "They're getting right back up."

"No, they're not." Sierra runs over to pistol guy and chops his gun arm off at the elbow. "They're turning into dust."

As if he can't even see her, that ghoul walks right past Sierra toward me. Her sword bursts out of his chest from behind a second later. He peers down, seemingly confused, then collapses into a cloud of grey powder.

"Their spirits are returning to the mausoleum and they're rematerializing there… or perhaps elsewhere in the graveyard." Eldon fast walks forward. "Not literally rising from where they fall. Hurry now, there's a break in their assault."

Sierra laughs. "Guess we killed them so fast they're all stuck waiting on the respawn timer."

"This is not *Call of Duty*," I say.

"No, you're right. These guys are much easier to kill," Sierra zips back over to stand beside Mom.

Eldon leads us up a twisting path of mossy dark paver stones to the face of an impressively large mausoleum. It's big enough to be a tiny house. He tries to open the metal door, though it doesn't budge.

"I got it." I slip around him, grasp the handle, and pull. The door opens. "There."

"How did you do that?" Eldon makes an impressed face at me.

I shrug. "If I reach for a door and expect it's going to open for me, it usually does."

The solid metal door abruptly flies open the rest of the way, bonking Eldon in the face—and

stopping on him as if it hit a stone statue.

"Ouch," says Eldon.

I sigh at the ghoul in the doorway, then stab him in the chest. "Rude."

The ghoul bursts apart into dust.

After giving the horrible smelling cloud a chance to dissipate, I step inside, entering a single stone vault room containing seven stone crypts, three on either side and one at the far wall. Wow, this is much nicer than the mausoleum I spent my first night of undeath in. More spacious. Still lacks in amenities though. No furniture, no power, no electronics to bust boredom with. No wonder ghosts are so restless. Society should start installing PlayStations or Xboxes in graveyards. That might cut down on hauntings.

Mom scoots inside the room and gazes around. "This is rather creepy."

"Yeah," says Sophia in a mousy voice. "This entire place is saturated with negative energy."

"Now what?" asks Sierra.

"We look around I guess. The curse focus has got to be in here somewhere." I head over to the crypts on the left. "Think it's in the big central tomb, or would that be too obvious?"

We spend a moment snooping over the crypts. Bethany's remains are apparently in the outermost crypt on the left. The rest appear to belong to Eldon's brothers—all four of them—plus his mother. Guessing the big one opposite the door belongs to the father.

Evidently bored, Sierra wanders back and forth, tapping her sword on the crypts.

A groan comes from the exit.

Ashley, barely even looking behind her, punches the ghoul in the doorway, sending it flying out of sight.

"Hulk smash," says Sierra.

Sophia, in the middle of the room, turns in place, gazing around like a tween girl brought to a horse farm trying to choose which pony she wants for her birthday present. Wait, no. She's nowhere near that eager. This is more like a race driver studying cars and trying to pick the one she thinks won't kill her.

When Sierra sword-taps the big crypt, the echo sounds much different than the others.

"Sierra?" I point at the big crypt. "Tap that one again."

She does.

Eldon's eyebrows go up. Ashley perks up, too. They can hear the difference.

"What?" asks Mom.

"That one sounds super hollow." I approach it.

Another groan comes from the doorway.

"I got this one." Mom raises her skillet in both hands and scoots over by the wall, hiding out of sight from the doorway.

As soon as a ghoul shambles in, she wallops it over the top of the head, crushing the entire skull like a giant egg wrapped in dried out leather.

My mother stares at the crumpled ghoul body until it disintegrates into dust. "This is oddly therapeutic. Work would be so much less stressful if I could crush the heads of idiots."

"HR would probably frown on that," says Sierra in a flat tone.

I fiddle at the crypt, trying to get the lid to come off.

"What do you think is in there?" Ashley walks up and proceeds to help me grab the lid.

"Definitely no coffin. Could be a little box with the curse thing in it." I grunt and push at the stone.

Something gives with a click. The floor rumbles. Not sure if one of us hit a concealed button by accident or if my 'lockpicking' power did something. Whatever. I'll take it. I don't need to understand what happened.

Ash and I jump back and drop into a fighting stance, ready for a ghoul assault.

The crypt lid slides straight backward, disappearing into the wall like a morgue cooler tray. The closer end cap of the crypt sinks down to the floor, revealing a stairwell leading to an underground chamber.

Sophia sees that, covers her face, and starts muttering, "No. I don't wanna go downstairs in the creepy mausoleum."

"You don't have to go down there." Mom puts an arm around her.

"Could've told you that would happen." Sierra elbow-nudges me.

Sophia sniffles, lowers her hands from her face, and sighs. "But I do. Sarah can't destroy the curse. They're gonna keep coming after her."

Eldon punches his fist through the chest of another ghoul rushing into the mausoleum. The body hangs on his arm for a second or two before collapsing. "Fortunately, they are not a great threat."

"They're far more of a menace to laundry machines than people." Sierra coughs. "We're probably going to have to burn these clothes. The smell is never coming out."

"I can fix that," says Sophia.

"Wait!" Mom holds up a finger. "I would rather you try that after we've changed and showered and our clothing is on the floor."

"Yeah." Sierra blushes. "She'd do it now and all our clothes would just disappear or something stupidly embarrassing."

"Guys..." Sophia rolls her eyes. "I'm not *that* bad at magic."

"You're scared." I rub her back. "And when you're scared, things tend to go a little haywire."

She grumbles. "Okay. Fine. Let's finish this." She points at the stairs. "You go first."

"Yeah, come on. The ghost tour is starting soon." Ashley bounces on her toes.

"Allow me." Eldon steps toward the stairs.

"Hang on." I tug him back. "This entire curse is about destroying you. Seems a little reckless to send you in there first. Appreciate the chivalry, though."

He fidgets. "If you are sure."

"Yeah." Feeling like some anime samurai girl, I hold my katana in a two-handed grip and make my way down the stairs.

Eldon follows right behind me.

The room downstairs is about half the size of the main mausoleum chamber, though it feels bigger because it houses only one crypt, a huge ornate one adorned with small angel statues and tons of occult symbols and carved writing. The same foreboding dread that hung over the mine where we found Eldon lurks in this room, too. I'm almost certain it's coming from the big crypt.

"Bingo," I whisper.

Light blasts into the space from behind, making my eyes water from the intensity. Good thing I didn't happen to be looking back at the time or I'd be blinded for a bit.

"Gah! Warn me next time," mutters Sierra.

"Sorry," whispers Sophia.

I mute my eyes the way I do when out in the city at night or driving. Going from total darkness with zero light to even mild dimness is crippling if I'm not prepared for the change. Once I stop seeing flashing spots, I peer back.

Sophia advances from the bottom step, hands out for balance, creeping along as if walking atop a frozen lake. A small amorphous cloud of light orbits around her head, no bigger than a grape. It's only about as bright as a miniature flashlight, except it's radiant and shining in all directions. Inch by inch, my littlest sister makes her way into the room, sneakers scratching over the dusty stone floor.

Down here, in absolute darkness, her tiny light seems way more powerful than it really is.

The craziest thing happens next.

No, they're not renewing *Firefly*.

All the carvings and such on the lone crypt gleam like bike reflectors when the aura of magical light gets close enough despite appearing to be ordinary stone otherwise.

"It's enchanted." Sophia points at the tomb.

Groans echo from upstairs.

Ashley, who is still up there, yells, "More ghouls. Wait. No. Same ghouls."

She doesn't sound worried, so I don't panic. "Try to chokepoint them in the door. Yell if you need a hand."

Sophia approaches the crypt and studies the writing on the facing end.

"Can you read that junk?" asks Sierra. "Doesn't look like English."

"I dunno. It's kinda cryptic." Sophia sets her hands on her hips.

I groan—as does Mom.

Sophia twists around and blinks at us. "What are you groaning about?"

"Wow. Just wow." Sierra shakes her head. "Dad would faint from happiness if he was here."

"Huh?" Sophia tilts her head.

Sierra points at the tomb. "The writing is *crypt*-ic?"

Sophia blinks, then bursts into giggles. "Oops. I didn't mean that."

I hold the katana up and bow my forehead in reverence. "To pun without knowing is the final stage of enlightenment."

"This is your father's doing." Mom moves up to stand by Sophia.

Both girls and I say, "Yes," at the same time.

"I think this entire thing is the curse." Sophia waves at the crypt. "All the writing carved into it is the spell."

"Can you break it?" I ask.

"Gonna find out." Sophia pretends to crack her knuckles, then widens her stance and holds both hands out at the crypt as if she's getting ready to do tai chi.

Klepto crawls under her hair to hide.

Not sure what to expect here. Is Sophia going to glow and float into the air? Something straight out of *Dragon Ball*? Will there be an explosion? Maybe we'll get lucky and the magic will just go away in a fizzle.

Sophia shakes slightly from exertion. She emits a faint snarling growl, the same sort of noise she usually makes when struggling to lift her book bag. I swear school is too demanding on kids. The books she has to carry for homework probably weigh more than she does.

Five seconds later, a deep, bellowing roar fills the underground chamber. The crypt lid shatters upward, sending two-inch-thick stone chunks flying in all directions. Amid a haze of smoke, the decaying remains of a man in 1800s era clothing claws upward from the box. He's huge... not like fat or muscular huge. I'm talking ordinary proportions but at least nine feet tall. Wild black hair stands up in a floof atop his head, as disheveled as his copious beard. Wow, this guy looks like an undead Rob Zombie after he spent two weeks wandering around a dust storm and then got electrocuted.

His skin is somewhere between paper white and grey wherever it isn't simply missing. Even though he doesn't have eyes anymore—only empty sockets full of shadows—I'm pretty sure this is the father from the painting we saw in the lobby back at the hotel. He's still giving off that 'I am rich and therefore much better than you' vibe.

King ghoul, so to speak.

"See?" Sophia gestures at him, remarkably unfazed. "I told you. Boss monster. Now, if you'll excuse me—"

She shrieks in terror and runs away from the crypt to hide behind me.

37

CURSES

YES, STILL SATURDAY

Some video games make their boss monsters abnormally large.

I'm not saying my unlife is a video game, though it's a good metaphor here. A bad guy in the game who is basically an ordinary human is somehow ten feet tall and massive just because he's a 'boss' fight... and no one in the game world notices the abnormal size in character. That's kinda what this dude is like. He's just... big for no reason. Maybe it's ego.

A constant cacophony of Ashley war cries and fleshy thuds echoes from upstairs. She sounds amused, almost giddy. I don't think she's having any trouble keeping the ghouls bottlenecked at the door.

King Ghoul points a grey hand tipped with long yellow claws at Eldon, then me while rasping, "Fiends!"

Sierra does a snotty impression of Chloe's voice and yells, "Cork sucker!"

Mom gasps. "Sierra Renee Wright!"

"I said *cork*." Sierra glances sideways at her. "C-o-r-k."

"Mom, she's referencing Chloe being called a fiend by that town guard."

"Oh. Yes." Mom takes a few breaths. "Sorry. I'm a little anxious right now. You said there wouldn't be anything dangerous."

I fold my arms. "I'm still not convinced there *is* anything dangerous. This guy looks impressive but he's not doing anything more than looming at us."

"Father?" whispers Eldon. "What has become of you?"

King Ghoul makes a face of confusion at Sierra, Mom, and me. "What the devil are you talking about?"

"It would take too long to explain." I wave dismissively. "Really not worth it. I'd have to explain the modern world, roleplaying games, magic, why it's hilarious that Chloe uses foul language... just a total project."

King Ghoul stares at me... as much as a guy with no eyeballs can stare.

"Holy shit, he talks," blurts Sierra.

Mom sighs.

The giant old undead dude turns his head to face Sierra. "Such language from an innocent child. What have you fiends done to corrupt her thus?"

"Seriously," says Mom in a flat tone. "I can't get her to stop swearing. Believe me, I've tried. However, it's not Sarah's fault. Don't blame her for it."

Sierra flails her arms. "Gah! Language isn't such a big deal. Why does everyone get their underwear in a knot over 'bad words'? Who cares if someone says shit? Get upset about homeless people being homeless, or bigotry, or violence, or any of a million other problems with society. Oh noes, the girl has said a naughty thing. The world is doomed! It's the future! Stop acting like me saying bad words is somehow worse than the dead coming back to life and trying to kill us!"

King Ghoul stares agape at her.

She points her sword at him. "Guess what, you old dusty fart-for-brains, girls can even go to school now and get jobs. And I don't even have to get permission from my father if I want to get married."

"Oh, no." I shake my head at the ghoul king. "You got her started. Might be better for everyone if you just crawled back into your crypt and went back to sleep."

He disregards me and snarls at Eldon. "I could not undo the fiend's foul touch upon you. There is no choice left but to destroy the evil you have become."

A severed ghoul head rolls down the stairs into the chamber, bounces off Sophia's leg, and bursts into a pile of dust.

Sophia shudders and makes a face as if she just stepped barefoot on dog poop. She does not, however, scream again. Progress.

"What happens now?" asks Mom.

"We have three choices." Sophia clears her throat and somehow finds the courage to step forward. "One, talk him into deciding his son isn't really evil and should be allowed to exist."

"Eldon?" Sierra glances at him. "Do you think it is acceptable to mix Skittles and M&Ms in the same bowl?"

Eldon turns his head toward her. He looks absolutely confused. After a moment, he stammers, "No?"

Sierra gestures at him. "There. He's not evil."

"Option two." Sophia holds up two fingers. "I try again to dispel the curse. He's going to get angry and attack us when I start. I can probably overpower the spell, but I don't know how ugly it's going to get. You'll have to keep him and his minions off me long enough for the spell to finish."

"It's already gotten fairly ugly." Mom winces. "No offence. You *are* decaying."

Wow. A zinger from the parental unit. Go, Mom.

"And option three." Sophia holds up three fingers. "Barbarian approach. You guys just try beating the crap out of him and see if that does it."

"Wretched fiends," hisses King Ghoul. "Your evil cannot stand against the wrath of the light. I shall rid this world of your foul taint."

Eldon takes a step closer to his father. "You cannot see reason, can you?"

"The guy cut your head off, chopped you into pieces, and put you in boxes." Sierra gawks at him. "I kinda think you're beyond talking it out at this point."

"It might have been a misunderstanding." Eldon attempts a hopeful smile.

The older Whittmore growls, smoky dust leaking out between his teeth.

"It appears not." Eldon bows his head. "I fear my father's irrational hatred of the undead has driven him beyond the point of reason."

"You think he's irrational?" Sierra glances back and forth between father and son. "He's just kinda standing there talking to us. He could've jumped out of his box and started fighting right away. Is he reasonable, or is this just monologuing before we have to fight?"

"He's not really monologuing," whispers Sophia. "Just kinda hissing and calling us fiends. For him to be monologuing, he'd have to be going into details about some nefarious plans and how we've unknowingly been helping him the whole time."

Eldon glares accusingly at King Ghoul. "Father is quite irrational. He despises what I've become to such a degree he has brought back our entire family, less Mother and Bethany, as ghouls… plus a great deal of his most trusted employees. Tell me, Father, did Mr. Farthing, or Jack, or Leopold agree to this eternity of drudgery?"

Sierra taps her sword against her sneaker. "Oh, good point. Yeah, a guy that raises a bunch of people into ghouls against their will because he's pissed off at his son's life choices is pretty irrational."

"It was not my choice," mutters Eldon.

"I know." Seirra looks up at him. "Just saying."

"Hey, that's stupid!" Sophia steps out from behind me to point at Mr. Whittmore. "You hated your son because he became an undead vampire?"

The elder Whittmore growls at Eldon. "Abomination. That is no longer my son. My son is dead."

"What the heck are *you* then?" Sierra gestures at him. "Why is it bad for him to be an undead, but it's totally okay for you to be undead?"

King Ghoul gawks at her.

"Such a dumbass." Sierra huffs.

Sophia walks right up to the crypt, seemingly having no fear of the guy anymore. "Yeah, my sister has a good point. If being an undead means he's no longer your son, does being an undead mean you are no longer you? You're so angry that you made *yourself* into an abomination."

King Ghoul stares at his hands for a moment in silence, then lets out this wail of anguish before exploding into a cloud of grey dust.

The blast is pretty epic. We're all covered in it, as if we'd been standing at ground zero of a flour mill blowing up.

"Whoa. Death by logic trap," I say, attempting to sound like a surfer dude.

Sierra cuts me a sideways glance. "Isn't it death by stereo?"

I gesture at the big crypt. "Parody license."

"Something happened!" yells Ashley from upstairs. "All the ghouls just turned into dust and I didn't even hit some of them."

"Dammit." Sierra drops her sword and scrapes the semi-sticky powder away from her eyes.

"Apparently," says Sophia, not bothering to open her eyes, "I missed an option four: a logic trap that makes the curse implode on itself."

"You didn't say we had an option four earlier." I chuckle.

"Didn't think of it." Sophia swats at herself. "Sierra's a lot smarter than she lets on."

Whatever face Sierra's trying to make at her is impossible to see beneath the coating of dust.

"Sec. Gonna clean this off," says Sophia.

"If we all end up naked, I am going to..." Sierra shivers. "Do something."

"Relax. I got this." Sophia raises one hand over her head, holds it there for a few seconds, then snaps her fingers.

All the dust in the room and on us jumps into the air, gathering into a mini-tornado before flowing into the empty crypt, leaving us clean. And hey, we don't even smell like rotting ghouls anymore.

Sierra peers down, sees her clothing is intact, then slouches in relief. "Nice. Okay, I was wrong. Maybe you are getting better at this magic thing."

"Are we done here?" asks Mom.

"Yep." Sophia heads for the stairs. "Totally done. The curse is gone. Eldon will no longer have all the ghouls throwing themselves at him."

Mom and I groan.

We make our way upstairs.

Ashley's standing by the door that leads outside, grinning at us. "We're not totally done. There's still a ghost tour. We've got ten minutes to get there."

38

GEEKS

SUNDAY NIGHT (FINALLY NOT SATURDAY)

*A*dmittedly, the ghost tour wasn't bad.

The tormented spirits of the Whittmore family and their employees found peace and no longer haunted the building. No idea if they got sucked back into the cosmic machinery to wait their turn at reincarnation or simply decided to go explore the world elsewhere as spirits. Whatever Sophia did worked well beyond her expectations. She attracted around twenty other spirits to the property who were all too happy to take up residence there and mess with the living.

Since Sophia could see them, the ghosts resorted to sneaking up on her for ambush jump scares in much the same way as an annoying little brother might. For everyone else, they did the usual stuff like making doors move or appearing as distant shadow people. According to my littlest sister, ghosts still need energy to feed on. Some get it from electromagnetic stuff. Others absorb it directly from the living. The new haunts she coaxed into the place seem to get their food by scaring the hell out of people in (mostly) non-malicious ways.

That hotel should do more than okay with their spooky tour business.

And yes, we told Dad about Sophia's unintentional pun. He's vowed to get a cake and celebrate the occasion of her first subconscious pun.

I'm relaxing at home.

It's 1:18 a.m.

Chloe and Ashley are loafing around with me on the living room sofa. We're all in PJs and have been marathoning *Sailor Moon* since the 'rents went to bed at midnight. Ashley and Chloe are clinging to plush animals. All three of us sing along with the theme music—quietly so as not to wake anyone—whenever the episodes change.

Yeah… we are hardly fearsome creatures of the night. Geeks for sure. Meh. It works for me. Just proves I am still who I was before all of this craziness started. I might be a vampire, but I don't need or want power.

So many people, alive as well as undead, seem to never be happy with what they have. They always want more. More stuff, more power, more living space, a change of scenery, whatever—their lives are never enough for them no matter how much they get. They never seem to just be able to enjoy what they have.

Me? I could exist like this—in some nowhere space of being a high-school-aged kid with only a handful of responsibilities, an eternal best friend, a little kid I'm babysitting for eternity, and be happy. Maybe it's wishful thinking to expect this house will *always* be my home. On a scale of infinite existence, there's a nonzero chance the day will come when I will have to say goodbye to my home forever. That hopefully isn't going to happen until long after the 'rents are haunting me as ghosts and the Littles are all off on their own somewhere. Maybe it won't happen until the Littles are haunting me as ghosts, too. It's pointless to waste time dwelling on dark thoughts of futures that might not even come to pass.

Hunter will likely join us in a few years. I hope. I don't expect Ashley to be jealous of him for competing with her for my time. She likes him but doesn't *like* him. No, we're never going to do anything super messed up like sharing him as a boyfriend. Ash is too much like my sister for that. For the time being, she's still going through her weird post-Transference mind storm nostalgia fit that's basically turned her into a fourteen-year-old, mentally. She's really putting the innocence in Innocent right now.

It won't last, though. Just like how I got over obsessively dwelling on my 'lost mortal life,' she will emerge at the other end of her rainbow unicorn plush tunnel and be back to herself. Not entirely sure how she'll end up. Will she be more like the way she was before her tryst with Aurélie? Will she be freshman-sophomore Ashley who could talk about sex but not without giggles and blushing? Or will she be senior-year Ashley who talked about sexy type stuff more than I really wanted to?

Time will tell.

Whatever happens, I'm sure we'll be fine.

In fact, the only thing I'm really worried about now is what's going to happen the day the red faerie finally catches up to Sophia. I can't imagine her PMS-raging. It's kinda scary to be honest. She might go the emotional route and shut herself in her room all day crying... or she might set off a nuclear explosion and shower all of Washington state in flaming kitten-shaped comets.

There is a whole lot of potential badness out there waiting for me and my family in the future, but I'm not going to waste too much time thinking about it. I've got a Chloe snuggling up to me, an Ashley laughing her head off at the television, and several thousand hours of Anime on DVD to watch. Oh, yeah, we also have lots of cozy blankets. I might not be able to pull a 'Count Dracula' and live in this house for thousands of years. Gonna try my damndest to, though.

Again, I am a teenager. I should not worry so much about the future.

So, I won't.

For now, I am home. And I am happy.

fin

ACKNOWLEDGMENTS

Thank you for reading Vampire Innocent #18! I am beyond grateful that so many of you have supported this series with your comments, emails, and reviews.

Sarah and company will return in the next book.

Additional thanks to Lee Sheridan for editing and Alexandria Thompson for the cover design.

ABOUT THE AUTHOR

Originally from South Amboy NJ, Matthew has been creating science fiction and fantasy worlds for most of his reasoning life. Since 1996, he has developed the "Divergent Fates" world, in which *Division Zero, Virtual Immortality, The Awakened Series, The Harmony Paradox, and the Daughter of Mars series* take place. Along with being an editor at Curiosity Quills press, he has worked in IT and technical support.

Matthew is an avid gamer, a recovered WoW addict, Gamemaster for two custom RPG systems, and a fan of anime, British humour, and intellectual science fiction that questions the nature of reality, life, and what happens after it.

He is also fond of cats.

Visit me online at:
    Facebook: https://www.facebook.com/MatthewSCoxAuthor
    Pinterest: https://www.pinterest.com/matthewcox10420/
    Goodreads: https://www.goodreads.com/author/show/7712730.
Matthew_S_Cox
    Email: mcox2112@gmail.com

OTHER BOOKS BY MATTHEW S. COX

Divergent Fates Universe Novels

Division Zero series

- Division Zero
- Lex De Mortuis
- Thrall
- Guardian
- Harbinger
- The Shadow Fixer
- Neuroshock

The Awakened series

- Prophet of the Badlands
- Archon's Queen
- Grey Ronin
- Daughter of Ash
- Zero Rogue
- Angel Descended

Daughter of Mars series

- The Hand of Raziel
- Araphel
- Ghost Black

Virtual Immortality series

- Virtual Immortality
- The Harmony Paradox

Prophet of the Badlands Series

- Prophet's Journey

- Prophet's Mercy

Divergent Fates Anthology

(Fiction Novels - Adult)

The Roadhouse Chronicles Series

- One More Run
- The Redeemed
- Dead Man's Number

Faded Skies series

- Heir Ascendant
- Ascendant Unrest
- Ascendant Revolution

Temporal Armistice Series

- Nascent Shadow
- The Shadow Collector
- The Gate to Oblivion
- The Queen of Discord
- The Burning Alchemist

Vampire Innocent series

- A Nighttime of Forever
- A Beginner's Guide to Fangs
- The Artist of Ruin
- The Last Family Road Trip
- The Phantom Oracle
- How Not to Summon Demons
- Ordinary Problems of a College Vampire
- A Vampire's Guide to Surviving Holidays
- An Introduction to Paranormal Diplomacy
- A Vampire's Guide to Adulting

- How to Stop a Vampire War in Six Easy Steps
- Ancient Vampire Death Cults and Other Annoyances
- Hunting Vampires for Fun and Profit
- A String of Seriously Unlucky Events
- The Summer of Completely Usual Strangeness
- Demonic Crisis Management for the Modern Vampire
- A Vampire's Guide to Work-Unlife Balance
- Eternity and You: Tips for the Young Vampire

Standalones

- Wayfarer: AV494
- Axillon99
- Chiaroscuro: The Mouse and the Candle
- The Spirits of Six Minstrel Run
- Sophie's Light
- The Far Side of Promise anthology
- Operation: Chimera (with Tony Healey)
- The Dysfunctional Conspiracy (with Christopher Veltmann)
- Of Myth and Shadow
- The Girl Who Found the Sun

Winter Solstice series (with J.R. Rain)

- Convergence
- Containment
- Catalyst
- Catacombs

Alexis Silver series (with J.R. Rain)

- Silver Light
- Deep Silver
- Silver Quarrel
- Silver Crucible
- Silver Heart

Samantha Moon Origins series (with J.R. Rain)

- New Moon Rising
- Moon Mourning
- Haunted Moon

Vampire For Hire series (with J.R. Rain)

- Moon Master
- Dead Moon
- Lost Moon
- Vampire Destiny
- Infinite Moon
- Vampire Empress
- Moon Elder
- Wicked Moon
- Moon Blade

Maddy Wimsey series (with J.R. Rain)

- The Devil's Eye
- The Drifting Gloom
- Dark Mercy
- Primal Wrath

Samantha Moon Case Files series (with J.R. Rain)

- Blood Moon

Immortal Operative (with J.R. Rain)

- Broken Ice
- Broken Wing

Four Elements series (with J.R. Rain)

- The Elementalist
- The Black Rose
- The Wakefield Curse

Witches series (with J.R. Rain)

- The Witch and the Hangman

Zeb Clemens series (with J.R. Rain)

- The Beast of Devil's Creek
- Wanted: Undead or Alive

Young Adult Novels

The Eldritch Heart Series

- The Eldritch Heart
- The Cursed Crown
- The Sapphire Soul

Evergreen Series

- Evergreen
- The World That Remains
- The Lucky Ones
- Nuclear Summer
- The Nuclear Frontier
- The World We Make
- The Threat Unseen

Progenitor Series

- Out of Sight
- Out of Mind

Diary of a Teenage Fey

(Short story series)

- Elder Horror
- The Hag of Barrow Falls
- Babysitter's Nightmare
- Lharakki

- Bauble for a Soul
- Simulacrum
- Amorphous
- Manticore

Standalones

- Caller 107
- The Summer the World Ended
- Nine Candles of Deepest Black
- The Forest Beyond the Earth

Middle Grade Novels

The Adventures of Ubergirl series

- My Dad is a Mad Scientist
- Aliens Ate My Homework
- The End of all Halloweens
- Dr. Infinity and the Soul Smasher

Tales of Widowswood series

- Emma and the Banderwigh
- Emma and the Silk Thieves
- Emma and the Silverbell Faeries
- Emma and the Elixir of Madness
- Emma and the Weeping Spirit

Standalones

- Citadel: The Concordant Sequence
- The Cursed Codex
- The Menagerie of Jenkins Bailey

www.ingramcontent.com/pod-product-compliance
Lightning Source LLC
Chambersburg PA
CBHW060221030726
47499CB00004B/1146